ALSO BY THE AUTHOR

A NEW YEAR'S TALE

by Nancy Farmer

Portal, Arizona

Library of Congress Control Number: 2013908018

Acknowledgments:
Permission to quote copyrighted material in chapters three and
forty-two is gratefully acknowledged: *In Our Time* by Eric Hoffer.
Hopewell Publications: Titusville, New Jersey, 2008.

Verses by Li Po in chapters twenty and thirty-two are from *The
White Pony*, edited by Robert Payne. John Day Company: New
York, 1947.

The quote in chapter twenty-five comes from the *Tao Te Ching* by
Lao Tzu, translated by D. C. Lau. Penguin Books Inc.: Baltimore,
Maryland, 1963.

The quote in chapter three comes from *The Bhagavad-Gita*, translated by Swami Prabhavananda and Christopher Isherwood.
Vedanta Press: Hollywood, California, 1972.

For my brother, Dr. Elmon Lee Coe, who graciously allowed me to use his image for Cubby Willows (and who has been known to read to ducks).

And for Harold, *mi vida*, without whom none of my books would have been written.

CONTENTS

CAST OF CHARACTERS

LIVE PEOPLE:

TOMBUDZO (TOM) SEAWORTHY: Janitor at Burton, Barton, Gerbill and Slithe Laboratory
VIOLETTA: Tom's wife
CEZARE, ATALANTA, PHAEDRA, JERONIMO and THAÍS: Tom and Violetta's children
DR. CUBBY WILLOWS: Entomologist
FRIETCHIE: Beauty salon operator and hot tomato
EZEKIEL: Frietchie's love slave
BOGOMIL: Ex-prison guard from a salt mine, currently an orderly in an Alzheimer's hospital
MR. YEE: Inventor of Ten Thousand Happiness Elixir
NING, FAN and LUCKY: Mr. Yee's children
ERIC HOFFER: Philosopher
THE WICHITA LINEMAN
GINZBERG ROSHI: Abbot of a Buddhist monastery

DEAD PEOPLE:

DR. GERBILL: Entomologist, friend of Cubby
SYBILLE: Gerbill's wife
MR. STRICKLAND: Cubby's high school science teacher
MISS FEENY: Cubby's first grade teacher
UNCLE SHUMBA: Tom's uncle
BALTHAZAR, MELCHIOR and CASPAR. Tom Seaworthy's ancestors, a.k.a The Three Wise Men
THE MHONDORO: Spirit of Tom Seaworthy's tribe, a.k.a. Big Daddy
MR. YEE'S MOTHER
BOGOMIL'S GREAT-GRANDMOTHER

BOOK ONE: DISPOSABLE PEOPLE

CUBBY WILLOWS, AGE SEVEN

One: *TOM SEAWORTHY*

B Y DAY Burton, Barton, Gerbill and Slithe Laboratory was alive with sound. When you passed a door you heard coffee percolators, the ping of computers, and the chittering of rats in cages. From the courtyard lab technicians discussed last night's TV, while beyond the double security fence rattled the noises of factories and dense traffic on Sasquatch Avenue.

But now it was night. The factories were silent and only sirens and gunfire echoed in the distance. It was now, in this velvet quietness, that Tom Seaworthy was reminded of his childhood. His father's farm lay buried beneath the industrial site—forty acres of cherry trees, corn, strawberries, lavender and mustard. Through the years the factories had crowded in until the cherry trees had died, and then they covered the trees until all that was left was the old farmhouse where Tom still lived.

At night the ghost of the farm appeared. When Tom climbed to the roof to check the security cameras he could see it. The dark alleys became irrigation canals and the buildings vanished beneath the shadows of trees. Bats fluttered around a lighted barn where Tom's father tended a cow in the throes of giving birth.

In the present time the soft whoosh of floor polishers filled the chemical-scented air. A janitor was assigned to each level of the lab and Tom, because he was the most senior, had charge of the top floor where the most important scientists were. He was alone most of the time, except for chance encounters with other janitors on the stairs. They would utter greetings, exchange a joke and move on like animals encountering one another in a forest.

In a week Tom would retire and never see them again.

It was strange to spend forty years in the company of people who would forget you the minute you walked out the door. It was depressing to realize that in all those years he hadn't made a single friend, except for Dr. Gerbill who was dead.

Superficially, Tom resembled the other janitors. He was dressed in the gray uniform that marked him as a menial. He had dropped out of high school and done a stint in the Navy. He was an African-American. But there the resemblance ended. Tom was a Seaworthy and they had been set apart by the old gods of Africa. His real name was Tombudzo. This had caused him no end of ridicule in grade school and so he quickly learned to shorten it.

There were never more than two hundred Seaworthys in the world at one time. They didn't produce many children. Tom was lucky because he had five sons and daughters who were all intelligent and loyal. Among the gifts granted by the old gods were happy marriages and worthy offspring.

When Tom was finished polishing the floor of the main hall he started on the labs. He saved the worst for last. This was crowded with antique equipment that worked fitfully. You never knew what you were going to find in Dr. Willows' lab—a wandering scorpion, a giant hornworm munching a tobacco plant in the dark or, once, a pile of preying mantis heads. You cleaned around these things because you never knew what purpose the doctor had for them.

The windows were so filthy you would need a trowel to scrape the dust off, but Tom left these alone. Scientists, especially one as eccentric as this one, reacted badly to changes in their habitat. The fluorescent light flickered erratically and drove him crazy every time he saw it. He'd itched to replace the fitting for years, but the doctor liked it that way.

When Tom was finished, he paused to look through the pages of Dr. Willows' lab notebooks. Hundreds of them lay in an old bookcase bolted to the wall above the scintillation counter. They were a wonder to the janitor, who admired the copperplate handwriting and illustrations as fine as engraved prints. They should have been in an art gallery, Tom thought.

He turned and his foot collided with a foam mattress jammed under a table. And there was Dr. Willows himself curled up like the family dog. This happened regularly when the man became too absorbed in his work to go home. The sight of the thin, ungainly figure with its gray beard fanned out over the edge of the mattress, filled Tom with tenderness. Night after night for forty years he'd cleaned around the Doc and the man had never awakened. They'd probably exchanged only a dozen words in all that time.

It gave him a twinge to realize that he'd never see that comforting presence again. The Doc was retiring, too, and tomorrow was the last day for him. It was a new Senior Law. Old folks were forcibly shuffled off to make room for the young, and what the retirees did afterwards was of no concern for the government. Die, hopefully.

The depression that Tom had been warding off returned. He'd lived in a small, safe cocoon, obstinately refusing to think about the end. *I'll tackle that problem tomorrow*, he always said, but the evasion didn't work anymore. The end was nigh, as the sign that loony carried outside the bank proclaimed.

Tom went to the drinks machine and bought a box of orange juice. He put it next to Dr. Willows' head as he'd done for many years. Something about the sleeping man stirred Tom's pity. Dr. Gerbill had said that Dr. Willows didn't inhabit the same world as the rest of mankind. When you saw the childlike delight with which he greeted a box of cockroaches, you knew you were dealing with someone different from the usual run of humans.

Tom finished and prepared to go home. He studied the parking lot for a long time. Gangs usually didn't make it past the first security fence, but it was a mistake you only made once. In the distance a wall of searchlights made a curtain of light to the south of the city. It was coming from Freedom Stadium and was a rally for the Youth Patrol.

Tom used his ID card to unlock the door and put his foot out to hold it open. He put on night-vision goggles to look for patches of heat in the shadows and dialed up his electronic ear to detect sounds. Revved high enough you could hear a heartbeat. Finally, satisfied, he dashed across the parking lot to his truck.

*　　*　　*

He drove through the warehouses. Tall buildings loomed over the alley and a tide of rats flowed away from the headlights. Tom remembered this wasteland when it was open country.

A stream framed by oaks once meandered through fields and the boy Tombudzo lay on his stomach to watch water striders skate over the surface. At night he listened to what he called the farm news through the bedroom window: Cottonwoods rustled. Coyotes yipped. Cattle shifted uneasily. A breeze told him that a daddy skunk had jumped on a lady skunk before she was in the mood.

All that was left was a deteriorating farmhouse surrounded by an industrial site. A fence topped with electrified razor wire had been installed by Tom's daughter Atalanta. It was the only way he dared to leave Violetta alone, now that the children had moved away.

He rolled to a stop in front of the security monitor in the gate. A needle of light scanned his retinas and laser beams fanned out along the alley, searching for intruders. A rat screamed as it fried. "Password," the gate said in a tinny voice.

"*Mhoro*," said Tom, giving a greeting in a forgotten African language. The gate clicked open and he drove to a back door leading to a disused bedroom. The room had once been inhabited by his daughters Atalanta, Phaedra and Thaís—Violetta had a fondness for exotic names—and the smell of their cosmetics lingered in the air.

They were fine children, all of them. Tom missed them, but he knew they weren't safe in the city. Since the Diminished Culpability Act had passed, neither were he and Violetta. They would have to move soon. They were being forced out as surely as the coyotes and cattle had been long ago: Move or die.

No matter how hard Tom worked at making repairs to the old house, time was against him. The walls of the back bedroom sloughed off paint like dandruff. The linoleum was pocked with the scars of old furniture. The glass in the windows had flowed slowly downward, as glass will over many years, to present a warped view of the outside world.

And yet, no matter how ephemeral the repair jobs were, Tom couldn't resist doing them. Maintenance was at the core of his being. He could no more have ignored a rusty hinge than Dr. Willows could have tolerated a faulty incubator. *I wonder where the Doc will go?* thought Tom, thumbing through the books on an old bookcase. Years of varnish had coated the shelves with a glaze like fried chicken skin and summer heat had cracked it. Tom felt the shadowy presence of his father in the bedroom, shaking his head over the deterioration. *Sorry, Dad,* Tom apologized.

Dad ran his hand over the book case and held up a palm, coated with dust. And for a moment he was really there, as solid and dependable as he'd been in life.

"Shit!" cried Tom, dropping his book.

Violetta was watching a bedside TV and didn't look up when Tom came in. "You'll never guess what happened on *Diversity Village* tonight," she said. "Monica stole Letisha's baby and passed it off as hers, but Monica's husband is sterile and so—what's the matter, Shug?" Tom was leaning against the door frame, breathing heavily.

"I just saw Dad."

"You mean in a picture?"

"No. I mean he was standing in the back bedroom checking out the dust. He looked absolutely real."

Violetta switched off the TV. "Is he still there?" she said.

"Of course not! It was a hallucination."

"I only asked," said Violetta, " because it's impolite to walk out on your father when he's visiting."

"Damn it, Letta! This isn't a joke! I'm worried that my mind is going soft like Uncle Shumba's." Tom sat down on the bed and rubbed his eyes. "He saw visions."

She sat next to him and massaged his shoulder muscles. "He saw visions all the time because he was a drug addict."

"At the end he was sober." Tom shivered, remembering the emaciated man at Chupacabras Hospital. Shumba had been amazingly cheerful for someone who was dying. His weight was down to ninety pounds and his eyes were as yellow as a dragon's. *I've seen the old gods,* he told Tom. *They're going to throw a party for me when I reach the other side.*

Glad to hear it, said Tom, struggling to keep back tears. *I guess they'll ask you to play the drums.* Shumba's drumming was famous.

Not this time. I'm the guest of honor, said his uncle. *The Mhondoro himself is going to play and the Rain Queens will dance.* He seemed to have a clear idea of what to expect.

That's going to be some party, said Tom, trying to remember which god the Mhondoro was.

Remember, I've left you the farm, said Shumba. *The monks will take care of it until you arrive. Don't leave it too late.*

I won't, lied Tom. He had no intention of moving there unless he was desperate.

Shumba laughed softly as though he knew Tom was jiving him. It turned into a terrifying coughing fit and Tom rang for the nurse. She immediately called the doctor. *You can't hide from the spirits,* whispered Shumba between racking coughs. The doctor ordered Tom outside and he never saw his uncle alive again.

"He died fifteen years ago," said Tom, coming back to the present.

"You need to get out more, Shug. You spend too much time on the Internet," advised Violetta. "There's a series on TV about the work of the Youth Patrol. The members check out neighborhoods for code violations, substandard housing and so forth."

"That's all this country needs, more snoops," said Tom.

"Tonight's show was about seniors who live alone. There was a woman who kept ninety-three cats in an apartment and a man who collected newspapers until all he had left was a tunnel going between the bed and the toilet."

Here it comes, thought Tom.

"At first it was really upsetting. The Youth Patrol kicked down their doors and dragged them outside. I don't know why they had to be so violent. I suppose the man and woman weren't cooperating. It came out all right in the end, though. They were moved into a nice-looking government retirement home, where they could get free meals and everything."

"There's no such thing as a free lunch," said Tom.

"My mistake," Violetta said. "Those people got what they were *entitled* to. What we're all entitled to from Senior Security."

"I won't move into a government rest home."

"It's not like the old days," said Violetta, warming to the topic. "There's a communal dining hall and enrichment courses to keep your brain sharp. They have dances every week. A social facilitator sets you up with instant friends."

"I don't want instant friends," said Tom.

"Instant is better than nothing, which is what we got. Anyhow, we don't have to move into a government home. With your pension and savings we could afford Joy Meadows."

No, no, no! thought Tom, but he didn't say it aloud. He was too tired for this argument tonight. "What happened to the cats?"

Violetta frowned. "Don't change the subject. My point is, people get weird when they don't have enough company and sometimes they see their daddy in the back bedroom. Your brain isn't going soft, Shug. You're lonely."

Tom bit back a reply: *Maybe the woman was happy with her ninety-three cats*, he thought. *Maybe she didn't want to be rescued.* But he couldn't blame Violetta.

After the kids moved away there was literally nothing for her to do. The streets had become too dangerous to visit friends, if she even had any left in the city. The stores had closed. The bus system had died. The church had turned into a 12-step program. If anyone was going crazy from loneliness it was Violetta.

She couldn't get a job. She was the most loving, warmhearted caregiver Tom had ever seen, but she had no paperwork to prove it. Kindergartens demanded a Ph.D. before you were allowed in the front door. Fat lot of good a Ph.D. did, Tom thought. Most of the kids he saw acted like they'd been raised by dingoes.

"You aren't listening," Violetta said.

"I'm thinking," said Tom. "We already have a place to retire and it won't cost us a dime. My uncle's ranch is big enough for the kids to visit us for as long as they like."

"That old place," said Violetta, shuddering. She remembered it from the disastrous vacation Tom wished they hadn't taken.

She rose—for a traditionally built woman she was extremely graceful—and led the way to the kitchen. They had a midnight feast of pot roast, candied yams and baby peas flavoured with mushrooms. The walls of the kitchen were decorated with drawings the children had brought home from school. Violetta changed them to go with the season and now Tom noticed that they involved Christmas trees. Funny, he'd forgotten all about Christmas, or rather Gifting Day as it was called now. It had been boiled down to an anonymous mélange of Hanukkah, Kwanzaa, Yule and a dozen other holidays celebrating midwinter.

The air was fragrant with the cherry pie Violetta was heating in the oven. She herself was wearing a gorgeous purple caftan and her dainty hands made circles in the air as she described the soap operas she'd been watching all day. Tom thought she was the prettiest thing he'd ever seen.

"Speaking of cats," Violetta said, "someone threw a dead one over the fence again. I don't know where they find them. It's the third time this week."

Two: *CUBBY WILLOWS*

CUBBY WILLOWS was trying to enjoy himself. He didn't like official get-togethers and removed himself from such events as quickly as possible. The music was too loud, the catered food too salty, the champagne—produced at the lab's experimental vineyard—too weird.

But this was Cubby's party, the first anyone had thrown for him in forty years. He felt obligated to be happy. The courtyard had been made as festive as possible by the secretaries. Paper streamers draped the gray cement walls, balloons bobbed over snack tables covered with biohazard bags. A faded cardboard Santa hung from a wire next to the figure of Uncle Gunnysack, a new bestower of holiday gifts from Haiti. Cubby's colleagues were perched on empty animal cages with plates of hors d'oeuvres and glasses of weird champagne.

Cubby's boss, Dr. Slithe, signaled for silence and a secretary turned off the tape recorder. "Dr. Willows has been with us for forty years," Slithe began. "In all that time he has not missed a single day of work. He has given generously of his evenings, weekends and vacations for research. I believe I am justified in saying that Burton, Barton, Gerbill and Slithe Laboratories would be a far less esteemed establishment without the presence of such a dedicated scientist."

There was a sprinkling of applause. Slithe grinned boyishly. He was one of those men who would maintain choir boy looks into his 90s and whose hairline would never recede. It was said that he took yearly trips to Shanghai, where he was implanted with the testicles of unwary sailors. Cubby, of course, had not heard the rumor.

"Dr. Willows' papers have been enthusiastically received both here and in Eastern Europe," Slithe went on. "He was given the Golden Aphid Award by"—Slithe consulted a note card—"the University of Belarus. It is with great pleasure that I honor our respected colleague with this plaque showing our heartfelt appreciation for his years of service."

Cubby stumbled to his feet. His boss handed him a slab of wood laminated with a certificate. "Speech! Speech!" someone called.

"No! An imitation!" someone else shouted amid general laughter.

Cubby cleared his throat and looked out over his audience, many of whom had not been born when he started work. He did not recognize them and he was almost certain they didn't know him. He never came out of his lab. His single social skill was an uncanny ability to make insect noises.

"I give you," Cubby said, "the mating song of *Gryllus assimilis*". Whereupon he produced an amazing likeness of the low, drizzling love-call of a cricket on a summer night. He followed it with the shrill cry of a cicada, the monotonous buzz of a blue bottle fly, and finished with a selection of bee hums, from *planning-to-swarm* to *oh-my-god-what-happened-to-the-queen*.

Everyone cheered. Cubby sat down amidst applause and accepted a glass of champagne from genetically engineered grapes. Those grapes would never fall prey to the glassy-winged sharp shooter. Any sharp shooter that stuck its beak into those vines would keel over in a convulsive fit, an enormous boon to the California wine industry.

Cubby allowed himself to fade into the fabric of the laboratory as gratefully as a bee slips into its hive. What kind of individuality does a bee need, after all, thought Cubby. It exists to work. It needs no conversation beyond the wiggle-dance that says *the honey is here, is here, is here*. It is surrounded by its fellows. Somewhere, deeply buried, is a gigantic queen whose presence permeates the nest but who needs no flattery, no candle-lit dinners and no anniversary gifts. She didn't even need sex, having wrenched what she required from an unlucky drone as a teenager.

Best of all, you didn't have to talk to her. Cubby had minimal conversation skills. If he could have communicated with pheromones, he would have been completely happy.

After a while the party wound down and everyone drifted off to his or her work station. Cubby was unusually lucky in that he had his own room—a relic of earlier times when the earth was not so densely populated and there was space for everything, and time. Cubby's lab was full of equipment that worked slowly and erratically. Only he was able to get results from them. His windows were fogged up with years of oily dust so that the interior was in perpetual twilight. No matter. The fluorescent light buzzing in the ceiling was adequate.

All was arranged according to Cubby's likes. If you had looked in you would have seen (going clockwise) a microscope, a gas chromatograph, a scintillation counter, a lab bench covered in linseed oil, Cubby, an incubator, a fridge, a rack of field samples, the chemical cabinet and so on back to the microscope. Round and round they went with Cubby fitting himself in as neatly as a caddis fly larva into its little silk bag.

Four o'clock came. The senior scientists left, secure that their work would be carried on by underlings. Five o'clock. The secretaries and a few of the lab technicians departed. Six. Dr. Slithe came by. "Carrying on to the last I see," he said, smiling. Seven. The rest of the technicians left and the first of the janitors arrived. Regular as the equinox, Cubby thought, pleased by the orderliness of things. At eight Tom Seaworthy arrived.

Cubby was surprised, for the man avoided any scientist who was still working. Tom was his own age, though he was more weathered. His face was scarred from a long-ago fight and his scanty beard parted on one side of the divide and continued on the other. His left hand was missing a finger. Cubby knew little about the janitor, but he had always liked him. Tom worked silently, disturbing no experiment and rearranging no papers. Every night he waxed the hallway, pushing his polisher from one end of the building to the other with a smooth, relaxing sound.

"How was the retirement party?" Tom asked. Cubby looked up, startled. It was unlike the man to speak.

"Okay," he replied cautiously.

"I cleaned up the mess," the janitor offered. "Mauled sand-wiches, greasy paper plates, cigarettes floating in champagne. I've seen five-year-olds with better manners. They left me a snack which I put into the bin. You never know what's in the stuff around here."

Cubby had never heard him say anything so long and com-plicated before. He didn't know how to respond.

"They say Slithe drinks the champagne as a preservative," Tom went on. "That's why he never gets any older. My theory is that he's made a deal with Satan like Dorian Gray. Somewhere in his house is a portrait that gets older and older. How else can you explain a man who looks like a Gerber baby food ad?"

Now Cubby was astounded, not only by the criticism of Dr. Slithe, but by Tom Seaworthy's knowledge of literature. Who could have guessed that a janitor read books? And then Cubby was ashamed of his snobbishness. He struggled to think of some-thing to say.

"You left this behind," said Tom, handing him the plaque of appreciation. "Mind you, I'd do the same. They'll give me one when I retire next week, the tight-fisted bastards, and I intend to put it down Slithe's pants. It'll be the first woody he's ever seen. Don't look like that, Dr. Willows. I won't really do it."

"You—you're retiring next week?" Cubby managed to say.

"Sure. The new Senior Law. Step aside and leave a place for the next sucker, but I won't be sorry to go. That reminds me. There's a rumor going around that you're moving to a whorehouse in Brazil and plan to spend the rest of your days drinking rum cocas with a naked showgirl on each knee."

"N-no. Not that," Cubby said, aghast.

"Thanks. I'll tell the others. It'll put their minds at rest." Tom grinned widely, showing uneven, yellow-stained teeth. "I won't move any of this stuff till you're out of here, Dr. Willows. Take your time, 'cause I'm here all night." He went out the door, calling to another janitor at the end of the hall.

Cubby sat in a kind of shock. *Move stuff?* His stuff? He looked around the room at the microscope, the gas chromatograph, the incubator. They didn't work well—he was the first to admit it—but they were not *totally useless.* But now he remembered half-heard conversations, of how crowded everyone was and how space was needed, and of someone shushing someone else when they saw him.

He should have asked to keep the equipment. Better that than see it hauled off to the dump! But in reality he had no place for it. His apartment was tiny, and besides, what would he do with it? His job was to catalogue insects, to boldly go where no entomologist had gone before (or at least process the samples sent to him by such explorers). All his work, *his whole life*, lay in a scant thirty papers gathering dust in some library. Who cared that the Peruvian braconid wasp had two sub-basal spots on its abdomen rather than the four sported by its neighbor the Paraguayan braconid wasp?

A silent avalanche poured down in Cubby's mind. He had just attended his retirement party, something he knew of course, but had preferred to forget. When he went home tonight, Tom Seaworthy would roll a hand truck through the door. He would load up the scintillation counter, the sample rack, the chemical cabinet. It wouldn't matter if something broke. Much worse things would happen at the dump.

Cubby broke out in a sweat. What about his notebooks? He had been trained long ago—he could still see the high school biology teacher in his mind's eye—to keep such perfect records that if he fell down dead, the next scientist could pick up his work and continue on without a pause. But now people kept information in computers. They sent it all over the planet. No one had the patience for beautifully constructed lab notebooks. *They would throw his books out.*

Cubby, feeling unutterably wicked, made a selection of his finest work. There were too many to take all, but he managed to load twelve of the best into a box. This was stealing, for a scientist's research belonged to the lab and every pore of Cubby's body revolted against it. But he had to do it.

Last of all, Cubby fell back on the comfort of routine. He cleaned and sterilized the work bench. He made sure the incubator and refrigerator were at the correct temperatures. He lined up the dissecting instruments and placed the chair under the desk. Then, struggling with the heavy box of lab notebooks, he turned out the lights and closed the door.

Cubby walked home unless it was after dark. Then he

usually slept in the lab, but stealing the books made that impossible. He hailed a cab and the driver cursed him when he discovered the trip was only six blocks.

The apartment was on the edge of the industrial part of town. The border was a noisy, disreputable street called Sasquatch Avenue. A line of bars and cheap restaurants lined one side and on the other, factories loomed in a gray twilight like the Communist side of Berlin before the wall came down. It was on the Communist side that Cubby lived.

Strictly speaking, his building was not zoned for apartments. A factory filled the lower floors, but on the roof was a small structure that must have served as an office at one time. There was a bedroom, a sitting room and a cramped kitchen that segued into the bathroom. Cubby could sit on the toilet and keep an eye on whatever he was cooking in the microwave.

Cubby reached this place by a fire escape at the back, and a difficult time he had of it, too, hauling the precious lab notebooks up the ladder. At the top he unlocked a metal door and switched on a bare light bulb hanging from the ceiling.

From there the evening proceeded in its usual manner. He stacked the disturbing notebooks behind a saggy easy chair and poured himself a gin. The sounds of Sasquatch Avenue were muted. The speeding cars, sirens and breaking bottles were gentled by the massive building in front. A pool of security surrounded the easy chair.

The very act of climbing the fire escape was like leaving the known world and ascending into a zone of peace. Little had changed in the forty years Cubby had lived there. The furniture came from his parents' house and the fixtures, with the exception of the microwave and TV, were old. The plumbing in the apartment was unreliable and water chugged ponderously from deep within the building to fill his rust-stained bath tub. But contentment is a matter of perspective. Such amenities would have awed Archimedes.

Cubby microwaved a dinner and settled in front of the TV. He watched a program about Egyptian mummies. Egyptologists kept finding more and more of these tucked under the shifting sands of Saqqara. Few, unfortunately, were of any quality. Everything got stuck in the sands of Saqqara—cats, monkeys, herons, crocodiles, as well as the lower-class servants. It was like rush hour traffic in the afterlife.

By now Cubby was drowsy and he crawled into the fat comfortable bed he had inherited from his parents. It had accommodated five generations of Willows and as Cubby sank into the familiar dust of his ancestors it seemed to welcome him. He dreamed of mayflies dancing over a sunlit pond.

*   *   *

Cubby sat up abruptly. A sound like the hum from a contented hive radiated from the next room, and a golden light filled the doorway. *Fire*, he thought wildly, but the hum had no urgency. He heard the clink of glasses and the sound of a champagne bottle being opened. He rose and put on his bathrobe.

At least a dozen people were standing in his living room, and when he entered they all raised their glasses and cried, "Well done, Cubby!"

"Who are you?" he said, squinting at the intruders. Light floated in the air like mist, a most unusual effect. He sniffed to be certain it wasn't smoke.

"Surely, you recognize me," said a tall, cadaverous man behind the easy chair.

"Mr. Strickland?" said Cubby.

His high school biology teacher was turning over the pages of one of the lab notebooks. "Excellent," said Mr. Strickland. "The data is laid out in a coherent manner. The writing is legible and the entries dated properly. Your argument that fleas taste their food source before feeding seems well-reasoned."

"Y-you taught me how to keep records," Cubby stammered.

"Indeed I did, lad. Remember, if you fall down dead another scientist should be able to take your records and continue working without pause."

"I remember," said Cubby fervently.

Now he saw other mentors going back to his earliest years. "You were a good little fellow to have in class," said Miss Feeny, his first grade teacher. "So obedient and reliable."

"You volunteered to clean the chalkboard after class,"

remembered his second grade teacher.

"And your homework assignments were always on time," added his third.

"Thank you," Cubby said, embarrassed. It had been years since anyone had noticed how painstaking and careful he was. He was not used to so much praise. No one, in fact, had paid attention to him since the Golden Aphid Ceremony in Belarus.

He remembered the uncomfortable flight on Aeroflot (or Aeroflop as some wags called it), the grim stewardess, the bags of bread and cheese she threw to the passengers as though feeding rats. But ah! The welcome he received on the ground made up for it. He basked in the cheering applause of his colleagues. He thoroughly enjoyed the tour of the broccoli farm where his aphid control methods were in place, and for once he was not tongue-tied. "Did you know," Cubby told his fascinated audience, "that aphids are *born pregnant*?" All was tucked into Cubby's memory to be pulled out and cherished at need. He looked around for the disheveled gentleman who had given him the award, but he wasn't there.

At the far end of the room, where the window looked out across the dark roof of the factory, stood three men in lab coats. "Dr. Willows! Come and join us!" they called.

It was Burton, Barton and Gerbill, the founders of the lab Cubby worked for (*had* worked for, he reminded himself). Burton and Barton's coats were a spotless white as befitted the lords of such an establishment, but Gerbill, a good-natured German with a strong accent, always seemed flecked with whatever he was working on—moss, leaf mold, guinea pig blood.

"You never missed a day of work," said Burton.

"Week ends and holidays, too," added Barton.

"Vell done, Cubby!" said Gerbill.

Something nagged at the back of Cubby's mind, something he didn't want to bring out into the open. But it wouldn't be pushed away like the lab notebooks behind the easy chair.

"You're all dead," he said.

"Ve are," agreed Gerbill with his endearing accent. Cubby remembered that field trips with him always ended up in a beer hall. It was amazing how Gerbill found them, even in the depths of the Mojave Desert.

They were hunting for the Mexican honey ant whose colonies included specialized workers called "repletes". Repletes hung from the roof of the nest as bloated bags full of nectar. They never went outside. They never joined clubs, made love or took up sports. Their whole lives were spent suspended from a ceiling as a sort of ATM for hungry ants. At the end of the day Gerbill had led Cubby to a beer hall in Barstow, complete with homesick Germans banging steins and a blonde singing *Lili Marlene*.

"This is a dream," Cubby said.

"It is und it isn't," said Gerbill. A great fear fell on Cubby then. To what kind of celebration had he been invited, hosted as it was by the dead? He tried to wake up, but the party went on relentlessly with more food being produced from who knew where, and more bottles of champagne being opened. The praises flowed around Cubby, warming and chilling him at the same time. The principal of his high school, who had written a glowing recommendation to get him into college, said, "Never did I have such an orderly student. You were never late for class, not once."

And Cubby thought *They speak of me in the past tense.* He went back to bed and pulled the covers over his head. The party went on unabated in the next room.

Three : *UNCLE SHUMBA*

THERE ARE MOMENTS when a seemingly trivial action changes the course of one's life. Sitting behind a particular girl in biology class, for example. Two seats over and you would have met Enid Glock, fallen in love and married her. You would have gone from strength to strength, becoming CEO of your own company by age 28. Then, in an economic downturn, your stocks would plummet. Your house would be foreclosed. Enid would leave you for a plastic surgeon. You would observe, from your place in a homeless encampment, as this new husband made her progressively younger until her eyebrows migrated to her hairline and her mouth resembled that of a gasping carp. We take our consolation where we can.

But you sat two seats back instead and met Fiona Farnsworth. From there your life unfolded like a seamless highway with neither peaks nor valleys to disturb it. You never became a master of industry, neither did you end your days in the gutter. Once, during a near-accident your life flashed before your eyes. Normally this takes thirty seconds, but in your case only two were necessary.

For Tom, this moment happened when he was twelve years old. Unknown to his father, he had skipped school and followed his Uncle Shumba to an anti-war demonstration in Berkeley.

*   *   *

Uncle Shumba walked with the well-oiled stride of a big cat padding through the jungle. Tom often tried to copy this movement. It was so confident, so *cool*, but his legs and body wouldn't cooperate.

"Years of dancing," said his uncle, noticing the boy's efforts. "Years of dancing. You'll grow into it." He carried the *tambour*, the African drum he was going to play at the anti-war demonstration. It was covered with animal skin and had a strange feral odor.

"I wish I could play," said Tom, hurrying to keep up. "Dad says it's a waste of time for me to study music. He says you're the only one with *juju* in his soul."

Shumba turned and held up his hand like a traffic cop. "Hold it right there. Your dad got no call to discourage you. *Juju* comes in all sizes and it looks different depending on who's got it. Maybe you aren't meant to be a musician. Maybe you're good at carpentry or fixing cars."

Tom shook his head. He wasn't good at anything and he'd helped his father enough with the farm to know he hadn't an aptitude there.

"*I* believe in you," his uncle said, warming Tom's heart. "I got the shadow skin from the old gods of Africa and I see things nobody else can. The old gods are interested in you."

"I hope not," said Tom. Dad said that Shumba was a good man, but he was crazy. He had something called—the boy had to search for the word—*schizophrenia*. It was what happened when the old gods were interested in you.

Shumba laughed comfortably. "What *you* want doesn't signify. If the spirits want you, they'll get you." He lit up a reefer right there in public with people all around. Tom began to think skipping school had been a bad idea.

Women naked from the waist up were clapping and chanting *make love, not war*. They wore flowers in their hair, just like the song. Raggedy-looking men were cheering them on, saying *right on* and *tell it, sisters*, just like the amen corner at church.

"What are they doing?" Tom asked his uncle.

"Krishna dances with the milk maids," said Shumba mysteriously.

"No, come on," begged Tom. "That doesn't look like an anti-war demonstration to me."

"It's part of the pattern. It's coming together."

Shumba was beginning to ramble and Tom realized that he was stoned. Dad said his brother was hooked on anything he could sniff up or swallow. But Tom still liked his uncle, crazy or not, and there was no question that other people admired him. Right now he was dressed in a green-and-red caftan, his hair radiated like a black sun, his neck was festooned with *juju* charms and his wrists were ringed with elephant hair bracelets. He was the most *happening* thing on the street and hippies were already gravitating toward him.

Shumba sat down on the sidewalk and patted the ground for Tom to sit beside him. "Before I begin playing, I want to teach you another word in our language," he said. This was an ongoing lesson where Tom was supposed learn the ancestral speech of his tribe. The location of this tribe was in a mysterious place called The Land Between the Morning and the Evening Sky. Tom was never able to find it on a map, and it was possible that Shumba had made the whole thing up. "Today's word is *kunyumwa*. Repeat it."

"*Kunyumwa*," said Tom, obediently.

"*Kunyumwa*," echoed the hippies around them.

"What's it mean, brother?" one of them said.

Shumba looked around, his smile taking in the audience, the flower girls, the sunlight, the wisps of pot smoke curling up. "*Kunyumwa* means *to sense that something is wrong*. It tells you when things are about to get dangerous, when the elephant is going to charge. You can feel it in the air. You can feel it here." His uncle patted his stomach. "I'm an expert and right now I don't feel any *kunyumwa* at all."

"Right on! Everything's totally mellow," the hippie agreed.

Shumba began to play the *tambour* and the sound rolled out like an earth tremor. Tom's ribs vibrated and his heart beat in syncopation. The rhythm followed its own logic, never repeating itself, just growing and growing like a jungle vine snaking through the trees and carrying birds, animals and people with it until the boy realized that he was dancing, *had* been dancing for he didn't know how long.

The hippies were dancing, too, and the girls with flowers in their hair. That was the effect Shumba had on people when the spirit was in him. He made you feel like the sun had just come up. Everyone *grooved* and *spaced out*, aided by the joints that were passing around. A girl held a cigarette to Shumba's lips.

In the distance Tom heard sirens. He grabbed his uncle's sleeve. "Let's get out of here."

"Where's *here*? Where's *out*?" Shumba's eyes had turned red and unfocussed.

"I think the cops are coming."

But his uncle was deep inside the jungle vines and couldn't hear him.

"Come on! Dad's gonna kill me if I wind up in juvie," Tom begged.

"*There was never a time when I did not exist, nor you, nor any of these kings,*" Shumba murmured. "*Nor is there any future in which we shall cease to be.*"

"What kings? What are you talking about?" Tom was beginning to get scared. He could hear the sirens getting closer.

Shumba suddenly came back to the present and extracted several dollar bills from a string bag around his neck. He crammed them into Tom's hand. "For the bus fare," he said. Then he went back to whatever landscape he had been contemplating.

When the cop cars rolled up Tom bolted, but he forced himself to stop a short distance away. He heard shouts and screams and the thump of bottles being thrown. Someone yelled, "Kill the pigs!" Everyone was streaming toward the action and suddenly hundreds of people filled the street. Tom fought his way back and caught a glimpse of Shumba being loaded into a police van. He was grinning as though somebody had just told him the best joke in the world.

What am I going to tell Dad? Tom thought. *He'll find out I skipped school.* But somebody had to bail Shumba out or—worse—get him out of Chupacabras Asylum. It wouldn't be the first time his uncle wound up there. Cops shoved through the crowd and Tom suddenly sensed *kunyumwa* all over the freaking place.

He ran until he was out of breath. He found himself on a quiet avenue shaded by liquid amber trees, his heart pounding and his body covered in sweat. This part of the campus was entirely peaceful. Only a faint whiff of tear gas drifted on the breeze.

I sure showed a lot of class back there, the boy thought

miserably. *Left my uncle the minute things got tough. I am such a loser.*

He had no idea where he was. He didn't know which bus to catch and he was suddenly, ravenously, hungry. He took out Shumba's money. Three dollars. Just enough for bus fare.

Shumba said you could live off the land by going through garbage cans. Tom looked into the nearest can and saw a heap of old, snotty tissues on top of a half-eaten sandwich. He had to sit down on the curb to keep from throwing up. He was never going to make it as a hobo.

He was never going to make it as anything. His grades were lousy. He knew his parents were disappointed in him. He just couldn't seem to get it together. And now he was going to get his ass whipped for playing hooky. *I am sooo dumb.*

Tom wiped his eyes, furious at himself. *Come on. Think.* He walked into the nearest building to look around. It was eerily deserted, as though everyone had been sucked up by a flying saucer and he was the only human being left. *That's a cool fantasy,* the boy thought. *I could raid all the rich people's houses. Yeah.* Tom tried a few doors. Locked. He drank from an ice-cold drinking fountain. He looked for change in the public telephones. Around a corner he discovered a candy machine.

Tom always carried a rolled-up ball of wire in his pocket for emergencies, and with very little effort he hooked an Almond Joy out of its slot. He got to work on freeing a bag of peanuts.

"Hold it right there!" A security guard shouted.

Tom fled up a flight of stairs and through hallways and up more stairs and still more stairs with the man pursuing him. He dodged through an open door and crouched behind it, gasping for breath. On *Bonanza*, the bad guys always rode past the arroyo where the good guy was hiding, but the maneuver didn't work here. Tom could see the guard's shadow on the frosted glass of the door.

"Excuse me, sir. Did you see a boy run in here?"

Tom looked up and to his horror saw an old white man seated at a table. The man was massive, not with fat but muscle, and his large hands grasped a book he could easily have torn in two. He was looking straight at Tom. "Did you lose a boy?" the old man asked.

The guard laughed—apologetically, Tom thought. "Not exactly, sir. A little punk was stealing candy out of the machine."

"Candy," the man said thoughtfully. "I have always personally liked candy, although the doctor says I should not eat it. No, I haven't seen the boy."

"Well . . . sorry to have bothered you."

"I am here to be bothered," the man said. The guard left. After a moment, the man got up and approached the door. Tom braced himself to flee. "I've been sitting here all morning waiting for a visitor," the man said, calmly, closing the door. "No one came. They are all walking around the streets, shouting, carrying signs. People in the grip of passions. Would you like to share my lunch?"

Tom unfolded himself, uncertain of what to expect.

"Sit there." The man indicated a chair and bent down to retrieve a bag from the floor. "Fettuccini. I picked it up from an Italian restaurant on Telegraph Avenue. They were shuttering their windows in preparation for the peace demonstration." He divided pasta and garlic bread onto paper plates. "I don't have enough utensils, but you can use the fork and I will make do with the spoon."

"Thank you," Tom said. He had never eaten fettuccini before, but it smelled wonderful.

"My name is Eric Hoffer, and you?"

"Tom Seaworthy."

"Go ahead, Tom. Eat. Do you know, when I was young I believed that if I went without food for a single day I would die."

"Really?" The fettuccini was as good as it smelled. Tom was having difficulty remembering his table manners.

"I thought it was like putting gas into a car. If a car runs out of gas, the engine stops."

"That makes sense," said Tom. The garlic bread was heavenly.

"It makes sense for machines," Mr. Hoffer corrected. "People are not machines. At any rate, one day I was too poor to buy food and I sat down and waited to die. I was very surprised when I didn't. Did you manage to get any candy?"

"Um, yes. I know stealing is bad. Do you want me to give it back?"

"That would be difficult now. Do you read many books?"

Tom was startled by the change of topic, but he answered. "Not really."

"You haven't felt the need for it yet. When I was your age I was blind."

"*Blind?*"

"My mother fell down the stairs while carrying me in her arms. She never recovered. When she died, my eyes stopped working. I think maybe I didn't want to see. When I was fifteen my sight returned, but I was so afraid I would go blind again, I read as many books as possible. It is a habit that has never left me."

The man handed Tom paper cups and sent him to the drinking fountain in the hall. Tom looked both ways very carefully, but the security guard had gone. When he returned, he took out the Almond Joy and divided it in two.

It was a day that forever remained etched in Tom's memory. The old man and the boy conversed as though they had known each other all their lives. Mr. Hoffer took everything Tom said with great seriousness and at the same time filled his head to overflowing with ideas. They went from discussing cave paintings in France to medieval cities in Italy where everyone was an artist, even the boys who herded donkeys.

"What did you mean, you were waiting for someone to visit?" Tom ventured to ask.

"The university pays me to talk to people," Mr. Hoffer replied. "Four days a week I work on the waterfront loading ships. On the fifth I come here."

"They pay you for that?"

"Yes. Anyone can come in and ask me questions. Today, as it happened, everyone was busy breaking shop windows or burning draft cards. I felt quite dishonest taking the university's money until you showed up. Do you like school?"

Again, Tom was derailed by Mr. Hoffer's shift of topic. "Not much," the boy admitted.

"I would divide the school day in two," the man said, "with the morning given to reading, writing and math, and the afternoon to learning skills. Retired carpenters, masons, plumbers, mechanics and gardeners would be the teachers. It is most fitting that the human hand, a most unique organ, should come back into its own and again perform wonders."

Tom looked at his hands and thought *yes, they are wonderful*. He glanced at the clock and suddenly realized that several hours had passed. "Oh, jeez. I've got to go home."

"My friend is picking me up. She can drive you." Mr. Hoffer tidied up the scraps left over from lunch and put his book into the pocket of his jacket. On the way home he told Tom about the first book he had ever studied, the *Essays of Montaigne*. It was a thousand pages long with small print and no pictures, and he had read it three times while being snowed in at a gold mine. "Always buy something thick," Mr. Hoffer advised. "It's more economical."

From that day on Tom always carried a book with him. Although his school career was short, in time he became far better educated than anyone at Burton, Barton, Gerbill and Slithe. No one there realized it and now that he was retiring, no one cared.

Hoffer's dream of retired craftsmen passing on their skills to the young had died long before, along with the old philosopher himself.

Four: *THE TACO TRUCK*

CUBBY WOKE at 6 a.m., his usual time. Without thinking, he moved through the morning routine: Tooth brushing, flossing, shaving, showering. Before doing aerobic exercises he observed himself in the mirror on the back of the front door. For a man of sixty-five he was in splendid condition, though pale from not going out into the sun for many years. He had given up field trips when Gerbill died.

Cubby's hair was gray, but healthy. His beard was abundant, his teeth well cared for. His back was straight and he had not shrunk as many older people do from loss of bone mass. He was still a comfortable five-foot-nine. "Yer a handsome devil, *arghhh*" he said, imitating his alter ego Captain Tarantula. Odd. He had not thought of Captain Tarantula in years. It was a persona he had donned to approach girls in high school.

It was much better than approaching them directly as Cubby Willows. If he was rebuffed (and he generally was), the salty-mouthed terror of the seas took the blame. Captain Tarantula did not care. There were wenches a-plenty in other ports, *arghhh.*

Cubby breakfasted on oatmeal with raisins. A glance at the clock said 6:45 and he automatically looked out the window to judge the weather before going to work. Except that the weather didn't matter. He wasn't going to work. Not today, tomorrow or ever.

Cubby was swept with panic. It reminded him of a story he had read long ago of some poor criminal in England who had been hung in chains. It was a refined form of torture where a man was suspended from a gibbet like a silkworm larva, to dangle until he died of exposure or thirst. *Not going to work* was like being hung in chains.

(This particular criminal had lost a shoe as he was hauled up and for some reason this upset him more than anything else. Anyone could see a lost shoe was unimportant to someone who was never going to walk the earth again. But there you are. People often don't worry about the things that matter.)

Cubby had several very bad moments until he realized that *not going to work* didn't mean that he *couldn't work*. After all, factories as ancient as this one were full of insects. For years he had intended to study the behavior of cockroaches. They were far more intelligent than people gave them credit for, learning complex mazes to climb up from the boiler room to a favorite piece of cake on the fourth floor.

He would buy mason jars. He would place a male and female in each one. He would observe the placement of egg cases, the attitude toward the young, the breakdown of law and order as the jars filled up with roaches. The project cheered him immensely. He dawdled happily, pulling out a note pad to plan the experiment. He cleared off a shelf in the living room for mason jars.

At 9 a.m. a most horrible din rose from below. It sounded like a giant piston pounding into the earth and with each blow the room shook. A metallic whine, loud and persistent, accompanied the impact and the smell of hot metal drifted in the window. Cubby realized that he had never been home when the factory was operating.

He hurried to the door. At the bottom of the fire escape hulking machinery rumbled back and forth on errands he could not fathom. The noise made his heart flutter. Cubby dressed rapidly and climbed down the fire escape. A sign said *Hard Hat Required* and to emphasize it one of the machines swung an iron ball on a chain in his direction.

Cubby normally walked to work through the industrial sites. At 7 a.m. it was a peaceful abode of birds and the brave weeds that dared to twine their stems about the chain-link fences. By 9 a.m. all had changed. The factory district was a cauldron of booms, hisses and noxious fumes.

Cubby fled to the street and was astounded by the amount of traffic that had sprung up on Sasquatch Avenue. Cars, buses, taxis, garbage trucks, and an ambulance keening its siren filled the street like a column of army ants on their way to devour a hen house.

There was no traffic light. Cubby had not needed one in the middle of the night when he made his forays to a 24-hour grocery store. Now he stood on the edge of a thundering river and knew that a great gulf had been fixed between him and the world.

How had it happened? Yesterday he had been a gainfully employed man of regular habits. Today he was of less consequence than an ant whisked away on a picnic plate. Ants do not survive long, no matter how well you feed them, away from their nests.

Cubby started walking down the street, trying to calm the panicky throbbing of his heart. He thought there was a traffic light several blocks to the north, but he wasn't sure. A few factory workers hurried past, taking no notice of him. He, of course, was too shy to speak to them.

Presently he came to a taco truck.

It is not generally known that taco trucks are the only food source on California industrial sites. Some workers may bring lunch from home, nutritious meals prepared by loving hands, but the sad truth is that carrot sticks cannot defend you against the desires of the flesh. Your body cries out for cholesterol. Your taste buds clamor for monosodium glutamate. The taco trucks understand this and they lie in wait outside factories, schools and even hospitals where triple by-pass operations are taking place.

Cubby went up to the window and observed the tamales nestled behind smudgy glass, warm in their little lard blankets.

The vendor was listening to salsa music with his eyes closed.

"Excuse me," Cubby said politely. "Could I purchase one of your cheese and green chili tamales."

The vendor ignored him. His finger tapped a jittery rhythm.

"Can you hear me?" enquired Cubby, raising his voice slightly.

The vendor blinked his eyes and suddenly came alert. "*Ay! Muchacho! Digame qué pasa?*"

"Wazzup," said a chunky teenager in baggy pants, tipping up a battered skateboard with an over-sized sneaker. He was accompanied by five other shambling youths. They reminded Cubby of hyenas converging on a carcass and he moved aside hastily. The first teenager leaned into the window, filling up the space. The others crowded behind, placing orders.

"It happens to all of us," observed Mr. Strickland, sitting on a cement wall next to an anemic flower bed. In the daylight he was almost transparent. "We step aside and hand the lab notebook to the next generation."

"You aren't real," said Cubby, annoyed rather than frightened. It was one thing to dream about a man thirty years gone and another to find him sitting next to a taco truck. Clearly, something in yesterday's champagne had been off. It wouldn't surprise him if Slithe were using his colleagues as guinea pigs.

"Provided the writing is legible and the entries dated properly, the research can go on without you," the high school teacher continued. His voice was furry, like a distant radio station in the middle of the night.

"I don't wish to be rude, sir—" Cubby had always been respectful to his teachers—"but you're a hallucination. Besides, I'm not dead."

"You're retired. A man's work *is* his existence."

"I don't have a job, which is an entirely different thing from not working," Cubby argued, thinking uneasily of the incubator and scintillation counter crushed to a lump at the city dump by now. *They* were certainly out of a job. "Retirement has freed me for the research I've always wanted to do. I'm going to make a study of cockroaches." He began to describe how he would trap the insects and place one male and female in each mason jar. He would feed them fruit cake (a roach favorite in his experience).

Mr. Strickland faded from view.

"I'm not that boring," Cubby said, somewhat hurt. But after all this was an illusion and it was foolish to be offended. This day had been so unusual! For forty years everything had hummed along in an orderly fashion with only a few exceptions—Gerbill's field trips and the Golden Aphid Award. Some would have found the routine oppressive, but Cubby wouldn't have had it any other way.

The teenagers were half a block away by now, rumbling back and forth on their skateboards. For a moment the air wavered and Cubby saw a pack of hyenas moving across an African savannah. Bitter-green acacia trees floated above a heat haze. A vulture wheeled in a bleached sky. The alpha hyena carried a bag of *chimichangas* in his jaws.

Where had that come from? Cubby shook his head. Something had definitely been in the champagne. The dead had a party in his apartment last night and today he met his old biology teacher beside the taco truck. But Africa? It was more the kind of illusion Tom Seaworthy would have.

Cubby had no way of knowing that the movers and shakers in the spirit world were beginning to stir. The old gods of Africa, who enjoy *chimichangas* as much as anyone, were following the scent. The boys went to an abandoned house to smoke dope and feed. The spirits watched them, becoming more distinct as they savored the aroma. They remembered the feel of hot, rich food between their teeth and the sensation of well-filled stomachs. They reached out in the dark.

Cubby stopped in the front foyer of the factory to buy a turkey burrito and a bag of cheese nips from a vending machine. He climbed the fire escape and stuffed wads of wet toilet paper in his ears to muffle the blows of the piston. The sound still vibrated through his rib cage and the air carried the odor of exasperated metal.

Five: *TOM'S RETIREMENT PARTY*

TOM SPENT the entire night after Dr. Willows' party cleaning his lab. It was incredible the amount of stuff the man had squirreled away. Tom found a matchbook with Russian on it and a napkin from one of the beerhalls Dr. Gerbill liked to frequent. Gerbill had taken Tom to beerhalls, too, but Tom could never quite relax in a room full of *übermenschen* banging steins on the tables.

It was strange how the old Nazi had taken to him. *You are smart,* Gerbill had said. *You haff the big brain which none of the others do, except for Dr. Willows.* Tom had reminded him that the others had Ph.D.'s up the wazoo. *Ach, they are robots. You are the real deal, as the Americans say,* Gerbill had insisted. Tom had liked the old man very much, even though he'd been in the Hitler Youth. According to Gerbill that had been like a bad first marriage, the kind where you wake up in Las Vegas and don't recognize the person in bed with you.

In some ways Dr. Gerbill had reminded him of Eric Hoffer, the way his mind detoured into interesting paths and of course in his physical presence. In Gerbill's case, the bulk wasn't muscle, but fat. Both men were minus snobbery about work.

No task was trivial according to Hoffer. In particular, maintenance was the most important job anyone could do. Without it cities crumbled and civilizations died. What good was it to plant an orchard and not water the trees? Or build a skyscraper and let the elevators break down? At the end of every great culture was a failure of attention where no one cared to repair the thousand little things that fell apart.

Tom cherished this idea because, after all, he was a maintenance man. He thought the rot had already set in America. Look
at the graffiti, the vandalism, the hordes of teenagers devolving
into apes. Look at the Youth Patrol hunting down the elderly to
force them into Protected Villages. Tom had seen the Villages on
TV. They were filled with old people looking relentlessly happy.
Jaunty music played in the background. A voice-over warbled
about everyone's joyful lives.

If it was so joyful, why was the perimeter fence electrified?

Tom thought long and hard about this and many other questions. And therein lay the problem with his making friends at
work. The other janitors ran like scalded cats from new ideas. The
few times Tom had been lured to a tailgate party, he'd killed the
conversation with some nugget of information gleaned from the
internet. Take the Wollemi pines, for example.

Not long ago someone had found prehistoric trees in a hidden
valley in Australia. They were thought to exist only as fossils, but
one tiny grove had hung on through comet strikes and ice ages.
Tom had been wildly excited by the discovery. Imagine that grove
waiting and waiting for the right moment to emerge, he told the
other men. It made you think there were places all over the world
with stuff everyone had forgotten about. It was like finding a time
machine.

But the others—they were at a Forty-Niners' game and
everyone was wearing the team colors except Tom—stared at him
as though he'd cut the cheese in the elevator.

Fuck 'em, Tom thought. He put the polisher away and
fetched a hand truck for Dr. Willow's equipment. There was work
here to keep him busy for the rest of his tenure at the lab. Slithe
wanted the place gutted.

Tom unplugged the incubator, noting that it had been set for
a precise temperature. Wasn't that just typical? Dr. Willows knew
he'd never set foot in here again, but he'd left everything in perfect
order for the next person. Hell, he'd even lined up the scalpels.

Tom felt vaguely guilty. It was like the time he packed up
his grandma's house after her funeral, finding dresses sixty years
old and cologne bottles with a ghost of scent in their dry interiors.
Tom didn't get rid of the cologne bottles for many years, and
then only because his daughter Atalanta wanted them for a

science project.

He loaded the incubator and scintillation counter and left the rest for another night. The bench had deep indentations where the machines had rested and a layer of insect detritus had been pressed into the linseed oil surface. Tom carefully cleaned the wall behind.

He climbed onto the bench to reach the windows and pulled long, shaggy mats of dust from the glass. Outside, security lights flooded the lab's courtyard where the farewell party had been held. When Tom turned around, he saw the foam mattress jammed under a table.

Damn. Tears came to his eyes. It was as though aliens had abducted the Doc to the mother ship where they would conduct outrageous experiments on him. No one would ever see him again. Tom would never see him again.

He noticed that the book shelf had been disturbed. For a moment he thought something had been stolen, but then he realized that Dr, Willows had taken a few notebooks with him. There were at least two hundred left. *I'll bet he wanted them,* Tom thought. *I should have offered to carry them for him.* Now it was too late. He had no idea where the man lived.

One of the other janitors hailed Tom as he rolled the hand truck to the elevator. "I've inherited your job," he called. "Thanks for the recommendation."

"Glad to help," said Tom genially. The lab paid him extra to take old equipment to the dump.

*   *   *

Tom's retirement party was much humbler than Dr. Willows' had been. He was only a janitor, after all. Instead of chicken and ham the secretaries laid out platters of Moo Meat, an invention that had earned millions for Burton, Barton, Gerbill and Slithe. It was derived from cattle hooves and had no nutritional value whatsoever. Dr. Barton had created it as a diet food and used it to preserve his boyish figure. When he died later of a massive heart attack, the walls of his arteries were found to be coated in a substance very much like Moo Meat.

Covertly, Tom removed the contents of his sandwich

and dangled it in front of a rat cage. The creatures inside ignored it. *Smart buggers*, he thought.

Dr. Slithe made a short speech and presented him with the appreciation plaque. Very soon afterwards everyone deserted the courtyard because it was past five and all the scientists were going home. *On my last day you'd think they'd have the courtesy to clean up after themselves,* Tom thought, gazing at the scattered paper plates and slicks of onion dip on the floor. But why would they? Most of the scientists didn't know who he was and after tonight they'd never see him again.

Once Tom checked out at midnight, his pass card would be invalidated. Forty years of his life would disappear under the sea with barely a ripple. If he wanted to see his fellow janitors, he'd have to wait for them outside.

Not that Tom had close friendships with any of them. Most of the time he was as invisible as Dr. Willows, and that gave him a twinge of melancholy. Only Dr. Gerbill had ever bothered to broach Tom's natural reserve, asking him questions about his life and sharing tidbits of his own.

After polishing the floors for the last time, Tom dropped the appreciation plaque into an incinerator. It was midnight and the parking lot was awash with the kind of storm they called the Pine-apple Express. Tom put on a yellow slicker, rain pants and boots. He couldn't see much on the security cameras and his battered old truck seemed a mile away. He wondered whether thugs were lying in wait for him.

I am sixty-four years and three hundred and sixty-four days old, Tom thought. *Tomorrow I will become a Senior Citizen.* It was a boundary as profound as the one you crossed at age eighteen. At eighteen you put away childish things and learned to drink whiskey and pick up women. You had years of glorious adulthood where you didn't have to go to bed at a reasonable time. You were free at last, even though there were annoyances such as finding work. You could take part in the bounty life had to offer.

At sixty-five this bounty was taken away. Oh, not all at once, but you soon realized that the goodies had only been on loan. The old age repo men came for your eyesight, hearing, and teeth. The government made you renew your driver's license every year and suddenly it became much harder to sign contracts. You had to prove your mental competency every time. The first ads from Joy Meadows showed up in the mail.

Tom closed the door for the last time.

The parking lot suddenly jumped out at him. The shadows, the glinting rain, the hoods of cars outlined by security lights were sharply defined. The air smelled tropical. Water poured out of gutters with a sound like the beat of drums. Tom felt a surge of happiness so long missing that he hardly understood what it was. Forty years of floor polishing contracted to a dot and vanished.

Why do I feel so good? thought Tom. He had no way of knowing that the spirits, who had so bedeviled Uncle Shumba, had waked up. The old gods of Africa, for whom time is elastic, had finally remembered Tom Seaworthy's existence.

A group of thugs was indeed lying in wait for him, but their attention had been diverted by a darkness looming up by the fence. *Mhoro*, whispered a voice in their ears. *Makadii*, responded another. *Makadiiwo,* answered a third. Then a fourth voice rolled out across the parking lot *Mwaaaaaahhhh!* like the side of a volcano breaking open. The gang members fled, dropping their knives and Saturday night specials.

Tom froze with his hand on the truck's door. The footsteps were running away, thank God. The thugs must have been spooked by the lab's security guards. He got inside and started the lengthy process of getting the vehicle to move.

Six: *A VISITOR IN THE NIGHT*

CUBBY HAD FALLEN into a deep sleep and when he awoke it was the middle of the night. He had passed out in his clothes. This left him looking no more rumpled than usual, for it is part of the culture of scientists to pay no attention to fashion. They are soldiers of the intellect and care not for the petty concerns of personal hygiene. Their uniform is the lab coat and acid holes add to their reputation in the same way blood stains enhance the allure of a Hell's Angel jacket. Without their lab coats some scientists are indistinguishable from homeless bums.

"Now that I'm retired, I can wear the same outfit every day," Cubby mused, staring up at the bedroom ceiling covered with a fretwork of cracks, and blotches where the rain came in.

"I can wash my clothes in the bath at night and sleep naked while they dry. Or," he thought daringly, " I could simply *stay dirty*." This was a childhood fantasy—what boy hasn't dreamed of dispensing with baths? Captain Tarantula cared not two pins about filth, sloshing around the bilge as he did with his parrot crapping on his shoulder, *arghhh!*

For a few moments Cubby basked in delightful freedom, but he knew he needed to get supplies. He donned his backpack and set off across Sasquatch Avenue.

What a difference night made! The bars were open and cars crawled along the street looking for women in crotch-high skirts. Everything happened in slow motion and Cubby was easily able to pass among them. The 24-hour store had an ATM inside. Order had been restored.

Glassy-eyed people stood in the cough medicine section, reading the labels very slowly. Teenagers were being watched by a security guard in the aisle where Cubby collected a fifth of gin. He considered for a moment and added two bottles of bock beer to his shopping cart. Odd. He hadn't drunk beer for years. He glanced at a newspaper headline that said, *Boys Committed to Chupacabras Hospital After Bad Drug Trip.*

Cubby loaded up with TV dinners, frozen vegetables and whole wheat crackers. Everything was chosen with an eye to durability because he didn't make this trip often. He had food delivered on Sundays to the bottom rung of the fire escape, from where he could carry it to his apartment. His mail box was there, too, not that Cubby ever got anything but catalogues.

(Once Gerbill had visited him at the factory, but had been unable to negotiate the fire escape. They had shared a turkey burrito on the bottom rung. "Get a cell phone, for Gott's sake," his colleague had implored. "For to call in late or sick."

"I'm never late and my health is excellent," Cubby had said.

"Ve are all mortal, foolish boy. You vill die up there like a helpless bunny, from the flu, the heart seizure, the stroke. I am too fat to climb that goddamn ladder to check up on you." And so Cubby, touched by his concern, had got a cell phone. But it was Gerbill who had died instead.)

Now Cubby was glad of this innovation. In recent years the trek across Sasquatch Avenue had become more threatening. No one had ever bothered him and perhaps no one ever would, but you never knew. Cubby was like a moth that had lived so long with asphalt and cement its wings had taken on those colors. It could cling to the grainy surface of a sidewalk unseen. Yet accidents did happen. A foot could descend on the wrong spot. It was this thought that drove Cubby to order most things by phone.

The store clerk scanned Cubby's purchases and the entomologist loaded the backpack himself, He saw that the clerk had turned his attention to the next customer. Or had Cubby ever had the man's attention? He had certainly not smiled and said "paper or plastic" as he was doing now. To him Cubby was a string of TV dinners followed by a credit card.

Vaguely disturbed, Cubby went out into the street. Gang members tattooed like Polynesian warriors stood in the alleys. Their lips were curled back over their teeth in a snarl, and their eyes were narrowed as they contemplated the passers-by in a kind of trance. Cubby had seen this kind of behavior before.

Males of many species open their mouths in a peculiar grimace known as *flehmen*. In this way they shut off the normal perception of smell and expose a small opening in the roof of the mouth. This is called the Vomero-Nasal Organ, or VNO. It detects the presence of females in oestrus, as the VNOs of these gang members were doing now. They would not detect Cubby any more than they would notice a gray moth resting on cement. Even so, Cubby hurried past.

He was out of breath by the time he reached the fire escape. He had to climb three floors, pausing to rest on each landing, before he reached the door and was able to collapse into the easy chair. Peace settled over him then as he contemplated the mildewed walls and sagging bookshelves. The dear old furniture was exactly where he had left it. The pictures from his parents' house brought with them a light from other years. Cubby himself starred in many (*such a good little fellow*) with his dog Jingle Bell. Jingle Bell was a joint birthday and Christmas present, for the dates were the same.

Most children feel cheated when their birthdays coincide with a major holiday, but at the Willows' residence Yuletide went on for an entire week. Cubby was kept far too entertained to feel he was missing out on anything.

"Bock beer, mine favorite!"

Cubby looked up to see Gerbill sitting in the straight-backed chair that had belonged to his grandmother. (Cubby only had two chairs and, until now, had only needed one.) "How are the beer halls in Heaven?" he asked.

"Not bad, but between you and me mortality is vat makes a good beer hall. Vat good is *Lili Marlene* without the sadness?" Gerbill popped open a bottle and helped himself.

"So are you . . . my guardian angel?"

"Nothing so high. I'm just visiting." The German drank deeply and wiped his mouth with a flourish. "Now that," he said appreciatively, "is good mortality." They sat in silence, as they often had when working together.

(One of their most famous papers was titled "The effect

of cephalectomy on the performance of the male mantid". Cubby had noticed that female praying mantises often nipped off the heads of their suitors. It seemed counter-productive. But the two scientists found, through exhaustive experimentation, that the removal of the head actually *enhanced* sexual performance. "Just like humans," Gerbill had marveled.)

"You never came here when you were alive," Cubby said when Gerbill reached for the second beer.

"Being dead gives you wings."

"Yes, well, I've been wondering about that." Cubby was reluctant to bring up the subject, but he was beginning to worry about his sanity. "I saw Mr. Strickland today."

"Ja, he told me." Gerbill pulled out the pipe he'd carried in life and packed it with tobacco. He lit it, using the elegant gold lighter Cubby remembered from years past. Cubby smelled the rich maple aroma and tinge of sweat that Gerbill insisted came from nubile island girls who picked the tobacco.

"Mr. Strickland's dead."

"Thirty years ago. Heart failure," said Gerbill, puffing his pipe.

"See, that isn't right. Believe me, I'm grateful you're visiting. In fact I've missed you a great deal, but this is something I expected on the other side. How can I see you if I'm not dead?"

Gerbill paused to finish the second beer and looked around for more.

"I'm sorry. I'll order a six-pack tomorrow," Cubby promised.

"Two vas just right," the German said, graciously. "Tell me, Cubby. How many live people do you know?"

The question shook the room like a silent lightning bolt. The walls went white, then dark. Cubby had trouble adjusting his eyes. Then all was normal again. "I know . . ." he faltered " . . . Dr. Slithe."

Gerbill made a rude sound. "Slithe is not someone you can know. He is a conditioned response. You have seen the little kitties the Japanese make out of plastic and fur? You pet them and they purr. You speak nicely and they mew. That's what Slithe is—a robot kitty designed to get grants from foolish businessmen. He is not anyone's friend."

"Well, then . . . " Cubby paused. He remembered his lab, the gas chromatograph, the scintillation counter—*dear* old scintillation counter. It was at the dump by now. *Wait, wait,* he thought frantically. There were the secretaries—what were their names? And the junior lab technicians—Ashok or Khalil or something. The visiting scientist from Brazil—or was it Belize? "I know Tom Seaworthy," he said at last.

Gerbill's outline wavered slightly and became firm again. "Yes. You do know Tom Seaworthy," he said, making Cubby feel as proud as if he'd won a spelling prize in grade school. "He is someone you should know better. You should track him down."

Cubby blushed, aware that in all the years he had listened to the comforting swoosh of Tom's floor polisher, he'd never had a conversation with him. Yet the integrity of Cubby's work depended on the man. Without Tom, no waste baskets would be emptied. No burnt-out lights would be replaced or paper towels left in the dispenser. A lab deteriorated in a hundred ways every day. Cubby tidied up, but every night he left some chaos behind.

In the morning it was gone. Tom also understood how far he could go. He carefully vacuumed between the boxes, test tubes and insect cages. He moved no papers and disturbed no arrangement, no matter how bizarre—a heap of praying mantis heads, for example.

"I think I've left things too late," said Cubby.

"Understand this, mine boy," Gerbill said. "The fewer live people you know, the more *dead people* will show up on your doorstep. You have seen the old men on the street, talking, talking, und no one's there. But someone *is* there. The vife or mother, who can tell? Only, you can't see them. Ve humans can't live alone. If the living are not with us, the dead will come. May I visit tomorrow?"

Cubby was rattled by this sudden shift. "Yes. Yes, of course. I'll order more beer. Same time?" he added, wondering what time meant to a departed spirit.

"It vould be nice to have some of those little sausages wrapped in pastry. Und a few chocolates." Gerbill looked down shyly. "If I could bring my vife . . . "

"Wife?" said Cubby, staring at him blankly. In all the years of working together Gerbill had never mentioned a family. Of course Cubby had never asked. "I—I'd be honored to meet her."

"Pumpernickel with cream cheese is also good," came the German's voice, tapering off into the wind blowing across the roof shingles of the factory. Cubby blinked. The room was empty. And so were the beer bottles.

Seven: *NURSE DEE DEE AND THE SKY CAPTAIN*

TOM SQUEEZED the microscope and chemical supply cabinet between the incubator and scintillator in the back bedroom. Violetta hadn't complained yet, but she soon would. He didn't like the mess either, but it was only temporary.

He had Dr. Willows' address now and looked forward to seeing the man's delight at being restored to his old friends. The secretaries at the lab had refused to give the address to him—what business did a janitor have to call a senior scientist?—but Tom had hacked into the main frame. He was proud of his computer skills. He could cruise around data streams like a shark checking out a New Jersey beach. He knew the salaries and employment history of every person at Burton, Barton, Gerbill and Slithe. He knew that Slithe had altered his birth certificate and was four years past the required retirement age. He learned of several lawsuits involving the side effects of Moo Meat.

To Tom's amazement, he found that Dr. Willows lived only a few blocks away. All these years and he'd never suspected that the man was a neighbor! It would make it easy to return the old equipment, for Tom had decided not to make a profit out of this last batch. He smiled, thinking about how pleased the entomologist would be. *They're like family to him. I swear.* Tom had also rescued the doctor's lab notebooks.

Violetta was preparing a special retirement feast for him, including a Virginia ham and chocolate cake. He kissed her appreciatively and she shooed him out of the kitchen. He settled onto the sofa to watch a muted TV.

"Letta!" he called after a while. "Could you bring me a beer." He heard a chair scrape and the fridge being opened. A moment later Violetta sailed into the living room in a bright, flowered caftan that reminded Tom of a tropical sunrise.

"Don't drink too much before dinner," she warned.

"Have one yourself, Letta. I'm celebrating."

"I'm working. Food doesn't fix itself."

"Just one little sip." Tom temptingly held out the bottle of malt liquor. Violetta graciously took a drink and snuggled next to him on the sofa.

"When are you getting rid of that junk in the back bedroom?" she asked.

"Soon."

"Oh, look!" squealed Violetta. "It's an infomercial for Joy Meadows."

Shit, thought Tom. He saw candy box houses with flower-lined walkways and brilliant green lawns. A camera panned over a golf course dotted with impossibly fit seniors.

Violetta unmuted the sound.

The infomercial music had just enough form to keep you interested, Tom thought, but not enough to reach any conclusion. He'd heard such motivational melodies before in department stores. They meandered through your head like a line of ants on the way to some infinitely sweet pool of honey.

Psychologists had learned that people tended to leave a store when a piece of music ended. But if they looped it again and again, shoppers lingered and bought more. By experimentation, psychologists had discovered which instruments and rhythms motivated a customer to reach for his credit card.

The Joy Meadows melody had a different goal, however. Tom listened intently, trying to figure out its message. "Do *you* have what it takes to be a citizen of Joy Meadows?" said a young woman with enormous breasts filling out the front of a nurse's uniform. Tom flinched. He'd been so caught up in the music he hadn't noticed her. Next to her was a surf god in an airline pilot's uniform. Air Viagra, Tom guessed. Together the pair formed the image of what old people yearned for, a youth where colonoscopy bags and bifocals did not exist.

"Hi! You can call me Sky Captain," said the man.

"And I'm Nurse Dee Dee," the woman chimed in.

"Wouldn't you like the security of knowing that you don't have to fear the sound of breaking glass in the middle of the night?" said Sky Captain. "Mr. and Mrs. Senior Citizen, life isn't what it used to be. Crimes against the age-enhanced have escalated 37% in the last six months alone. Murder is the third most common cause of death after heart attacks and cancer."

The scene in the background shifted from Joy Meadows to a dark alley with indistinct shapes hulking behind trash cans.

"Looks like our neighborhood," said Violetta.

The camera moved in to show an elderly woman sprawled on the ground. Her dentures and glasses lay shattered nearby. "She had only five dollars in her purse," said Nurse Dee Dee. "It wasn't enough to satisfy the gang members who ambushed her."

"Safety Tip #1," advised Sky Captain. "Always carry at least $50."

"If only she had lived in Joy Meadows," Nurse Dee Dee mourned. "No one in our managed care living arrangement has ever fallen prey to gang violence."

"What in hell is a managed care living arrangement?" said Tom.

"Our perimeter has the same sensing devices they use at the Pentagon, and 24-hour security guards with dogs on patrol. But don't let that worry you!" Sky Captain grinned, displaying perfect teeth. "You'll never notice the tireless guardians who watch over you. All you need to think about is the next exciting shuffleboard tournament or the barbeque your neighbors are holding." The scene lightened to show Joy Meadows again with its immaculate lawns and pink signposts reading *Begonia Boulevard* and *Lilac Lane*.

"You'll have state-of-the art health care providers like me to handle those naughty sniffles or take your blood pressure," promised Nurse Dee Dee. Tom thought that if he got too close to her spectacular cleavage, his blood pressure would go through the roof.

"Let's face it," said Nurse Dee Dee. "Life brings changes and as we age, our friends disappear. We don't go out any more. Sometimes it seems like the whole world has turned its back on us."

"You can say that again," Violetta said.

"But here at Joy Meadows life begins anew. No one needs to be lonely. Each person or couple is matched by computer with neighbors who share the same interests. It's like getting instant friends! And you don't have to worry about finding things to do. With dances, craft classes, yoga, sing-alongs and swimming, you won't have enough hours in the day to fit them all in."

"Best of all," enthused Sky Captain, "there won't be any kids to criticize your golf swing or how you look in a swim suit. Those little squirts are banned! So take a free vacation on us, Mr. and Mrs. Senior Citizen. Spend two weeks in our enhanced enrichment habitat and we guarantee that you won't ever want to go home. Remember, our gates are always open for America's most cherished resource."

The camera panned to show happy couples having sundowners, dance floors where all the men looked like Lawrence Welk, swimming pools with chubby ladies kicking in unison. The music swelled and Tom realized he'd been listening to it without realizing it. His malt liquor bottle had slipped from his fingers and spilled its contents on the floor. He grabbed the remote and muted the TV.

"I'd love to have a two week vacation," sighed Violetta.

"Where do they get phrases like *enhanced enrichment habitat*?" Tom complained. "It doesn't mean a goddamned thing."

"It means a place with gardens and swimming pools and—and—friends." Violetta was beginning to tear up.

"Aw, jeez. If we lived there, we'd have to sign away all our assets, Letta," Tom said, looking at the spilled beer and wondering how it had happened. "Our kids would have to give a month's notice before they visited and they couldn't stay more than a single day. I looked it up on the internet."

"We have five loyal and loving children," his wife said. "I know they wouldn't mind a little paperwork."

Which was true, Tom thought. It was one of the gifts granted to the Seaworthy clan by the old gods of Africa. Uncle Shumba might have been crazy, but he was right on the money about that. Seaworthy children never went through awkward teenage phases or neglected their parents in old age. They were completely reliable. "We've already got somewhere to retire, Letta," he said. "My uncle's ranch."

"It's so lonely," said Violetta, sighing . "You can hear coyotes in the middle of the day. Do you remember how we used to go to movies before the kids were born? We used to walk there and still see stars in the middle of the city. It was so nice doing things in a crowd instead of an empty room with an old TV. The laughter was better. And the popcorn! You could smell it before you saw the theater. I used to burrow my hand to the bottom of the bucket where the butter was."

Tom felt the ground slipping beneath his feet. Of course his gentle wife had suffered from isolation. Modern life had been cruel to women like her. For centuries such people had been the custodians of what is in Arabic called *hanan,* or unrestricted, unlimited tenderness. Letta had it in full measure. This quiet nurturing seemed unimportant until it was gone. Then it became clear that *hanan* was what held families together and, by extension, societies and governments.

"You fight dirty," said Tom.

Violetta smiled tearfully.

"All right, all right! I'll go this far: We can take a *one* week vacation in Joy Meadows, but at the end of it we're coming home." Violetta left him and went to prepare the special retirement dinner.

Eight: *RAPTOR MART*

TOM SLEPT THROUGH the day and woke at five p.m. as he had for forty years. He gazed up at the discolored ceiling. The Pineapple Express thundered outside and a small dark patch elongated and became a drip. Tom watched it grow until it detached and fell to the floor. He waited. The patch grew again. It was a repair job he'd neglected, but now he had all the time in the world to do it.

He could sand the bookcases in the back bedroom and replace the fried chicken varnish with something new. He could rewire the security fence, maybe fry whoever was throwing dead cats into the yard.

Tom smelled breakfast from the kitchen. He could feast on waffles, sausages, biscuits with chicken gravy and—a concession to health—a glass of tomato juice. And he wouldn't have to hurry. He could eat a second breakfast if he liked, or a third. Free at last.

Violetta kept the same hours as Tom, filling the time he was away with sewing, cleaning, cooking and soap operas. Sometimes she called one of the children, but the phone wires were frayed and begrudging. Technically, there weren't supposed to be telephones at all, since no one was supposed to be living in the industrial site. Factories and labs used the internet. As for letters, the post office had dried up long ago.

Now and then Cezare and Jeronimo, the Seaworthy sons, showed up with equipment from Cezare's engineering firm. They unstrung the old lines and installed new ones. This was completely illegal, but no one questioned it. Tom had once walked up to workers at the meat packing plant next door to ask whether he could buy directly from them. They looked straight through him. It wasn't hostility, just a kind of blindness. Tom had noticed that people under a certain age had trouble seeing old folks.

And so once a week Tom and Violetta made a trip to Raptor Mart, a warehouse that funneled shoppers through confusing aisles where you were tempted with ten pound bags of frozen frog legs, Mother's Day cards in packs of fifty, and gallon drums of KY. Tom guessed that you could assemble an entire space station if you poked around Raptor Mart long enough. It had been Violetta's only outing for years.

Now, as Tom slathered his third waffle with maple syrup, he saw his wife watching. "It's going to be rough having me around all the time, Letta," he apologized. "I've read about couples that were perfectly happy until the old man retired."

Violetta smiled. "That doesn't apply to us, Shug. Now that you're here we can do all kinds of interesting things. Go to church or the park. Visit people."

What church? What people? Tom thought. You couldn't put a foot down in the park without being stabbed with a hypodermic needle. "We could go to Raptor Mart," he suggested.

"We could," said Violetta.

"Or we could go to a French restaurant and a movie," he hastily added.

"I'd love that! Except that I don't have a thing to wear. A good restaurant wouldn't let me in wearing a caftan and sneakers."

"We'll go to Raptor Mart and buy you a new dress and me a shirt with real buttons on it," Tom said. "Then we'll drive around until we find a place with waiters so snooty they have assistants to carry their menus. I don't know what's out there anymore." And he realized, with a stab of guilt, that he hadn't taken Violetta anywhere for years. Time had slipped by without him even being aware of it. He'd been stuck in a little valley like a Wollemi pine.

Late that afternoon Tom fitted himself into a pair of pants that he hadn't worn since he was thirty. *Not bad*, he thought, looking at himself in the discolored mirror that had been in the family for three generations. He was as fit as a man half his age and with any luck, bell bottoms had come back in style.

Poor Violetta wasn't as lucky. All she had was a closet

full of caftans, most of which were only good for housework. Her shoes spread comfortably around her generous feet, and their original color was only a distant memory. "You can't polish sneakers," she said, sadly.

"Don't you worry. We'll get you new stuff," Tom promised. It was with a great sense of adventure that they set out. The trip to Raptor Mart was a familiar journey, but afterwards they would explore new territory. "Do you think that movie theater on Wendigo Way is still there?" inquired Violetta.

"I don't know. We can look." But when they rolled past all that was left was a burnt-out shell. The whole street was lined with boarded-up windows, yards full of trash and broken street lights. "There's got to be movie theaters somewhere," Tom reassured his wife.

Raptor Mart was crowded with shoppers. "Get your Hoochie Cream here," a loudspeaker blared. "Tighten your love pocket like a sixteen-year-old!" Another speaker shouted, "The first five people at the bakery aisle will get a free chocolate cake!" The path in front of Tom and Violetta cleared as shopping carts thundered off toward the promised treat.

"Shall I—" began Violetta.

"No," said Tom. "You know how tired you get running from place to place."

They found the women's clothing section, but the styles had changed since Violetta had bought her last dress. Spandex was in, with panels cut out for a peek-a-boo effect. It could have been sexy, Tom thought, if the colors had been good. Brown, beige, muddy purple, bruise yellow and dried scab were the hues in favor this year. It made everyone look like an accident victim.

And of course spandex was the last thing a traditionally-built woman could tolerate. "Do you wanna try a spray-on style?" said a clerk, holding up a can from a large display. "Works for everyone. You can keep spraying until the problems are hidden." She waited while Violetta curiously inspected the can and then, suddenly losing interest, wandered off without waiting for an answer.

"How can you spray on clothes?" wondered Violetta.

"First, you have to get naked," said Tom, reading the instructions on a can. "Shake well and apply layers until everything is covered. Avoid the face and—I'm not making this up—the lady parts."

"No!" exclaimed Violetta.

"Says it interferes with natural processes. You can wash it off with a special soap that they sell here." And now that Tom was aware of how spray-on clothes worked he realized that the clerk had been mostly covered with the stuff. "I think this is the wrong department for you," he said.

They walked for what seemed like miles. They passed a display of Gifting Day decorations, on sale since the holiday had been a week ago. Santas, shamans, Hanukkah candles, small Wicker Men with sacrificial victims inside, and Uncle Gunnysacks in various sizes.

"I looked these up on the Internet," said Tom, holding up an Uncle Gunnysack with long, skinny legs and a psychotic expression. "According to the original legend, he doesn't bring presents. He uses the sack to carry off kids to eat."

"I hope the children never hear that story," Violetta said, shocked.

Finally, they found a deserted aisle labeled *Seniors*. Here were the caftans, the muumuus, the bell-bottoms. "Shit," said Tom, reading a sign that said *Remember the good old days* by the bell bottoms. He found a Hawaiian shirt with World War II airplanes on it and Violetta found a silky, black caftan with chrysanthemums. She added black sneakers.

The check-out line moved slowly past food carts wafting the seductive odors of popcorn, chocolate chip cookies and deep-fried donuts. Violetta finally caved in and got a bag of popcorn. She was fading fast.

"Stop that!" cried Tom as a group of girls elbowed Violetta in the stomach and squeezed ahead of her.

"Oo! She's like a pillow!" one of them exclaimed. "Feel her tits." Another girl poked Violetta in the breast. Hard.

"See how you like being pushed," shouted Tom, shoving the girl back. Too late he realized she was wearing spray-on clothes. Her skin felt cold and snaky.

"He harassed me!" shrieked the girl. "He's a dirty old man!"

"Old fart alert! Old fart alert!" screamed the others.

Two security guards appeared and pulled the Seaworthys out of line. "I'll have to see your I.D." said one.

"The old ones come in here to cop a feel," the other said.

"I was the one who pushed that girl," Violetta insisted. "Here's my I.D." Tom was about to protest, but her frown silenced him.

The guard scanned the card with a device he unclipped from his belt. "Two years older and I'd have to detain you," he said, handing it back. "You have to leave the store."

"But we wanted to buy something," cried Tom.

"Not today. Get moving or we'll have to ban you."

Violetta, with surprising energy, grabbed Tom's arm and pulled him through the crowds. The young people in line jeered and laughed. Tom and Violetta got outside and he clicked on his GPS to locate the truck. "Letta, that wasn't right. I was the one who caused trouble."

"You're sixty-five," said his wife. "You're officially a Senior. If someone accuses you of breaking the law, you'll get hauled off to Chupacabras Hospital."

Tom felt the bat wings of depression approaching on the wind. He'd managed to shove the problem of age to the back of his mind. "That bad, huh?"

"That bad," agreed Violetta.

"I wanted to take you somewhere nice."

"We'll drive around, Shug. It's nice being out of the house. We'll look for a movie theater. Find a take-away." Violetta climbed, with some difficulty, into the truck. It was night now and the street lights flickered uncertainly. Tom felt for the bear spray and blackjack he kept under the seat.

"Maybe we shouldn't have come out so late," he said.

"Just drive," said Violetta. And so they went up and down the streets, looking for some oasis of light where they could find food or entertainment, but there was nothing. The taco trucks were shuttered and dark. The movie theaters were nonexistent. Only the all-night groceries and drug stores were open. And the booty shacks, of course.

In the distance a curtain of searchlights pointed up into the sky. "What's that?" said Violetta.

"It's a Youth Patrol rally," said Tom. "You won't like it."

"Let's get a little closer. It's so bright and pretty. I'd like to find something to make the trip worthwhile."

And it was beautiful, Tom thought, that pouring of energy into the heavens. The electric bill must be fantastic, but it was as inspiring as a man-made aurora. As they got closer he could hear the singing. Once, long ago, such things happened in churches. He remembered an Easter Sunday as a boy, only now it was called Bunny Day and the original meaning was lost. His parents had taken him to a service on Angel Island. It was before dawn and the congregation had sat at the edge of the water, facing east. Across the way was Berkeley and beyond, silhouetted against a rosy sky, were the dark hills of Tilden Park.

The sky brightened and suddenly a bead of sunlight appeared between a gap in the hills. The whole congregation rose and raised their voices in praise. *He is risen! He is risen! Hallelujah!* It was a timeless celebration of life appearing in different forms throughout history. So the ancient Egyptians must have stood at the edge of their desert, and so the Celts must have watched the dawn between the pillars of Stonehenge. So, perhaps, did birds and other wild creatures turn toward the east and rejoice because the night was over.

The streets became more crowded as Tom approached Freedom Park. Youth Patrolmen in their black uniforms stood on every corner and stopped people afoot. They approached Tom's truck and suddenly the whole demeanor of the night changed. Tom had been in a near-trance, watching the curtain of light and remembering that Easter sunrise. Now he could see the bowl of the arena at Freedom Park. It was filled with black-clad men.

Kunyumwa, said a voice in Tom's ear. It was a word in the Old Speech, but Tom couldn't remember what it meant. He was aware of a shadow between himself and Violetta, a shadow with a crazy, shit-eating grin.

Kunyumwa, said Uncle Shumba. *It tells you when things are about to get dangerous, when the elephant is going to charge. You can feel it here.* Tom felt the very slightest of pats on his stomach. He wrenched the wheel of the truck to the left and ran over the sidewalk, scattering Youth Patrolmen as he turned. He bumped back onto the street and sped up. The truck was old, but it was very powerful when it got into the sweet spot that trucks liked. Tom raced into the darkness as he listened for gunshots behind.

Round and round the streets he went, driving by instinct and by something else he did not understand. It was as though he had a co-pilot telling him where to go. At last he came back to Sasquatch Avenue and fitted into the traffic. Now he drove sedately as he maneuvered into the deserted industrial site where the old farmhouse lay. His body was soaked in sweat.

Violetta said nothing until they got to the security gate and Tom gave the password. "Could you tell me what just happened back there?" she said.

"*Kunyumwa*," said Tom. He looked so agitated that she wisely kept her silence and merely went inside to heat up leftovers and uncap a bottle of malt liquor.

56

Nine: *SYBILLE*

CUBBY ORDERED an express food delivery in the morning. It cost extra, but he wasn't worried about money. His parents had left him well-off. How well-off he didn't know, never having inquired into the matter. Month by month, year by year, a firm of accountants took his money to clubs on Wall Street where investments of easy virtue lounged. At least that was how Cubby understood it. It was a kind of escort service for money, though how the escorts reproduced was a mystery to him. The same accountants handled his insurance, his tax and now his senior security. His parents had set up the system when he was in college because they wanted him to concentrate on his studies.

And Cubby had concentrated. He graduated *summa cum laude* at Harvard, achieving a Ph.D. with a dissertation on synchronized flashing in fireflies.

(This little-known phenomenon occurs in the mountains of Tennessee. It is the insect equivalent of a rock concert. The male fireflies show up around 8:30 p.m., flashing on and off, watching one another to get the tempo right. The females, hot little groupies that they are, observe from the ground. By 9 p.m. the males are flashing in unison and the females go wild.)

With such a promising beginning, Cubby's parents expected him to have the Nobel Prize by age thirty. But thirty came and went. Cubby settled into the routine at Burton, Barton, Gerbill and Slithe. He did nothing else outstanding. He did nothing terrible either, and after a while Cubby's parents resigned themselves to his quiet, unassuming ways. He was happy. That was the important thing for they loved him very much.

Now Cubby laid out the trappings for a party, the first one he had ever organized. Naturally, he was nervous. He vacuumed and dusted relentlessly. He rearranged the two chairs, realizing too late that he needed a third. He fetched a crate from the industrial yard down below, covered it with an old sheet, and hoped for the best.

Once down in the yard he noticed how quiet the factory was. It was a relief, of course, but how strange that no one was working on a Wednesday. It *was* Wednesday, wasn't it? Cubby checked the calendar. It must be one of those new holidays like Kwanzaa or Tet. He worried that the store might not deliver, but just at five he saw the van drive up.

Cubby had described what he wanted over the phone to the deli. One box contained pigs-in-blankets, another, slices of pumpernickel slathered with cream cheese, a third, chocolates. To go with these were cold beef tongue (Cubby remembered how much Gerbill had enjoyed that), smoked gouda and ham. Two six-packs of bock beer finished the list.

Cubby laid the food out on Chinese willowware dishes he had inherited from his grandmother. He remembered evenings at his grandmother's house. He still had her oak table that could be fitted with extra leaves to accommodate extra guests. There were always many visitors in his grandmother's house—his parents, his aunts and uncles, great-aunts and great-uncles and elderly cousins dressed in formal clothes that smelled of cedar.

What good times they were! The conversation never flagged. The laughter never stopped. The table was covered by a white cloth crocheted by his grandmother. Her signature dishes—fluffy mashed potatoes and midget peas with carrots—were on the side board.

Afterwards, they put records on the Victrola. Even then, Victrolas were a thing of the past, and the music was scratchy and out of style. They listened to "Red Sails in the Sunset" and "Beyond the Blue Horizon", his mother's favorite, while they played canasta. Cubby was never made to feel the slightest bit excluded from this adult world. He wasn't bored by the stories, not even on the fourth or fifth retelling, because they were a kind of music that could be listened to again and again. His exploits at school were given great attention because all the relatives were interested in him. He was the only child.

Families start out with two individuals and, as the generations pass, grow larger and larger, forming a pyramid of descendants. But sometimes the reverse is true. For one reason or another fewer are born into each generation. Cubby's great grandparents had had eighteen children, the eighteen had produced seven offspring. His parent's generation had only produced one. Him.

Cubby shook himself. He was surprised to find his face wet with tears, and that made no sense because the memory had been a happy one.

Darkness had almost fallen. A storm had blown in from the Pacific, the kind they called The Pineapple Express, so that the air was both warm and wild. Water sucked up from a coral atoll beyond the blue horizon poured down upon the factory, and wind stripped off long shreds of tarpaper.

The phone rang.

Cubby almost dropped the bowl of chocolates he was carrying. With shaking hands he placed it on the little gateleg table he used for pinning out dead insects.

The phone kept ringing, six . . . seven . . . eight times. Cubby had no answering machine. He didn't need one because no one ever called him and he couldn't imagine who might be doing so now. He hadn't answered a phone in twenty years. The very idea terrified him. It was hard enough talking to strangers face-to-face. Finally, the ringing stopped.

The phone sat in its cradle, recharging its battery. If Cubby picked it up it would feel warm like a live thing, but he didn't pick it up. He covered it with a towel and busied himself arranging plumes of wild fennel in a vase.

*   *   *

"This is vunderful," exclaimed a voice behind him. Cubby turned to see a young man with blond hair. His face was flushed as though he had just returned from a hike through snowy mountains, and he smiled delightedly at the array of pigs-in-blankets, pumpernickel slices and ham. It was the response to food that told Cubby who it was.

"You look different," he said.

"Ach! I have given you the surprise. You see, my vife departed before I grew old. This shape is what she is used to." Gerbill circled the feast, exclaiming over every dish.

The implications of his statement suddenly dawned on Cubby. "Your wife departed—"

"Ja, she died young. She vas so disappointed not to spend the years with me. I told her, *you're lucky. You missed the kidney stones, the cancer.* Wild fennel! The best kind with the aphids on!"

"I picked it downstairs."

Gerbill knelt down to examine the bright green insects clustered on the stems. Here and there an individual had swelled and turned into a brown husk where a parasitic wasp had laid its egg. The whole mass quivered as dozens of tiny suckers probed the fennel's sap.

A hand reached from beside Gerbill—she must have been there all along, but Cubby hadn't noticed her—and touched the flowers with the tip of her finger. She was so fair she could have materialized from a snowdrift. Her hair had only the faintest hint of gold to distinguish it from white. Her skin was that shade you saw in the heart of a pale pink rose and her eyes were the color of forget-me-nots. In spite of her anemic appearance she radiated—yes, *radiated*, Cubby thought distractedly—warmth. He felt he could tell her anything, be anything, and she would smile indulgently. He was transfixed.

"This is my friend Dr. Willows," said Gerbill. "My vife Sybille."

"Please call me Cubby," said Cubby, hypnotized.

Gerbill bent over the fennel, clicking his tongue. "This certainly brings back memories. During the war ve were all so poor, starving actually. Ve ate everything. Aphids are a good source of protein. Of energy, too." Gerbill produced a jeweler's eyeglass from his pocket and examined the insects closely. "See. There is a drop of honeydew being extruded from the anus."

Sybille shuddered entrancingly. Cubby wanted to say something, but her closeness scrambled his wits. To cover his confusion, he knelt down and pointed out a ladybird larva shaped like a tiny dinosaur, eating one of the aphids.

"There's ants running around, too," he said. "They move the aphids to new plants, just like farmers driving cows to a fresh pasture. Did you know," he added, warming to the subject, "that aphids are *born pregnant*?"

"Und you thought women had it tough," Gerbill told his wife.

"Yes," babbled Cubby. "Aphids can actually give birth to live young. They reproduce parthenogenetically, which means—which means—"

"They don't screw around," finished Gerbill. Cubby's face turned hot, but Sybille didn't seem offended. He pulled out the easy chair for her and a box for her to rest a plate. Then the party began in earnest with both Gerbill and Cubby vying to entertain Sybille. Gerbill remarked on the crocheted table cloth and Cubby revealed that his grandmother had been a seamstress in New York.

"She made clothes for Lady Astor," he bragged, watching for Sybille's approval. "Once, she sewed a thousand seed pearls onto a single evening dress."

"It must have weighed a ton," laughed Gerbill, and Cubby agreed that Lady Astor must have been rolled onto the ballroom floor on a hand truck.

All in all, it was an exhilarating party. Cubby felt younger than he had in years—almost as young as his guests, who flirted and fed each other slices of pumpernickel. For once he was not tongue-tied, holding forth with as much eloquence as he had at his grandmother's dinners. Sybille's admiration warmed him like a fire.

But after a while, as entomologists tend to do, the men fell into a discussion of midges and mayflies, crickets and katydids. They compared taxonomy and the position of spots on butterflies' wings. It was dull stuff, but not to them. Sybille listened contentedly.

The sky outside the window shifted from the muddy glow of neon lights to the furry gray of dawn. The Pineapple Express had settled in and rain thundered down. Cubby could not even hear the traffic on Sasquatch Avenue. He might have been marooned in a mountain chalet with rivers foaming on either side. He felt enormously secure, for he knew that his chalet was anchored to a spur of rock.

"It's late und ve must go," Gerbill said, gazing

regretfully at a half-eaten plate of beef tongue.

"Late?" murmured Cubby, wondering how time was measured in the realm his guests inhabited.

"I promised Sybille a visit with her family in Austria. The adults can't see her of course, but the little ones do und she likes being around them. Ve never had kids."

"The little ones?" said Cubby, waking up.

"Babies, you know. They talk to us until they learn to speak properly. You have no idea how full infants' lives are with all the coming and going of their dead relatives. Ve try not to overdo it because it can make them quite nervous."

Gerbill's wife pulled his arm and pointed toward the window.

"Soon, my dearest," soothed her husband.

Cubby could well understand that a baby might cry in the middle of the night with dead people hanging over its crib. No wonder new parents hardly got any sleep. "You'll come back tomorrow, won't you?" he said. "I'll order more food."

"Ach, well, that's a little awkward." Gerbill looked down, embarrassed. "Ve have a lot of relatives. In Germany, in Austria, even Argentina Ve like to touch base and anyhow Sybille is most fond of the babies—but ve'll be back in a week or two."

The light outside the window was strengthening. It would never be bright on such a stormy day, but dawn was clearly not far away. Cubby vaguely remembered stories about ghosts having to depart before the sun rose.

Sybille pulled Gerbill's arm so forcefully she knocked over a bottle onto the crocheted tablecloth. Gerbill quickly righted it. "It vas a vunderful party, Cubby. Really vunderful," he said. "I always thought of you as the son I never had." Then, as if embarrassed at revealing so much, Gerbill hurried away. Or rather, he and Sybille faded through the window and reappeared briefly on the rain-lashed tarpaper outside. The storm quickly covered their traces.

Cubby slumped to the floor. He realized that Gerbill and Sybille had a right to visit others, but somehow he'd formed the impression they were *his*. He'd imagined that they would come every night, that there would be more celebrations. Cubby had never been to so many parties in his life and he'd discovered a taste for them. He knew he was being unreasonable. Of course Gerbill and Sybille's relatives missed them, even the babies. It was still humbling to realize that dead people had a better social life than he had.

Cubby felt an emotion so unusual he had trouble putting a name to it. His life had been as orderly as a well-maintained stream. Emotions had rarely stirred it and he didn't care to go poking around the sludge at the bottom. Sludge was the home of obscure, creeping things. If you disturbed it mud swirled up, contaminating the bright surface where sunbeams danced.

Cubby had been the center, and genetic end, of a large and adoring family. His relatives' allegiance had been unquestioning, and by extension he expected Gerbill and Sybille to be equally devoted. Now he understood that this was not so. The emotion Cubby was struggling to name was *jealousy*.

He dragged cushions from the easy chair to make a bed on the floor. The truth was, he had drunk far more than he was used to and wasn't sure he could make it to the bedroom. For the first time Cubby wondered if his own relatives moved restlessly through his rooms at night. If so, why couldn't he see them? And did he want to see them? Did he really want his parents, grandparents and elderly kinfolks sitting around, drinking beer and eating pigs-in-blankets?

Not yet, thought Cubby, choking back tears. The tears were part of the sludge at the bottom of the stream and he willed them to subside. Cubby had never mourned his relatives. He had accepted the disappearance of one after another of them as though they had merely stepped into another room and would presently reappear. He did not truly believe they were dead.

The phone rang, slightly muffled under its towel. Cubby waited patiently for it to stop. When it fell silent after twelve rings he snuggled into the cushions and listened to the rain pounding against the walls of his apartment. A new leak appeared in the corner near the door. It was a small one that didn't threaten his books. Soon he fell asleep.

Ten: *THE COCKROACH EXPERIMENT*

FOR A MOMENT Cubby didn't know where he was. He looked around for the gas chromatograph and scintillation counter before realizing that he wasn't on the floor of his lab. The new leak had trickled across the floor to soak the cushion under his head. Empty beer bottles lay everywhere, and one had tipped over on his grandmother's table cloth, leaving a dark brown stain. As Cubby sat up a frosting of cockroaches scurried from plates of half-eaten food.

His head throbbed. His bones ached and he had the beginnings of a cold. The lamp glowed dully in the gray light from the window.

Cubby staggered to the bathroom to draw a bath, but here another unpleasant surprise awaited him. The water was cold. The pilot light in the boiler was out, and when he tried to relight it nothing happened. The gas had been cut off.

The electricity was still on, though, and by heating a kettle on the stove Cubby managed a meager, if unsatisfying, sponge bath. A cup of coffee restored his spirits. *Captain Tarantula wouldn't have minded waking up in a crowd of cockroaches,* he thought. Captain Tarantula could have slept in a nest of fire ants. He could have drunk twelve bottles of beer—that was how many Cubby counted on the floor—and pissed them away over the fire escape.

Cubby put the living room back into as much order as he could manage, although the cream cheese had been mashed into the rug, and the daisies on his grandmother's tablecloth had turned brown. Cubby put the tablecloth into the tub to soak. The left-over food had clearly been feasted on by the hordes of cock-roaches. Cubby wasn't as averse to the presence of insects as most people. He'd eaten termites, grubs and even the fat-bodied spiders one found sitting on orb webs in the fall of the year. It was a point of pride with entomologists that insects were as delicious as ham-burgers. Even scorpions were edible if you nipped off the stings.

(Once Cubby and Gerbill had cooked up a Chinese recipe for scorpion soup. The Chinese raised scorpions in small, home-based "ranches" and sold them to men with erectile difficulties. Cubby had no erectile difficulties, though of course this had not been tested on the battlefield, as Gerbill put it. The recipe went as fol-lows:

1/2 cup of vegetable oil
30 live scorpions, washed
1/4 lb pork tenderloin
garlic, fresh ginger root, salt and pepper.
Heat oil in wok. Stir-fry the scorpions. Add the pork, garlic, ginger, salt and pepper and stir-fry until done. Slowly add a pint of water, a handful of raisins, a handful of cranberries and a grated carrot. Simmer for 40 minutes.

Cubby and Gerbill had served it during lunch break at the lab. It was even less popular than the Chirpy Jerky, made with dried crickets, and one of the secretaries threw up.)

Not every insect is suitable for food, however. Cockroaches have the annoying habit of defecating while they eat, leaving an indelible odor. And so Cubby wasn't anxious to finish the pum-pernickel bread and beef tongue. Their presence, though, reminded him of his plan to study their habits.

He remembered seeing, during the abortive journey to the taco truck, a cardboard box of large bottles near the garbage cans. The factory workers threw out all sorts of useful things—useful to Cubby, that is, who could winkle out wires and batteries for vari-ous experiments. Lately, it seemed, there had been more trash than usual and no one had bothered to remove it.

Cubby put on his army surplus raincoat and the backpack. The rain was coming down in sheets and perhaps that was the reason no one was at work in the factory today. As he went out the door, the phone rang again. Its peal was quickly lost in the storm and anyhow Cubby's attention was focused on keeping his hands and feet from slipping on the fire escape. The air was a lot colder than he had expected.

The bottles were still there, although the box had disintegrated. Cubby loaded up all that would fit into the backpack and made the perilous ascent to his apartment. Back and forth he went until he had twenty-four wide-mouthed jars with lids. It was an acceptable number for an experiment. But by the time he stumbled into the living room for the last time he was thoroughly chilled. His hands shook so much he was afraid to line up the bottles in case he broke one.

Cubby stripped naked and lay under an electric blanket until he recovered. The apartment was furnished with three space heaters. He turned them all on and soon the rooms were so comfortable that he didn't need to dress again. He squatted on the living room floor, trapping cockroaches, examining them with a jeweler's eyepiece to ascertain the sex, and placing one male and one female in each container. These he labeled with numbers. He supplied the new couples with chunks of pumpernickel bread and cotton balls soaked with water.

Now came the enjoyable part. Cubby opened a new notebook and painstakingly described his experiment, drawing a picture of a sample bottle:

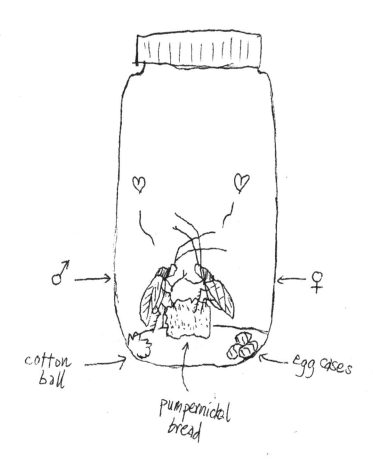

cotton ball

egg cases

pumpernickel bread

He wrote at the top of the first page: *An Enquiry into the Social and Nesting habits of Blatella germanica, the German Cockroach, in an Enclosed Environment Beginning with an Index Mating Pair, by Dr. Cubby Willows.*

The first paragraph read: Blatella germanica *is a gregarious insect with a large reproductive capacity and few natural enemies. It is fond of kitchens and bathrooms, fitting into the lives of humans with the practiced ease of a domestic animal. Indeed, one may say* Blatella *has been domesticated through long centuries of association with us. Perhaps the earliest Neolithic housewife (cave wife?) found them skittering across her mastodon cutlets when she arose in the morning. Perhaps Neanderthals (who originated from the same German valleys) stamped fruitlessly on the cheeky little invaders.*

Cubby put down the pen with a sigh. It was a fanciful opening, but for once he need not emulate the dry-as-dust scholarly journals. This was his experiment. He would write a popular book about it. He might even do a children's book, *Blatty and the Neanderthals*. The time was overdue for a rehabilitation of cockroaches.

The phone rang again. Cubby barely heard it. He entered observations into the notebook, with the date and time. *The males and females in bottles 6 and 15 have developed a dislike for one another, while those in bottles 3, 7 and 21 have already engaged in mating behavior. Is it possible that cockroaches have preferences? Are there unpopular cockroaches? Are there some who never get dates? Note to self: In next experiment swap mates.*

*   *   *

The days passed. Food was delivered on Saturday and Cubby dressed long enough to go down and fetch it. The rest of the time he spent comfortably naked, like a savage on a tropical island. The rain continued to pour. It was a comforting sound, separating him from the rest of the world. He dined happily on ramen, TV dinners, V-8 juice and canned tuna. The cockroaches dined on pumpernickel bread. The female in bottle 6 ate the male. This dropped the sample size to 23, but much activity was observed in the remaining containers. Egg cases had already appeared.

Cubby knew that one energetic female was capable of producing 200,000 offspring in a single year. The bottles would fill up quickly and the stress of crowding and constant stimulation of mating pheromones would soon become apparent. Just imagine the effect of 100,000 receptive females in one little bottle! But of course cannibalism took care of that problem long before it happened.

In the evenings Cubby drank gin and watched television. A week went by. Two weeks. Gerbill and Sybille did not reappear, but no exact time had been established and he did not give up hope. He laid in a supply of bock beer just in case.

The rain stopped.

Cubby climbed down into a landscape of destruction. Sometime during the storm the gangs on Sasquatch Avenue had invaded the factory. Windows had been shot out, trash was strewn everywhere and a side door of the building had been wrenched open. Cubby nervously peered inside. The vending machine had been looted, but there was little else to tempt a thief.

Attempts had been made to destroy the factory inside, but those machines had been built in an era when American industry was still strong. Their wires had been whelped in Cincinnati. Their cogs had been forged by men nourished by the vast cornfields of the Midwest, and their metal had been purified in the coal fires of Kentucky. They would never decay.

Cubby was swept with awe as though he had stumbled into a cathedral. The machines were as overpowering as the colossi guarding Abu Simbel in Egypt, and their vast shadows filtered the sunlight like gods. Cubby had a keen appreciation of such creations. They were logic made manifest. They were the visible workings of the human mind.

An engineer building a bridge, for example, sent out the first feeler of metal in the same way a philosopher cast forth an idea. It hovered in space. It interlaced with other strands. Logic followed logic until you had a complete structure, which might be a theory, a new religion or a bridge. All these years Cubby had lived in the factory's loft, as unaware of the grandeurs below as a moth perched on the Statue of Liberty. He was ashamed of his lack of curiosity.

And then he noticed a sign dangling on the front door. It was a large yellow sheet of metal pockmarked with bullet holes and hanging crazily by one strand of wire. The sign said: CONDEMNED.

Condemned? How could that be? Cubby's heart caught in his throat. How could anyone doom those magnificent dinosaurs inside? But the original dinosaurs had died, hadn't they? All it took was one meteor. Cubby felt so distressed he had to hold onto the chain-link fence to keep from fainting. And then he noticed another thing: The gate, which had stood open day and night for forty years, was padlocked shut.

It must have been done that very morning for the slide marks were still fresh in the mud. Now, Cubby realized, the supermarket truck could no longer deliver his food and—horrors!—he wouldn't be able to get out! A Y-frame of barbed wire at the top of the fence made certain of that.

Cubby walked around the perimeter, looking for an opening and finding none. He forced himself to think rationally. There had to be a solution. They wouldn't seal up a useful factory with no plan to remove its equipment. (But they *had* condemned his gas chromatograph and scintillation counter.) Cubby heard Gerbill's voice murmuring, *Ve are all mortal, foolish boy. You vill die up there like a helpless bunny, from the flu, the heart seizure, the stroke.*

Cubby looked around sharply, but no one was there. There was only the rubble of the factory yard and the puddles shivering from traffic on Sasquatch Avenue.

Get a phone, for Gott's sake, came the whisper.

Of course. The phone was upstairs. He could call for help, although he was unsure who to contact. He remembered a song his great-uncle used to play on the piano while his mother sang: "Hello Central, Give Me Heaven". There were quite a few people he could talk to in Heaven, but no one in the immediate vicinity.

Cubby climbed the fire escape, trying to remember where he'd put the phone. It had awakened him in the middle of the night. He'd been unusually foggy-headed and the noise had sent him staggering from the easy chair, where he'd passed out, to the bathroom where he—

Dropped it into the tub with his grandmother's table cloth.

Cubby fished it out. He couldn't get a dial tone, so he wrapped it in a towel and put it into the cupboard behind the laundry soap.

The tub smelled sour, perhaps because of the warm temperature in the apartment. Three space heaters made the air as tropical as a Tahitian summer. Cubby stripped naked and went into the living room to look at his cockroaches. He turned on the TV for company and was pleased when it produced languid Hawaiian music. The nature channel was screening a show about global warming. The sea level was rising and some of the South Sea atolls were about to disappear beyond the blue horizon.

*   *   *

Voices shouted. Wood splintered as it was wrenched apart and suddenly the room was full of people. Cubby sat up on the cushions where he'd fallen asleep.

"He's still in here!" one of them called. Cubby shivered in the cold wind blowing from the doorway and reached for a towel.

"This—place—*reeks*!" groaned another fireman. "It's like that old lady's house with the cats."

"Only this guy keeps cockroaches. Hey, old timer, do you eat those?" The first fireman laughed.

"Cockroaches have a rank odor that makes them unpalatable to most people," Cubby said. "Although they are considered a delicacy in Japan."

"You don't say. What's the idea lying of naked in a heap of beer bottles? And why didn't you answer the phone?"

"I didn't want to talk to anyone," Cubby said reasonably.

"Geez Louise, you should smell the bathroom," someone called.

"We've been trying to contact you for weeks. Now that the building's condemned it's illegal for you to stay here," said the first fireman. A paramedic came in from the fire escape. He crossed the room swiftly and opened a window.

"I pay my rent," said Cubby.

"Yes, and you can also rent a cabin on the *Titanic*. This building is coming down."

"Coming down?" Cubby said faintly.

"How much do you drink?" asked the paramedic, hunkering down to take Cubby's pulse.

"Oh, I didn't drink all those," said Cubby, wishing he'd disposed of the beer bottles. "My friend Dr. Gerbill had most of them."

"Yeah, right. Did he fly through the window?" said the medic.

Cubby was about to say yes (*death gives you wings*)

when he realized it probably did look odd to find a naked man surrounded by bottles of alcohol and cockroaches. Admitting to dead visitors would make it worse. "This is actually an experiment," Cubby explained. "I'm a retired entomologist and I was studying the social habits of insects. Cockroaches are basically gregarious. If you put sixty in a cage with three matchboxes, most of them will crowd into one box and leave the other two empty. They like company, but there comes a point at which the instinct switches off—"

"I think it's a cognitive problem. He seems healthy," said the paramedic.

"Alzheimer's?"

"Or alcoholic dementia."

"I'm perfectly sound," Cubby insisted. "You may call my former boss Dr. Slithe."

But the men didn't seem to hear him. They hurried him into the bedroom where the paramedic dressed him hurriedly and then strapped him—strapped him!—onto a stretcher to be lowered over the fire escape. Cubby protested. He tried to explain. He told them he was perfectly capable of climbing down, but nothing got through. It was as though once they'd decided he had Alzheimer's, a shutter came down. No matter how carefully he constructed his arguments all they heard was *quack . . . quack . . . quack.*

"Don't you worry, gramps," said the orderly in the ambulance. "We're going to take you to a nice, safe place."

The last thing Cubby saw before they closed the ambulance was the door of his apartment lying in ruins.

Eleven: *JOY MEADOWS*

TOM RESISTED calling Joy Meadows for as long as possible, but Violetta eventually wore him down. The first thing he discovered was that the free vacation had to be two weeks long. "Why is that?" he demanded. "Maybe we won't like the place."

"Two weeks is fine," whispered Violetta, who was sitting next him.

"That's our policy," a female voice on the other end of the line admonished him. "Important decisions, such as where you are going to spend the rest of your life, can't be done hastily. After all, you didn't get married after only one date."

But Tom had. Seaworthys did that kind of thing. When he first met Violetta, he knew that this was the lady who would make him happy for the rest of his life. It was another one of the gifts from the old gods of Africa.

"Maybe I don't want to book at all," Tom argued, but he looked down at Violetta's stricken face and revised his decision. "If we do come," he smoothly added, "I want to know what strings are attached. I'm not signing any documents."

"Goodness, Mr. Seaworthy. You *are* paranoid!" Tinkling laughter took away some of the insult. "You'll only need to sign an insurance waiver in case there's an accident—not that anything has *ever* happened during an orientation period. Everything at Joy Meadows is designed for the differently abled. *And* you will be assigned guides to see to your every need and answer questions."

"Guides?" said Tom, scenting danger.

"They'll stay around only as long as you want them. I

must congratulate you, Mr. Seaworthy, on being so proactive. Your sixty-fifth birthday was only two weeks ago."

"How did you know that?" said Tom.

More tinkling laughter. "It's our business to serve the public. From your phone number alone I can access your and your wife's birthdates, number of children, health records, traffic violations, military records, and federal and state income taxes. By the way, don't worry about Violetta being only sixty-two. We're flexible."

Tom's alarm system was beginning to overload. "You can get all that from a phone number?"

"For starters," said the woman. "Goodness! If we're going to take care of you, you don't want us to be *ignorant*."

"Maybe, but—"

"We'll expect you tomorrow then. Check-in time is from two to four p.m.. Pack light. Anything you forget we can provide free of charge. And congratulations, Tom. We're always delighted to welcome new members to Joy Meadows."

"I'm not a goddamned member yet!" yelled Tom, but the line had gone dead. He sat down on the sofa, the phone held limply in his hand.

"Are we going? Did you make them angry?" implored Violetta.

"Oh, we're invited. Does flypaper say no to a fly?" The woman—and Tom realized she had never identified herself—knew a hell of a lot for someone who had just met him. It had not escaped him that she had shifted from using his last name to the more familiar, and slightly patronizing, first name when she was certain she had a customer. "I don't like this, Letta. I smell *kunyumwa* all over the place."

"*Kun*-what?" said Violetta, flipping through the Joy Meadows catalogue that had come in the mail that morning. "You said that word when we got back from the Youth Patrol gathering."

"It's one of Uncle Shumba's words. It means 'premonition of danger'."

"Oh, I remember! He tried to teach you the Seaworthy ancestral language. That was so sweet."

"Except that I never knew whether he was making it up. *Rufaro* meant happiness. *Utiriri* was patience. *Ganja* was the weed he smoked all the time. *Matzivariva* meant 'to look away when you don't want to see something you don't like'."

"Wow! They even had a word for that," said Violetta.

"The trouble was, the words never really got strung together," said Tom. "I could never hold a conversation, although Shumba did. He used to talk to people I couldn't see." Tom looked around at the old farmhouse and saw dozens of flaws he hadn't noticed before. The factories were closing in and the Pineapple Express hadn't added to the cheer. A refrigeration unit switched on in the nearby meatpacking plant and the lights dimmed.

Even in the gloom Tom could see blotches where water had seeped in. The floor was warped and if you dropped a marble in the living room it would roll all the way to the kitchen. He couldn't remember how many times he'd had to rewire Violetta's oven. Every time he pulled it out, rust showered over the floor.

Sunlight seemed to pour out of the Joy Meadows catalogue as Violetta turned the pages—luminous rooms painted in fresh cream, yellow for the kitchen, a patio with lime green chairs, a pitcher of lemonade beaded with condensation. It was always summer in Joy Meadows and the Pineapple Express was turned back at the border.

"So when do we go?" asked Violetta.

"Tomorrow—damn it! that doesn't give me time to deliver Dr. Willows' equipment," Tom said.

"Deliver? I thought you were selling it."

"Not this time," Tom admitted. "I felt, well, kind of nasty stripping down Dr. Willows' machines that he'd cared for all these years and probably misses. I thought I'd give him the chance to keep them."

Violetta leaned against him. "You're a good man, Tom. I'm so glad I married you."

"Shucks. And I thought this was only a ten thousand-night stand."

"I guess Dr. Willows can wait another two weeks," said Violetta, leaning a little more purposefully.

"I'm sure he can," Tom said, putting his arm around her. "It isn't as though he's going anywhere."

*   *   *

Tom aged five years every time he got onto the freeway. First he had to insert the old truck into the traffic stream on Sasquatch Avenue. You had to make it to the far right lane before the avenue split in two on the outskirts of the city. Everything to the left was swept onto a monster conduit called the Corridor to the North. If you got onto the Corridor to the North you might as well kiss your loved ones good-bye. You were never coming back.

Once Tom had maneuvered into the correct lane, faster cars nudged the bumpers of the old truck and their drivers screamed insults. Someone hurled a cup of yellow liquid onto the windscreen.

Violetta had her feet braced against invisible brake pedals. One hand clutched the door handle and with the other she scanned for road signs with binoculars. Tom was too near-sighted to read them before they flashed by.

"You make a good co-pilot, Letta," he said.

"Thanks. What's that funny smell?" said Violetta.

Tom realized that the yellow liquid had dripped into the air vents. It wasn't lemonade. "Open the window," he began and then, "No! Don't open the window!" A car full of gangbangers had squeezed between the retaining wall and the truck, and were attempting to herd Tom and Violetta into the main stream. But old trucks, slow as they might be, were made of solid American steel. Tom shimmied the heavy vehicle sideways and knocked the car onto the next off-ramp.

"Tom!" cried Violetta, shocked.

"Do you think they got our license plate?"

"They almost went over the side! They were too busy." Violetta was silent for a while, scanning the road ahead. Several more towns passed, although what marked them off from one another was a mystery. As far as Tom could see, the landscape was an unbroken mass of tract homes and strip malls. The lowering gray clouds began to rain and washed the piss off the window.

"You can't afford trouble," Violetta said at last.

"What should I have done? Let them push us in front of a tanker?"

"You've turned sixty-five."

"Don't you think I know it? Those goddamn kids sure as hell knew it and took out a hunting license on me. Fuck the Senior Laws." Tom knew he shouldn't yell at her, but she didn't understand what it meant to cross the invisible boundary between manhood and senility. Even Tom hadn't understood it before it happened. One day he was a respected member of the community, and the next an old coot with a bull's eye on his chest.

Seniors could no longer count on an elastic court system to forgive their trespasses. At sixty-five all infractions were taken seriously. If you really screwed up, you found yourself in Chupacabras Hospital with a catheter jammed up the yang. And then there was the Diminished Culpability Act.

The Diminished Culpability Act was a lawyer's wet dream. The amount of liability a person incurred for a crime depended on the age or health of the victim. It made a weird kind of sense. Sentencing was regulated by how many useful years of life had been destroyed. Murdering a twenty-year-old was a heinous crime, killing a sixty-five-year-old much less so.

This led to a quagmire of legal decisions. Clearly, a person with terminal cancer had a shorter life expectancy than someone without it. What was the equation to say how many years of prison you got for killing someone who probably wouldn't have survived six months anyway?

The interesting part was what happened when someone reached the age of seventy. Three score and ten was the life span allotted in the Bible, and the government made sure you didn't hog more than your share. Killing a seventy-year-old earned a murderer two years max in the slammer. An eighty-year-old only racked up two weeks of community service. Tom couldn't remember the last time he'd seen an eighty-year-old.

"Letta, I'm sorry I swore at you," he said.

"That's all right. This traffic would make Mother Theresa snap her beads."

Her generosity of spirit made Tom's eyes mist up. He blinked several times to clear them.

"Look!" cried Violetta, pointing at a sign. "The road to Joy Meadows is five miles ahead."

Tom realized that the monotonous tract homes had

disappeared. Gentle hills covered with amber grass spread out on either side, with here and there groups of cattle sheltering beneath oak trees. The meadows were splotched with yellow stands of mustard. Even in winter California managed to produce flowers.

It was beyond beautiful. It brought back Tom's childhood with aching force, and the summers he'd spent on his uncle's ranch. It had been years since he'd been out there. Why had it taken him so long? Why had he been satisfied to let the city grow up around him like scar tissue?

"There's the off-ramp," said Violetta.

They came down into a country lane lined with cottonwoods—remnants, Tom guessed, of an ancient farm. A stream meandered through fields, now near, now far, glinting where it caught the sky. A red-tailed hawk watched them from the top of a telephone pole. Tom pulled over and opened the windows.

Rain mingled with the distant rumble of traffic, but beyond this was a faint rustle. "That's the cottonwoods," Tom said. "Every tree makes a different sound when the wind blows through it. Cottonwoods patter, pines hiss, palms rattle and bay trees whoosh like waves coming in to shore."

"I had no idea you were so poetic," said Violetta.

"It's not poetry. It's called being alive and I'd forgotten about it until this minute. I used to listen to cottonwoods at night when I was a kid. Our house was in the middle of a pasture then and I left the window open."

"Can't do that anymore," said Violetta.

"The crickets sang all night and if they went silent I knew coyotes were walking around. When the wind blew, the sounds and smells of the farm came into my bedroom It was like getting a news report. By God, I've been asleep for forty years. I've been cleaning up people's messes with no more awareness than a hamster on a wheel."

"Don't be so hard on yourself. You raised five wonderful kids," said Violetta.

"You did most of it. When they grew up and moved away, I let you sit day after day in that empty house."

"I never blamed you, Shug."

Tom looked out at the rain. Rivulets poured out of the saturated ground and formed a stream at the side of the road.

"Maybe I am too hard on myself. All week I've been eating my guts out about turning sixty-five and now I see that it was foolishness. What does sixty-five mean to a cottonwood? What does unemployment mean to a hawk?"

"I'm so glad you're feeling better," said Violetta.

Tom breathed in the cool, sweet air and felt it circulate through his body. "When you live in places like this, numbers don't mean shit."

"We can easily visit here from Joy Meadows," said Violetta.

Tom's enthusiasm faded. What he wanted didn't involve a managed care living arrangement with pre-selected friends and a golf course. But he looked at his wife's eager face and shelved his reply. "I guess we'd better move on," he said.

Twelve: *NONI AND NGWENYA*

TO TOM'S AMAZEMENT, Joy Meadows was not a glorified trailer park where old folks went to die. An arm of the Sacramento River had been dammed to create a lake. In the middle of this was a magical island, gleaming as though the Emerald City had been plunked down into the middle of Kansas. The muted colors of the fields faded next to red-tiled hacienda roofs, glowing white walls, and lawns the color of crème de menthe.

"It's beautiful!" cried Violetta, as delighted as a child at a fireworks display.

"What happened to the rain?" said Tom. He had parked at the top of the last hill to take in the fantastic scene before him. The Joy Meadows people really had stopped the Pineapple Express at the border. Some barrier arched over the island, turning back the downpour. Hard as Tom looked, he couldn't see anything solid. Lights floating under the barrier turned the community below into a bubble of summer at the bottom of a drab, dark day.

"How in hell did they do that?" he said.

"Who cares?" said Violetta, training her binoculars on the sight.

"I care. There has to be some form of energy pushing up and that means it's going through the air. It'll go through your body, too, like a big old microwave."

"Stop trying to spoil things," scolded Violetta. "You don't know how the TV gets into the house and you still watch football."

"Actually, I do know," said Tom. "I spent enough time

at Burton, Barton, Gerbill and Slithe to be suspicious of anything scientific. I always ask questions. I bet they got a bunch of two-headed rats running around Joy Meadows." But he stopped himself before he upset his wife. She was so obviously happy and it was the first time she'd been anywhere in years.

Tom drove down the hill to a wall with large doors that he assumed gave access to a bridge. Three men stepped out of a small kiosk and approached the truck. *Guards*, Tom thought with an instinctive surge of dislike.

"ID," one of the men barked.

"We have reservations—" began Violetta.

"You, too, lady. We need an ID."

"Are you sure you don't want a passport as well?" Tom said sarcastically. He'd seen thugs like these before. They were dressed in urban camouflage, a kind of uniform that took on the color of whatever you were close to. Right now they looked like rain-soaked mud.

"Nobody goes anywhere without an ID," growled the guard, leaning into the window on a meaty elbow. Tom was about to shift into reverse when two other people suddenly materialized.

"You must be the Seaworthys," cried a young woman, clapping her hands like an African woman Tom had seen on TV. She wore a long red and white patterned dress with a headscarf to match. She was as pretty as Tom's youngest daughter Thaís and his heart warmed to her.

"My name is Noni and this is Ngwenya." Noni indicated her companion, an elegant young man in a green and yellow caftan. "Don't pay attention to our watchdogs. They look after our safety and we love the dickens out of them." She playfully squeezed the arm of one of the guards.

"If you would be so good as to show an ID, we can get on with the total immersion experience." Ngwenya grinned, displaying teeth that seemed to glow in his dark face. Tom was hypnotized by them. He detected a slight accent.

"Are you from Africa," he asked.

Ngwenya responded with a belly laugh so whole-hearted that Tom smiled in spite of himself. "Bless you, *Sekuru*! You have found me out. I am indeed from the green land of Africa.
Let me show your ID to these men so I can be your guide."

When the formalities were done the great doors opened to reveal a parking lot, but no bridge. "What's going on?" Tom said, once more suspicious.

"It is nothing," Ngwenya assured him. "You see, we do not allow outside vehicles onto the island. So many are not smog-worthy and our elders suffer from infirmities of the lung. For their health we have provided them with electrical golf carts. You, too, shall have one to go wherever you wish."

"Can I have one, too?" said Violetta.

"Of course, *Ambuya!*" responded Noni. "We do not practice gender discrimination here."

So Tom parked the truck. They would travel, Ngwenya informed him, by boat. "It is a most pleasurable experience," the African said. "The trip by water is said to enhance the feeling that you are leaving this world behind and entering a realm where dreams come true. We will dock at the Alhambra lifestyle module for an Andalusían feast. From there we will take you on a tour of the island to choose the location of your total immersion experience. I would recommend Timbuktu. Many African-Americans find it spiritually rewarding."

"Oh, Tom," murmured Violetta. "You always wanted to go to Africa."

"That's what Joy Meadows is," Noni said softly. "A chance to catch up on the experiences you missed during life."

"Without the risk of dysentery!" Ngwenya gave another of his resounding belly laughs. He loaded the suitcases onto a boat that Tom realized had been copied from a painting in an Egyptian tomb. It was so fanciful and beautiful, floating by the prosaic cement dock, that it really did seem like a craft built to transport you to another realm. It was made of bundled reeds with the ends curled up in the shape of lotus flowers. Two comfortable seats faced a single seat in the middle and a long oar was suspended from the back. Ngwenya, looking for all the world like a young pharaoh, took his position by the oar.

Tom had always loved Egyptian history. As a boy he had imagined himself the master of a sunny estate with walled gardens and a lotus-filled pool.

"I have to ask you," Noni interrupted his thoughts. "Do either of you have a pacemaker?"

"No. Why?" Tom tore his attention away from the boat.

"We pass through an energy barrier and sometimes that causes problems."

"Is the energy barrier what keeps the rain out," Tom asked.

Noni giggled. "My goodness, *Sekuru*! Don't ask me anything about science. I barely understand how to get the cotton out of an aspirin bottle."

"Why do you keep calling me *Sekuru*? That isn't my name." Tom smiled to show that he wasn't offended.

"It means *grandfather*," explained Ngwenya. "It is a central tenet of African culture that elders are revered above all others and so we honor you with the title. *Ambuya* means *grandmother*."

"And I really am a grandmother," Violetta said happily. She gasped when the boat moved under her as she stepped aboard. Tom steadied her.

She's never been on a boat, he realized, remembering all the times his father had taken him fishing on San Francisco Bay. Why hadn't he ever taken Violetta for a boat ride? Years and years had gone by with her daily round of raising children, cooking, cleaning, Sundays at the park—until it filled up with drug addicts—and trips to restaurants until these, too, became dangerous. Violetta's world had shrunk to a few rooms in the middle of an industrial site.

Only once had Tom taken her on a vacation, when she was pregnant with Cezare, their first child. They had gone to his uncle's ranch beyond the Mirage Mountains and while Tom had been perfectly happy, Violetta had reacted badly to the solitude. She'd grown up with ten brothers and sisters. The empty desert frightened her.

Then, too, Shumba wasn't the most restful man to be around. He played the drums incessantly and fell into strange fits where he spoke with people no one else could see. His walls were covered with spooky African masks and mummified animals.

The worst had been the cats. Violetta normally liked cats, but these lurked in the shadows or wound up in unexpected places, such as a drawer she was reaching into. You could never count them. They moved incessantly and, all being black, when they were massed together it was difficult to tell where one ended and the next began.

I'll make it up to you, Tom promised silently.

Ngwenya poled the reed boat away from shore. Presently, they passed through something that made Tom's skin tingle as though ants were scurrying over him. The energy barrier, he supposed. At the same time the music began, the almost-melody he'd heard on the TV advertisement.

Does that go on all the time? Tom thought. *It's like being stuck in a fucking elevator.* But none of the others seemed to notice and Violetta was absent-mindedly smiling. She leaned over to trail her fingers in the water.

The lake was dark and waveless under a shrouded sky, but as they approached the island, the lights beneath the invisible canopy cast a silvery sheen. The shore behind became dim and insubstantial. The air grew warm.

They tied up beside other boats and climbed a flight of steps to a courtyard with a fountain. Noni and Ngwenya led them to a charming restaurant with brass lamps and caged birds hanging from the ceiling. It was empty except for a pair of old men seated before pitchers of sangría. They seemed oblivious to all around them and Tom suspected they had been drinking for a long time. A waiter sprang up from behind the bar.

Tom and Violetta were offered salt-free, sugar-free, low cholesterol and high-fiber options on the menu, but neither of them had any dietary restrictions. Tom turned the menu over, looking for the price list.

"You need not worry," said Ngwenya,. "All is *gratis*. Free."

"That's very generous," Tom said, "but if we're going to live here we have to know whether we can afford it."

"You can afford to eat out all the time," said Noni. "That's the wonderful thing about Joy Meadows. Once you sign up *everything* is free."

"Once we sign up . . . " Tom trailed off when he saw Violetta's warning frown. He had no intention of signing his possessions away because it would make them utterly dependent. It was true that the farmhouse was practically worthless and that his pension was small, but they were his, earned with his own hands or the hands of his ancestors. He didn't want to feel helpless.

And there was his uncle's ranch. That had been in the family since time out of mind and no papers had ever been involved in the transfer of this property. Tom doubted whether any record of the ranch even existed. Shumba had said that the place belonged to the spirits and you didn't try to sell what the spirits owned. Bad *juju* to do that. Bad *juju* all around.

"There's a concept in African society called *ujima*," said Ngwenya. "Have you heard of it?"

"*Ujima*. Something to do with *Kwanzaa*." Tom had never bothered with that holiday. He thought it was a marketing ploy to get shoppers into the malls.

"It means *cooperation*. It's how a village works. When a job needs doing everyone pitches in. If one person is poor, the others share their resources. Some people who become citizens of Joy Meadows are rich and their money helps maintain members who don't have as much. We have no class differences here." Ngwenya spoke with quiet passion, like a missionary pointing out hygiene to a bum.

Tom felt embarrassed and annoyed at the same time. "I guess I didn't understand," he said.

"Don't give it a second thought," boomed the African in his resonant voice. "Now we can get on with the pleasant task of eating. Let me recommend the *mishmishaya*, lamb with apricots, or *hamam meshwi*, grilled pigeon. For dessert I always have the pistachio nougat . . . "

After lunch they went back to the boat and sailed past the haciendas of Spain and the pavilions of Arabia. Lavender, yellow and ivory-striped tents clustered along the water. Next, they saw a New England fishing village with bone-white cottages and nets hung out to dry. Tom learned that within the encircling waters of Sacramento Lake were twenty lifestyle modules where seniors could enjoy experiences they had only dreamed of. Nor was this the only Joy Meadows, though it was the prototype of the line. The franchise had spread (or metastasized, Tom thought) throughout the United States.

"Some people prefer a simple life style," said Noni as they came to a lakeside beach. "This is Woodstock."

Tom saw aging elves, geriatric nymphs, ancient wizards (but they were supposed to be ancient, weren't they?) and a few withered hippies. Next to the water a group had dispensed with clothes and were seated around a bong. Two seniors were on the sand engaging in—

"Are they really doing it?" Violetta put her hand over her mouth.

"Each module follows its own rules," said Noni blandly. "That's why we're going to ask you to fill out a questionnaire, to find your best fit."

They came to the main office, disembarked, and were ushered into an orientation hall. The questionnaire they were given was long and involved, often asking the same thing in several places. Did they expect many visitors? Were they afflicted with serious health problems? What kind of insurance did they have? There was the preference test, e.g.: *Which would you rather do: (A) Shoplift a sweater; (B) Write a bad check; (C) Drink vodka until you pass out; (D) Have sex with a stranger.*

"I don't like any of those," said Violetta.

"It's merely to measure your level of risk-taking. Pick the one you dislike least," explained Noni.

By the time the paperwork was finished, Tom and Violetta were tired, but they weren't allowed to rest. They were taken on a tour of the island's interior. Ngwenya drove a golf cart, with Noni, Tom and Violetta sitting behind, as he pointed out objects of interest. Round and round they went, past swimming pools, fitness gyms, club houses, cafeterias and craft centers until Tom was thoroughly confused about their location.

Most of the neighborhoods were the same under a veneer of foreignness. Timbuktu boasted an African marketplace, but the grass houses were completely modern inside. It was here that Tom realized that they had left their luggage behind in the orientation hall. Ngwenya assured him it would be delivered as soon they chose a module.

They stopped at a German beer hall for dinner. By now Tom was so exhausted his vision was beginning to blur. He stared unhappily at the plates of sausages and opted for bock beer instead. Poor Violetta put her head down on the table.

"What do you think, *Sekuru?*" said Ngwenya. "Your questionnaires say you could fit in almost anywhere, but I still think Timbuktu is the best."

"Please stop calling me *Sekuru,*" Tom said, too tired to be polite.

"Okay, Tom. We're here to please you." Ngwenya smiled, showing fluorescent teeth.

"We only mean to be respectful," added Noni.

"I know," Tom said. The beer hall was a reasonable copy of the ones Gerbill had dragged him to, but something was missing. The waitresses were suitably blonde and practically bursting out of their dirndls. The heavy wooden beams of the ceiling were hung with ropes of garlic and onion. The beer steins were overflowing with foam. But the hall lacked Nazis. *That's what it needs*, Tom thought sleepily. *More Nazis.*

And then he realized that the music he had first noticed when they passed through the force field was still playing. It wasn't the oom-pah beat of a genuine beer hall. The melody was circling his brain like a mosquito deciding where to bite and he hadn't noticed it *for hours*.

A man sat in the shadows at the other end of the room. He was overweight and seemed to be perspiring heavily, although the light was too dim to be certain. *Dr. Gerbill*, thought Tom, shocked. The man pointed at the door. *What do you want me to do, Doctor? Leave?* But of course it was another hallucination, like seeing his father in the back bedroom and Uncle Shumba in the truck. Tom relaxed slightly. He couldn't face dragging Violetta away and driving all the way back to the city.

"Timbuktu sounds like the right place for us," he said. "I think we should go there now."

"Are you sure? There's lots of interesting things to do," said Noni.

"My wife is so tired, she's fallen asleep. Please, please let us go to bed."

"You're the boss," said Ngwenya, standing up, and when Tom looked at the other end of the beer hall, Dr. Gerbill had gone.

Somehow, they managed to rouse Violetta and get her back onto the golf cart. Ngwenya drove in silence until they reached the stylish grass houses and jungle gardens of Timbuktu. Tom and Violetta's dwelling was already lighted, their suitcases unpacked and the clothes hung in the closet.

"We'll check up on you in the morning," said Ngwenya, helping Violetta to an easy chair.

"Not too early," said Tom distractedly. If only these

relentlessly cheerful people would go!

"I'll bring you a breakfast basket," promised Noni.

Later, Tom got Violetta to eat some of the food he found in the refrigerator and she woke up enough to take a shower. Afterwards, they shared a bottle of Zimbabwe red. They each had their own king-sized bed and Violetta found a complimentary chocolate box on her pillow. Tom found a box containing Viagra.

These fuckers don't leave anything to chance, he thought, angrily shoving the box into a drawer. He collapsed onto the bed with a pillow over his head. But the music still got through.

Thirteen: *MUSIC AT NIGHT*

T OM HAD LOST track of time. He couldn't remember how long they'd been at Joy Meadows. Was it yesterday they'd gone to a fireworks show? Or was yesterday when they had the golf cart race? Noni and Ngwenya arrived in the morning with suggestions for new entertainment. After years of dreary solitude, this attention went to Violetta's head. She bloomed with the new social life and Tom couldn't bring himself to remind her that they weren't staying permanently.

Noni had insinuated herself into their lives so completely that he could hardly imagine her out of it. She was smart and pretty like their youngest daughter, as well as sensitive to their every need. The Seaworthy children would certainly approve of her if they came to visit. *When* they came to visit, Tom reminded himself. He'd meant to call them, but somehow hadn't found the time.

As for Ngwenya, Tom was less enthusiastic about him. He insisted on dragging Tom to Afrocentric events to help him discover his roots. Tom already knew about his roots. They were far stranger than anything Ngwenya could imagine.

There was always a subtle sales pitch behind everything the African said, and Tom found himself coerced into doing things he didn't really like. Once he woke up to find himself signing some kind of form. He couldn't remember where it came from. He tried to read it, but Ngwenya snatched it away. "You are a most suspicious man, *Sekuru*," the African accused him. "It is merely a petition against human rights violations."

"Stop calling me *Sekuru*," said Tom, but he didn't have

the energy to argue. That was another thing. He'd fallen into a kind of lassitude where it was easier to coast along than resist Ngwenya's projects. Besides, he didn't want to spoil Violetta's vacation.

Every morning Noni brought them a breakfast basket with cinnamon rolls, orange juice and a thermos of hot coffee. She insisted on making them omelets or anything else they might find interesting. Violetta accepted this with gratitude and spent the morning on the verandah soaking up the sun. Or what passed for sun. Tom didn't trust what came out of that artificial sky.

Timbuktu produced its own little newspaper called *Drum Beat*, and Noni read tidbits aloud to them over breakfast. Sharhonda, one of their neighbors had won a prize for making a mosaic out of seed corn. Kenyatta, her hulking husband, was a much-sought-after dance partner. (Tom and Violetta had gone to a dance, but the atmosphere made them uneasy. Unmarried seniors prowled the floor for fresh conquests and the married ones weren't far behind. Perhaps it was all that Viagra on the pillows.)

"Soon, *Ambuya*, you'll be winning prizes of your own," predicted Noni. "You have such a beautiful singing voice."

"She does?" said Tom. Vaguely he remembered that long ago his wife had belonged to a church choir.

"Yes, indeed. I have signed her up for the Joy Meadows Glee Club."

"I hadn't sung for years until yesterday," said Violetta, giving Noni's cheek a fond pat.

"What happened yesterday?" said Tom.

"Sharhonda had a birthday party. Well, it wasn't really a birthday party. They were celebrating their first three months at Joy Meadows. You were at the gym."

Tom realized uneasily that they were beginning to spend a lot of time apart. Noni would take his wife to a "just for girls" event, while Ngwenya would ferry Tom off to a "guy outing".

For example, Tom had started going to the gym after breakfast. He worked up a sweat and then had a nice, cooling swim. Ngwenya had supplied him with a suit. After Tom's initial shock at seeing his own, aged body in daylight, he thoroughly enjoyed himself.

They would come together for lunch in one of the

restaurants—Chinese one day, Indian the next. In the afternoon Tom and Violetta split up to attend lectures or movies or one of the many classes taught on the island. Tom was studying ancient Egyptian history and Violetta had opted for jewelry-making. Evenings generally found them together at a party. But always they were attended by their polite, solicitous guides.

Had they been there six days? Or nine? Tom couldn't remember.

Noni always opened a bottle of wine for them before she left at night and much as Tom and Violetta enjoyed her company, it was a relief to be by themselves. They discovered each other again—minus the Viagra. Tom realized how many activities had been allowed to lapse during their years at the old farmhouse. In Joy Meadows, falling asleep was easy.

Staying asleep was the problem.

At first Tom thought it was caused by all those years working a night shift. After all, he had a forty-year jet lag to overcome. But then he realized that he woke up at exactly 3:18 a.m., not a moment before or after. His heart would be pounding and he would be covered with sweat. Every night he got up quietly, so as not to disturb Violetta, and went outside.

The sky was evenly dark, not a star anywhere. The little lights lining the walkways had gone out. Tom looked up at the gray canopy with something close to panic. It was like the lid on one of Dr. Willows' bug bottles. Outside, anything could be happening. The Pineapple Express could still be thundering down or it could have blown away with a full moon riding a few straggling clouds. He couldn't possibly tell.

The air was perfectly still, not like during the day when a gentle breeze wafted the smell of freshly cut lawns. Now it was stagnant, with a hint of machine oil. Tom's alarm grew. He wanted to wake up Violetta, let her soothe his fears, but just as he was about to do this he suddenly felt better. The breeze started up. The little lights came on again. He went back inside and saw that the digital clock read 3: 33. He fell asleep almost at once.

It was only in the morning that Tom realized that during those fifteen minutes the music that always filled the air of Joy Meadows had fallen silent.

BOOK TWO: A GATHERING OF ELDERS

Fourteen: *CHUPACABRAS HOSPITAL*

ON THE WEST perimeter of the city from which Cubby was being extracted lay a river. It had begun life as a canal, but years of erosion had widened and blurred its outline. Farm run-off fouled its waters. Oil flushed into it from garages. Richly laden with both pollutants and fertilizer, the river could not decide which ecological niche to occupy.

Sometimes it bloomed with mats of blue-green algae; sometimes it filled with water hyacinth whose leaves choked out sunlight and turned the water into a fetid sludge. But recently, due to an influx of rain from the Pineapple Express, it was—briefly—a picturesque California river. Thousands of tadpoles sported in its brown waters. Frogs crouched on its banks, croaking their little three-chambered hearts out until folks nearby fired shotguns into the reeds just to get some sleep.

It was called the Chupacabras River. On its far side a small community had grown up, also named Chupacabras. It was filled with adobe houses and ramshackle yards full of children's toys and old cars. At its center was a hospital surrounded by a barbed wire fence. Most of the adults in town worked there, and grateful they were to have jobs that required no formal education or proof of citizenship. Many came from places where you could be shot for bad-mouthing the government, and they thanked God every day for the freedom they enjoyed.

Ezekiel Gratz was the only orderly who'd been born in the U.S.A.. He was paid a true minimum wage instead of what the bulk of the work force received. The doctors who ran the facility realized they needed one person who spoke English to order supplies. As for the rest, Tagalog, Turkish, Serbian and Spanish were fine because they didn't need to understand their patients. The inmates of the government hospital had Alzheimer's Disease. They couldn't understand anybody.

Ezekiel noted the arrival of Cubby Willows ("Doctor" had been lost during the transition) in his log book shortly after noon. Cubby was put into the Orientation Ward. It was the darkest part of the hospital, watched over by an ex-prison guard. This was officially for security reasons, but actually to break the spirit of whoever was put there. Little light penetrated the grimy, heavily barred windows. The care was fitful and begrudging. The food horrible. Alzheimer's patients, it was presumed, had no taste buds.

Ezekiel forgot about Cubby for some hours. His work load was heavy and a sewage leak in the kitchen occupied his interest. Eventually, though, he felt an obligation to check up on the new arrival. His first impression was of a thin, undernourished man with gray hair and a beard lying as still as an Egyptian mummy. Then he realized that the patient was strapped down. This sometimes happened to newcomers before it became clear they were non-violent. Or it happened because Bogomil, the orderly in charge, enjoyed tying people up.

To Ezekiel's eye, Cubby didn't seem dangerous. He looked for signs of dementia and found none, although the man did appear to be listening intently to something Ezekiel couldn't detect. All he could hear was the whine of Bogomil's vacuum cleaner down the hall. "Hello," said Ezekiel.

Cubby noticed him for the first time and broke into such a sweet, trusting smile that Ezekiel was disarmed. "I'm having trouble sitting up," said Cubby.

"That would be the restraints," said Ezekiel.

"I don't need them."

And at that moment the afternoon sun moved just far enough to send a ray of light through the grimy window. It was muted to be sure, like looking at the moon through toilet paper, but it created a mysterious aura around Cubby's head. Ezekiel was startled. It reminded him of the halo that enfolded saints in the churches of his youth. He felt a superstitious awe, and guilt—long suppressed—surfaced in his heart.

For the Hospital of Chupacabras existed for only one reason. The aging, graying population of the U.S. had strained its social security system to the breaking point. The young were not willing to forfeit a third of their income to care for parents and grandparents, and so new laws had been passed. Any elderly person deemed a liability was automatically cared for by the State in a government nursing home. It sounded compassionate. The young proclaimed it the final, loving care bestowed by a grateful community, but in fact all such government institutions were hospices for the dying.

The staff were of minimal skills. Medicines were watered down. Hygiene was almost nonexistent and entire hospital wings succumbed to dysentery. If you didn't die of an overdose, you perished from an empty oxygen tank or moldy intravenous drip or a backed-up catheter tube. None of this was planned. It was simply built into the government system. It takes a village to kill a grandparent.

All this floated to the surface of Ezekiel's mind and he found himself undoing the straps binding Cubby, fluffing up the man's pillow and digging into his pockets for an energy bar he was planning to eat himself during break.

"Thank you," said Cubby. The afternoon light moved on. The aura vanished, but the gentle smile nourished by years of unconditional love still hovered on Cubby's face.

Ezekiel left, feeling shaken. He met Bogomil in the hall. It was unclear what nationality Bogomil was, but the man understood at least six Eastern European languages. Ezekiel knew catchphrases in all of them. "You leave new patient alone. No hurt," he said in Serbian.

"I do how I like," replied Bogomil.

"You hurt, I bring shit on your head."

"I listen, son of incestuous dog," replied Bogomil, who knew Ezekiel had the power to do this.

"Your mother was mounted by camels," said Ezekiel, continuing on to his next job of shooting rats in the pantry.

*   *   *

Cubby felt much better with the restraints off and he rubbed his arms to restore circulation. "You were a such a good little fellow," said Miss Feeny, his first grade teacher, sitting at the end of the bed. "So obedient and reliable."

"Obedience is not always good," argued Gerbill, who was looking out the murky window. He was back in the form Cubby was used to, having left Sybille with her relatives. "Not so good to follow orders in the *Hitler Jugend*."

Cubby understood that Gerbill had been a member of the Hitler Youth because once, in one of the beer halls they visited, he got drunk enough to admit it.

"It vas at first like a sports club, most jolly. Much hiking in the woods, much singing, the nice girls with the pigtails coming out to give us flowers. But it vas setting us up."

"Setting you up how?" said Cubby, who had only a hazy idea of world events outside of locust swarms and boll weevil invasions.

"First with the breaking windows," Gerbill said morosely. "What boy does not enjoy breaking windows? Then with the beating up. I did not like it, but who vants to be called a sissy. They softened you up gradually, making you get used to one thing before moving on to the next. Then with the killing—" Cubby looked up, startled—"which I did not do. It vas a Lutheran minister with radical ideas. The others beat him to death. I vas supposed to take his daughter to the *polizei*."

"Obedience and reliability are the hallmarks of a good student," said Miss Feeny complacently, patting her dead-black hair that was always lacquered into submission with hair spray. The theory among her students was that it wasn't hair at all, but a space alien that had taken up residence on her head.

Gerbill prowled the room, observing the cold cement floor, the cracked mirror over the wash basin, the hanks of gray hair wedged under the wall skirting. He looked out into the hall where Bogomil was vacuuming the same section of floor over and over. "This place is a death trap," he said. "I vill tell you how it was in Germany. There is a parasite called the lancet fluke."

(Cubby knew all about the lancet fluke, but he liked listening to Gerbill's discourses, familiar or not. The lancet fluke's eggs begin life in the liver of a sheep, passing out through the bile duct to nestle in a pile of excrement. Not a promising beginning you might think, but even sheep shit has its fans. Snails graze on it and swallow the eggs. These hatch in their intestines, producing creatures called *cercariae* that irritate the hosts so much, the snails surround them in slime and cough them up. Soon the grass is covered in tiny slime balls with many *cercariae* inside. Few people have seen a snail cough or even know that it's possible.)

"Now comes the interesting part," said Gerbill. "An ant eats a slime ball and while most of the *cercariae* move to its gut, one goes to the head where it changes the chemistry of the brain. It whispers to the ant, *Climb up high. You vill like it. The view is lovely.* The ant climbs to the top of a grass stem and waits. It is obedient. It is following orders. Sooner or later it is eaten by a sheep and the whole process begins again. That is how it vas in Germany then. Hitler vas the lancet fluke and every German had this little voice in his head saying *Climb up high. The view is lovely.*"

"Well, I'm quite sure I don't want to hear about the bodily processes of sheep," said Miss Feeny, fading into the distempered wall of the Orientation Ward.

"She never did approve of bodily processes," Cubby apologized. "I wish I could leave, but they took my clothes." He was dressed in a threadbare hospital gown that opened at the back. All his belongings had been confiscated, including his credit card. Bogomil had asked for the PIN number, but Cubby had been too dazed to reply. "I don't even know where I am," he said.

"You were never certain of that," said Gerbill, sighing. "My poor foolish boy, you should have made friends with the living. You need Tom Seaworthy, but unfortunately right now he is out of our reach. We must make do with what we have."

"With Bogomil?" said Cubby. The ex-prison guard had stripped him with the efficiency of an army cook pulling the skin off a chicken.

"The other one. Ezekiel. He has a soul buried in there somewhere."

The sun was setting now and the gloom in the bedroom was profound. The lights were controlled by a central switch, but Bogomil didn't activate it until he could no longer see. Since he had spent years working in a salt mine his eyes functioned at the same level as a feral cat.

But Gerbill, like many ghosts, shone with a spectral glow so that the room was not entirely cheerless. The light wasn't bright enough to read by and it was an eerie green. Still, it gladdened Cubby to see it hovering next to his bed.

"The daughter of the Lutheran minister, the one you were supposed to arrest . . ." Cubby began.

"Of course I did not hand her over to the *polizei*," Gerbill said, knowing exactly what question Cubby was going to ask. The dead don't need to work things out logically. All the actions they took while living exist in an endless present for them, nor are they allowed to forget them. This is both their Heaven and Hell.

"I took Sybille away," Gerbill continued. "Or rather we escaped together. We went into the forest, running, running, we did not know where. We ate turnips from abandoned farms und drank from horse troughs. The war ended. We did not know. We starved until she grew weak. In the dead of winter with snow everywhere she died."

"So you didn't know her long," murmured Cubby, thinking that was why Sybille had been so beautifully remote and why she never spoke. She wasn't quite real to Gerbill either.

"Love does not need time," Gerbill insisted. "Love is once und forever."

Fifteen: *FRIETCHIE*

FOR FRIETCHIE, love was frequent and temporary. She wouldn't have had it any other way. But as she aged, the urges of youth lost their hold on her. She could go an entire week without dragging home some hapless barfly.

Not that she wasn't extremely fond of Ezekiel. Him she regarded with a tenderness born of fellowship. She would never break a beer bottle over his head or take out a restraining order against him as she had for others. For it was a curious thing that men passed up women far more comely and good-natured to pursue Frietchie's rough charms. She'd had her share of stalkers.

Her hair stood out like an alpaca's. Her feet swelled after a long day at work. She had a fondness for fuzzy pink sweaters and leather miniskirts. She was almost sixty-five years old and men still followed her down the street like demented hounds.

(Gerbill would have said she had "veffs". He'd done an experiment on "veffs" as a young man and had come up with fascinating results. More about this later.)

But Frietchie was devoted to Ezekiel. When he was in residence in her mansion (courtesy of husbands #2, 5 and 6), she waited on him like the chief *kadine* of the Grand Turk. She listened devotedly to his stories. She fed him snacks and anticipated his every need. Few men could have withstood such attention, and certainly not one with as little will-power as Ezekiel. The twenty-year age difference barely registered on him. It didn't hurt either that Frietchie had neutralized Bogomil on the second day of Ezekiel's job at the hospital.

Bogomil had introduced himself to the new orderly by smashing his fist into a wall next to Ezekiel's head. It was a method that transcended language and had worked well on Turks, Filipinos and Vietnamese. Bogomil figured it would work well on Americans, too, but he hadn't counted on Frietchie.

Frietchie in a good mood lit up a room like a tropical sunrise. In a bad mood, the San Andreas Fault could not inspire more dread. She had a direct line to whatever female character could reduce a man to oatmeal and she instinctively channeled that fearsome creature.

She assumed the persona of Bogomil's great-grandmother who had shared his bed as a child and made his nights dreadful with groans and death rattles. Frietchie didn't remotely resemble the great-grandmother, but Bogomil recognized the voice.

What Frietchie said was: *If you ever hurt Ezekiel you'll have me to deal with.*

But what Bogomil heard was: *Child . . . child . . . fetch me the chamber pot . . . yes . . . hold it there . . . ahhhh!* A spectral hand clutched his hair, the exhaled fetor of infected gums swept over him as though a grave had opened up. He was reduced to gibbering terror and never threatened Ezekiel again.

Now Frietchie eagerly awaited Ezekiel's arrival. She was well off, having plucked the excess income from eight husbands, and from having her own hair-dressing salon in the snazzy part of town. You might wonder why anyone would have her hair done by someone whose own style resembled a lint trap, but Frietchie inspired confidence. She could turn a forty-year-old virgin into the Serpent of the Nile in thirty minutes. Women staggered out of her salon in a daze. Often the spell lasted long enough to transform their lives.

Frietchie had made Ezekiel a feast of oysters on the half shell, T-bone steak and a cake oozing with dark chocolate. She herself was on the half shell in her new Frederick's of Hollywood gown. But when Ezekiel arrived he slumped into a chair and flicked open a bottle of beer with hardly a word.

A young woman would have been angry. Frietchie was far too wise for that. She threw a bathrobe over the drafty gown and settled herself across from her morose lover. "Bad day?" she commented.

"Sometimes . . . " he paused, thinking it out, and took a long draft of beer. "Sometimes I hate my job."

Well, who wouldn't hate that job, thought Frietchie, depriving old folks of happiness and driving them to an early grave. (She automatically subtracted herself from the ranks of "old folks".) What went on in the hospital didn't bear thinking about. She remembered how well her parents and grandparents had been cared for, but such things didn't happen anymore. With the new Senior Laws, young people had turned into brutes who should have been drowned at birth.

The government fawned on them. Every opportunity was provided for them, but the streets were still thronged with homeless youths. It wasn't *their* fault they couldn't drag themselves out of bed before noon or sign their names correctly on a welfare check. It was Society's. Parents and grandparents insisted on keeping their money, the selfish old farts.

The young had voted in increasingly oppressive governments. Frietchie wasn't quite sure how it had happened, but gradually life had become much more precarious for the elderly. (Again, Frietchie automatically subtracted herself this group.) And now there was that ominous Youth Patrol poking their noses into what little joy was left.

"You might find another job," she said, knowing that Ezekiel couldn't. He'd barely passed high school—not his fault. It was how his brain was wired. Reading was beyond him, but his hands could build anything.

Ezekiel didn't bother to argue. He opened another beer bottle. "I saw a man today who was so . . . angelic. Bogomil had him strapped down, but the man was as harmless as a moth. Even his name was appealing, Cubby Willows."

"Wait!" cried Frietchie, grasping Ezekiel's arm so hard that he yelped. "Are you saying Dr. Cubby Willows is a patient at the hospital?"

"Ow!" yelled Ezekiel, rubbing his arm. "Maybe he's a doctor. I didn't see it on the admission papers."

"What does he look like?"

So Ezekiel, with one eye on his distraught mistress, described Cubby's gentle smile and the aura of sanctity that had hovered about his head.

"Son of a bitch," murmured Frietchie. Her eyes went soft and unfocussed. She was fifteen years old again, with the biggest crush in creation, just throwing herself at the gangly, unsophisticated boy whose smile made her feel all creamy inside and who hadn't the slightest inkling of the power he exercised over her. "Son of a bitch. Captain Tarantula," said Frietchie.

*   *   *

The lights had finally been turned on, not that it made much difference. The 25 watt globes were only bright enough to attract mosquitoes from the nearby river. The frogs were in full cry—*Croak! Croak! Croak!*—sending a melancholy message to the patients in the hospital. The floors were dark, with here and there a piece of equipment to snag the ankle of someone attempting to reach a bathroom.

But Cubby had excellent night vision. He'd spent many years hunting insects after dark and his hearing was keen as well. He could detect the nearness of a wall by the air molecules bouncing between his ear and its surface. Thus he maneuvered his way easily to the bathroom. He also had access to another sense once common among our ancestors, but atrophied through lack of use: An instinct for water. Cubby correctly identified the drip of a leaky water faucet and traveled up a gradient of humidity until he had located it. He did this effortlessly, not realizing that the skill was unusual, not to say creepy. It certainly creeped out Bogomil.

The ex-prison guard was standing in the hallway when he became aware of a shape moving rapidly towards him. It flitted to one side, fitting itself neatly between him and the wall, before disappearing into the bathroom.

The hair rose up on Bogomil's arms. He himself had good night vision, but it was the *assurance* with which Cubby moved that woke an atavistic fear. It was like the bats that had lived in Bogomil's ceiling as a child. Those creatures, too, had moved with complete confidence in the dark, only brushing the child's face with a puff of air. His great-grandmother said they went forth to drink blood.

I make hurt, thought Bogomil, listening to Cubby's

moth-like rustlings in the bathroom. It was his usual reaction to fear, but this time caution halted him. This particular patient was under Ezekiel's protection and by extension, Frietchie's. *I bring garlic for wear around neck*, he decided, flinching as Cubby flitted past him on the way back to bed.

"Vell done," congratulated Gerbill when Cubby returned. "You scared the *scheiss* out of that bully."

"Was that Bogomil in the hall?" Cubby said vaguely.

"Indeed it was," said Mr. Strickland, his old biology teacher. Mr. Strickland was hovering near the ceiling, observing the mosquitoes. "*Culex pipiens*, if I'm not mistaken."

"You are correct. Some of them are carrying West Nile virus," said Gerbill, floating up to confirm the diagnosis. The dead can smell mortal illness the way we detect ozone in the air after a thunderstorm.

Cubby waked up. He liked nothing better than a discussion of insect-borne diseases, and all three scientists settled down for a vigorous conversation. Gerbill said he'd seen dead crows in the fields and Strickland, who was an avid bird watcher, had noticed blue jays, robins and a hawk as well.

(The West Nile virus circulates between birds, horses and men in the bodies of mosquitoes. It doesn't harm the mosquitoes because that would be like a bank robber shooting out the tires of his getaway car. The virus needs those wings to get to the next blood bank. Flocks of sentinel chickens are kept all over California to detect the spread of the disease, much in the same way canaries used to be kept in coal mines. There had once been a flock of chickens at Chupacabras Hospital, but the staff had barbequed them during a Fourth of July celebration.)

A shotgun blasted away at the reeds in the distance. It was Bogomil attempting to soothe his unease by silencing the frogs. The croaking stopped, but after a couple of minutes it started up again. The frogs were used to Bogomil. They knew he couldn't hit them.

Sixteen: *THE SECRET OF THE SEAWORTHYS*

L ONG AGO, at the same time Tom was being driven home by Eric Hoffer, his Uncle Shumba was being taken to Chupacabras Hospital. In those days it was still an insane asylum and Shumba was well acquainted with it. It took Tom's father two weeks to spring him. By that time Shumba had been filled up with anti-psychotic drugs and was about as responsive as a banana slug. He lay in the back bedroom for weeks, being cared for by Tom's mother. Gradually, the drugs drained out of Shumba's system.

Tom sat beside his bed day after day, reading to pass the time. He had tried to check *The Essays of Montaigne* out of the library and was told that it wasn't for children. Tom sneaked the book out anyway, but after working on it for several days he realized that the librarian had been correct. He selected *Rats, Lice and History* instead, mainly because he had a pet rat.

It was full of Latin and Greek words that Tom had to skip, but it repaid his efforts with a gross story about how a scientist had carried a pill box full of lice inside his socks to keep them warm. This convinced Tom that scientists were crazy, a viewpoint that was reinforced later when he worked for Durton, Barton, Gerbill and Slithe.

Now he was reading *Microbe Hunters* by Paul de Kruif and finding it every bit as enthralling as a detective story.

"I'm back," said Uncle Shumba. Tom was so startled that he dropped the book. It had been weeks since his uncle had done anything but groan.

"I'll get Mom," the boy said.

Shumba held up his hand. "Not yet. I want to talk to you."

"Jeez, I'm sorry I left you," Tom said. "I feel so bad about it."

"Don't worry about it. The whole thing was pre-ordained."

"Pre- what?"

"Means the old gods had it planned. Actually, I been back a while, but I thought I'd play dead and collect myself. Sheee-it, that was a bad trip! Don't ever let strangers put stuff into your veins." Shumba hitched himself up to a sitting position and Tom quickly put a pillow behind his back.

"What do you mean, the old gods had it planned?" Tom asked cautiously.

"I was visited by the Mhondoro himself before the anti-war demonstration."

"Who's that?" Tom fetched the tray Mom had left and put it within his uncle's reach.

"He's the Big Daddy of the spirit world. I told you that before, kid. Listen up. The Mhondoro said, *Take that boy to the anti-war demonstration*, and I said, *What for?* And he said, *Never you mind. You get the boy there and I'll do the rest.* So I did. You don't argue with Big Daddy. It ain't intelligent."

"I ran away," Tom said. He felt so guilty about leaving his uncle and letting him get shot up with anti-psychotic medicine.

"Ah! But where did you run *to?*" Shumba said, so Tom told him about having lunch with Mr. Hoffer and about how he suddenly liked to read books and about the scientist who kept a pill box full of lice in his socks.

"I don't know what that's gonna lead to, but one thing is certain. The old gods got their eye on you," said his uncle. "And now it is my solemn duty to tell you the story of why the Seaworthys are so special." He took a swig of Tom's mother's excellent coffee and cleared his throat.

The Secret History of the Seaworthys

Once upon a time (said Uncle Shumba) in the land between the morning and the evening sky was a city made of stone. It was ruled over by a great king named

Mutapa. Mutapa had built his palace on a high hill and in the middle of this palace was a tower where he dreamed his dreams and planned his plans.

At the base of the hill were the abodes of his people, the barracks where his soldiers lived, his storehouses, and his fields and farms. Beyond them lay the gray-green mopani forest stretching all the way to the sea.

When Mutapa stood on the tower he could see the shadow of the sea at the edge of his empire. It was there that he traded gold to ghost-colored men from across the water. They brought him silk, jewels, mirrors and spices, but the men themselves were forbidden to enter his land.

One day the high priest came to the king. He said that he'd been given a vision by the Mhondoro, the spirit of the tribe. The king's wife was pregnant with twins. The female twin would have the ability to control the rain. The male would become a great spirit medium.

But the law of the land forbade that both should survive. Twins were against the natural order and if both lived, terrible misfortune would befall the land. Therefore, asked the priest, which one should they kill?

Mutapa considered the problem for a long time. Rain was the gift of life, without which no one could prosper. On the other hand, a spirit medium could defend his people from enemies. Which was more important?

Mutapa stood on his tower and fed the royal vultures as he pondered. No enemy had ever been able to stand against him, but he had no more control of the weather than the lowest peasant. Therefore, the girl was more important.

But when the children were born, the boy grasped Mutapa's thumb and the king's heart melted within him. He could not bring himself to kill his son, and so he sent the male child with a generous gift of gold to the ghost-colored men. He told them to take his son beyond the sea so that the curse could not reach his land. He called the boy Tombudzo, which means 'suffering', and the girl who remained behind Modjadji, 'she who must be obeyed'.

The men took Tombudzo away, but soon they returned with an army and invaded the land between the morning and the evening sky. They led away Mutapa's people as slaves. The city of stone fell into ruin. Modjadji and her mother fled to a secret place in the hills where there is always mist, and where her descendants, the Rain Queens, rule to this day.

The End

"Tombudzo was raised as a companion to an Italian prince," said Shumba, "and when he grew up, the old gods appeared to him. They gave him the shadow-skin that makes you invisible. They kept his foot from the precipice and most importantly they kept him and all his descendants safe in the midst of their enemies."

"Ohhh," Tom said softly.

"Nobody ever ruled over Tombudzo or has ruled over any other Seaworthy. We are protected. We have long, happy lives full of contentment. No Seaworthy has ever had an unhappy marriage or an ungrateful child, but in return we must obey certain rules. Now and then the spirits appear to one of us with a command *which we must obey*. If we don't, the protection extended to us will vanish and our tribe will disappear like raindrops fallen into hot sand.

"One day the spirits instructed Tombudzo to climb the tower of Pisa and drop a grape and a pebble. Galileo was walking underneath at the time. He was struck by Tombudzo's pebble and grape simultaneously and the laws of modern physics were born."

"That's all he did? Drop a grape and a pebble," said Tom, disappointed. He'd been hoping for something more spectacular. After all, he was named after this ancestor.

"Don't bad-mouth what you don't understand," Shumba admonished. "The biggest things in this world start out little. We Seaworthys are the pebble that starts an avalanche in world events. Where do you think penicillin came from?"

"Arthur Fleming found it on a Petri plate," Tom said, who had read this recently.

"But who put it on his desk? Who drew his eye to the ring of dead bacteria around the penicillin?"

"I don't know. A lab technician?"

"Exactly!" said his uncle with satisfaction. "Your

great-grandfather Balthazar was the technician in that lab."

Tom's mouth fell open. He remembered Great-Grandpa. He was a fierce old man who had owned the ranch before it passed on to Shumba.

"Another Seaworthy revealed how sound travels along a wire to Alexander Graham Bell. One of our ancestors told Elias Howe such a frightening story that he dreamed about being speared by Zulu warriors. When Howe woke up he invented the sewing machine needle. Who do you think whispered the word *peanut* into George Washington Carver's ear?"

"A Seaworthy?" guessed Tom.

"Correct. The most important advances in civilization have come through us."

Tom suspected that the story had been cooked up in Shumba's fertile brain while he was coming off the anti-psychotic medicine, but the boy was too happy to see his uncle awake to argue about it. He rotated the tray so that Mom's loganberry pie was within reach. "Want me to cut that up for you?" he asked.

"Thanks," said Uncle Shumba. "My hands are still shaky. I see my backpack in the closet. Would you —"

"Dad threw out the marijuana."

"Oh, well. Too much to hope for," Shumba said.

Tom cut the pie and spooned whipped cream over it. His uncle had become alarmingly skinny during his convalescence. "Did Dad ever . . . you know . . . see anything weird?"

Shumba's laugh sprayed bits of loganberry pie over the bed-spread. "That's good. That's really good. If your father ever saw a spirit he'd break a two-by-four over its head. But he's a good man, Tombudzo. He keeps the world safe for the rest of us."

Tom wasn't sure he liked being included in the *us* his uncle was describing

Seventeen: *THE HOT TOMATO EXPERIMENT*

A S BOGOMIL LUNGED through the mud on his way back to the hospital, a car eased into the parking lot. Visiting hours were long past. From two to four in the afternoon the door of the waiting room was propped open. A heap of dusty pamphlets —*Carcinoma for Beginners, Self-Examine Your Hemorrhoids,* and *Why Do They Call It the Cough Test?*—were provided for those lingering to see whether Uncle Edgar could be located among all those beds. But in fact no one ever visited the hospital twice. What was the point? It upset the kids, and Uncle Edgar only had one thing to say: *For God's sake get me out of here!*

At four the door was closed again. The passengers in the car weren't concerned about that, however, because they had keys. They opened a side entrance and made their way through the long, winding halls. The odor of T-bone steak wafted through wards accustomed only to gelatin and toast. Essence of chocolate cake drifted into the nostrils of men and women who had not tasted it in years.

The sense of smell is the last memory to disappear and, indeed, can resurrect all other memories by its power. Who does not recall the cocoa served to you in a china mug by your grandmother? Who cannot remember the bacon frying in her kitchen? And from there we move to the flowered curtains at her window, the garden with her prize rose bushes, and last of all to the woman herself called back from beyond the blue horizon.

The passage of the visitors caused a stir and a murmur throughout the Alzheimer's wards, but all too soon the life-giving odors dissipated. The bright Sundays of yesteryear faded. There was only the monotonous croaking from the marshes and the incoherent curses of Bogomil struggling through the mud.

"Vat is that delicious smell?" cried Gerbill, distracted from a dissertation on botfly infestation. He and Strickland made way for the visitors, and Cubby sat up, blinking at the flashlight Ezekiel waved at his face. The woman with him arranged a row of votive candles in the window. There's something about candles that brings out the best in a place. Cubby's ward was a vile, distempered cellblock, but the wavering flames turned it into a sanctuary.

Gerbill and Strickland faded to spots of brightness on the wall plaster, although Cubby could still see them. His attention was taken up by the woman. She seemed familiar.

"Oh, Cubby, you probably don't remember me. I've changed so much," sighed Frietchie. "A lot of water under the keel, eh, Captain Tarantula?"

And Cubby saw past the frazzled hair, pouchy cheeks and yellowed teeth to the girl who had put herself in his way after chemistry class. Quite simply, he did not see any difference between Frietchie then and now. Ugliness wasn't something he understood. To him his elderly grandmother had been as attractive as a Hollywood starlet, which meant that he didn't understand the allure of a starlet either. "*Arghhh*, me proud beauty. So ye've struck your sails in my port," he said, fitting into the role of Captain Tarantula.

"Permission to come aboard, sir," she replied, wiping her eyes. "I've brought marvelous booty: T-bone steak, oysters, and—and—oh, Cubby! How did you land up here?"

"I'm not quite sure," said Cubby. "I was doing experiments with cockroaches. I really have to get back to see how they're doing. The factory where I was living has been condemned."

"You're such a pill!" said Frietchie, weeping openly now. "How can you worry about bugs when you're in so much trouble?"

"If I don't worry about them, who will?" Cubby said reasonably. "They're Captain Tarantula's faithful companions, bilge mates on the long nights at sea, *arghhh*. Is that chocolate cake?"

"Yes, dearest. You must eat to get your strength back." Frietchie cut up the food and fed it to Cubby as tenderly as though she were ministering to a child. Ezekiel paced in the shadows, unsure of whether to be jealous or not. Gerbill and Strickland watched in amazement.

"Vat did the American soldiers used to say? *Va-va-voom! That is one hot tomato!* I am thinking Cubby has got himself a tomato," marveled Gerbill.

"He'd be better off with a tomato hornworm," Strickland observed. "He never did understand women."

"Bah! She has veffs. No man can resist veffs."

"Come again?" said Strickland and so Gerbill explained the experiment he'd performed as a young man.

(After the war he'd managed to complete his education, choosing entomology because it had nothing to do with politics. But he had not counted on the cachet of Nazi scientists for Americans. Everybody wanted one—General Motors, Westinghouse, Walt Disney, and especially the newly established Burton and Barton Laboratory. Entomologists were at the bottom of the scientific peck order. They didn't do sexy research like the chemists and physicists. They didn't make nerve gas or atom bombs or kill anything except bugs. And so Burton and Barton wanted to enhance their company's status by hiring Gerbill, even though he'd only been in the Hitler Youth. It was all they could afford.

Gerbill's first project involved moths. Moths were pitching woo under every green tree in California and wreaking havoc on the state's agricultural profits. You could blast a ten mile bug-free zone around a farm and the little bastards still found their way across. Gerbill theorized that the females, like good German housewives, stayed home. It was the males who crossed the sexual Siegfried Line in search of adventure. In this he was correct. The *Ceanothus* silk moth can spread his lovely rose-red wings and flap as far as thirty miles to find the elusive fair one.

Gerbill believed that desire traveled through the ether much as soap operas traveled over radio waves to reach the ears of neglected housewives. If he could find the signal, he could jam it. Thus was born the Veffs Project—"veffs" being the way Gerbill pronounced the word "waves".

He erected a tent in an alfalfa field and asked two hundred college boys to identify the gender of the person hidden inside. Sometimes it was a woman and sometimes a man and sometimes the tent was empty. He discovered that most of the answers were random, but very occasionally a woman would inspire the correct identification from every single male. Those were the hot tomatoes with veffs.)

Alas, Cubby had no veff detector. Frietchie fed him morsels of chocolate while Ezekiel paced up and down in the shadows. Cubby soaked up her adoration like a kitten being groomed by its mother, but he had no idea what it meant. He only knew that it made him feel nice and he radiated good will. It was this innocence that had so besotted his elderly relatives and which also worked its charm on stray dogs and cockroaches. In religious paintings such generalized benevolence is shown as a halo.

"*Donner und blitzen,* he has no idea vat is going on," exclaimed Gerbill.

"Told you," Strickland said smugly.

Frietchie packed up the food and dusted the crumbs from Cubby's beard. "We have to get him out of here tonight," she said.

Ezekiel reappeared from the shadows. "Oh, no! It's more than my job is worth!"

"You know they'll microchip him tomorrow."

"If I'm caught they'll microchip *me.*" Ezekiel fell silent at the ominous look on Frietchie's face.

"There are only two witnesses, you and Bogomil. Both of you can stay at my place," she decided. "Get up, Cubby dearest."

"They took my clothes," he protested, trying to close the gap in his hospital gown.

"There's nothing there I haven't seen before. Where's Bogomil? He can help us move your things out of that factory. I'll bet anything he ripped off your credit card." Frietchie went in search of the ex-prison guard and cornered him in a broom closet. She explained what she wanted, but all Bogomil heard was *Child . . . child . . . fetch me the chamber pot.* He followed her down the hall like a zombie.

Soon they were tiptoeing through the crowded hospital. From here and there came cries. A few patients pressed fruitlessly on alarm bells, but the staff were tucked up in their beds and heard nothing.

To Cubby the wards seethed with visitors. Spectral shapes hung over every bed causing moans of fear. The dead are not always wise. They want desperately to reassure their relatives, but their presence only adds to the confusion. "I suppose that's what happens when Sybille visits the little ones," Cubby remarked to Gerbill, who was keeping pace in the air.

"Ja, I keep telling her to keep her distance, but she is so loving."

"Who's Sybille?" asked Frietchie, looking around to see what had prompted Cubby's odd statement.

"Gerbill's wife. She died in the snow long ago," explained Cubby.

"And Gerbill—?"

"Over there. He's dead, too." Cubby pointed.

"Oh, brother. He's delusional," muttered Ezekiel. "I am so screwed."

"Why are these people here?" Cubby insisted. "They sound so unhappy." In all his life he had never seen such a scene, for his relatives had disappeared one by one without his realizing exactly what had happened. The others had shielded him from it.

"It's a hospital, darling. Keep walking," Frietchie said. Soon they were outside in the cool, clean air. Cubby wanted to go back for a second look, but Ezekiel firmly steered him to Frietchie's little sports car.

They all squeezed inside and drove away with the engine complaining at the extra weight. Bogomil filled up the back seat. Ezekiel, Cubby and Frietchie crammed into the front. The frogs in the marsh croaked mournfully. The dead crooned over their frightened relatives in the Alzheimer's wards.

Eighteen: *THE RATTLESNAKE GODDESS*

ONCE CUBBY GOT an idea into his head it was impossible to dislodge it. That's what made him a good scientist, but he was beginning to get on Frietchie's nerves with his constant, low-key nagging. "We have to go back," he kept saying. "I'm sure those people are in trouble. Their relatives were very upset."

"*What* relatives?" snarled Frietchie after the sixth pass of this argument. She had to keep her mind on the potholes that ate into both sides of the Chupacabras road.

"Those spirits hanging over the beds." Cubby explained. "They mean well, but most people aren't ready to talk to the dead until they're dead, too. It's what I was telling Gerbill—"

"Oh, brother," groaned Ezekiel.

"Plea*s*e don't tell anyone you see dead people," said Frietchie. The car rattled over a cattle grid and on through farm land. The cool, sweet smell of alfalfa drifted into the window. It was a welcome relief from Bogomil who, even fresh from a shower, had an odd medicinal odor people found disturbing.

(Cubby could have identified it, had he not been so consumed with the Alzheimer's patients. It was the scent of the Arizona desert tarantula, the kind with a seven inch leg span. Tarantulas live long, solitary lives and the males do not become sexually active until they are ten years old, oddly enough at the same age Bogomil became sexually active. There is no conclusion to be drawn from this.)

"Gerbill says that if you don't know enough live people, the dead will visit you instead," said Cubby. "That's why I see them. I haven't had much of a social life and it's clear the hospital patients don't have any at all. I should explain to them what's happening so they won't be frightened."

"Cubby, listen to me," said Frietchie. "If you walk in there they're going to lock you up. They'll microchip you and then they'll drug you. Chupacabras Hospital is the home of the living dead."

"They . . . microchip people?" Cubby faltered.

"It's called *belling the cat*," explained Ezekiel. "If you try to escape it sets off an alarm."

Cubby was astounded. He'd never taken much notice of the outside world, assuming that its laws and customs were the same that had existed in his youth. If asked who the president was—one of the cardinal questions used by doctors to assess mental alertness—he would have had to look it up. Such things were not important to him.

"But why?" he asked, bewildered.

"For humane reasons at first," said Ezekiel. "Alzheimer's patients tend to get lost. So do kids and pets. Microchips were very trendy a few years back, but then the government figured out that you could keep track of everyone with them. Only, it isn't legal to force it on adults unless they're disenfranchised."

"Which includes anyone who's incurably ill, insane, incarcerated or old," said Frietchie. The car struggled up a hill to another cattle grid.

Cubby sat still, digesting this information. He understood now the strange transition that had happened after the firemen discovered him in his apartment. At first they were polite, but then, having decided he had Alzheimer's, they had *disenfranchised* him. "Is it possible to get enfranchised again?" he asked.

"It isn't easy," said Frietchie. "Generally folks don't live long once they've become wards of the state."

Cubby looked out the window. They were approaching the first lights of the city. It was a nice part of town with large estates and well-kept lawns, much prettier than where he'd been living on Sasquatch Avenue. He hadn't been out here for years and it awakened happy memories of his parents' house.

The house had had an old garden planted higgledy-piggledy with whatever took anyone's fancy. Tomatoes grew next to tiger lilies, fig trees wrestled for space with pomegranates. Paths wound around ramshackle structures for chickens, a machine shop, an extra piano room for Cubby's great-aunt to pound out her love songs. Through this tame jungle Cubby hunted for bugs with his dog Jingle Bell.

He remembered getting up before dawn once to watch a meteor shower. His father had arisen, too, to barbeque breakfast hotdogs in the back yard, and the sparks had flown up like a tiny meteor swarm of their own. Since then, his relatives had flown away, too, somewhere among all those stars.

"I'm not good at making friends," said Cubby.

"*I'm* your friend," Frietchie responded at once.

"That's awfully nice of you. He's my friend, too. He gave me an energy bar this afternoon." Cubby turned his luminous smile on Ezekiel.

"It was a mistake," muttered Ezekiel, slouching down as much as the space allowed.

"Yesterday I didn't know anyone except forty-eight cockroaches—no, wait. Forty-seven. One of the females ate a male. Now I have you and I feel so happy. Perhaps those people in the hospital only need someone to visit them."

"No, no and no," said Frietchie. "You're not going near that place again."

They went down a winding avenue with old-fashioned street lamps and houses set back behind high fences. Frietchie pulled up in front of one and Ezekiel hopped out to key in the security code. He was the only man who had ever been entrusted with this secret, and he carefully blocked the numbers from Bogomil and Cubby.

Cubby was listening to the rustle of a midnight breeze in the poplars lining the street. He heard the whirring flight of a sphinx moth and a sudden challenge from a male cricket encountering another male cricket. How beautiful it all was! Why had he spent so many years on Sasquatch Avenue where little could be heard except traffic?

But it was not in his nature to regret things. His apartment had its own charms, not the least of which were cockroaches. "Did you know," he said, marveling at how everything worked together, "that if you count the number of chirps a snowy tree cricket produces for thirteen seconds and add forty, you get the temperature in degrees Fahrenheit?"

"No, Cubby dearest, I did not know that," murmured Frietchie, easing the car through the gate. It closed and locked behind them.

Bogomil looked around unhappily at the space in which they were trapped. He didn't like the koi pond overhung with wisteria. The gardenias and jasmine with which Frietchie surrounded her veranda filled him with dismay. They were beautiful and beautiful things, in his experience, were enemies and would attack him. *I not like*, he thought in the pigeon language he employed even in his brain.

Frietchie had a shrewd idea of the environment that would put Bogomil at ease. She had him drag a mattress to the utility room and gave him a blanket, a supply of canned food and a bottle of vodka. "I expect you to be ready for work after breakfast," she said and closed the door.

Bogomil curled up happily next to the glowing flame of a hot water heater. He had Spam, much Spam, his favorite food. He had vodka. The room reminded him of the Siberian hovel he had grown up in. Life was good.

For the others, Frietchie opened the French doors on the verandah and let the fresh air of the garden into the house. It was a beautiful place, courtesy of husband #2, with improvements by husbands #5 and #6. It was based on the floor plan of a Moroccan castle, with hanging lamps and a fountain splashing in a courtyard. All the furniture was comfortable, the floor was covered with lush carpets, the walls were festooned with romantic tapestries. Would it have won prizes in interior design? Of course not. It was too open-hearted. It was the house equivalent of Ava Gardner strolling barefoot through an Italian street trailing a mink coat.

"You must rest tomorrow, Cubby," Frietchie said, pouring him a glass of champagne. Cubby had never had champagne before and was enchanted by the bubbles. "Ezekiel, Bogomil and I will collect your belongings."

"If I can't return to the hospital," he said, letting the bubbles fizz under his nose, "perhaps I can call and offer my advice. I'm sure the doctors want to know why their patients are so frightened."

"There aren't any real doctors," said Ezekiel, downing

his glass of champagne rapidly and refilling the glass. He was beginning to wonder how long Frietchie would keep Cubby.

"It's a hospital, isn't it?" said Cubby.

"It's an assembly line," Frietchie said somewhat sharply. "You feed people into one end, move them along a conveyor belt and drop them off into a dumpster at the other end. If you call Chupacabras Hospital they'll arrest me for absconding with one of their patients. Do you want that?"

"Of course not," said Cubby, shocked. "You're my friend."

"Good. Keep it in mind. I want you to spend the day looking for creepy-crawlies in the garden and watching TV. I think it gets the Nature channel."

"What if I write them a letter—"

"Cubby!" Frietchie's voice rose to a shriek. In the utility room Bogomil heard it and crossed himself. "Cubby, you must not call, write, e-mail or even *think* about the hospital! What you can do—" she fussed in a desk drawer and came up with a notebook "—is make a list of the bugs in the garden. I'm dying to know what's out there."

Cubby took the notebook and saw to his delight that it had at least two hundred pages. He at once began making plans to explore the relationships between the various plants and insects.

Frietchie showed him to a bedroom with a bedside lamp and gave him a set of yellow silk pajamas left over from husband #5. She and Ezekiel retired to the other end of the house, to what she referred to as the Mistress Bedroom. There they disported themselves until they fell into an exhausted slumber.

But Cubby stayed awake all night, making diagrams and identifying the moths that fluttered around his bedside lamp.

*   *   *

Frietchie awoke to the sounds of splashing and looked through the bedroom curtains. Bogomil was washing himself in the koi pond. She rapped on the glass and he sprang out at once, dripping water weeds. "Get out of there, you behemoth!" she screamed. Ezekiel came up behind her and shaded his eyes at the sight of Bogomil's buttocks wreathed in algae.

"Would you mind running the garden hose over him?" Frietchie implored. "For God's sake tell him to leave the koi alone."

Grumbling, Ezekiel put on a bathrobe and staggered outside. By the time he got there, Bogomil had already discovered the hose. He was spraying himself lustily while rubbing the thatch between his legs.

"No eat fish," Ezekiel said in Bosnian.

"I pick teeth with fish bones, scrawny goat-boy," Bogomil responded.

"You hurt, Frietchie tack Bogomil skin to gate."

A shadow passed across the ex-prison guard's face. "I hear, degraded catamite of a gravedigger's donkey."

Ezekiel went inside, wishing he knew more Bosnian. Frietchie had laid out a sumptuous breakfast. She was on the phone, explaining to the hospital that Ezekiel and Bogomil had been quarantined with measles. "You can't do that! We'll need medical certificates," Ezekiel protested.

"You'll have them," she said tranquilly. Husband #4, with whom she was still on good terms, was a gynecologist. She reasoned that it didn't matter who signed the certificates, so long as it was a doctor.

She took a bucket of scrambled eggs, Vienna sausages and canned sauerkraut out to Bogomil. It was all mixed up together, but she thought he wouldn't mind and he didn't. It was so close to the food Bogomil's mother had cooked for him on feast days that tears came to his eyes. For a moment he was swept with a strange sensation. Was it typhus? Was it tape worms? He realized with a surge of alarm that it was *love*. Bogomil shook himself to get rid of the spooky emotion.

Last of all, Frietchie left a tray by Cubby's bed with a note and a rose in a bud vase. He was curled up like a caterpillar in a cocoon. The notebook had fallen to the floor and at least twenty of its pages were filled. "Sleep tight, darling," whispered Frietchie, planting a kiss on his soft gray hair. "I won't ask the bedbugs not to bite. You'd probably like them."

"Is it safe to leave him alone?" said Ezekiel as they drove out the gate.

"You don't know Cubby," Frietchie replied. They were

sitting in the front of the sports car and Bogomil, as before, was in the back. He didn't smell as good as he had the night before. Perhaps it was the sauerkraut. "If you give Cubby a problem, he's riveted. There's nothing he loves more than collecting data."

"You seem to know a lot for someone who only had a crush on him when she was fifteen."

"I love the smell of jealousy in the morning," said Frietchie, checking her global positioning system to find the garage where she had arranged to rent a van. "I kept tabs on Cubby because he was an ideal, a holy grail if you like. As long as Cubby was out there I could still believe in the innate goodness of mankind."

Ezekiel stifled a laugh. If the doctor was a holy grail, he was a seriously cracked one.

Frietchie had brought tools to break into the factory, but when they arrived the gate was wide open and a mob of workmen were hauling out the last of the giant machines. At once a foreman waved his arms and ordered them to leave. "*Es peligroso*, dangerous!" he shouted.

"We've come to get Dr. Willows' belongings from the apartment on the roof," explained Ezekiel.

"No can do! *Peligroso*! Go boom!"

"Go boom?" echoed Ezekiel.

"Let me handle this," said Frietchie. She climbed out of the van. Several workmen stopped what they were doing and watched. Frietchie explained in Spanish what she wanted and the foreman said very politely that he was sorry, but that the building was wired with explosives. As soon as the last equipment was removed it would be blown up.

"*Necesito obtener las cosas de mi amigo*," Frietchie said. "I must get my friend's belongings."

"*No es posible*," the foreman said regretfully. "It is not possible."

Frietchie then began to explain further how she needed Cubby's things, and her voice changed imperceptibly and the foreman began to look unsure and the workmen began to appear uneasy. They were all good Catholics, but buried in their DNA was a memory of an older, less forgiving, religion. They heard in Frietchie's words the ancient, clotted voice of Coatlicue, the Aztec Rattlesnake Goddess.

Coatlicue had a head formed of two opposing rattlesnake heads and wore a skirt of writing serpents. Around her neck were the hands, hearts and skulls of her children. She drew men to the darkness between her thighs as a jaguar hypnotizes a fawn with its remorseless eyes. Unbelievable pleasure lay there, but to reach it they must first pass beneath her skirt. The rattlesnakes hanging from her belt had fangs that folded up into their jaws like switch-blades.

What Frietchie said was *Favor de ayudarme.* Please help me.

What the work crew heard was *I am Coatlicue who devours the living and whose hands are claws to dig graves.*

"Okay-fine," murmured the foreman, his eyes distant and unfocussed. Soon everyone on the work site was climbing up and down the fire escape to retrieve Cubby's belongings. Bogomil loaded them into the van. Ezekiel relaxed in the cab with his eyes closed. He'd seen Frietchie in action before and knew that he needn't lift a finger.

Nineteen: *UNCLE SHUMBA'S SOLUTION*

THE MIRAGE MOUNTAINS are in a remote corner of California. By some error (perhaps a surveyor's coffee mug tipped over) they are depicted on maps as having only one side. The Corridor to the North thunders past them, but few drivers bother to look out of the window. This is a pity. The mountains are beautiful and wild. The Modocs hunted here and something of their fierce spirit still remains.

Once seen, the mountains are not forgotten. They return in dreams and occasionally people are impelled to climb them under a compulsion only dimly understood. It is then discovered that the mountains do have another side.

Beneath forested peaks lies a fertile belt of farmland and through the years a thriving community has grown up. Except for one item these people do not trade their goods with the outside world. Early in the nineteenth century a group of Dominican monks built a monastery and planted vineyards along the foothills. They made a wine that later became the justly famous Mirage brand.

Mirage Wine is not like any other alcoholic beverage in the world. It doesn't make you drunk. Rather it gives you, as the label states, "more abundant life". Remember how you felt as a child on the first day of summer vacation with the sun shining through the window and the smell of pancakes from the kitchen and your dog panting with excitement as he crouched at the foot of your bed. That's what Mirage Wine gives you.

On the far side of the farm belt lies a long, shallow lake

separating it from a very different territory. Here is desert, bitter green shrubs and tracts of alkaline soil extending all the way to the Farther Hills where no one goes. Hot springs boil up, sending plumes of steam into a faded sky, and coyotes howl in the middle of the day. Yet there are houses even here. At some time in the remote past a Seaworthy crossed over the Mirage Mountains and found this barren place to his liking.

It was impossible to grow crops in such ravaged soil, but the first Seaworthy discovered unusual properties in the water. A few drops added to the insipid wine then produced by the Dominicans, caused a momentous change. The wine suddenly came alive, which was amazing since the water itself was bitter. Perhaps it contained the same ingredient that vitalized Gerbill's beer halls. Mortality.

The Seaworthys traded their water to the Dominicans in exchange for caretaking duties. If no one was in residence, monks maintained the property. They fed the chickens and cats, and cleaned the rooms. But they refused to sleep in the main house. It was entirely too unwholesome for Christians and the sound of drums in the middle of the night gave them nightmares.

Uncle Shumba was drumming now, his eyes rolled back in his head. Black cats lay all over the furniture, purring for all they were worth, but the Seaworthy ancestors were growing restless. They floated in midair, watching Shumba and wishing they had better news for the Mhondoro.

"At least we know where Tom is," said Balthazar.

"Fat lot of good that does us," grumbled Caspar. Melchior said nothing and only stared disapprovingly at Shumba's careless behavior.

All three knew that the Mhondoro didn't take kindly to excuses. Nor did he, when he materialized a few minutes later. "*Mhoro, Sekuru,*" the ancestors greeted him.

"*Mhoro,* my children," responded the deep voice of the spirit of the tribe. "Have you found my child Tom Seaworthy?"

"Sort of," began Balthazar.

"Only we can't reach him," finished Melchior.

"THAT'S NOT GOOD ENOUGH!" thundered the Mhondoro, making the ground tremble and the cats scurry away in all directions. Shumba kept drumming, however, lost in a world of his own. "Has he been at the *ganja* again?" said Mhondoro.

"I'm afraid so," said Balthazar, relieved by the change of subject.

The Mhondoro kicked the drum across the room. Shumba looked up, bemused. *"Mhoro, Sekuru,"* he said.

"What am I going to do with you? You don't take anything seriously," complained the spirit of the tribe. "Never mind. You're awake now and we need to talk. Did anyone bring beer?"

Caspar produced a crate of Eight Ball Stout. Balthazar had helped himself to French fries and ketchup from the monk currently staying on the ranch. The spirits settled down with gusto.

"All right. Tell me about Tom," said the Mhondoro after he had mellowed out a little on beer.

"There's an island in the middle of a lake," Melchior said. "It appears to be a village set aside to honor the elders, but I can't see what's going on inside. Have you been able to discover anything, Caspar?"

"New residents arrive every day," said Caspar. "No one leaves. I've only been able to manage glimpses because the island is guarded by spirit poison."

"It's a kind of music that paralyzes your will," Balthazar explained. "It's as formless and pervasive as swamp gas and when we get close to it, we feel faint."

"I have encountered such things in elevators," remarked the Mhondoro.

"Dr. Gerbill got through briefly, but he was sick for a week afterwards," Melchior added.

"Every night the music stops for a few minutes," said Caspar. "Supplies are brought to the island and waste is taken away. We've been waking Tom up then, but we can't materialize fast enough to communicate with him."

The Mhondoro thoughtfully opened another bottle of Eight Ball. The liquid disappeared down his shadowy throat. "How long has he been there?"

"He and Violetta went there two months ago," said Balthazar. "As far as I can tell, they are being cared for like prize cattle."

Melchior passed around the bucket of French fries heavily slathered with ketchup. "We Africans love our cattle," said the Mhondoro, licking his fingers appreciatively. "They gladden our hearts and we know each one by name, but we know they are not people. When famine comes, we sometimes have to kill them to feed our children."

Everyone, including Uncle Shumba, looked sorrowful about that. All the Seaworthys liked cattle and the ones living in cities regularly visited county fairs to admire livestock.

"There is," Balthazar began tentatively, "a kind of famine in this land. The young no longer work as their ancestors did and so the fields have become barren. They do not care for their elders anymore. They drive them away like stray dogs. Children remain children forever, stretching out their hands for food. If the elders grow too weak to feed them, who knows what will happen then?"

The Mhondoro's aura deepened to red and the ground shuddered. The ancestors, except for Shumba, fled to the ceiling where they bobbed up and down among the fetishes. "Are you suggesting that the young will feed upon the old?" cried the Mhondoro. "What kind of people are they? This island must be destroyed and our child Tombudzo rescued. It must be torn open like an evil hornet's nest and thrown into the fire."

The other spirits were silent. They didn't care to point out that, as spirits, they had no power to tear open anything. They had to work through the living.

"Well?" demanded the Mhondoro. "What have you layabouts to say for yourselves?" The ground shivered with another earthquake. The resident monk, who was sleeping in a shed, fell out of bed and began to pray fervently.

Shumba by now had retrieved the drum and ran his fingers lightly over the skin. It sounded like raindrops falling on parched earth. "We need help, *Sekuru*" he said, playing the riff again.

"Shumba, stop messing around," scolded Balthazar, but the Mhondoro held up his hand.

"Help from where?" he asked.

Shumba ran his fingers back and forth, creating the sound of a storm approaching in the distance. "We need the Rain Queens, *Sekuru*. We need the ladies in on this. They got the power. They got the lightning in their pretty little hands."

*   *   *

All of Tom and Violetta's children had gathered in their old home, alarmed by the absence of their parents. "Why didn't they leave us a note?" said Cezare, the oldest. "Why don't they call?"

"Maybe they can't." Thaís, the youngest, started to cry again. Jeronimo handed her a box of Kleenex.

"We've checked all the hospitals and combed the neighborhood—God, what an awful neighborhood!" said Atalanta, who had gone knocking on nearby doors armed to the teeth. "Why did we let them stay here so long?"

"Dad didn't want to move," Jeronimo reminded her.

"And Mom didn't want to go to the ranch. I wonder if that's where they are?" said Thaís.

"I called the Mirage Monastery. The line was bad, but they managed to understand me." Cezare poured fresh coffee for everyone. They'd been low on sleep for days. "The abbot said that the ranch was deserted except for a resident monk. He said they'd had a few small earthquakes recently."

"Can't you get any action out of the cops?" Thaís said tearfully.

Atalanta snorted. "They don't do anything for people over sixty-five. They made a half-hearted effort with Mom, but beyond a general computer check, nothing. It's the new Senior Laws."

They were sitting in the living room that had been so carefully maintained by Tom and Violetta through the years. A mobile made by Atalanta in grade school still hung from the ceiling. Jeronimo's first effort at building a spice rack sat drunkenly on a shelf. Everywhere were traces of the children's past and it made them sad to see the care with which their vanished parents had preserved them. The house itself, though, was falling apart.

No matter how often Tom repaired the roof, new leaks opened up. The Pineapple Express, in its passage, had left discolored blotches all over the ceiling. It had warped the floor boards and grown mold on Violetta's rag rugs. Nothing could disguise the fact that the place was on its last legs.

"One hopeful sign," said Cezare, warming his hands on his coffee mug, "is that the house hasn't been vandalized. And

Mom and Dad packed suitcases before they left."

One Seaworthy child was missing from this gathering. Phaedra was unusually sensitive to weather and right now she was suffering the mother of all migraines in the back bedroom.

Unlike many migraine sufferers, she didn't fall ill at the approach of storms. Quite the opposite. Fine weather found her peaky and nervous, and with the departure of the Pineapple Express, poor Phaedra had been laid low. Ripples of light danced across her vision. Her stomach roiled as though she were standing on the deck of a fishing boat with diesel fumes blowing in her face. Her head pounded like a drum. As the attack intensified, she began to hallucinate.

There really *was* a drum and the rippling lights resolved into a huge bonfire. She could see Uncle Shumba sitting on a log in a forest clearing, banging away for all he was worth. Phaedra had never seen him in real life, but his skinny body, dreadlocks and manic expression were unmistakable.

"Hi, Baby Girl," said Uncle Shumba, whaling away at the drum. It was a hollowed-out tree trunk covered in skin. "Wanna dance?"

The last thing Phaedra wanted was to get out of bed, but the rhythm caught her and her feet began to move. Surprisingly, this made her feel better. She was good at dancing. She undulated her body and waved her arms. She tossed her head, making the beads on her braids glitter in the firelight.

Now others came out of the forest and joined her. They were handsome women in brightly colored dresses with scarves to match. Their necks were festooned with beads and their skin shone with oil. They grinned at Phaedra and she smiled back, happy to have found so many aunties and grandmas. She knew instinctively that these were members of her family.

"You can do it, Baby Girl," crooned Shumba. "You can pull the clouds out of the sea and send them wherever you want."

Where should I send them? Phaedra thought dimly. Her body, running with sweat, was almost as shiny as those of her relatives. One of the women took her hand and danced away with her through the air. They flew over the forest until they came to a great river coiling through deltas until it emptied into a lake. At the center of the lake was an island.

Here, said the woman, still holding Phaedra's hand. The girl reached out over the sea and pulled. Clouds boiled up, fat with rain. They flickered inside as their power built. Phaedra had never felt so happy in her life as when the first lightning bolt fell, making the dome over the island glow.

*   *   *

When twins had been born to the line of Mutapa, lord of the land between the morning and the evening sky, one child was sent away into exile. He was Tombudzo, founder of the Seaworthys, and a great spirit medium. The other, Modjaji, fled into the mountains to become the mother of the Rain Queens. But the ability to call rain did not entirely vanish from Tombudzo's line. Now and then a Seaworthy girl was born with extra-sensitive nerves. She would require much silence and solitude. She would suffer from headaches during balmy weather, but feel strong during hurricanes.

These girls never possessed the ability of a true queen of Africa, but with help they could manage thunderstorms. Modjaji's descendants in the spirit world had banded together. Being spirit, they could do nothing physical, but they could work through someone with talent.

*   *   *

Phaedra sent bolt after bolt onto the island until the glowing dome collapsed. Rain poured into the opening. She sighed with happiness and returned to bed. She slept for hours and awoke, bright and cheery, to greet her exhausted brothers and sisters.

Twenty: *MR. YEE*

WHEN CUBBY AWOKE, he immediately noticed the rose Frietchie had left. It had two dainty holes in one of the leaves where a sawfly larva had feasted. The note said, *Make yourself at home. We'll return as soon as we've got your stuff. XXX Frietchie.*

Cubby puzzled over the meaning of XXX, but then his attention was drawn to the blueberry muffins, Swiss cheese, orange juice, and thermos of coffee on the breakfast tray. He hadn't eaten well for some time. He devoured every morsel, including the butter pats, and lay back contentedly on the soft bed. The air in the room was fresh, unlike the diesel-soaked vapors of Sasquatch Avenue.

The bed smelled fresh, too, not that Cubby resented the dusty residue of generations of Willows in his own bed. The residue made him feel safe, like a den in which successive packs of wolves have laired. But he had to admit it felt wonderful to lie in clean sheets. He looked around, hoping to see Gerbill, but his old friend had apparently gone off on a trip.

Thoughts of being clean reminded Cubby of having a bath. His hygiene had left much to be desired since the gas had been turned off. He inspected the bathroom. What delights! He found a spotless white shower stall, fluffy towels and soap without the little black specks that Cubby's soap seemed to collect. Hot water, too!

Cubby floated out of the bathroom in a cloud of steam, but then he couldn't find anything to wear. His old clothes were at the hospital and all he had brought with him was the embarrassing hospital gown. The closets were locked and so he had to put on the yellow pajamas again. He found a purple bathrobe and fuzzy pink bedroom slippers in Frietchie's bedroom.

Cubby collected his notebook and went out into the garden. Water striders skated across the koi pond, bees worked industriously on flowering thyme, butterflies wafted about depositing caterpillar eggs. Cubby busily made notes. The koi followed him hopefully, their noses poking above the water.

He found a lawn chair under a wisteria and settled down. He thought of all that had happened since he'd retired—parties, visits from old friends, the appearance of new friends. For a man who'd had no social life at all, it was bewildering. Cubby thought about the gas chromatograph and scintillation counter and found, to his surprise, that he no longer missed them. Frietchie and Ezekiel had taken their place.

The wonder of this made him put his pen down. Gerbill was right. Humans could not live without other humans, and now that Cubby had discovered them, he felt a great longing to meet more. Where was Tom Seaworthy, for example? Why hadn't Cubby paid attention to the man when he had the chance? He realized it was because he'd thought of Tom as just another piece of equipment.

The janitor had performed his chores so flawlessly that he required no more attention than a well-oiled engine. Cubby felt something so unusual it took him a moment to realize what it was. *Shame.* He remembered that when he slept on the floor of the lab, he sometimes woke to find a box of orange juice by his head. Tom had done it and yet Cubby had never thanked him.

He must be in the phone book, thought Cubby. He searched through the house, opening drawers and looking into cupboards, but couldn't find a directory anywhere or, for that matter, a phone. There wasn't a computer either, although he was almost certain he'd seen one the night before.

(And this was because Frietchie had removed everything she thought could get Cubby into trouble. She had learned the technique with husband #1, who was a wealthy alcoholic. Whenever he was out of the house she used an alcohol-sniffing dog to locate his bottles and systematically destroy them. But even a pack of hounds couldn't discover all of husband #1's hiding places, and he was found floating in the koi pond one morning. Since he had beaten Frietchie up and she was his only heir, the death wasn't as traumatic as you might think.

Frietchie always maintained that the first marriage was like the first pancake you made for breakfast. First pancakes were always misshapen and the best thing to do was throw them away. The second, third, fourth, fifth, sixth, seventh and eighth ones generally came out better.)

Cubby, frustrated, returned to his seat under the wisteria vine. He noted the birds caroling in the trees. He observed a jumping spider lying in wait on a grass stem. Frogs called from the koi pond, *krek ek . . . krek ek.*

Frogs. Cubby paused with the pen hovering over the page. He identified them as Pacific Treefrogs (*Hyla regilla*) that weren't, in fact, found in trees. He wrote the information down. They made a cheerful noise, not at all like the melancholy croak of the bullfrogs in the Chupacabras River.

Cubby's pen hovered again. A memory of long, winding hospital halls came back, along with the throngs of dead relatives hanging over beds. He found suddenly that his eyes were blurred with tears. He had never encountered such anguish before and the existence of it shook him to his very core.

Cubby had been shielded from such knowledge by his loving relatives. He had never been taken to a sickbed or to a funeral. His family members had simply disappeared one by one. Later, when Gerbill died, it had happened when Cubby was receiving the Golden Aphid Award in Belarus.

Grief was what he was experiencing now, not for himself, but for the Alzheimer's patients who didn't understand that their relatives only wanted to comfort them. He knew he could help them. He could tell them how pleasant it was having dead people around. But without a phone Cubby couldn't do anything. He got up at once to go in search of Frietchie's neighbors who must surely have a way to contact the outside world. It was then he discovered that the front gate was locked with no way to open it from the inside.

The wall was at least ten feet high. Even with a ladder —and Cubby wasn't strong enough to wrestle one into position—he couldn't get down the other side. He studied the gate lock. It had ten buttons and the number of combinations for that many digits, as Cubby well knew, was astronomical. It would take him years to stumble upon the correct one. And yet there might be a solution. His methodical mind clicked through the possibilities. He tapped one of the buttons and it gave a musical beep. Ah.

Frietchie thought she had covered all the ways Cubby could get into mischief. She didn't know about his keen sense of hearing. This was a man who could distinguish between the hum of an Asian tiger mosquito (A above middle C) and a salt marsh mosquito (G above middle C). He never confused the love call of a Caribbean fruit fly with that of a Mediterranean fruit fly. His score on identifying katydid chirps was perfect.

When Ezekiel had keyed in the code for the gate lock, Cubby had appeared to be wool-gathering. He was, in fact, listening to a breeze, a whirring moth and a pair of belligerent crickets. He was also registering the little beeps Ezekiel was producing. Now he poked around until he recreated that sound sequence. The lock clicked. The gate slid open. Cubby was free.

*   *   *

Mr. Yee walked slowly down the sidewalk, relishing the movement that oiled his joints. His daughters, Ning and Fan, followed behind, ready to fend off roving bands of children. They had pepper spray in their purses and cell phones speed-dialed to 911. This was a generally safe neighborhood, but you could never tell.

They followed the same routine winter and summer. In cold weather Yee barely moved at all, but he persisted. Moving was good. Once you stopped you were dead. He could have exercised in the spacious garden of Ten Thousand Happiness, his mansion, but danger sharpened his wits. He also enjoyed savoring the power he had over his children.

Ning and Fan were almost paralyzed with boredom, but they knew better than to complain. If they did, their father would shower them with the insults they had endured since childhood. It was strange how these insults still hurt. Ning and Fan were middle-aged, successful businesswomen. They'd grown up in California, not some backwater Chinese village in the seventeenth century. But their father's voice stripped away their self-esteem as neatly as an ape peeling a banana. Their husbands were afraid of Yee's tongue, too. Everyone was.

Sometimes Ning and Fan entertained themselves with unworthy fantasies of turning their backs if a gang of thugs attacked. It would not take much force to finish off their ninety-year-old father. But then they remembered the consequences if he should, God forbid, survive. Yee still held grudges for wrongs done to him half a century earlier.

Yee paused to contemplate a mushroom forcing its way through a layer of asphalt. "The most submissive thing in the world can ride roughshod over the hardest thing in the world," he quoted approvingly. "Observe, daughters, and be enlightened."

Ning and Fan dutifully observed the mushroom. Ning's feet hurt. She should have worn sneakers, but she had to go straight to the office as soon as they had delivered *Ba Ba* back to the house.

Yee crept on. As a young man he'd been busy buying and selling, laying traps for competitors, and channeling money as skillfully as a farmer irrigating his fields. At the end of the fields, thought Yee, enlarging on the figure of speech, was a Great Wall damming up all that lovely money into Yee Enterprises. Now that he was old, he could afford to appreciate the natural world he had exploited so ruthlessly. His money was secure in spite of the melon-headed sons and daughters God had seen fit to curse him with.

Stirred by the spring sunlight and by the red-winged blackbirds rioting in a tree nearby, the old man silently quoted Li Po:

> *My friend is dwelling in the eastern mountain,*
> *Delighting in the beauty of valleys and hills.*
> *In the green spring he lies in deserted forests,*
> *And he is fast asleep when the sun rises.*

What wonderful refinement! No one today could come up with sentiments like that. Imagine having such a friend, thought Yee. You could drink tea in the moonlight together. You could talk all night about music, poetry and beautiful women.

The women Yee had known were more like machines

designed to eat money and shit lawsuits. Still, he appreciated the female form, especially during the fifth month of pregnancy. It was after the morning sickness and before they started lying around like sick cows. If Yee ruled the universe he would have made all women five months pregnant all the time.

Alas, Yee had no friend to drink tea with in the moonlight. He'd alienated everyone he hadn't ruined or driven to an early grave. He arrived at a tiny park and slowly moved across the grass. When he reached his favorite spot under a jacaranda tree, he curtly signaled for his daughters to withdraw.

"We'll wait, *Ba Ba*" said Ning. "It isn't safe for you to be alone."

"Go where I do not have to contemplate your ugly faces," said Yee, taking the first stance of his *tai chi* exercises. "I don't wish my meditation to be polluted by your brainless conversation." Ning and Fan gratefully trotted away and Fan took a flask of gin from her purse.

The old man went through the exercises feeling, as always, his spirit align itself with the trees and the wind. Suddenly, he heard a shout and opened his eyes to see a troop of small boys on bikes barreling toward him. "Old fart alert!" one of them screamed. Then they were on him, going round and round, bewildering him with their dizzy speed and delivering air punches at him.

"You stop!" bellowed Yee in the voice that made his children and ex-wives tremble, but the boys only laughed.

"Fart face! Poo-poo head! Crap eater!" they yelled, going round and round. Yee's heart fluttered and he tried to call for help. But at the last minute when he thought he would die there in the midst of these ten-year-olds, they suddenly broke off the attack and zoomed away. All but one. That one was being held by the strangest-looking person Yee had ever seen.

He was a tall, skinny man in a purple bathrobe and fuzzy pink slippers. He didn't look strong, but he had the boy in an odd grip that stirred a memory in Yee's mind. *He was using Praying Mantis Kung Fu.*

In the thirteenth century the abbot of Shaolin Monastery had invited eighteen martial arts masters to improve the fighting ability of the Shaolin monks. One of these masters had perfected the movements of the predatory insect. The school of fighting existed to this very day and Yee had observed matches where it had been used with deadly and satisfying results.

In fact, Cubby—for it was he in the fuzzy pink bedroom slippers—knew nothing about martial arts. He knew a great deal about praying mantises, however. He'd often observed them swaying back and forth, the better to see their prey. They moved slowly, not unlike a man practicing *tai chi*. When they were within range, they struck rapidly with both arms gripping their prey, immobilizing it. At that point they delivered a bite to the neck and proceeded to devour their victim alive.

Cubby had no intention of following through with this interesting behavior, and he certainly wasn't strong enough to hold an active ten-year-old. But the sheer *weirdness* of the Praying Mantis Grip had completely demoralized the boy. He blubbered and begged for mercy.

"You hold him," panted Yee, picking up a large stick. "I'll beat the crap out of him."

Cubby suddenly woke up. He'd been mildly surprised by the success of his maneuver "You can't beat a child," he said.

"Wanna bet?" snarled Yee.

Cubby opened his arms and the boy tumbled to the ground and scurried away—but not before Yee had delivered a heavy blow. "*Ba Ba*! Father! Are you hurt?" shouted Ning and Fan, spraying the air uselessly with pepper spray.

"Turtledung daughters," muttered Yee, dusting himself off. "Never there when you need them."

Ning and Fan halted, and Fan covered her mouth. "That man's got women's clothes on," she giggled.

"Please control your loose mouth," growled Yee and Fan sobered up. But she was correct, the old man thought. There was something definitely whorish about his rescuer's clothes. Still, he owed the man gratitude. "Thank you for capturing that rotten duck-egg brat," he said to Cubby, bowing slightly, "although I admit to disappointment for not breaking a tree branch over his head. I am Yee Ssu."

"Hello," said Cubby. "Do you have a telephone?"

Yee was startled. "Everyone has a telephone."

"Not me. I need to call Chupacabras Hospital."

"That's a loony bin," whispered Ning.

It would explain the clothes, thought Yee, but the man didn't look insane. Yee was an extremely good judge of character and this person seemed more unworldly than crazy. "Is the hospital where you live?" he said cautiously.

"Oh, no!" Cubby laughed. "I want to tell the orderlies how to calm the patients. They were so upset last night with all their relatives visiting. I can't find Frietchie's phone and she's not home. Oh, look! *Coprinus comatus.*" He bent down to observe a patch of the same fungus Yee had seen pushing its way through the asphalt.

"Did you say Frietchie?" said Yee.

"These are more commonly known as the Shaggy Mane Mushroom. They're very good eating if you get them young," explained Cubby, brushing leaves and dirt away from the fungi. "You have to be careful to get them on clean soil because they can soak up diesel. Gerbill used to fry them for breakfast when we were on field trips." Cubby picked one and held it up for Yee to inspect.

The old man sniffed it. "*Mao-tuo quisan,*" he murmured "My mother used to cook them." The hovel Yee had grown up in floated into his mind, along with the image of his mother slaving over a brazier of hot coals. He hadn't thought of her for a very long time. He hadn't wanted to. He'd deserted her to come to America, and she was lying somewhere under a demolished building, courtesy of an earthquake. He hadn't even offered sacrifices at her grave site.

"*Mao-tuo quisan.* I must write that down," said Cubby. "*Mao-tuo quisan.* If I forget you'll have to remind me. My notebook is at Frietchie's."

Yee shook himself. It was like having a boil probed after the ache had subsided into the background. His mother had foraged for mushrooms, his favorite dish. He was her only child and she had lavished all her scanty resources on him. "You're staying with Frietchie?" Yee repeated, thinking that the man didn't look like the usual shred of human debris that Frietchie dragged home.

"She's my friend. By the way, I'm Dr. Cubby Willows." He extended his hand. Yee took it, bracing himself for the inevitable pain, but Cubby applied no more pressure to Yee's arthritic bones than a moth.

"Please accompany me to my house, Dr. Willows. You are most welcome to use my phone, but I'm surprised Frietchie doesn't possess one."

"She probably does. I just couldn't find it. Shall I gather these—*mao-tuo quisans?*—for your breakfast? I'm very well up on fungi and these are perfectly safe." Yee nodded, bemused. Cubby filled the pockets of the purple bathrobe with them.

They began the long, slow trip back to Ten Thousand Happiness. Yee had named it after the energy drink that had earned the bulk of his fortune. Ten Thousand Happiness Elixir, according to the label, was brewed from ginseng gathered in a remote Tibetan valley and mixed with water that had been struck by lightning. It could revive the manhood of an Egyptian mummy.

A tiny pinch of the ginseng had once come from Tibet, but the rest of it was grown in Petaluma. And water was always getting struck by lightning. Just look at it lying around during thunderstorms.

Yee expected Cubby to get impatient on the slow journey, but Cubby warbled on about things they passed as joyfully as the red-winged blackbirds in the trees. Everything was of interest to this strange being—the temperature, the quality of light, the caterpillars dropping down on tiny silk threads. (*Sabulodes aegrotata*, Cubby explained, the common inchworm.) He informed Yee that Shaggy Mane Mushrooms had been used to make ink during medieval times. "The caps turn into a black liquid if you keep them," he said.

And gradually an unaccustomed feeling came over Yee. It took him a while to realize that it was *contentment*. For years he had struggled for money and status. He had the biggest house in the neighborhood. His children were the best educated, his ex-wives the best dressed. He had a bank balance that made his business rivals gnash their teeth. But it was never enough. There was always the possibility that someone would outdo him and then *he* would be the one gnashing his teeth.

Cubby didn't concern himself with such things. He was clearly a cultivated man (despite his strange attire). See how he discoursed on the weeds that bordered the walk. To him there was no such thing as a weed. Everything was equally interesting and acceptable. He was content to observe the myriad beings with no thought of turning them into money-making elixirs.

What a simple, yet profound, attitude!

For the first time in his life Yee had met someone with whom he couldn't compete. Then he understood that *this* was the friend Li Po had written about in his poem. This was the man who delighted in the beauty of valleys and hills, and who lay in deserted forests in the green spring. Cubby was as unworldly as a buddha.

"Do you like tea?" Yee said, shyly.

"Yes," replied Cubby, turning his luminous gaze on him. The two men entered the ornate gate of Ten Thousand Happiness. Ning and Fan raised their eyebrows at each other from behind.

Twenty-One: *THE COFFIN SHIP*

TOM HAD BEGUN taking longer and longer afternoon naps. There was nothing specifically wrong with his existence, but he felt a dead sameness creeping over the days. How many shuffleboard matches could a man endure? How many bingo nights and barbeques? It wasn't that they weren't fun. They were, in the same way a slice of pecan pie covered in whipped cream was fun. You tasted the sweetness. You felt the butterfat kissing your taste buds on its way to your arteries.

Then it was over. You had accomplished exactly nothing. *I'm being an old coot*, thought Tom. *What in hell does any pleasure accomplish? The longer you can stay happy, the longer you can keep the spiritual colonoscopies at bay.* But he was having a spiritual colonoscopy right now and he didn't like what it was telling him.

His soul was lumpy with tumors. They might be benign. They might not be. It was going to hurt like hell to find out.

The only time Tom was happy was when he was dreaming. As soon as he fell asleep he found himself polishing the floors of Burton, Barton, Gerbill and Slithe. He felt a deep satisfaction at smoothing out the surface. If it was done well, you could see the drinking fountains and candy machines reflected. The soft swoosh of the polisher filled the air with music, and when Tom was done he went to Dr. Willows' lab to carefully clean between the insect cages.

Tom sat up abruptly. He remembered something Eric Hoffer had written when he, too, had retired: *In my dreams I still load ships.* Work. That was the solution. Work was the measure of mankind and without it people's souls got lumpy. A job well done was the most satisfying thing you could do, and it didn't matter whether you discovered a cure for cancer or cleaned up after the people who did.

The door flew open and Violetta ran in, followed by Noni and Ngwenya, and flung herself onto the bed. "Oh, Tom! She's gone! I went to see Sharhonda and when I knocked a complete stranger came to the door. She didn't know who Sharhonda was. And *they*—" Violetta pointed at Noni and Ngwenya "—won't tell me what happened to her."

"Please, *Ambuya*, let me help you," said Noni, kneeling.

"Leave me alone!" shouted Violetta. Tom had rarely seen his wife in such a rage. She was a forgiving woman, but she was intensely loyal and would fly at anyone who threatened her loved ones. "Sharhonda was the best friend I've had in years. She wouldn't have left without telling me, and she wouldn't have gone without a good reason. I think she's sick. She's in the hospital and I want to see her."

Violetta was shivering and Tom put his arms around her. He was seriously worried that she might wind up in the hospital herself if she didn't calm down.

"Sometimes people leave," Noni said soothingly. "They decide to visit their children or they just want to travel. It isn't unusual."

"Is that what happened?" demanded Violetta.

"We aren't allowed to give out confidential information," said Ngwenya. "It's part of the contract. Believe me, *Ambuya*, you wouldn't want us blabbing about how many mai tais you put away."

"I don't drink mai tais!" screamed Violetta. "And stop calling me *Ambuya*!"

"It's all right, honey. We'll get to the bottom of this." Tom hugged her and looked up at Noni and Ngwenya. "Maybe you'd better go."

"I'll send over a health care provider," said Noni.

"Just go," said Tom. When they had left, he took a wash cloth and bathed Violetta's face. She was still shaking and that didn't seem right at all. He'd never seen her lose control so completely. Come to think of it, he didn't feel good either. He was so blindingly furious at the whole Joy Meadows situation that his heart fluttered and his body was soaked in sweat. He felt like he'd gone five rounds with Mike Tyson. And then he understood.

The music, that constant infernal music, was trying to dull his mind. He could feel it taking apart his will power, the same way it made him too tired to resist Ngwenya's plans. The very act of fighting against it made him tremble.

The health care provider arrived, a Nurse Dee Dee clone, and was relentlessly cheerful and insulting at the same time. "Come on, Granny," she warbled. "Let me take your temperature and pulse. I think you need some quality time with Mr. Sandman before you get back on the dance floor."

Why did everybody talk to old people as though they were retarded? thought Tom. But he was relieved when Violetta took the sleeping pill and lay down.

"You, too, Grampa," said Dee Dee #2.

Tom hesitated and then accepted the medicine offered to him. Dee Dee #2 watched him drink the cup of water she handed him.

When she left, Tom spat out the pill. Some of it had dissolved. Hopefully he hadn't swallowed too much. He knew now that they would have to leave, but he guessed that Noni and Ngwenya wouldn't make it easy. He rubbed his forehead, trying to concentrate. Could they swim far enough to reach shore? Violetta could float and he could tow her.

Tom's eyesight began to blur. Damn! He went to the dresser and pulled out the drawers. *I'm not sober enough to pack*, he realized. They'd have to abandon everything—and what was this? The bottom drawer was full of shiny little Viagra boxes. One for each day. At least sixty.

Tom staggered back to bed and squeezed in next to Violetta. The room was pleasantly dark. The ceiling was covered in imitation palm fronds and Tom had the impression he was lying in a jungle hut. The walls were a mellow yellow.

My ancestors lived in a place like this, Tom thought. *They didn't have freeways or the IRS or the Youth Patrol trying to kick in the front door. All they had to worry about was lions. But they knew what the lions looked like and where they lived.* A distant headache told him that his blood pressure was high.

He took Violetta's hand. "Are you awake?"

"Mm," said Violetta.

"Was Kenyatta missing, too?" Kenyatta was Sharhonda's husband.

"I think so."

"Well, that's a good thing," Tom said. "If they're both gone, it means they probably did go on a trip."

"Mm," said Violetta. Tom could hear her breathing slow to the rhythm of sleep, and soon he was drifting off as well.

*　　*　　*

People were arguing and at first Tom couldn't understand what they were talking about. "I say we give them another month," said an unfamiliar male voice. "The children haven't had time to forget them."

"*Aiwa!* The Seaworthys have noticed the departure of their neighbors and will not be easy to contain. The old man is as cranky as a mamba with an infected tooth."

I love you, too, Ngwenya, thought Tom. He didn't open his eyes.

"The old woman is in fine health," said Noni.

"I hope so. Sharhonda wasn't worth shit," said a fourth voice that took Tom a moment to recognize: Dee Dee #2.

Thunder rolled. It was the first time Tom had heard anything from the outside world and it seemed to take his visitors by surprise, too.

"What in hell is that?" said the unfamiliar male voice. "The energy field isn't supposed to come down for another hour." Tom opened his eyes a slit to see a man in a white coat. A doctor.

"The sky was perfectly clear when I went outside," said Noni. "We brought in a new couple today who haven't yet chosen which module they'd like. I'd say they'd fit in here."

"Why do we wait?" Ngwenya argued. "We have the contract signing over the Seaworthy property."

Wait a minute, thought Tom. *When did that happen?*

"Their vital signs are excellent," pointed out Dee Dee #2. "There's a recipient for the female's heart in Oakland. That's worth a quarter of a million dollars right there."

My God, these people are going to kill us, thought Tom. His mind raced and he tried to remember some of the street fighting techniques he'd learned in the Navy.

More thunder, louder this time.

"Very well," said the Doctor. "I'll sign the deportation order and send a crew to load them onto the coffin ship." Tom heard footsteps and the door opening and closing. He opened his eyes to see Ngwenya alone, sitting next to the window.

Tom sprang up and was immediately swept with dizziness, but he kept going. He leapt on the African and jammed his fingers at the man's throat for a killing blow. Ngwenya easily deflected him. "So you're awake, old mamba. I should have expected it." He twisted Tom's arm and forced him toward the beds. Tom brought his heel back to connect with Ngwenya's balls.

The African screamed and let go, but he recovered too quickly for Tom to get the upper hand. "I am much too clever for you," snarled Ngwenya. "I could snap your neck like *this*—" he twisted Tom's head until a sheet of white light flashed across his eyes.

But it wasn't pain. It was lightning. The air outside the window turned incandescent and in that brief instant Tom saw Violetta rise up and throw Ngwenya against a wall. Another lightning bolt snaked through the ceiling and incinerated him.

The thunderclap following made the house shake and both Tom and Violetta cowered with their hands over their ears. A dreadful smell of burning meat filled the air.

For a moment they were paralyzed. The room alternated between black and white as the storm raged. Tom's ears were ringing, but he recovered enough to hear rain sloshing against the walls. "Violetta," he said, reaching out to touch his wife crouching on the floor.

"Oh, Tom, I feel so sick," she moaned.

"Don't look at him. Ngwenya got what he deserved."

"That isn't the problem. The pill made me sick. I had to throw up in the wastebasket."

"You did?" said Tom with dawning hope. "When?"

"Soon after we went to bed."

So she didn't have much of the medicine in her system.

She must have been awake during the earlier conversation and certainly alert enough to attack Ngwenya. Good old reliable Violetta! "Can you walk?"

"I think so. Where can we go?"

"Anywhere but here." Tom grabbed his jacket with the truck keys and a sweater for his wife. There was too much to carry, but he dumped the contents of a dresser drawer into a plastic bag. A two month's supply of Viagra. Maybe he could use it to bargain their way out.

The scene outside was utterly wild and chaotic. Branches had been ripped off the trees. The power was out and the only light, apart from lightning, came from a dozen fires struggling with the rain. Old people had left their houses and were wandering around, dazed by the storm.

"Is it breakfast time yet?" one of them said fretfully.

"Come with us," said Tom, taking the man by the arm and trying to get the attention of his woman friend. But the couple wandered off.

"At least that damn music is gone," said Tom, going back to fetch Violetta. For the first time in weeks his mind felt clear. He took his wife's hand and they began walking through the rain. He had no idea where to go. The geography of Joy Meadows had never been clear to him, but he guessed that if they kept moving they would eventually come to the lake.

They were soon soaked to the skin. They walked past Mexican haciendas and Japanese teahouses. The storm was doing dreadful things to the rice paper walls. Violetta staggered. "Sorry, Shug. I'm still dizzy."

Tom despaired of finding a way out before his wife collapsed, but then he saw a golf cart beneath a tree. Its parking lights were on and its single occupant glowed gently. Tom saw a tangle of dreadlocks and a toothy grin.

"Uncle Shumba?" he whispered.

"My man!" Shumba said heartily.

"I'm hallucinating," Tom said.

"I do it all the time," his uncle confided. "Now you can't let this nice lady walk when she's feeling poorly. I scored you a golf cart from that shed."

Tom saw a building burning fitfully. Inside were the

skeletons of many golf carts. So that was where they went after dark. "Are you really here?"

"Depends on where 'here' is. You drive this sucker and I'll navigate."

"Of course I'm here," said Violetta. "I'm standing right beside you." She couldn't see or hear the spirit, of course, because she wasn't a Seaworthy. She climbed gratefully into the back seat of the golf cart

"Turn left at the next street," said Uncle Shumba.

Tom obeyed. He passed more wandering seniors and he wondered where their keepers were. Perhaps they spent the night on the mainland. He wanted, and at the same time was afraid, to reach over and touch Uncle Shumba. What would he feel?

"I've gone crazy, haven't I?" he said.

"Craaaazy!" agreed Shumba, not calming his fears a bit.

"You're just tired," said Violetta.

They came to a part of Joy Meadows Tom hadn't seen before. A warehouse loomed up next to the road and a ramp went down to the deck of a small ferry boat. Two lights, placed on either side of the bow, reminded him unpleasantly of eyes.

"The coffin ship," said Shumba.

By now the rain had lessened and a break in the clouds to the west revealed a full moon riding toward dawn. Pale light outlined the black coffin ship and Tom saw a fume of white vapor rising from its deck. "What's that?" he wondered.

"Dry ice," said Shumba. "They use it to keep the bodies nice and fresh."

"It looks like mist," said Violetta, who of course couldn't hear the spirit.

"Where's the crew?" Tom asked, alert to a new danger.

"They won't be a problem." His uncle smiled. "They're in the warehouse with the doctors and nurses. They just delivered a cargo of dry ice. When the lights went off and the fans stopped blowing, why that building just filled up with bad air. Wasn't nobody able to find the exit."

"Carbon dioxide," murmured Tom. He'd read warnings about dry ice at the lab. Heavier than air, carbon dioxide could build up in enclosed spaces. You couldn't smell it, you couldn't detect it until a fatal sleepiness crept over you. "Are they dead?"

Shumba's toothy smile assured him that they were.

"Who's dead?" cried Violetta. "What are you talking about?"

"I was just wondering where the guards were. Don't worry about it," Tom said. "I can probably operate that boat."

"Just keep the windows open and the breeze in your face," advised Shumba. "*Chienda zvako*, my man. That's *good-bye* in the old language, and by the way *ngwenya* is the old word for *crocodile*. You would've known that if you'd been paying attention." He faded from view in the moonlight until the last thing Tom saw of him was a crazy grin.

"Come on, 'Letta," said Tom. He helped her step aboard and kicked the remaining blocks of dry ice over the side. Then he cast off and started the engine without a single hitch. "I've still got it," he said, flexing his hands. She clung to the rail as they eased out onto the lake. By now the cloud cover had withdrawn completely and stars swarmed overhead in a black sky. The moon was low in the west.

The interior of the guard post was lit. Tom could see three dark shapes watching his approach.

Long ago, during the first heady months after meeting Eric Hoffer, Tom had read everything he could lay his hands on. One of the books was a collection of Greek myths. In it he learned about a three-headed dog that guarded the entrance to Hades, to keep anyone from escaping. But a few heroes did manage to escape. The solution was to feed the dog something so tasty that he would forget all about his duties. Tom had a good idea of what that thing might be.

He docked the coffin ship. "Hey!" growled one of the guards. "What are you doing here? Where's the crew?"

"Free Viagra!" yelled Tom, tossing the slippery boxes around. "Get yours before the other man does!"

"Shit! It *is* the old folks' Viagra!" The guards scrabbled on the ground, shoving each other and grabbing as many as possible. Tom hurried Violetta past and found his old truck. It was often sluggish until it was warmed up, but amazingly, like the coffin ship, it roared into life. With a silent thanks to the old gods, Tom gunned it out the far door and up the hill away from Joy

Meadows.

The eastern sky was brightening by the time they reached the cottonwoods where they had stopped on that first day. Tom pulled over to rest his thumping heart and gear his nerves up for facing the freeway. He rolled down the window to smell the sweet, predawn air.

Violetta burst into tears. "What are we going to do? They've got the contract for our house and who knows what else? They'll track us down. They'll make us go back."

Tom realized that she'd been holding her panic in check, but now had reached the breaking point. "Don't you worry about a thing, honey," he said, hugging her. "We've still got the ranch. There isn't anyone in the world who can take that away from us. It belongs to the old gods of Africa. Ain't nobody gonna get the better of them," he said, echoing Uncle Shumba.

"I wish it were true," she sobbed.

"Oh, it is," said Tom. "I didn't used to think so, but I do now."

Twenty-Two: *HUNGRY GHOSTS*

T AKE THIS OFF-RAMP," said Frietchie. Ezekiel veered to
the right and she directed him to a sanitary lane behind a row
of townhouses.

"Do you know someone here?" he enquired.

"My sixth husband," she replied tersely. Ezekiel knew that
#6 had been one of the bad divorces, involving a much younger
woman. Frietchie opened the back of the van and an odor com-
pounded of sauerkraut and Arizona desert tarantula drifted out.

"Hand me the bottles," Frietchie instructed Bogomil. She
tipped the contents over the back fence of one of the townhouses.
Moldy pumpernickel, cotton wads, egg cases and fertile cockroaches pattered down the other side. "Born free, little buddies,"
she called. "Go forth and multiply." Cubby's cockroaches quickly
overcame their fear at being thrust out into the world. They made
their way through the comforting shadows of the yard.

Frietchie's sixth husband had no interest in gardening and
had covered his yard in ivy. It looked attractive and was easy to
maintain, but beneath, in the green darkness, snails proliferated.
Snails are the very favorite food of rats There was a constant
rustling and chittering as predator hunted prey.

Through this jungle crept the cockroaches. They had sensitive antennae that detected the presence of food ahead. They had
delicate bristles, or *cerci*, protruding from their backsides to
perceive the slightest air movement. They were able to scurry out
of the paths of foraging rats.

At last they reached the source of the enticing smell and

entered the townhouse of Frietchie's sixth husband. He was a French chef. At the moment he was lying down, having spent many hours preparing a feast for a Saudi prince. The dishes for this feast sat in boxes, waiting to be loaded into the prince's limousine.

Cockroaches can eat almost anything—cigarettes, paper, dog food, grease and, as we have seen, each other. They like beer, too, especially Eight Ball Stout because it is full of healthy B vitamins. Roaches will even, if pushed, nibble your eyelashes. But they prefer *haute cuisine*. Now four of them discovered a bowl of tahini and settled in. They would be transported, like exotic decorations, to the prince's hotel room and wind up in an ambassador's pita sandwich.

The other forty-three cockroaches wisely chose to hide under the kitchen stove until dark. They passed the time playing slap-and-tickle and a few more egg cases were started. One female German cockroach (and these were good Germans) can produce 200,000 offspring in a single year.

Meanwhile, Ezekiel drove the van back to Frietchie's house. "How long is Cubby going to stay?" he asked carefully.

"I don't know," Frietchie admitted. "He puts an incredible kink in my life style, but I can't set him out on the sidewalk. He has no place to go. He was so happy in that dump over the factory. Damn it, why did they have to go and blow it up?"

"The firemen said he wasn't doing well on his own."

"He wasn't on his own," said Frietchie, laughing. "He had Gerbill and Sybille."

"He was squatting naked in the middle of a roach colony. The firemen said the room was so hot it was a wonder he didn't get heat stroke."

"Cubby has never been like anyone else," Frietchie said. "In high school he built a nest in a tree and slept in it all night to see what birds felt like when they got up. He ate pebbles until the biology teacher explained to him that he didn't have a gizzard."

"That sounds crazy."

"It's just Cubby being Cubby."

They drew up in front of the gate and Ezekiel jumped out to key the lock. The garden was deserted as far as he could see, except for red-winged blackbirds singing in the trees. The air was warm with the scent of jasmine, honeysuckle and gardenia. It was a setting made for love, he thought, if he could get rid of the house guests.

"Cubby dearest!" sang Frietchie, going into the house. "Come and see the treat we've brought you."

Ezekiel drove the van to the back where he and Bogomil carried Cubby's bed into an empty garage. A fume of dust rose from its covers as generations of Willows ancestors protested at the disturbance.

(When Tutankhamen's tomb was opened, Howard Carter discerned a subtle perfume in the air as though an unseen fair one had just passed through the room. It faded as he went deeper in. He discovered a delicate peacock fan and a wreath of flowers. But as he watched, the iridescent colors of the feathers dimmed and the flowers crumbled into dust.

For over three thousand years they had waited. The fan had waved over the boy king and his courtiers, whose spirits had emerged from wall paintings and statues. The flowers, left by his grieving subjects, had remained fresh. Banquets had been held under blazing torches visible only to the dead. Naked dancers with cones of perfumed fat on their heads had performed to the sound of flutes and drums. When Carter opened the tomb the spirits left in a long, muttering procession and he never even knew they had been there.)

"Did you hear something?" said Ezekiel, rubbing his ears.

"I hear—" The hair stood up on Bogomil's back. He felt the muttering in the air around him. He smelled a distant echo of pipe tobacco, potpourri and witch hazel, and heard the rustle of antique clothes. Then the impression faded. Cubby's relatives settled back into the bed. "I hear Frietchie," said Bogomil.

"I can't find him!" she wailed from the garden. Ezekiel and Bogomil hurried to her side. "Look! There's his notebook," she said. "The last entry is dated three hours ago, something about a tree frog. Oh, damn! It must have reminded him of the frogs at the hospital. He's probably trying to get there now. Cubby! Where are you?" She poked distractedly under the bushes.

"Find bug-man soonest," ordered Ezekiel and Bogomil nodded. Hunting humans was a skill he'd perfected in the salt mine. He prowled the perimeter, looking for escape tunnels. *Find bug-man soonest,* he thought happily. *Make bug-man do ca-ca in pants.* Ezekiel rechecked the house in case Cubby had got trapped in a closet. But after a half-hour's frantic searching they had turned up nothing.

"He must have opened the gate," Frietchie conceded. "He's so *damned* clever. Why couldn't he have waited till we got back?"

"Maybe he missed his cockroaches," suggested Ezekiel.

"We'll have to search the neighborhood—" Frietchie stopped. A faint *beep boop boop beep* came from the gate. It slid open to reveal Cubby in purple bathrobe and fuzzy pink slippers.

"I made a friend. Can he come in?" Cubby said, exactly like a boy asking if he could bring home a stray Rottweiler he'd found in an alley. Beyond, idling its motor in the drive, was Mr. Yee's black stretch Hummer. His son Lucky was driving.

Yee's Hummer appeared in the avenue whenever the old tyrant wanted entertainment. He cruised the neighborhood, rolling down the window to jeer at people who didn't meet his approval. Frietchie had frequently been the object of his scorn, but she didn't retaliate. It wasn't worth the bother. The bastard had to drop dead of spleen someday.

"Yeah, sure, he can visit," Frietchie said, resigned. The Hummer rolled in.

"I see you got a new boy-toy," said Yee, pointing at Bogomil. "Looks durable."

"Thanks for bringing Cubby back," Frietchie said, refusing to rise to the bait.

"The pleasure is mine. It is unusual to find a jade pendant concealed in a urinal, but value is undimmed by setting."

So Cubby had made a good impression, thought Frietchie. "How's the blood pressure? High?" she said hopefully.

Yee laughed, a dry sound like a rat chewing into a wall. "My blood pressure is most serene, thank you. I came to see whether Cubby has anything to wear besides hooker clothes. He wants to go for a drive."

Drive? thought Frietchie, alarm bells clanging.

"I asked Mr. Yee to take me to Chupacabras Hospital," Cubby said.

"Whoa! No! That's the one place he can't go," cried Frietchie. She took a deep breath to steel herself for the ultimate sacrifice. "Wouldn't you like to come in for a cup of tea, Mr. Yee? It's going to take a few minutes to find something in Cubby's size. Besides, we've been neighbors so long. It's a shame we haven't gotten to know one another better." Her fingernails were digging into her palm, drawing blood.

"Regretfully, I must turn down your American floor-sweepings tea, but I would accept hygienic bottled water," Yee said pleasantly. "I admit to curiosity about the local pussy house."

"Ezekiel, be a dear and find Cubby something to wear," Frietchie said, choking back a response. She watched Lucky lift his father out of the Hummer. The old man insisted on making his own slow way down the drive. Good, thought Frietchie. It would take at least ten minutes for him to reach the living room. She needed a stiff drink.

Once Yee was ensconced in the most comfortable chair, Frietchie presented him and Lucky with a tray of the softest snack she could find. Yee waved his son away with a gesture that reminded her of a tomcat guarding a bowl of tuna. He picked up a peanut butter cracker, removed the butter with a long fingernail and inserted it into his mouth. Frietchie hurriedly handed him a napkin. Too late. Yee had already wiped his finger on her brocaded chair. "Nice pussy house," he remarked.

"I'm sure you're an expert," she said. "Now about that trip to Chupacabras—"

"I wasn't born yesterday," said Yee. "Chupacabras is one of the thirty-six Buddhist hells, the one named after the sound of popping blisters. I only wish to deflect Cubby while I think of a solution to his problem. He was most upset about the hungry ghosts."

"Hungry . . . ghosts?" said Frietchie.

"We Chinese have a much better way of dealing with them. We throw them parties and burn spirit money for them to use on the other side."

Frietchie was speechless for a moment. "You don't actually believe in such things?"

"I could give you a psychological explanation or treat them as literary symbols, but yes. I believe there is another heaven and earth beyond the world of men. Cubby can see into it directly. In his opinion, the dead are trying to comfort their relatives in the hospital. He wants to explain this to the Alzheimer's patients so they won't be afraid."

"He can't go there," Frietchie said. "They'll microchip him."

"I know. This is very good peanut butter, by the way." Yee had massacred several more crackers and his fingernail was mired with brown sludge.

"Thanks. Would you like the bottle?"

"Why not?"

Frietchie brought him the bottle and watched him dig in. She'd have to have the chair professionally cleaned.

Yee washed the peanut butter down with bottled water and pushed the tray away. "I've lived a very long time," he said meditatively. "I think I may say that I'm a success. My house arouses intolerable envy. My children are subservient, my enemies are in prison, and my ex-wives no longer bedevil my ears with useless complaints. I thought I was contented until I met Cubby."

Frietchie nodded. Cubby had that effect on people. There was something so innocent about him.

"This first thing he did was cook me a breakfast of *mao-tuo quisan* mushrooms he gathered in the park."

"Good grief! I hope they weren't poisonous," said Frietchie.

"No, no. I have every confidence in his expertise. I hadn't eaten them since I was ten years old and they brought back memories—" Yee paused to wipe his eyes. "I became a child again. The colors were brighter, the sun warmer. It was as though fairies had wafted me off to one of the Blissful Realms."

Frietchie heard a choking sound from the chair where Lucky was struggling to keep a straight face.

"There's more to life than running up gambling debts on my credit card," snapped Yee. His son stopped grinning. "Cubby told me about the patients at Chupacabras hospital and under the rainbow-hued spell he'd cast over me, I agreed to help him."

"I don't see how you can," said Frietchie. "It's dangerous for anyone over sixty-five to approach that place. The Senior Laws, you know. Put one foot wrong and they can lock you up."

"I know," sighed Yee. "It's just so hard to turn Cubby down. I'm nine-tenths certain that he's an Immortal."

"An Immortal?" echoed Frietchie.

"*Xian*," Yee said in Chinese. "It means someone who

has escaped the bounds of earth. He, or she, is described in several ways: A bird in flight that leaves no trail or a mountain sage who rides on clouds. He is immune to heat and cold, untouched by the worries that beset the rest of us, unconcerned with how others perceive him. He has the trusting face of a child and acts spontaneously without forethought."

"Sounds like Cubby all right," Frietchie murmured.

"Of course there is a one-tenth possibility that he's a complete loony. I can't make up my mind," said Yee.

A red-winged blackbird hopped to the door of the verandah and Frietchie tossed it one of the mangled crackers. She'd never thought much about the supernatural, but what Yee said was interesting. All those years ago, she had never understood *why* Cubby attracted her. He had zero social skills and she had to grit her teeth to get past the Captain Tarantula routine. She wasn't lured by sex (or not much, anyway). Maybe there was something to that Immortal business. Being with Cubby was like looking through a high window into another world where people might actually ride around on clouds.

"I did the best I could," said Ezekiel, ferrying Cubby into the living room.

Frietchie passed a hand across her brow. He was dressed in the jogging suit Husband #1 had been wearing when he drowned in the koi pond.

"Lunch!" cried Cubby, descending on the tray of mangled crackers. "I forgot to ask, Frietchie. Were my cockroaches all right?"

"Dearest," she replied slowly, "did you know that if you love something, you have to set it free?"

"I didn't," said Cubby, his mouth full.

"It's one of the cardinal rules of married life. Your roaches looked so miserable I couldn't bear to keep them bottled up. So I found them a good home with my ex-husband. He's a chef in an exclusive French restaurant. I'm sure he'll have tons of snacks for them."

Yee laughed so explosively his son had to prop him back up in the chair.

"Thank you, Frietchie," said Cubby. "Did you notice whether they had egg cases?"

"Indeed they did," she replied gravely. "There were enough for ten French restaurants."

* * *

Gerbill was right, Cubby thought happily. It was good to know live people, although he wished he could introduce Gerbill to his new friends. He should have done it at the hospital, but things had moved too quickly. Remembering the hospital, he said "I made a list of things we should do for the Alzheimer's patients."

Frietchie looked appealingly to Yee.

"Chupacabras is like flypaper," Yee said bluntly. "If you go there, you'll stick to it. It's a death camp for old people."

Cubby was appalled. He hadn't realized he'd been in so much danger. He was further dismayed when he was told about the Senior Laws. "Why doesn't anyone complain? People make the laws, don't they?" he said, remembering uncomfortably that he'd never voted in a single election.

"They used to vote for representatives who made the laws," explained Frietchie. "We had some control over the process, but now we have computer-generated candidates."

Cubby was thoroughly baffled by this and so Frietchie switched on the TV. An amazingly handsome man, whose face shifted subtly from Asian to African to Caucasian as the predominant race, was talking about Universal Health Care. *No Senior left behind*, he said in a caressing voice. *We're here. We care. We're the Empowerment Party.* Frietchie muted the sound.

"That's the Homeland Channel with the current President, Soko Mogador. No one is sure whether such a person really exists. The Homeland Channel plays his message over and over, but when we get close to an election, he'll deliver longer speeches based on opinion polls. His image is derived from the same polls, which is why his appearance keeps shifting. The Fairness and Diversity Party candidates are basically the same."

"They aren't real," murmured Cubby.

"They're as real as public opinion."

Cubby felt as though he'd wandered into quicksand. "Who . . . " he paused, thinking it out. "Who's in charge?"

"Everyone and no one," said Frietchie. "Public opinion is a shifting concept. It's influenced by what people see on TV. One starlet with big tits and a room temperature I.Q. can influence an election if she supports a candidate at the right time."

"You're smart for a good time girl," said Yee with grudging admiration.

"Thank you. I try to hide it," said Frietchie.

"The change happened years ago because of the rapid transfer of information," Yee continued. "Everyone knew too goddamned much about everyone else. The standards by which real candidates were judged were so exacting that no one could measure up. It made sense to create a composite person who reflected the needs of the party. He or she is called an Icon. There's the Fairness Icon, Diversity Icon and Empowerment Icon. One makes it to the presidency every four years, but there's no difference."

"Who goes to Washington?" said Cubby, who remembered vaguely that real people had walked the halls of Congress.

"No one." Frietchie gestured to show empty hands. "Everyone does everything over the internet these days. Washington has turned into a ghost town."

Cubby thought he saw Gerbill in the garden, gazing into the koi pond. He raised his hand in greeting before he realized it was only Bogomil urinating.

"Every two years we get the election crisis," Yee said. "Mouse pox, global warming, a meteor headed for Earth. Everyone goes into a panic. The fornicating government uses it to get more power. Ten years ago we had the social security crisis."

Frietchie suddenly noticed what Bogomil was doing and shrieked. "Ezekiel! Get him out of there! Jesus and Mary, I paid five hundred dollars for those koi!" Ezekiel ran out to the garden, followed by Frietchie. Bogomil retreated, grinning impishly.

Yee helped himself to a last finger load of peanut butter and took a swig of bottled water. "The polls said young people were angry because we seniors wanted the money we'd fed into the system. What system? Letting pigeon dung congressmen handle your money is like asking Jaws to take care of your hamburger. There wasn't any money. The only solution was to keep us from asking for it, and so Congress voted in the Senior Laws.

Social Security turned out to be a goddamn ponzi scheme and we were left holding the bag."

*   *   *

Cubby was sitting on his old bed in Frietchie's garage. Everything was crowded together, not unlike Tutankhamen's belongings after the priests had rescued them from tomb robbers. Everything was there except the cockroaches, even his grandmother's tablecloth. It was steaming in a bucket, having turned brown with mildew. Cubby was sorry about that. He loved his grandmother and she had loved him, carefully embroidering the tablecloth with her arthritic hands and presenting it to him on his seventh birthday.

It might seem strange to give a seven-year-old a tablecloth for his birthday, but Cubby wasn't like other children. He saw at once the weeks of effort that had gone into his gift. It was as precious to him as his dog Jingle Bell, a present on the same occasion.

He had a bedroom in Frietchie's house—and a beautiful place it was, too, with a window onto the garden and the sound of the fountain coming in. But he needed to get away by himself, to think over what he'd learned from Frietchie and Mr. Yee.

The garage was dark. The only light came from the partly-open door, and that was how Cubby wanted it. He was surrounded by his books, pictures and furniture. He had changed from the sweat shirt once worn by Husband #1—heavy with the unmistakable odor of koi pond—to a T-shirt that read "Siberia: Land of Opportunity". It was a relic of the Golden Aphid trip. What a good memory that was, Cubby thought. And so was his retirement party where he'd done an imitation of *Gryllus assimilis,* the common field cricket. And so, too, was the sound of Tom Seaworthy's floor polisher he half-listened to as he slept on the floor of his lab.

What had happened to Tom Seaworthy? thought Cubby, burying his nose in the comforting dust of the bed. Of all the live people he had worked with only Tom stood out. Cubby wasn't sure why.

"It's a matter of soul," said Gerbill.

Cubby sat up. His friend was perched on a stack of dishware that would have collapsed if he'd been alive. But the dead can sit anywhere.

"Most of those people are little robot kitties like Slithe," said Gerbill, making a rude noise. "They don't know they are alive und when they die they don't know that either. It is vat your new friend Yee calls 'hungry ghosts'."

"I'm so glad you're back! Would you like to meet Mr. Yee?" said Cubby.

Gerbill laughed, a good German beer-belly laugh. Cubby had always admired it. "Yee does not vant to meet spooks just yet. It vould give him the heart seizure."

"We certainly don't want that," agreed Cubby. "I wish I'd remembered to get Tom's address."

"He also is looking for you."

"That's nice of him. But he'll probably go to the factory and I suppose that's gone."

"Ja. Ka-boom. Most satisfying to watch."

Cubby felt a vague pain in his heart. He would not have enjoyed seeing his home destroyed and he preferred not to picture it now. It was still there in his memory, the dear old fire escape, the loose shingles outside his window, the marvelous machines he'd only discovered at the last. "I should go to the lab and ask them for Tom's address."

"They vould not give it to you. They are vat you call tight-assed control monkeys, but don't worry. Tom is looking for you und he won't give up. He is driven." Gerbill's eyes twinkled at some hidden joke.

"What exactly *are* hungry ghosts?" Cubby enquired.

"Ach, we are all somewhat hungry. We regret the things we did not do und crave the things we did not have. That is why Sybille hangs over the little ones' beds. She vanted a child. She cannot resist them now. But Yee is talking about a very special kind of spook. They are the ones who can never get enough. They consume day and night, but they are never satisfied. They are afraid to stop feeding because for them there is nothing else."

Cubby stared at his friend in sudden understanding. "That's who's in charge of the government!" he cried. "That's what an Icon is! That's public opinion! Hungry ghosts!"

Gerbill wafted down from the stack of dishware and settled companionably on the bed. "I always knew you were a bright boy, Cubby," he said.

Twenty-Three: *THE SPIRITS ARRIVE*

TOM WAS SO exhausted by the time he reached home, he could hardly keep his eyes open and Violetta had passed out against the truck's door. He thought he was hallucinating again when their children swarmed out to meet them.

"Where have you been?" cried Atalanta, the tallest and most athletic of the children. She'd spent two years in the Navy, like Tom, and was mechanically inclined as he was. "We were so worried! We've been calling hospitals!"

"Why didn't you leave a note?" demanded Thaís and burst into tears. Violetta immediately joined her and the two of them clung to one another, sobbing.

"It was awful! Awful!" said Violetta. "They wanted to cut my heart out and Ngwenya tried to break Tom's neck. Then the lightning came down and—oh!" She was too overcome to continue.

"It's all right, Mom," said Cezare. "You lie down and recover." He and Atalanta helped her walk.

Jeronimo looked into the truck for suitcases and found none. "It's a long story," said Tom. "I need to lie down, too."

For the next few hours both he and Violetta slept, rousing to half consciousness when Thaís or one of the other children checked to see if they were all right. It was afternoon before they staggered into the kitchen to be greeted with a sumptuous feast.

"We're celebrating your return," explained Cezare, pulling out their chairs.

It was like the old days, Tom thought, the whole family

around the big wooden table, the air full of the voices of his children. They had worried about him and Violetta! They had left their own families and jobs to look for them. You couldn't beat Seaworthy children for loyalty.

When the meal was done and the dishes cleared away, they all went to the living room. Tom described what had happened at Joy Meadows. Violetta joined in occasionally. At first, the children asked questions, but after a while they merely listened in stunned silence.

"Your mother," Tom said, "was a lioness. When Ngwenya tried to kill me, she sprang up and threw him against the wall. Then—" He swallowed. Shock was beginning to set in. He described what happened next.

"I've never seen anything like that lightning," said Violetta. "It was like it was *hunting* Ngwenya. The storm came out of nowhere and tore open Joy Meadows to save us. It was a miracle."

"This happened last night?" said Phaedra. Tom looked at her fondly. She was the one they worried about, with her finely-strung nerves and headaches. She was the one they all protected.

"Yes, Baby Girl," he said, using his favorite name for her.

"That's what Uncle Shumba called me."

"*Shumba?* When?"

"In my dream." Phaedra revealed how she'd been suffering from a migraine and had hallucinated about her aunties and grandmas coming to dance with her in the forest. "Then one of them flew with me to an island in a river. Uncle Shumba said, *You can do it, Baby Girl. You can pull the clouds out of the sea and send them wherever you want.* So I did. I called up a big old thunderstorm and put it right over the island."

Tom stared at her, his thoughts racing. "It's like you had ESP," Violetta said. "That's exactly what happened last night. The storm blew up out of nowhere and when we took the boat to the mainland, the clouds had all gone away. You've discovered a new talent, honey."

It isn't a new talent, Tom thought. *It's very, very old. She has the blood of the Rain Queens in her and Shumba somehow woke it up.* He studied her with more than a little concern, thinking of the lightning setting fire to buildings, the dead doctors and nurses in the warehouse, Ngwenya. "I wonder if that storm at Joy Meadows is on the news," he said.

But Jeronimo flipped through the channels and found nothing. "They're not going to tell us anything," he said. "Joy Meadows is a huge franchise and nobody's going to rock the boat."

"If they're killing people, we should go to the police" Atalanta said.

"The cops don't care about seniors." Jeronimo paused at an ad for President Soko Mogador. *We're here. We care. We're the Empowerment Party.* The President was a well-rounded black woman with a gospel choir in the background. "I hear there's a new Senior Law that says people over sixty-five are no longer allowed to own businesses."

"What's the world coming to?" said Violetta.

"One thing's for sure," Tom said. "We're getting out of here. I don't want to be around when Joy Meadows arrives to collect on the bill."

*　　*　　*

The next morning, Tom Seaworthy loaded his truck with Dr. Willows' belongings—the microscope, gas chromatograph, scintillation counter and incubator as well as insect samples, slides and notebooks. At least a hundred notebooks.

I hope he's got room for all this, thought Tom. He knew where the doctor lived now and vaguely remembered the old factory building. Dr. Gerbill had said the only way in was via a fire escape and Tom wondered how he was going to offload the machines. Dr. Gerbill had found the fire escape impossible to climb. *It is like living in a tree house*, the old Nazi had complained. *He vill die up there, the silly billy. No one vill know.*

Dr. Gerbill was a decent man, Tom thought, in spite of his background. He was unfailingly polite and the only scientist who'd shown interest in Tom's ideas. But poor old Gerbill had dropped dead of a heart attack in his lab. Tom had found him with his face resting on the eye pieces of his microscope. It was a classy way for a scientist to go.

Now Tom fired up the engine and waited for the truck to shudder into life. It took a few minutes to warm up, just like

Tom himself. He saw Cezare carry a box to a van. The children and Violetta were packing up the house.

The truck settled into an even rhythm and Tom drove through the warehouses to Sasquatch Avenue and squeezed himself into traffic. An SUV on pimped-up tires vibrated its displeasure behind him. Music consisting of screams rolled out the windows and teenage boys shouted obscenities at him. Tom hoped they were going deaf.

He couldn't find the factory. He drove back and forth several times before he realized that a pile of rubble was what he was looking for. *Oh, my God,* he thought, rolling into a yard seething with bulldozers, backhoes and workmen. *I hope they got Dr. Willows out first.* Tom had no illusions about the unworldly scientist's ability to notice when something was taking a chunk out of his building.

A foreman ran out, waving his arms. "*Vaya! Vaya!* Is not allowed!"

Tom opened his window. "I'm looking for Dr. Cubby Willows. He used to live . . . there." He pointed at a fume of dust rising above the rubble.

"Is second person to ask about Willows. Others take his stuff away."

"What others?"

The foreman wiped his forehead, remembering Frietchie. "*Era mujer—una mujer reguapa. Pero no joven.* She not here. He not here. Please go."

Tom left, working through his hazy Spanish. A woman had taken Dr. Willows' belongings, a *foxy* woman, but not young. *You dog,* thought Tom, pleased. He'd made a joke about Cubby retiring to Brazil with a showgirl on each knee because it was the last thing anyone could imagine.

Tom was disappointed that he couldn't get rid of the machines, but he certainly couldn't deliver equipment to a hole in the ground.

He went home to help with the packing up. Violetta was weepy at seeing her keepsakes disappearing into boxes and crates. "The house looks like a plucked chicken," she mourned.

"Our stuff will look better on the ranch," Tom said, which was exactly the wrong thing to say.

"It'll look lonely out there with nothing but buzzards to see it," she cried.

"Nobody sees it here," Tom said incautiously.

"You don't understand!" Violetta stormed at him. "This is where it belongs. This is where my children grew up and where they left their little fingerprints and love all over the walls. You think it can be loaded into a truck like an old couch. Well, you can't move love!"

Tom retreated to the living room with a bottle of beer and sat down in front of the TV. They wouldn't be taking the TV. There was no reception on the ranch. He watched a football game with the sound off.

I wonder if Letta would like a makeover at one of those fancy beauty salons before we go, thought Tom. *She's always talked about it, but I could never spare the money. Nothing like having your heart almost cut out to rearrange your priorities.* He finished his beer and got it a friend from the refrigerator.

The living room was dark even though it was the middle of the day. Light shone into the window on only one day of the year, the winter solstice, when the sun briefly crossed a crack between towering, factory walls. *It's like Stonehenge*, thought Tom. *Here comes the sun, folks. Don't forget to set your watches.*

December 21 was a long way off and the little ray of sunlight was still trapped behind a warehouse. The only illumination was the muted TV where football players milled around. A siren wailed on Sasquatch Avenue.

Mhoro, said someone behind his back. Tom felt as though an electrical shock had gone through his body.

Makadii, said another voice.

Makadiiwo, answered a third. *Mhoro, Sekuru.*

A much deeper voice that seemed to shudder in the air made Tom break out in a cold sweat. *Mhoro, my children*, it said.

He does not speak the language of the ancestors, said the first speaker.

It is to be expected, said the deep voice.

"I promise . . . never . . . to drink malt liquor again," whispered Tom. He wanted to turn around. He wanted to reassure himself that the room was empty, but he couldn't move.

Heh! He wets his loincloth like a child. There was a

sound of ghostly laughter.

"You're not there," said Tom.

Yes, we are, said the voices, laughing. *Turn around child-of-Tombudzo so that we may address you.*

Tom turned around, shading his eyes. After a moment he lowered his hand. On the far side of the room were three dark shapes and behind them was a much taller fourth. The light of the TV flickered on spotted cloaks, feathered hats, a spear glinting, bone necklaces. As Tom's eyes adjusted, he was able to see faces, though not clearly. The three in front seemed friendly enough. The one in back made Tom feel as though he'd just been dropped off a cliff. It was like being observed by a lion.

"H-hello?" said Tom.

Makadii, they responded. *You have waited long, but not as long as we.*

"I guess not. Can I get you something to drink?" Tom didn't know why that came into his head, but it seemed the polite thing to do.

That would be welcome, the spirits replied and so Tom went into the kitchen and got the rest of the beer, a bag of tortilla chips and salsa.

Masviita! Thank you! cried the spirits, clapping their approval.

Mielie chips. I have not had these before, said the big, scary one. *The relish is good also.*

"Glad you like it," said Tom. He watched as the beer disappeared down shadowy throats and the chips were munched silently. *Silently,* he thought with a tremor of fear. When the spirits were finished, they dusted off their hands and once more became businesslike.

We have come with your task, child-of-Tombudzo, one said.

"I hope I can oblige," said Tom, uneasily.

We'll be there to see that you do.

"Okay."

We have seen the plight of the elders. We have heard their cries for help, said one of the spirits who looked vaguely familiar. But of course they would be familiar, thought Tom. They were all Seaworthys. They were one, big happy family going back to the land between the morning and evening sky.

You have been chosen to save them, said the familiar ancestor.

"Now you see, that's a problem," Tom said. "I'm kind of over the hill myself and with the Senior Laws—"

You have been chosen, the spirit said relentlessly.

"How am I supposed to do that? I'm on the run already and I've got Violetta to take care of and—"

YOU HAVE BEEN CHOSEN, said the big, scary one in a voice that seemed to come at Tom from all directions. The air turned red and the ground trembled. Beer bottles rattled across the floor. Too late Tom remembered what Uncle Shumba had told him long ago: *You don't argue with Big Daddy. It ain't intelligent.*

"Okay," he said humbly.

The air cleared. *You will find Cubby Willows. You will invite him and the people he is with to your ranch.*

"You know Dr. Willows?" Tom said, astounded.

Masviita for the beer and chips, whispered the small spirits.

Nice relish, said the big, scary one. They faded into the darkness.

"Wait! Wait! I don't know where Dr. Willows is," cried Tom, but the room remained dark and empty. In the distance gunshots broke out on Sasquatch Avenue.

Twenty-Four: *CUBBY TAKES CHARGE*

CUBBY SAT by the koi pond savoring the vibrant activity of the garden and occasionally making notes. A hummingbird swooped furiously around a mockingbird, who barely noticed his tiny assailant. A blue jay chased a squirrel out of a tree. Water striders skimmed across the pond and a pair of wild mallards dozed under a tree. Frietchie loved all living things. She rarely discouraged anything from moving in.

On one level, Cubby's orderly mind went over the problem of the Alzheimer's patients, the Senior Laws and the presence of hungry ghosts in the electoral system. But his attention was also drawn to the beauty around him. Most of it would have seemed beautiful to Frietchie, too. Some of it—such as the observation that the mallards were probably not lazy, but full of parasites—would have horrified her. Cubby made no judgment calls. He was as entranced by a thorny-headed worm digging into a duck intestine as he was by the outer receptacle covered in malachite-green feathers.

Twenty-two thousand parasitic worms reside in the digestive tract of an average duck, with different species claiming different stretches of turf. The gang war is continuous. Tough species drive out wimpy ones to the lower bowel where the pickings are slim.

The mallards twitched uncomfortably. Cubby wrote in his notebook. A tapeworm, he mused, is much like a hungry ghost inside one's own body. Stretched out, a worm could reach sixty feet, but it was usually folded and looped through a host's intestine. It was a long, thin tube of hunger with no mouth and no digestive system. It simply let the good times flow, selecting this or that nutrient from the bounty. Each segment of the worm, and there could be thousands, was a little bag of genitalia, both male and female. Each could mate with itself or avail itself of a sexy loop of worm nearby. Happy, happy parasite! Not for it was the angst of getting a date on Saturday night.

"Cubby!" said Frietchie. He woke to see her kneeling on the grass before him. "Cubby, something dreadful has happened. Yee's here and all hell has broken loose."

Cubby looked up to see the old gentleman cursing richly into a phone. Lucky was hovering near him. "*Ta ma de*! Damn it! Get my lawyers over here! Send those shitty cops back where they came from!"

Cubby heard a woman's hysterical voice.

"Don't you talk back to me!" Yee shrieked. The woman continued to argue and he hurled the phone away. Ezekiel caught it neatly. "Turtledung daughters! Cuckoo eggs! My dishonorable ex-wives foisted them on me. Their fathers must have been street beggars. I'll disinherit them!"

"Dad, they can't order the cops around," said Lucky.

"Don't you start!"

Frietchie hurried into the house and returned with a bottle of beer and a glass. "You must calm down, Mr. Yee," she said. "You'll have a stroke."

"What's that? American goat piss? I want Chinese beer."

"It's Tsingtao," she said gently.

Yee squinted at the bottle and relaxed slightly. "You're okay," he said.

"I'm the best. Now settle down. The police don't know you're here and I'm sure Lucky can drive you to the lawyers' office. "

"Can't," said the old man. "My car is known everywhere."

"All right, we'll make a plan, but first we should all take a deep breath. I'll send for food. You sit by the koi pond and relax. Cubby, come with me." Frietchie led the way to the kitchen and called a Chinese takeaway before settling at the table. Cubby was impressed with how well she had handled everything and said so.

"Oh, Cubby, I'm not handling it well at all. Things are spinning out of control." She leaned her head on her hands. "The cops want to arrest Yee for child abuse. What happened in that park?" Cubby explained about the pack of boys on bicycles and how he'd grabbed one. "So you're involved, too, although they probably don't know who you are. Everybody recognizes Yee because he's always ratting out people from that behemoth he rides around in."

"I don't think Mr. Yee hurt the boy."

"If only because he was too weak." Frietchie grimaced. "The kid was healthy enough to run home and his parents called the cops. Do you know what this means? No, of course you don't. Hitting a child is the worst thing you can do in this society. Even *restraining* a toxic brat is grounds for a lawsuit and besides, Yee is ninety years old."

"The boys were attacking him," said Cubby, not understanding her point.

"He comes under the Senior Laws. The slightest infraction can cause him to be declared incompetent. He'll be sent to an asylum—they call them Sanity Enhancement Centers, the bastards."

Cubby's eyes widened. What was wrong with the world? Why would boys want to attack an old man in the first place and why would they be championed for doing so? When he was a child he'd loved old people. His grandparents, great-aunts and uncles, aged cousins and their friends had surrounded him with a gentle cloud of affection. He'd never had the desire to hurt them.

They had listened to his stories, sympathized with his concerns and taught him little tricks—like how to snap an apple in two with a quick twist of the hands, or to imitate a dove using a blade of grass. They were always there when his parents were busy, a protective outer ring. And beyond them, unseen, lay a more distant ring of the ones who had taught his grandparents how to snap an apple in two.

These rings radiate out to the beginnings of humankind. The elderly gradually become the ancestors, and the ancestors become the spirits that watch over us. It is what makes people different from the beasts of the field, for among beasts it is natural for the elderly to be abandoned when they grow feeble. Care of the old was as important the discovery of fire. How else could knowledge have been passed on from one generation to the next? How else could we have separated ourselves from the muttering bands of apes roaming the savannahs?

"We have to get rid of the Senior Laws," Cubby said. It was the logical conclusion and he was unfailingly logical. The Alzheimer's patients were suffering because of the Senior Laws and now Yee, his friend, was threatened. Therefore, the laws had to go.

It was a momentous decision that would have caused snorts of derision from the young parasites feasting off the bounty of their grandparents. What could an old geezer do against them? But they didn't know Cubby Willows. He was not merely an eccentric scientist with a fondness for cockroaches. He was an advance scout for the spirit world.

Gerbill, Mr. Strickland and Miss Feeny had looked out on the living and seen spiritual decay. Tom Seaworthy's ancestors had noted the loss of respect for elders and the destruction of families. Yee's forebears had observed that their descendants had become shiftless, no-good, egg-sucking hounds. Even Bogomil's great-grandmother had paused from her continual moans to see that her beloved Bogie was not prospering. In short, the whole spirit world was up in arms.

Frietchie smiled sadly and patted Cubby's hand. "Many have tried to change the Senior Laws, dearest. The problem is finding out who makes the decisions. When you try to track down a politician he turns out to be an Icon, or a secretary working for an Icon. You can't get your hands on the power structure."

"That's because the government is run by hungry ghosts."

"Please stop talking about ghosts," sighed Frietchie. "The government isn't going to go away if you feed it pumpernickel bread and cream cheese."

"That's what you give normal spirits," explained Cubby. "*Hungry* ghosts are different. Gerbill explained it to me a few minutes ago. They feed continuously and are never satisfied. They're like tapeworms, except that tapeworms sometimes do feel satisfied."

Frietchie laughed in spite of herself. "Only you would know how a tapeworm feels. Is Gerbill in the house now? This place is getting awfully crowded."

"He *was* in the garage." Cubby looked around.

Someone rang the gate bell and Frietchie switched on

the surveillance camera. "Ye Gods, it's Ning and Fan," she murmured. When the gate opened Yee's daughters streaked in and began to berate their father. A family shouting match ensued with Lucky joining in. Yee moved more vigorously than anyone had seen him do in years. He roared and cursed, waved his arms and hurled the Tsingtao bottle into the koi pond.

Frietchie, Cubby, and Ezekiel watched in amazement. None of them understood Chinese, but it was clearly a battle between Yee and his children. Finally, Lucky left the melee and came over. "Please accept my apology for this unfortunate disagreement," he said.

"What on earth is happening?" said Frietchie.

"Steps must be taken to safeguard the family business," said Lucky. "Father is about to be declared a ward of the state and before that happens, we must gain control of his assets."

"You mean, you intend to pick him clean," Frietchie said.

"Father was right. You do have a double-hinged tongue. We will of course place our esteemed elder in a comfortable retirement home. No expense will be spared. We go to draw up the papers now."

"Please leave him here," said Frietchie, who didn't put it past the Yee offspring to hand their irascible father over to the police. "We can discuss the situation later."

Lucky, Ning and Fan climbed into the stretch Hummer and departed. By now Yee had collapsed on a lawn chair. He lay there, groaning faintly, his eyes glazed and his fingers fluttering over his heart.

Ezekiel had a horrible suspicion that the number of household members had just increased by one. It wasn't enough to have Bogomil lurking around like a bad smell or Cubby soaking up Frietchie's attention. It looked as though Yee was on his way to being a permanent guest, too. Ezekiel morosely fished the Tsingtao bottle out of the koi pond.

When the take-out food arrived, Frietchie laid out steaming containers of shrimp, pork, chicken and tofu. She had chosen the softest dishes, in deference to Yee's delicate teeth, but he refused to eat.

"They want to take everything," he moaned, deep in shock. "They want to eat me up like shithouse rats. The house, the car, the bank account . . . " He shuddered " . . . my beautiful bank account that I watered like a lotus from the Western Heaven. They'll tear it up by the roots. I curse them. May they be reborn as maggots festering in a beggar's sores."

"Mr. Yee, I won't let them take you," said Frietchie.

Uh oh. Here it comes, thought Ezekiel.

"You can stay here until we find out how to protect you," she finished.

"You're a nice lady," whimpered Yee. "Why didn't I meet you when I was young?"

"Just lucky, I guess," said Frietchie.

"The problem is the Senior Laws," said Cubby. "We have to get rid of them."

Yee smiled painfully. "I know you mean well, my friend, but engaging in that battle is like rolling up one's sleeve where there is no arm. We have no weapons."

"I disagree. Everything has natural enemies," argued Cubby. "The aphid, for example, is prey to ladybugs and parasitic wasps. Once you introduce them into the system, the aphid population goes down. We need to find out what feeds on hungry ghosts. This is going to take time and so we have to remove ourselves from view and safeguard our resources. Mr. Yee, you need to transfer your money into my account before your children get hold of it. Give me the pass code and I'll keep it in a separate folder for you to use whenever you like."

Everyone turned to him in amazement. Cubby had seemed so insubstantial, like a moth fluttering in twilight. He had appeared far too weak to fight anything.

Yee became very alert. He had never—*ever*—trusted anyone with his pass code or with any of the labyrinthine tricks he used to hide money. His children were going to find it easier to extract a brick from the heart of the Great Pyramid than get their hands on his cash. But at the same time he couldn't touch it either. He would be at their mercy.

"You have an account?" Yee said.

"I have a whole foundation," said Cubby. "It's in the name of the Willows Trust. The power is controlled by the family. It isn't affected by the Senior Laws because you can't assign an age to a family. I've never made financial decisions, but I could. I'm the last of the Willows. I represent the family in the same way President Mogador represents the Empowerment Party. You could call me the Willows Icon."

"I could help you make decisions," said Yee eagerly.

"Shame on you! You are *not* going to take Cubby's money away from him," scolded Frietchie.

"I have no such plans," the old man said huffily. "I'm merely saying that I am a financial genius, just as Cubby is a genius where bugs are concerned. We can help each other." He helped himself to a serving of sweet-and-sour tofu and chewed carefully, removing a shred of pineapple from between his teeth.

On the minus side, Yee thought, if he was declared a ward of the state he would lose control of both himself and his fortune. That was intolerable. He might as well be dead. On the plus side, if he transferred his wealth to Cubby, he could still manage the account. Could he trust Cubby? Yee looked up to see a reflection from the koi pond shimmering on the entomologist's face. The man was nine-tenths an Immortal and therefore only one-tenth susceptible to greed. Yee had gambled with worse odds.

On the double-plus side, Ning, Fan and Lucky would tear their hair out when they discovered that their father had given away his estate. Yee smiled evilly.

"All of you go away," he barked in his peremptory way. "Go on. Shoo! Cubby and I have business."

BOOK THREE: THE NET OF HEAVEN

Twenty-Five: *THE NET OF HEAVEN*

THE OLD FARMHOUSE had been packed up, with only a few items of furniture left. Tom's children had gone off to explain the situation to their own families and to take leave from their jobs. They would return in two days with a convoy of vehicles. Tom was proud of them and more than a little touched by their devotion.

Violetta spent the last days cooking at the old stove and watching soap operas. She was somewhat puzzled by Tom's sudden ravenous appetite. He devoured five sandwiches at a go, and his consumption of taco chips and salsa was amazing. Also, he was obsessed with finding his old boss. He had settled into the back bedroom with a laptop computer, and every time she went back there, he flinched as though someone had said *Boo*!

"You mustn't stress yourself out, Shug," she cautioned him. "You said the doctor moved on with a foxy lady. I'm sure she made him forget all about his machines."

"Dr. Willows never forgets anything," Tom said.

Violetta shrugged and went back to the kitchen. The only thing she rationed him on was beer. Five bottles of malt liquor were more than enough for anyone.

Tom, meanwhile, was seriously worried about leaving town before locating Dr. Willows. As Uncle Shumba had said, when the spirits issued a command, it had to be obeyed. Otherwise, the Seaworthy tribe would vanish like raindrops into hot sand. He couldn't hand that legacy on to his kids.

Una mujer reguapa, pero no joven. A foxy lady, but not young. Tom turned the words over in his mind. The more he thought about it, the more he became convinced that she wasn't a girl friend after all, but a relative. The doctor must have had a family.

Tom followed dozens of leads to dead ends. He typed in the man's name in every way he could imagine. Nothing came up except scientific articles about scorpions and praying mantises. He accessed the Golden Aphid website and watched a video of Dr. Willows explaining that aphids were born pregnant. "I didn't know aphids were born," he murmured.

They can lay eggs as well as give birth, said the big, scary spirit who had taken up residence in the corner of the back bedroom, along with the three junior spirits. Tom had closed the door, but of course that didn't keep them out. *If all the descendants of a single aphid survived during one summer, they would form a line, four abreast, 27,950 miles long.*

"You're full of surprises," said Tom.

I got that statistic from Dr. Gerbill, said the big, scary spirit.

"So the dead hang out together," said Tom, clicking the mouse onto a new website. "What do you do for fun? Go out for pizza?"

Pizza is good.

"Damn straight. I should have asked this before. Do you guys have names?"

I'm your Great-Grandfather Balthazar, said one of the junior spirits.

Tom swung around. He hadn't been able to pin down the resemblance before because he remembered Balthazar as a fierce, old man. "I'll be damned! You *are* him, fifty years younger."

We can take any age we prefer.

"Are you all my relatives?"

I'm your cousin Melchior, several times removed, said the second spirit. *I was responsible for the steam engine.*

I'm Caspar from the seventeenth century, said the third spirit. *I was the first Seaworthy to set foot in America, but I didn't do anything important. That's how it is sometimes.*

"Tell me about it. I spent forty years polishing floors." Tom rubbed his eyes, thinking that maybe he really was losing his marbles. He'd been at the computer for a long time. Violetta knocked on the door occasionally, to bring snacks and to comment about the amount of food he was going through. Tom didn't want to explain why he needed all those sandwiches. Then the names struck him: Balthazar, Melchior and Caspar. The Three Wise Men. He was definitely losing it. "Let me see if I get this straight," he said. "You're my dead relatives."

Except for him.

"Who're you?" Tom asked the big, scary spirit.

The Mhondoro, the spirit said in a voice that echoed inside Tom's bone marrow.

"The *Mhon*—what?" said Tom.

THE MHONDORO. The floor shook.

"Don't do that!" Tom yelled. "Jesus! I'm only trying to figure things out."

He's the spirit of the tribe, explained Balthazar. *We call him Big Daddy.*

Now Tom remembered. Shumba had told him about the Mhondoro years before. "Okay," he muttered, wishing he had a bottle of beer, only he'd have to get five bottles. "Look, I'm exhausted. I've been tracking Dr. Willows for hours and every trail winds up going nowhere. Cubby Willows is a ghost. No one seems to know where he came from or where he's gone. Hell, nobody is even sure when he was born."

Tom looked up at the sound of spectral snickering. Suddenly everything fell into place. "My God, you guys knew all along, didn't you?"

The room shook with invisible laughter.

Tom accessed the records of births and deaths in the city, and typed in *Willows* without a first name. If he was correct, Cubby hadn't traveled far from his birthplace. Someone who lived forty years in a shack over a factory was not what you'd call restless. Nor did he vary his routine. He'd spent every single day, winter and summer, weekends and holidays, in the lab, except for those few times when Gerbill had lured him away. Tom knew Cubby's birth date because he knew when he'd retired.

And there it was, in the city's records: A home birth. Except that the name wasn't Cubby, but Wolfgang. Wolfgang Willows, Jr., the son of the richest man in the state. A quick search revealed a news article about the event, with a picture of Wolfgang Senior, a.k.a. Wolfie.

Everybody listen up, said Wolfie on that long-ago occasion, handing out cigars to his fellow tycoons. *This here's the Wolf Cub and someday he's going to make history.*

Of course.

The Wolf Cub had morphed into The Cub and then into Cubby.

"This calls for a celebration," said Tom, standing and stretching his arms and back.

You still have work to do, rumbled Big Daddy.

"Cut me some slack. The dead don't get tired, but this living person is on his last legs. I'm going to order pizza, take a bath and fall into bed. You can haunt somebody else until morning." Tom was afraid he'd gone too far. The spirits clustered together ominously and the air shivered with their conversation, but at last they arrived at a decision.

"We want the triple grand-slam pizza deluxe," said Balthazar.

"With the cheese-filled crust," said Melchior and Caspar.

"No anchovies," added Big Daddy.

$$*\quad*\quad*$$

"You have got to be kidding!" cried Frietchie when Yee told her. "He's the heir to the Wolfgang Willows fortune? I should have tried harder to get him into the hay."

"You wouldn't have succeeded," said Yee. *"He who excels in defeating his enemy does not join in battle."*

"What's that supposed to mean?"

"It's a quote from the *Tao Te Ching*. It means nothing and everything."

"Stop trying to confuse me," said Frietchie.

"Confusion gives rise to order and order to confusion. I can play the *Tao* game for hours," Yee said happily. "It drives Ning and Fan crazy."

"I can see why they want you out of the house."

"Seriously, Cubby is not someone you can control. In the *Tao* such a person is like water, seemingly weak, but able to wear down mountains."

"I suppose you're right," sighed Frietchie.

Yee was so buoyed up by the transfer of his assets to Cubby's account, he began a *tai chi* session under the wisteria arbor. His movements were smooth, like a man of fifty or, indeed, like a praying mantis.

Mantises hunt not only other insects. There are records of them bringing down lizards, mice and hummingbirds, a sure case of someone's eyes being bigger than his stomach. These colorful creatures stalk their giant prey by moving slowly and carefully—as Yee was doing now—their many-faceted eyes fixed on the chunk of protein frolicking before them. And then they strike! The sharp barbs on the mantis's legs go straight to the heart. The hummingbird falls dead, to be eaten at leisure.

Yee entertained himself with thoughts of his children having fits when they realized the money was gone.

It was late and the golden light of sunset flooded the city, making the sullen warehouses along Sasquatch Avenue shine with a glory not their own. For the first time in decades, light touched the polluted earth beneath Cubby's old factory. The workmen had watered it lavishly to keep down dust, and a bubble of cement, cracked by the incessant activity of bulldozers, opened up to the present time. A spadefoot toad awoke from his tiny crypt.

He crept out into a new world. Gone were the waving marsh grasses and forget-me-nots of his youth. He ate a fly he found dozing on a fragment of burrito left behind by the taco truck. Water soaked into his skin, reviving him. For sixty-five years he had lain beneath the factory, thinking slow toadish thoughts and dreaming slow, toadish dreams. Now he was awake. The soft air stirred his soul and presently he gave the love-call of the spadefoot toad so reminiscent of a bleating sheep. From a drain came an answering cry, for in the drowsy magic of that evening the last female spadefoot toad left in the city heard him.

Yee continued his exercises as the sun withdrew and blue shadows filled up the corners of the garden. He thought of the *Tao* as he often did in moments of great peace.

> *The way of heaven*
> *Excels in overcoming though it does not contend,*
> *In responding though it does not speak,*
> *In attracting though it does not summon,*

In laying plans though it appears slack.
The net of heaven is cast wide.
Though the mesh is not fine,
Yet nothing ever slips through.

If Yee could have seen her—and it would have been bad for his heart if he had—his mother sat in one of the blue corners and watched him lovingly. Bogomil's great-grandmother was lurking behind the hot water heater in the utility room. Gerbill smoked a cigarette—yes! Cigarettes are allowed in the afterlife!—as he observed Cubby, Frietchie and Ezekiel playing Scrabble. Cubby was winning.

Across the city, Tom Seaworthy fell into an exhausted sleep while Violetta clipped coupons and made plans to have a makeover at *Chez Frietchie*, the best salon in the city. It was a present to herself before they headed out to Tom's ranch in the country. *Ranch, my ass*, she thought. It was a miserable dump where the coyotes howled all night. Still, Tom would be happy and that was worth something. Big Daddy was sitting across the table from her, but she couldn't see him. She wasn't a Seaworthy,

The net of heaven was cast wide and now it was going to be pulled in.

Twenty-Six: *CHEZ FRIETCHIE*

TOM DROVE VIOLETTA to the salon in the morning. The seething traffic on Sasquatch Avenue made them both nervous and it was a relief to pull off onto a quiet street lined with ginkgo trees and little boutique shops. *Chez Frietchie* had a front wall made entirely of glass, and you could see inside to neon lights and mirrors and fuzzy pink chairs so deep they looked like they could eat you. Boy-toys in tight pants fussed over women so beautiful Violetta felt like a frog that had just hopped out of the gutter.

Too late she remembered that she hadn't made an appointment. Or maybe she hadn't wanted to. "It's going to cost $300," she said.

"You go and enjoy yourself," said Tom. "I'll wait in the truck."

"You won't be bored?"

"I'll be alone and in good company," said Tom, sensing that the spirits were lurking somewhere behind the seats.

Violetta took a deep breath and pushed open the tall, glass door of *Chez Frietchie*. She caught a glimpse of herself in a mirror and her heart dropped into her shoes. Her dress was shapeless. Her makeup was all wrong. She looked like a bag lady, although she'd been so pleased with herself when she left the house.

Violetta turned to go, but then a trashy-chic woman stood up from behind the counter and said, "May I help you?"

Yeah, help me, thought Violetta. *Send me to the St. Vincent de Paul down the street.* But she took another look and saw something behind the Day-glo lips, push-up bra and fringed miniskirt. This woman was *old*. And yet she was incredibly sexy, the kind of sexy that made construction workers fall off their perches. All this in spite of hair that looked like a dead squirrel.

Violetta had just encountered Frietchie's first rule of beauty: *The secret of sex appeal is to look available.* The second rule was: *Men have incredibly low standards that almost anyone can meet.* But if you were truly cursed in the looks department, rule number three said: *If you're too ugly to pass the low standards you can scare men into bed.*

Like all deep truths, the rules were both simple and elegant. Of course Frietchie aspired to create beauty, but she always held out hope for those who could not measure up.

She only went to her salon two or three times a week. Her services commanded such exorbitant prices that she needn't exert herself. Frietchie had trained her staff well, however, and a make-over by them was almost as popular. Right now, the star of the salon was a golden-skinned surf god called Lourenço Marques.

Frietchie had sampled Lourenço, as she sampled all her male job applicants, and found him disappointingly predictable. But he had a talent for African-American beauty problems. Now she evaluated the creature who had just entered her salon.

Frietchie saw a woman who had sadly neglected her bath oil regime. The woman's shoes—surely she wasn't wearing *sneakers*?—she was! Her dress was so loud you needed sunglasses and her fingernails were chewed down to the quick. Lourenço would have his work cut out for him. But there was more.

The woman's eyes were filled with shame. Frietchie had seen that look many times from ladies who only wanted to be forgiven for being a blight on the landscape. Most of the time such despair gave Frietchie a warm sense of financial security, but having Cubby in the house had altered her perceptions. *He* would like this woman. He wouldn't see the dried-out skin or pouchy eyes.

"Do you have an appointment?" enquired Frietchie.

"I shouldn't have come," Violetta said miserably. "We're moving to the country and I thought I'd do something nice. But who's going to look at me out there? Anyhow, you're probably all booked up."

"My first chair could take you."

"Really? But you've got to tell me honestly, could three hundred dollars make a difference to this?" Violetta indicated her body with a despondent gesture.

Three hundred dollars? thought Frietchie, scandalized. Three hundred dollars would barely cover a shampoo.

Someone opened a window across the street and sunlight reflected through the glass wall. Frietchie was proud of the pink neon surrounding the mirrors in her salon. The color brought out the best in most peoples' skin, but it wasn't doing a thing for this bedraggled creature. However, the unexpected sunlight rounded Violetta's cheek in a pretty way and brought a liveliness to her eyes that had not been apparent before.

Frietchie thought: W*hat would Cubby do*?

"Three hundred dollars would make an *enormous* difference," she declared. "I'll do your hair and makeup myself. Trust me, baby, by the time you walk out of here you'll need a chair and a whip to keep men away."

Violetta felt as though she were in a dream. *Chez Frietchie* consisted of twenty staging areas containing hitherto unknown therapies that sent her pulses racing: The Mayan Hummingbird Massage, the Fur-Lined Womb, the Kama Sutra Stimulator.

With the aid of Lourenço and one of his underlings, Violetta's ragged fingernails were filed, her toe nails soaked and clipped into submission. Her body was covered in red North African clay and she was laid on a soft bed with river-smooth stones resting on her acupressure points. When the clay dried, it cracked open like a fine pot to reveal skin as soft as an infant's. Violetta's hair was oiled and washed several times. Her hands were encased in gloves lined with mink oil and her feet were scrubbed with powdered apricot kernels.

Finally, when she was ready to melt from sheer contentment, Violetta was carried to a massage table by Bulbul, a Turkish furniture mover hired to deal with traditionally-built ladies. Bulbul gave Violetta a delightful tune-up, not too forceful but vigorous enough to set her nerve ends tingling. Then he carried her, wrapped in a bathrobe, to one of the fur-lined chairs. "You're going to be *spectacular*," said Frietchie, beginning to style her hair.

Violetta was as defenseless as a newly hatched chick.

She warbled on about Tom, her children, and the lonely ranch where she would soon be imprisoned without anyone to talk to except the coyotes. If left in this state too long she would reveal how she lost her virginity.

This is a secret the KGB and CIA have never discovered. Forget water-boarding. Hire, instead, a troop of good hairdressers, for there is no one more adept at finding out secrets. Frietchie listened idly until Violetta said, "Would you believe he *still* has that pile of junk from Cubby Willows?"

Frietchie halted, comb in midair. The sauna next door hissed. Lourenço dropped a clatter of scissors into a sterilizer. "Did you say Cubby Willows?" she said.

"Those old things are never going to work," scoffed Violetta. "Tom tried to deliver them to Dr. Willows' apartment and all he found was a hole in the ground."

"How did Tom get them?"

"Oh, he used to inherit all the old equipment from the lab where he worked. Every time someone retired, he hauled off the junk and sold it. But Dr. Willows was different. Tom said he lived in his own little world and looked upon the machines as family. I'm afraid he'll take them to the ranch and I'll have to train ivy over them."

Violetta knew she was babbling, but she couldn't seem to stop. She was just too happy and comfortable. "Tom says Dr. Willows used to spend the night in a gray sleeping bag and that he looked exactly like a caterpillar in a cocoon. That's not a criticism. The doctor was crazy about caterpillars. He would have been pleased to be mistaken for one—listen to me! I'm running on like a leaky faucet."

Frietchie put the comb down. "I'm feeling a little hysterical myself," she confided. "You see, I know where Cubby is."

Violetta sat up abruptly. "You do?"

"It's so strange. The last time I saw Cubby was when I was fifteen years old. Three days ago he moved in with me and here you are, come out of nowhere to look for him. I don't know much about astrology, but there has to be a humungous convergence of planets for this coincidence to happen."

"That's amazing," cried Violetta. "I should start reading my horoscope."

It wasn't the planets' doing, however. It was the net of heaven drifting through the beauty salon.

Big Daddy was watching Lourenço trim a fashion model's hair and wondering why these people didn't feed their women better. Lourenço could feel something dark and heavy nearby. He'd grown up in Mozambique and knew that the air was not empty, though it might appear so to Americans. It was thronged with scary spirits. It was as thick as blood.

Lourenço was so jittery, he kept dropping scissors and having to get new ones. Finally, he called an underling to finish the haircut, and there went the big tip. He disappeared into a store room with a bottle of brandy. Big Daddy sat down next to him in the dark.

"You know what?" said Frietchie, giving a last fluff to Violetta's hair. "This beauty treatment is on me. No, I insist. I'd be an idiot not to know when fate was trying to tell me something." She folded Violetta's fingers over the three hundred dollars. "You and Tom come to my house for dinner and we'll ask Cubby whether he still wants those machines—for heaven's sake don't cry! The fake eyelashes will come unglued."

Violetta bravely choked back sobs and thanked her benefactor again and again. She stumbled out in the black slippers Frietchie had substituted for the ugly sneakers, although she carried the sneakers in a paper bag. Violetta had never been rich enough to throw good clothes away.

On the way to Tom's truck men turned and leered at her. A road crew stopped its jackhammer and made kissy noises. At a bus stop a man immediately jumped up and offered her a seat. "Did I see that?" he said, intimately, bending down to breathe into her ear. "Did I see a nice, soft woman smile up at me?"

"You didn't see anything!" Violetta cried and, scared out of her wits, ran the rest of the way to the truck.

* * *

Back in the salon Frietchie felt bathed in light by her good deed, not that she was a stranger to good deeds. She simply wasn't used to doing them for women, but there you are. Cubby changed people. Just look at Yee, sweet as a baby's bum once he'd decided Cubby was an Immortal. Which reminded her she'd have to clear out another bedroom. The house was getting damned crowded and she didn't know where she was going to put Cubby's equipment.

Lourenço staggered out of the storeroom, looking haunted. Frietchie detected the odor of brandy. "Are you all right?" she said.

But before he could answer, several men in uniform came through the front door. They weren't the regular police that Frietchie bribed for this and that misdemeanor. They were the Youth Patrol, or YP, created by President Mogador to enforce the Senior Laws. Frietchie had only seen them on TV and frankly had not paid much attention.

Their uniform resembled that of a California motorcycle cop, except that it was entirely black. The Youth Patrol logo, a cupped hand holding a flame, was emblazoned on both sleeves with the motto *The Future Belongs to Us.* When on duty, as apparently they were now, they were kitted out with an array of sexy weapons. They were trim, they were buff. They were the latest word in S & M chic.

Bulbul, mistaking them for a new kind of border patrol, slipped out the back door.

"May I help you?" Frietchie said.

"Are you Senior Frietchie Paskowitz?" said one of the YP.

Senior? What's up with that? she thought. "Don't you mean *Señora?*" she said, batting her eyelashes.

"Don't get cute, granny. Are you or aren't you?"

"She matches the photo," said another YP, checking a vidphone.

Frietchie hadn't paid close attention to the news, figuring most of it was bogus, but she did remember a TV show about an old woman who lived in an apartment with ninety-three cats. The Youth Patrol had kicked down her door and dragged her away. The old woman was crying and the cats were all meowing and trying to follow her—really, it was very distressing. "I used to be called Frietchie Paskowitz. That was my first husband's name," she said cautiously.

"Look at this!" said YP #2, scrolling information on his vidphone, "She's had *eight* husbands."

Frietchie realized that she had better watch her tongue, but a wave of anger, the same anger that allowed her to subdue Bogomil and the foreman at Cubby's factory. radiated on the astral plane and was picked up by every male in the room. Bulbul, hiding in the alley, quivered with alarm. Female rage takes many forms—Kali who sent out *thuggees* to murder lonely travelers, Coatlicue who demanded human hearts, Medusa who turned men to stone—every culture has such a being in its pantheon. Frietchie knew little about theology, but she understood female power.

The problem was, such power required a gender to work on. The Youth Patrol had no gender. None at all. Zip. The part of the brain where such things existed was blank, unlike the hairdressers who had dozens of naughty impulses stored there. The YP members had grown up with televisions for mothers and computers for playmates, and so they identified with machines. The presence of living, breathing humanity made them edgy.

The hairdressers, answering Frietchie's subliminal appeal, left their clients and stood behind her.

"What are you? Some kind of fag hag?" said YP #2, eyeing them distastefully.

"Sometimes," Frietchie said, wondering what on earth was wrong with that. Somebody had to look after the poor darlings. They were forever getting into mischief in bus stations. "Anyhow, what I do with my spare time is none of your business."

"Everything about you is our business," YP #1 said. "You turned sixty-five today and that means, according to Federal Code SS9275-K, you're officially retired. Federal Code SS4719-A states that senior citizens can no longer own businesses. You have thirty days to sell this salon to someone younger."

"*What?*" shrieked Frietchie. Lourenço put his hand on her shoulder. The other hairdressers crowded closer. Bulbul hovered outside the back door.

"Any profit from this sale is taxable under capital gains legislation. Fifty percent is the usual levy. If you do not sell this place within thirty days, the property becomes forfeit to the government under Federal Code SS1158-W."

"You must be crazy! This is my shop. I paid for it. I made it the success it is." Frietchie had lost all caution.

"It's a new Senior Law," Lourenço whispered into her

ear.

"Well, I won't obey it! I never heard of such nonsense!"

The YP officer didn't bother to answer. He signaled and one of his men picked up a fur-lined chair and hurled it into a mirror. Glass shattered. Clients screamed. Bulbul burst through the back door, and Lourenço pushed Frietchie toward him. The hefty Turk swept her into his arms and fled.

"Put me down! I have to protect my salon!" Frietchie cried as he pounded down the alley.

"I protect *you*," said Bulbul. "The police, they everywhere. Look for me, look for you. I see the television, how they take old people away. You want to live, you run."

"I am *not* old," said Frietchie.

"You not old," Bulbul said loyally, "but they think so." He didn't stop until he had arrived at her little sports car parked several blocks away. Frietchie dissolved into tears and he held her until she calmed down.

"My beautiful salon. What's going to happen?" she moaned.

"You go home, have nice bath and think. We all your friends, remember."

"I do." Frietchie got into the car and switched it on.

"By the way, happy birthday," said Bulbul.

"Thank you, Bulbul. Your timing's off, but you have a beautiful soul." She drove away.

Twenty-Seven: *SANCTUARY*

TOM AND VIOLETTA drove along the tree-lined avenue, looking for house names. It was one of those upscale neighborhoods where it was considered vulgar to display one's address. The houses were called Kon-Tiki, Brigadoon or Shangri-La, and they were all hidden behind high walls. You were supposed to know who lived there. If you didn't, you didn't belong.

They passed a mansion called Ten Thousand Happiness after a well-known sex tonic. *Wonder what goes on in there*, Tom mused. He could have used some Ten Thousand Happiness after Letta came home. He couldn't believe how seductive she was. It was like being sixteen again.

She had washed off some of the makeup before they left the house. The attention she'd got from strange men frightened her and now she looked more like the old Violetta. Tom liked her that way, too.

"That's the place. Joie de Vivre," cried Violetta.

They pulled up at a gate with a black stretch Hummer parked in front of it. Tom identified himself to the two-way camera and was startled to see Dr. Willows' face appear. Presently the gate opened. The first thing they saw was a mob of middle-aged Chinese screaming at a very old man. The old man was seated on a lawn chair looking very pleased with himself.

"Drive in quickly!," called Cubby. "We have to keep the gate locked because of the police."

He conducted Tom and Violetta past the melee to a living room where a woman was slumped in an easy chair. It took

Violetta a minute to recognize Frietchie. Gone were the fringed miniskirt and Day-glo lipstick. Gone was the confident, cheery face. Poor Frietchie looked as though she'd been dragged through a carwash minus the car. Her hair was wet and stringy, her face woebegone and she was wearing a frumpy bathrobe.

"Honey, what happened?" said Violetta, kneeling by the chair.

"The Youth Patrol trashed my salon," moaned Frietchie. "Just after you left. They smashed the mirrors and threw the furniture into the street. Lourenço called me from the hospital. Poor darling! They broke his arm."

"Youth Patrol? Those are the people who are supposed to take care of seniors," cried Violetta, shocked.

"They take care of seniors the same way pest control companies take care of rats," Tom said.

"What did Lourenço ever do to them?" wailed Frietchie. "What did *I* do except turn sixty-five." Frietchie pulled the bathrobe tightly around herself and shivered. "It's just a number, damn it. I don't feel sixty-five."

"And you don't look it," Tom said generously. "By the way, I'm Tom. Violetta's husband."

Frietchie pulled herself together in the presence of male sympathy. "Oh, dear, I invited you to dinner, didn't I? I haven't prepared a thing."

"Don't you worry," said Violetta. "Point me toward the kitchen and I'll fix something. But first we need to talk." She made shooing motions with her hands. "You men take a hike. This is for women only."

Tom left willingly. He knew that no one was better at healing hurt feelings than Violetta and he didn't want to witness the tears such healing involved. Cubby took him through the house and a magnificent place it was, like a Moorish palace in a Hollywood movie. Tom admired the Persian rugs and Mogul paintings on the walls. Every window opened onto a garden. He was surprised when they left the house and walked toward a garage.

In the distance, the fight between the Chinese continued unabated. Tom suddenly registered that Dr. Willows had said something about keeping out the police. "A lot seems to be happening here," he remarked.

"Yes," Cubby said, taking him to the garage.

Inside was a jumble of dishware, books, pictures, a sagging easy chair and a bed. One of the pictures was of a dreamy-eyed boy holding a puppy. Tom squinted to make out the details in the dim light. It had to be Dr. Willows. The eerie thing was how little the man had changed.

"Mr. Yee's children are upset because he transferred his property to my account," Cubby explained. "They're negotiating a settlement. Would you like a beer? I have Tsingtao."

"Tsingtao is fine," murmured Tom. Negotiating? It sounded like the Yees were ripping each other's throats out.

Cubby indicated the easy chair and opened a small fridge humming on a work bench. The garage smelled of ancient dust —not an unpleasant odor. It reminded Tom of dried rose petals and wool suits that had been packed in trunks. "Why did Mr. Yee transfer his assets to you?" he said.

Cubby described how the boys on bicycles had attacked the old man and how Mr. Yee's own children wanted to send him to a rest home. "Giving me the assets was the only way to protect them. The family came this morning when Frietchie was at work and they've been fighting ever since. Yee told them he'd donated everything to a Tibetan monastery, but that wasn't true."

Cubby drank tranquilly as though a screaming mob in the front yard was the most normal thing in the world.

"And the police?" Tom enquired. His eyes had grown used to the gloom and he saw a heap of notebooks like the ones he had rescued from the lab.

"They want to arrest Mr. Yee for hitting a boy. Frietchie says that means he'll be sent to a government hospice for the dying. She's given him sanctuary."

"She's quite a woman, isn't she?"

"She's wonderful. She rescued me from Chupacabras."

"Really?" said Tom, thinking, *isn't that an insane asylum?*

"After a while Mr. Yee will tell his children he's giving them an allowance in return for protection from the police. He says it's the way Chinese negotiate. If you want to put windows into a house, everyone will say no. But if you say *Let's rip off the roof*, they'll say *Let's compromise and put in windows.* I'm sorry. I should have offered you a glass for that beer. I can get one from the kitchen."

"That's okay. I always drink out of the bottle." Tom was struggling to make sense of Cubby's words. He heard a lawn chair smash and Frietchie's voice rise above the others. Violetta must have helped her get her mojo back.

"Gerbill says we have to move out of the city," said Cubby. "I'm at risk, Mr. Yee's at risk, and now Frietchie is."

"If you break one more thing, Lucky, I'm calling Bogomil!" shouted Frietchie in the distance.

"Gerbill is dead, Dr. Willows," Tom said gently.

"Please call me Cubby. We're retired now and titles don't mean a thing. I'll admit I *was* surprised when Gerbill showed up, but he explained that if you don't know live people, the dead visit you instead. Oh, dear! She did call Bogomil."

Tom heard a startled shriek and a splash.

"Gerbill said you were looking for me," said Cubby. "I was afraid you'd give up when you found my apartment demolished. But then Frietchie told me about Violetta's visit to the salon. I'm so happy you've come."

"Well . . . I'm happy, too." Tom was disarmed by such direct friendliness. The noise was dying down in the garden and the Tsingtao was beginning to relax him. The garage seemed remote from the rest of the house, almost as though you were in another world. Cubby, age seven, smiled benignly from a picture on the fridge. In another photo a group of old-fashioned men and women stood around a man playing a piano. Cubby sprawled on a Navajo rug with his head resting on his hands. The same rug lay at the foot of the easy chair where Tom was sitting now.

"I should have got your address before I left the lab," said Cubby. "I didn't realize then how important it was to know live people. The night I retired my old teachers threw me a party—Mr. Strickland from high school, Miss Feeny from first grade. Burton and Barton were there, too."

Most people would have thought Cubby was crazy, but not Tom. He'd been serving tortilla chips and salsa to his ancestors.

"That was the last I saw of most of them. The dead usually associate with each other," Cubby continued. "Gerbill says that too much fraternizing with the living makes them nervous. Did you know he had a wife called Sybille? They ran away from the Nazis in the last days of the war and she died in the snow."

"He told me that once," murmured Tom.

"Everything has been so strange since I retired. I feel like the forty years I spent in the lab was a dream—a *good* dream of course. I liked working there. But now I'm awake and I've learned so much these past few days. It's clear that my mission in life is to get rid of the Senior Laws."

Tom smiled inwardly. Cubby challenging the legal system of the United States was like sending a moth to fight a grizzly. Stronger people had tried and ended up in old age homes or asylums. The only way to deal with the Senior Laws was to make yourself scarce. "I saved your lab equipment," Tom said. "It's at my house."

"You did?" Cubby's eyes shone. "The scintillation counter? The incubator?"

"Everything. The notebooks, too."

"How wonderful!" There was a luminous quality about Cubby now that Tom had never seen before. The light shining from the garage door was met by something from within the man. Tom suppressed a shiver. It was as though the energy gathered during the forty years Cubby had lived sheltered from the world was burning brightly now. Brightly and rapidly. "Do you want me to bring it to you?" Tom said gruffly.

"Not any more," said Cubby. "Believe me, I'm grateful for what you did, but I understand now that people are more important than things. I've made so many friends recently. . . Frietchie, Mr. Yee, Ezekiel, you . . ."

"Maybe we'd better go back to the house and make plans," Tom said.

*　　*　　*

Ning and Fan were weeping while their husbands stood by uneasily. Lucky was slumped on the ground, his Armani suit streaked with algae. "Bogomil! I said *restrain* him, not drown him," scolded Frietchie. "Damn it! I wish I hadn't sent Ezekiel to the salon. I need a translator." Bogomil smirked.

"The latest boy toy is useful," said Mr. Yee from his lawn chair. "Maybe I'll hire him as a bodyguard."

"The way you're going, you'll need all the bodyguards you can get. Oh, Tom!" cried Frietchie, coming forward to take his hands. "I'm so sorry you and Violetta caught us in a muddle. I was overcome with problems, but Violetta has been an enormous help. She's in the kitchen now, preparing dinner. Mr. Yee was just about to make a very generous offer to his kids."

"No more luxuries, you blood-sucking ticks!" Mr. Yee crowed. "No more fancy cars or designer clothes! You'll have to work for everything you get. Look up the word if you don't know what it means."

"*Ba Ba*, we do work hard," whimpered Ning, clutching onto her sister.

"Mr. Yee, remember what you promised me. No more bullying," scolded Frietchie.

"We can tell the cops where you are," said Lucky.

"If you do that, you won't inherit even the smell of a dollar bill," Mr. Yee jeered. "*Ai-ya!* It will be sweet to go to my ancestors with the laments of my offspring in my ears."

"Oh, come on," said Frietchie. "You know you're not going to disinherit them."

"I'll do what I like!" shouted the old man. "All you people go home. I want a nap. Beg harder next time." He gestured impatiently at his children.

They trooped out the gate, complaining loudly, and at the last minute Lucky turned. "I don't believe for one second that you gave everything to a Tibetan monastery. You hid the money, Pops, but you're not getting away with it. I, too, will enjoy the laments of my disreputable elder as the cops investigate his shady business practices."

"Get out!" shrieked Mr. Yee as the gate closed. "Did you hear what he called me? *Pops*? For that alone he loses his inheritance."

Frietchie's confidence sagged. "You know it's a bad idea to keep taunting them. You aren't really safe here. God knows what's going to happen now that I'm," she swallowed, "classified as a senior."

"Yeah, yeah. I know how far I can push them," said the old man. "I can get another two days of entertainment out of them."

Tom had been watching the Yees with horror. What kind of family was this, consumed with such malice and distrust?

Cubby, on the other hand, found them fascinating. They reminded him of the Dracula Ants he and Gerbill had studied in the Sierra Nevada.

That had been a most agreeable field trip, with Gerbill sniffing out an excellent brewery in an old growth Douglas fir forest. They'd sat in the courtyard with beer steins, and Gerbill had waxed lyrical about the *Wandervögel*, Birds of Passage, club he had belonged to before joining the Hitler Youth. "Ve lived under the sky, hiking, singing jolly songs and camping," he said. "Ve toughened up by throwing a fifteen-pound *Völkerball* stuffed with rocks at each other. Such fun!"

Dracula Ants, or *Amblyopone oregonensis*, are sluggish creatures that prey, by preference, upon centipedes. When they encounter a centipede—perhaps a brave mother attempting to protect her clutch of eggs—they close in, grasping her with their mandibles and stinging her into submission. Once she is paralyzed they drag her back to the brood nest, where they set about tenderizing her by chewing.

Once the centipede is softened up the ant larvae crowd around and eagerly bury their heads in her body.

But there is an unusual habit associated with these creatures. An adult Dracula sometimes grabs a larva and squeezes it roughly, turning it over and over to find a soft spot. It nicks the skin and drinks the hemolymph, or insect blood, that oozes out—not too much. Just enough to sooth hunger pangs. After a while most of the larvae in the brood nest are flecked with feeding scars. This behavior seems to have no ill-effect upon the species as a whole. It does foster insecurity and a permanently embittered state of mind.

Now Cubby discoursed on this happy memory and it was bizarre enough to take everyone's minds off the Yees' argument.

Violetta, meanwhile, had been busy in the kitchen. She was enthralled by Frietchie's spacious pantry, giant refrigerator and state-of-the-art equipment. It was a far cry from the dark kitchen in the old farmhouse and she was having the time of her life.

She loved dinner parties. Even more, she loved

company and when the others offered to help, she sat them down at the table. "Just talk," she said. "I work best on my own, but I do like listening to conversation."

Bogomil sniffed suspiciously and Frietchie, realizing that he felt threatened, sent him off to the utility room with a bottle of vodka and a block of Velveeta.

"I've been meaning to ask you, Cubby," she said. "Why, when you were so incredibly rich all these years, didn't you live somewhere besides that ghastly factory? Why didn't you buy a car? Or take vacations? I don't understand."

"Why take a vacation from work I enjoyed?" said Cubby, honestly puzzled. "What good is a mansion when my apartment was all I wanted? As for a car, I would have missed the early morning walks to the lab, the birds waking up, the crickets chirping, the spider webs hung with dew."

"I told you. He's an Immortal," said Mr. Yee, shaking his head. "Or nuts."

"But all those years I was dreaming," Cubby went on. "The world changed and I didn't notice."

"None of us did," said Tom, "although it seems to me that the world didn't change that much until recently. Where in hell did these new Senior Laws come from? My kids tell me there's a move to force everyone over sixty-five into so-called Protected Villages. Letta, tell them about Joy Meadows."

Everyone listened with horror as Violetta described the deadly purpose behind the retirement community. "I was completely taken in. I thought Noni was a friend, but she was scheming to harvest our organs just like the rest of them."

"After they got us to sign over our house and bank account," added Tom.

"They were going to get a quarter of a million dollars for my *heart*!" exclaimed Violetta. "If that's what goes on in Joy Meadows, imagine what will happen in the government-run villages. They'll be whisking out your kidneys as you come in the front door."

Frietchie looked stunned. "You mean . . . the government could take away my salon . . . my house . . . and *me*?"

"After the November election. That's what my kids say," said Tom. They heard the front gate open and

Frietchie's sports car drive in. A moment later Ezekiel appeared with news about the salon. The destruction wasn't as bad as feared. The hairdressers and Bulbul were cleaning things up, and were going to sleep in the salon to protect it from vandals. They thought it could be back in business in a week.

"But will *I* be back in business?" mourned Frietchie.

Violetta served up roast chicken with sage dressing, mashed potatoes, and baby peas with pearl onions. "There's ice cream for dessert," she said. "Mr. Yee, that chicken breast is as tender as butter." He was jabbing at it with a long fingernail.

"No *hoisin* sauce?"

"No *hoisin* sauce," said Violetta in the voice she had once used to tell Atalanta to stop picking on Phaedra.

Grumbling, Mr. Yee began to dismember the chicken, but wound up eating everything on his plate.

A phone rang somewhere. It took Tom a moment to realize it was the cell phone Cezare had insisted on giving him, and another moment to remember how it worked. "Hello!" he shouted, convinced that the tiny speaker couldn't transmit sound.

"Dad, you and Mom can't come home," said Cezare.

"*What?*"

"I said, you and Mom can't come home!"

"I can hear you," Tom said crossly. "You don't have to shout. Why can't we come home?" Violetta leaned closer to listen.

"The Joy Meadows people have taken it over. They won't let me in and they say you owe them thousands of dollars."

"To hell with that," said Tom.

"What's going on?" cried Violetta. Tom explained the situation and she burst into tears. "I told you they'd come for us! They want to cut out my heart!"

"Honey, I'm not going to let that happen. We'll meet the kids somewhere else."

"Where?" demanded Violetta.

"Hello? Hello?" shouted Cezare.

Frietchie took the phone from Tom. "You don't know me," she said, "but I'm a friend of your parents. They're having dinner with me right now and they can stay at my house until you're able to pick them up." She gave Cezare her address.

"He's coming in the morning," she said. "My God!

Everything is happening so fast. First Cubby, then Mr. Yee, then me and now Tom and Violetta are in the cross-hairs. What's gone wrong with this country?"

No one had an answer, although several spirits in the room could have supplied one if they'd been visible. The Mhondoro thought it was the decay of the family and Miss Feeny was certain it was the lack of discipline in grade school. Mr. Yee's mother blamed laziness and Gerbill thought that joy had gone out of people's lives. *Vat this country needs is more beer halls,* he said, *und healthy sports in the fresh air. Und lots of love.*

After dinner, Frietchie cleared out another bedroom and laid out towels and soap. Soon everyone had gone to bed.

Twenty-Eight: *THE CORRIDOR TO THE NORTH*

B UT TOM WAS too disturbed to sleep and wandered outside. He thanked his lucky stars that Frietchie had invited them to dinner. What if she hadn't? What if they'd been home when the Joy Meadows enforcers had arrived? He sat under the wisteria arbor and listened to tiny frogs cheeping somewhere in the papyrus next to the koi pond. Cubby would know what they were.

A mockingbird began to sing. Violetta used to call them feathered car alarms and put a pillow over her head when they began yammering in the middle of the night. But gradually the mockingbirds had disappeared from around the old farmhouse. It had been years since Tom had heard one.

What if Ezekiel hadn't been working at Chupacabras? Cubby would have died without anyone knowing what had happened to him. If Cubby hadn't broken out of Frietchie's garden, Mr. Yee would have had a heart attack when he was attacked by the children. If lightning hadn't struck Joy Meadows, he and Violetta would have become passengers on the coffin ship. If Violetta hadn't wanted to get her hair done, they would never have met Frietchie. *It sure is an amazing set of coincidences,* thought Tom.

Of course there were no coincidences. The net of Heaven was carefully sifting through the possibilities and choosing what to preserve.

The cool darkness of Frietchie's garden began to change. The pleasantly splashing fountain faded and even the mockingbird was muted. *I must be dreaming,* thought Tom, pleased to be dozing at last. He saw a hot sun beat down on fields of millet and smelled the dust of a land trampled by ghost cattle. He could see people bending and planting. They were singing in a lovely chant to accompany their work. He saw a grey-green forest in the distance, and lions that stepped back into shadow when he tried to look at them. Thunder rolled around the blue horizon.

A voice suddenly rose out of the earth and shouted, *Child of Tombudzo! Why are you wasting my time?*

"Jesus and Mary, don't come at me like that!" cried Tom in that far-off land between the morning and the evening sky.

I've told you what to do and yet you piss around eating ice cream! roared the Mhondoro.

"I'm on the case," Tom cried. "I'll wake up Cubby now and invite him to the ranch."

You must ask all of them. This task is for the elders.

"What?" said Tom.

YOU HEARD ME!

Tom found himself back in Frietchie's garden with his ears ringing and his bones shaking. Damn! Why couldn't Big Daddy leave a note? Next time the Mhondoro pulled a stunt like that, he was going to find the latest Seaworthy stroked out on the ground. Tom tasted blood in his mouth from where he'd bitten his tongue.

The bell on the front gate rang. Tom stumbled to the surveillance camera and saw a squat, black car and a group of policemen. Frietchie came out of the house and he waved her back.

"Yes?" Tom said politely into the speaker. "Can I do anything for you?"

"We're looking for a senior delinquent named Mr. Yee Ssu," said an officer. "His son says he's hiding here."

So Yee did push his kids too far, thought Tom. "There's no one here by that name," he said. "The owner is in the process of selling this property to the Wolfgang Willows Trust."

There was a hurried discussion outside. "Is there someone in charge I can talk to?" said the officer.

Tom remembered that they could see him as well, a raggedy black man in a bathrobe. "There's only me. The Willows lawyers should be here next week."

"It's only the janitor," someone complained.

"I'm a *maintenance* man," said Tom, irritated.

"Can you let us in?"

"No, sir," said Tom with what he judged was the right amount of humility. "I'd like to comply with your request, sir, but I'd lose my job. You understand."

Someone in the background said something about getting a search warrant, but the officer told him it was the middle of the night. "We can send the Youth Patrol tomorrow. They don't need no stinking warrant," he said.

"If I see the owner I'll pass your request along," Tom said, his heart thumping at the thought of the Youth Patrol breaking down the gate.

Frietchie was waiting impatiently on the veranda. "Who was it? What did they want?"

"We have a problem," said Tom.

They woke up Cubby, Mr. Yee and Violetta, and Tom explained what had happened. "I said the first thing that came into my head to buy us time."

"Maybe you had the right idea," said Mr. Yee. "Maybe Frietchie's estate should be merged with the Willows Trust to keep it from being confiscated." Everyone turned to look at him. "Why not? Cubby's relatives were financial geniuses. I should know because I'm a financial genius, too. They incorporated the Willows Trust in Antarctica which, according to international law, can't be owned by any government. It's the one place on Earth beyond the reach of god-rotting IRS agents."

"Is that even legal?" said Frietchie.

"No one will ever know," said Mr. Yee. "Cubby's father surrounded the Trust with so many firewalls even I was impressed."

"I hate like hell to lose control of my property."

"I think things have been taken out of our hands," said Tom, fetching the laptop computer and clearing a place for it on the table. Cubby sat before the keyboard, his hands poised like a concert pianist.

"I don't know . . . it's such a giant step," Frietchie faltered.

"You're in deeper trouble than you realize," said Tom. "If the Youth Patrol gets in they're going to find out that you're harboring a house full of fugitives. What they did to the salon will be a love tap compared to what they'll do here."

Frietchie shuddered.

"Come on, baby," encouraged Violetta. "Tom and I have lost most of our belongings, but you don't have to. Tom trusts Cubby. Mr. Yee trusts Cubby and you know he wouldn't even let God look after his piggy bank."

Frietchie still hovered.

"It's time for us to skip town," said Tom. "I'm officially inviting all of you to come to the Seaworthy Ranch."

"Do you mean it?" cried Violetta, her eyes shining.

"I do. It's out in the wilderness and it's not fancy. I'm afraid the buildings are basic, but there's plenty of room."

"Oh, goody! I'm going on a boy scout trip at age ninety. Rub two sticks together, get fucking merit badge," said Mr. Yee.

"It's not a dump," Tom said, offended. "The ranch has been in my family for generations."

"Some people live in dumps for generations."

"My God, Mr. Yee, can't you stop picking fights for one second?" cried Frietchie. "Tom has solved our problems. I'll admit I'm frightened, but I can trust Ezekiel to look after the house. Lourenço can take care of the salon. I say we put our finances in order and hit the trail."

She sat down. "I've got goose bumps in my stomach," she said, watching Cubby type in bank codes. "Everything I own is turning into blips on the internet. My worldly goods are vanishing into nothing."

"*A clay pot is called Something,*" Yee said tranquilly. "*You may hold it in your hand, yet it is the Nothing within that renders it useful.*"

"Please don't play the *Tao* game with me," begged Frietchie. "I'm upset enough."

After the transactions were done, Violetta opened a bottle of champagne and they drank a toast to their new life. "Do you suppose we've been called together for a purpose?" she said.

"I think we were meant to come together," said Tom. He didn't mention the *Mhondoro* or the secret of the Seaworthys. He didn't know how the others would take it. "I think we have a role to play in this world that has turned against us. I'm not sure how, but our task will be made clear to us as we go along." By now it was almost dawn and the wisteria arbor trilled with birdsong. A koi swished its tail in the pond. Bogomil grunted as he did early morning push-ups in the back garden.

"So, in light of our new adventure, what do you think we should do, Cubby?" said Tom.

"Take over the government," he replied, promptly.

"Yeah, sure. Why not?" said Mr. Yee, holding out his glass for more champagne.

*   *   *

A convoy of five moving vans rolled down Sasquatch Avenue in a formation large enough to intimidate the other vehicles. The five Seaworthy children were experts at maneuvering in traffic. They coordinated their movements like a lion pride working its way through a herd of wildebeests. No one challenged their right to dominate a lane or to spread out in an insulting wall before lesser drivers. It was the way to survive on the freeway and they enjoyed it.

Not so their parents. Tom ground his teeth and Violetta gave yips of dismay as the assemblage swung in front of a truck carrying bridge parts.

"You have to show them who's boss," explained Cezare, who was leading the convoy. "Otherwise, when you reach the Corridor to the North, you are lost."

The Corridor to the North was sixteen lanes wide, a mere baby compared to the sixty lane CanaMex Conduit sweeping from Panama City to Winnipeg. Entirely different weather systems existed on either side of the CanaMex. Trucks fifteen stories high and road trains as long as city blocks filled the lanes, pumping out hot gas and plumes of ozone. This formed a barrier in the atmosphere that turned back all but the highest clouds.

The Corridor to the North, and the Corridor to the South running parallel to it, were not as terrible. But they weren't for the timid. Not one of the seniors in the Seaworthy convoy had ever ventured onto them. It was one of those things that penned older people into smaller and smaller territories. As the corridors expanded, so the lands that had once been planted in life-giving orchards and fields shrank. Little islands of old people clung to their fogeyish ways between thundering rivers of traffic. Gradually they lost their hold and were swept away.

The passengers in the convoy reacted with alarm as Sasquatch Avenue split apart into two congested channels. But the Seaworthy children were already in control of the left channel and rose triumphantly to cross over the seething Corridor and join it on the opposite side.

Tom looked down and thought it looked like something from Dante's *Inferno*, the City of Dis where the souls of the wrathful fell continuously like rain. Violetta trembled as she cowered against him.

Mr. Yee, who was a passenger in another van, worked through his meditation beads and muttered a fervent prayer: *Hail to the noble Bodhisattva, Great Compassionate One! He who surmounts fear!* He added many flattering descriptions to get the Bodhisattva on his side

Cubby looked out at the maelstrom from his van with fascination. He had only the vaguest knowledge of cars beyond what Gerbill had forced him to learn. Gerbill had given up on him when the younger man's attention had been distracted by a butterfly and they had ended up in a ditch.

The Corridor's walls towered on either side with a meager strip of sky overhead. You could have been driving in the Amazon jungle or Alaskan tundra for all you could see, but that didn't mean the journey was uninteresting. Cubby asked Atalanta, who was driving his van, about the small machines skittering up and down the walls. She explained that they measured air quality. The air was never good and that was why—she pulled out a coil of tubing from the dashboard—they carried oxygen.

At intervals the Seaworthy convoy swept onto a side channel to a rest station. This was a bleak plateau covered in asphalt that offered a place to stretch one's legs and visit a toilet. Vending machines provided drinks and mummified sandwiches. It also offered a view of the sky. It wasn't a nice sky, Violetta thought as she massaged the feeling back into her legs. It was a dull yellow-gray and any bird that ventured into it would probably drop dead from the fumes.

The convoy rolled on. From eleven to twelve-thirty the sun shone into the Corridor and the temperature rose, due to the greenhouse effect. Cezare turned on the air conditioner. "Oxygen, Mom?" he offered, passing a tube to Violetta. She sucked on it gratefully. Her thundering headache subsided and she passed it on to Tom. They took turns, like smokers around a hookah, and eventually the sun disappeared over the western rim of the Corridor.

They had lunch at a rest stop with plastic bushes and an overpowering smell of grease. Tom, Frietchie and the others nursed glasses of fake ice tea while attempting to eat fried Spam sandwiches. Mr. Yee threw his sandwich on the ground.

Only Bogomil was happy. He'd gone into a kind of hibernation during the trip, like a spider trapped in a bottle, and felt delightfully rested. Lack of oxygen didn't bother him because he'd seen worse in the salt mines. Not only did Bogomil have his beloved Spam (and everyone else's after the first bite), but he'd found his favorite soft drink, the kind that tastes like cough syrup.

Cubby wrote in his notebook: "Amazingly—but we shouldn't be surprised by such resourceful creatures—these rest stops contain large numbers of cockroaches. I detected the tell-tale flavor in my sandwich. Also, I am fairly certain the pepper grains were not what they seemed." Fortunately, Cubby did not share these observations with anyone.

At last, when the strip of sky overhead faded and the mustard-yellow lights on the freeway walls switched on, the Seaworthy convoy left the Corridor for the last time. They came out into a tube town that existed solely for the purpose of servicing the Corridor. Motels, restaurants and casinos flashed giant neon signs to attract business, but Cezare had already arranged lodging. He led the vans to the Luga Chuga Lounge teetering at the edge of darkness on the eastern side of town.

It is a curious thing that people who have spent all their lives in the city have a fear of both darkness and silence. They leave the TV on continuously. They find comfort in the eternal glow of the microwave. For the gnawing question is always, *what's left after the music dies?* and the answer is: *You.*

For many people the thought of confronting *You* scares the living daylights out of them. Old people handle this situation better than the young. They are used to looking into the darkness and their expectations are not high.

Most travelers avoided the Luga Chuga Lounge because it was too close to the darkness. The hotel had never seen better days. It had always been an overflow refuge when other places were full, but to the weary travelers that night it seemed a paradise. Violetta swore that she would never enter the Corridor again, and Frietchie said she had aged ten years *at least* during the trip.

They settled onto the restaurant patio while the rooms were being made up, and a waiter brought them the standard Luga Chuga dinner—lukewarm macaroni and carafes of Mirage wine. The patio looked out onto the Mirage Mountains, now hidden by night, with only the beginnings of a cedar forest visible.

"This wine is excellent," remarked Frietchie, tracing a pattern in her cheese sauce with a finger.

"It comes from a vineyard on the other side of the mountains," said Tom. "I saw it once as a boy. Run by monks."

The conversation died. Everyone was exhausted and could hardly wait to get into bed, but Cubby sat up a while longer to gaze out at the forest. The view wasn't empty to him. He saw a line of Modoc warriors walking stealthily through the cedars at the foot of the mountain. They were spirits, of course, doing what warrior spirits enjoy most—scaring the crap out of people. Their destination was a boutique bed-and-breakfast just a little bit too close to the woods.

BOOK FOUR: THE NIGH AND FAR VALLEY

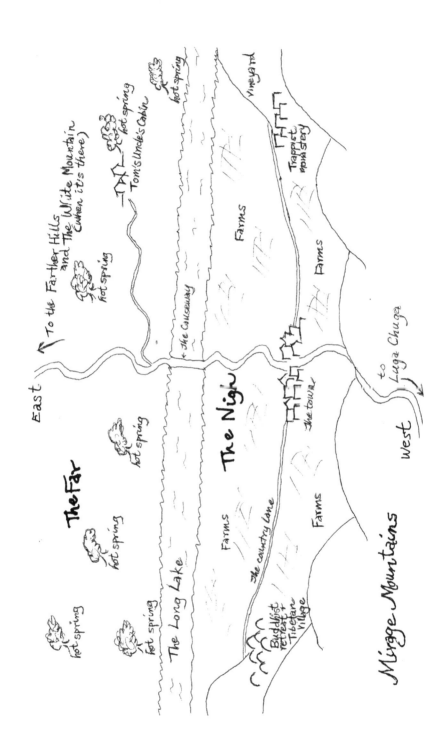

Twenty-Nine: *THE NIGH AND FAR VALLEY*

THE SUN ROSE on the far side of the Mirage Mountains and so the town of Luga Chuga was still enveloped in shadow when Cubby woke up. A blue haze hung over the streets and buildings. Clouds condensing from the warm fumes rising from the Corridor turned a sickly yellow, but it would be an hour before the sunlight reached the ground. A constant rumble emanated from the Corridor and was echoed back by the mountains.

"Vat a dump," said Gerbill, perched on the table next to the coffee machine.

"There's hair oil on the back of this armchair!" complained Miss Feeny, recoiling from her seat. "And it's hollowed out in the shape of a person."

"Vat you feel is the shape of Jedediah Bidwell. The hotel got it second-hand from his estate," said Gerbill.

"Nasty man! You're always trying to upset me!" Miss Feeny fled through the window.

Cubby had to admit the chair did have eerie hollows as though someone were still sitting there. "Is Mr. Bidwell—" he began.

"*Nein*, he hates that chair. He vould be happy to see it burned up und the town with it. He prefers to stay in the forest with the Modocs."

"I think I saw them last night," Cubby confided, opening the packet of free muffins the hotel provided. "Want one?"

Gerbill shuddered. "There are some things even dead people won't touch." So Cubby ate the muffins by himself and washed them down with gray coffee from the in-room coffee maker.

Everyone looked jaded and slightly ill in the wan morning light of the lobby. Frietchie paid at the desk, using the credit card for the Willows Trust. It sounded impressive and the clerk asked whether they might hold a convention at the hotel.

"If Hell is full up," said Frietchie. The remains of a complimentary muffin churned in her stomach.

"Hell always has vacancies," the clerk said morosely.

The convoy made its way out of town. The road into the Mirage Mountains was narrow and full of potholes. It wound around boulders and squeezed between towering cedars, and parts of it were only traceable by slash-marks on near-by trees. They skirted chasms where pebbles cascaded into abysses and crept up slopes that had the engines groaning in first gear. Once, Bogomil had to lift a wheel out of a pothole before they could go on.

There were no lay-bys, no passing lanes and after a while no tar. "Is this even the right road?" said Frietchie at one their rest stops.

"It's the only road through the Mirage Mountains," Tom said. "There's a country lane paralleling the mountains on the other side."

"We're overloaded," said Cezare. "Once we take out the furniture, the drive back should be easy." The seniors became quiet and thoughtful at this remark, for only the children were returning.

There's something extremely sobering about realizing that you are making your final move. There will be no more new houses. The rooms you live in now will be the last you will ever inhabit. The young may journey on in their thoughtless way, carelessly discarding furniture and friends in the belief that they can always find more. The old know better. You let go of things at your peril. Remember the picture book you had as a child, the one with the impossibly green meadow and the rainbow saturated in colors not of this world. Where is that book now? And if you find it, will your aged eyes be able to see those brilliant hues?

But in fact the meadow does not die. The arc of light against the clouds does not fade. The book is still there, waiting for you to open it and be transported anew. The reason is that you were not careless with your memories. You cherished each one and the people in them most of all. You didn't really discard anything, but merely put it away, to be taken up again when time is no longer a problem.

At Jedediah Bidwell Pass, the highest point on the road, was a picnic area. The tables were covered with a drift of pine needles, and a stream pattered down a ravine going into the valley. Mr. Yee made his slow way to the nearest table, breathing deeply of the good clean air. "It's so quiet," he remarked.

Tom turned toward the west where the polluted fumes of the Corridor were hidden by trees. "I can't hear traffic anymore."

Violetta spread her arms to the breeze ruffling the mountain trees and felt unaccountably happy. "All I ever heard on Sasquatch Avenue were sirens and gunshots. How could I have lived in such a place for so long?"

"I feel overdressed," murmured Frietchie. "I want to peel off everything and dance naked under the trees." She blushed. It had been years since she'd felt confident enough to dance naked in front of anyone, except in the garden during the dark of the moon.

"Uncle Shumba stopped at this place when he brought me here as a child," Tom remembered. "He used to say *lay down your troubles here, boy. Troubles belong to the city. They're like cockroaches and need filth to stay alive. There's no filth in the Nigh and Far Valley.*"

"The Nigh and Far Valley! What a name," said Frietchie, shivering slightly.

"Cockroaches don't really like filth," Cubby objected. "They're always grooming themselves. They smooth oil over their exoskeletons at least a dozen times a day. Did you know that cockroaches can survive an entire week without a head?"

"Good grief, Cubby, how do you scientists find out these things?" said Tom. "We should go on now. The ranch has been looked after by a caretaker, but I imagine we'll have to do some work to make it comfortable."

"I can't wait to get there," Frietchie exulted. "I'm *dying* for a hot bath and an oil massage for my tired, old exoskeleton."

Nothing could have prepared the travelers for their first sight of the Nigh and Far Valley. Even Tom and Violetta were surprised because they'd been young when they'd seen the valley before. To the youthful, life is a series of brightly colored pictures to be admired and discarded. Movement is everything. Young people are already reaching for the next experience before they have fully savored the current one.

The old are different. They stop and the scene deepens before them. The longer they watch, the more details appear and eventually they realize that the view is endless.

At the south end of the valley a vineyard covered a hillside, below which was a Spanish-style mission with red tile roofs. At the north end lay a collection of geodesic domes like giant mushrooms poking up through the soil. Between these two extremes were farms, patchworks on a green quilt, that were connected by the country lane Tom had mentioned earlier. Squarely in the middle was a town. This area, Tom explained, was called the Nigh. It was divided from the Far by a long lake.

The colors changed abruptly on the other side. The land there turned a muted gray and powder blue, and bitter green bushes dotted the plain. But the most astonishing things were the plumes of steam rising from a dozen places. Between these, dust devils writhed across salt pans, looking like wandering spirits. Tom said they would have to be careful when going for walks. Most of the hot springs and creeks were tepid, but some could be lethal.

"Is your so-called ranch in that wasteland?" demanded Mr. Yee.

"It's better than it looks," Tom said.

"Just what do you farm out there? Lizards?"

"Actually," Tom said reluctantly, "no one has ever raised much of anything out there. It's more like a spiritual retreat."

"I know what that means," scoffed Mr. Yee. "The plumbing doesn't work."

"I'm sure something can be worked out," Frietchie said. "Anyhow, *I* think the valley is perfectly beautiful."

And even Mr. Yee, looking out over the Nigh and Far Valley, so verdant on one side and so mysterious on the other, was strangely moved by the sight. It did look like a place inhabited by Immortals.

The Immortals had already moved in. Caspar, Melchior and Balthazar were occupying the main ranch house. The Mhondoro had draped himself over a lawn chair with a bottle of Eight Ball Stout and Shumba was trying out a few riffs on his drum. Gerbill and Sybille were exploring the wine cellar at the monastery and Mr. Yee's mother had discovered a moon-viewing garden outside the geodesic domes.

There are places where the spirits gather, much as holiday-goers flock to Waikiki. They, too, get tired of their everyday deaths and want to kick back. The Nigh and Far Valley beckons to them with the same allure as a Las Vegas nightclub calls to an aging rock star. It's a place where time runs sideways and lost opportunities are recovered.

The valley was self-contained and had little commerce with the outside world. The same families had lived there for generations. A few children moved away. A few outsiders found their way in. These often didn't know why they had suddenly walked out of their houses and traveled to the Mirage Mountains, but they were drawn to the Nigh and Far Valley like monarch butterflies drawn to the leafy groves of California.

Tom, Violetta, Frietchie, Cubby and Mr. Yee looked out to where the road crossed the Far and lost itself in the Farther Hills. No one knew where it ended, not even Tom. The Farther Hills faded into shadow in the distance, and at the very edge of the horizon rose a solitary, white mountain cloaked in haze.

Thirty: *TOM'S UNCLE'S CABIN*

A CAUSEWAY crossed the lake at its midsection, linking Nigh with Far, and the water was dotted with waterfowl that paddled away as Cezare led the convoy past. On the Far side grass disappeared entirely to be replaced with sagebrush and splotches of alkali.

They turned onto a side road wavering off between drifts of sand. Buildings as small as children's toys gradually grew larger as they approached, but even close up the buildings huddled together like castaways on a desert island. The main ranch house had been whitewashed recently, and a new red tile roof had been added.

Someone had taken great care with creating a garden, shoring up an enclosure with adobe walls and filling the interior with imported soil. Stands of broad beans, limas, zucchini, tomatoes and squash rioted within a businesslike chicken wire fence. Pipes ran here and there from a water tank perched on long legs, and a large outdoor hot tub had been constructed near one of the steaming springs.

"Will you look at that," said Violetta as they piled out of the vans.

"A hot tub! Oh, Tom, why didn't you tell us?" Frietchie cried.

"I didn't know," Tom said. "The Dominicans send a monk out to care for the property, but they never mentioned that this much work had been done. I wonder where the monk is."

"We'd better unload," suggested Cezare. "It's getting

late and we've got to get everything set up before sundown."

"Is that when the coyotes come out to eat us?" Mr. Yee looked around at the barren plain.

"There's no electricity, Mr. Yee. We can't work in the dark," Cezare explained.

"No electricity?" echoed Cubby. This was a problem that hadn't crossed his mind.

Bogomil and the Seaworthy children began hauling furniture out of the vans. There were a dozen cabins, as well as the main ranch house, so everyone had his or her choice of living quarters.

Cubby selected a building with an extra room for a lab. In the first spending spree of his life, he had bought computers, a telescope, a microscope and other scientific equipment. Frietchie had given him Turkish rugs from her mansion. She tried to give him a new bed, but there Cubby drew the line. His bed was enveloped with the memory of departed ancestors and he didn't want to abandon it.

When Bogomil plunked down the old mattress, a fume of dust filled with the twitterings of the Willows ancestors arose. They were annoyed at being disturbed, but eventually they settled down.

"No electricity?" said Cubby, holding the homeless plug of his computer. "How am I going to access the internet?"

"We'll work something out," said Frietchie. "Just look at those birds walking along the road!"

Cubby was immediately diverted by the natural drama unfolding before him. The plain that had seemed empty was in fact dotted with sagebrush, small ponds and reed beds. Now, in the late afternoon, Canada geese appeared from these refuges and gathered on the road in front of the ranch. They strutted up and down, honking and craning their necks as they complained about the newcomers. Soon all of them were gazing west toward the emerald fields of Nigh, and at some unknown signal they all took off in a long line toward the setting sun. Their mournful cries were echoed by the ducks on the lake.

Shadows slid across the land, reaching out from the Mirage Mountains, and in the distance a bell rang sweetly from the monastery. It was a strangely moving sound that made everyone stop and turn toward the lake glowing pink under high cirrus clouds. When the onlookers turned back they saw the shadow of the earth rising in the east. The White Mountain stayed visible long after everything else.

Tom, Mr. Yee and Cubby lounged contentedly on lawn chairs, watching the others work. An assembly line of Seaworthy children stocked the shelves of the pantry, while Bogomil put the house in order under Frietchie's supervision. Violetta heated dinner on a propane stove.

But in a distant shed, a man in a white postulant's robe huddled next to a chicken coop. The chickens muttered sociably at his presence for they liked him. He fed them well and let them run around outside when the weather was good. Having him sleep in their shed was new, but they figured it was just another human eccentricity.

When Uncle Shumba knew his time was drawing to a close, he alerted the Dominicans to send one of their members to care for the property. This was an arrangement welcomed by the monks, for it offered a safety valve. Things that one can escape in ordinary life become magnified in a closed setting. Someone sucks his teeth incessantly or passes gas or rocks back and forth while meditating. Men had been known to throw wine casks through windows for such provocations.

Monks who were suffering from nerves could escape to the ranch. There they spent blissful hours meditating and listening to the desert wind and coyotes. In return, they kept things tidy, fed the cats and didn't disturb the fetishes in the main house.

The person who'd been minding the ranch for the past three years had arrived at the monastery late one night. He'd been wild-eyed and frantic, shaking as though he had a fever. The abbot took him in.

The man had suffered terribly. The abbot could see it in his eyes, and all of the monks were appalled by the marks on his body when he changed into the robe of a postulant. For on his shoulders, chest and back ran seams of scar tissue forking like the imprint of a lightning bolt. They asked him what had happened and the man shrank away. He wouldn't tell them. He *couldn't* tell them because he was mute.

He was about forty, strong and tanned as though he'd been working outdoors. He fitted himself into the monks' routine as though he'd been there all his life. He cleaned and cooked and farmed tirelessly. He prayed at the appointed times, or at least appeared to. He was incapable of speech, so no one was quite sure.

The other monks developed the theory that the man had been an electrician stringing wires when he'd been struck by lightning. They called him the Wichita Lineman.

For a long time the Wichita Lineman went about his duties flawlessly. But one night a rare thunderstorm had torn apart the sky and the Lineman had torn apart the monastery. Thereafter, he'd been assigned to the Seaworthy ranch.

He was happy there. He painted, planted, weeded, laid pipes, and hung drapes. He replaced the metal roof with the tiles the monks manufactured at the monastery. The cats adored him. The spirits did, too, although he couldn't see them. Now, in late afternoon, he had watched with consternation as five moving vans pulled up and men and women unloaded furniture.

A monk had come out to warn him of the Seaworthy invasion, but the Lineman couldn't understood him. When people talked to him all he heard was *buzz buzz buzz* like the mutter of voices on a telephone line. "I'm sure you'll be welcome to stay," said the monk. "There's a dozen cabins here, so you won't be tripping over anyone's toes."

Buzz buzz buzz is what the Lineman heard.

When the vans pulled up he fled. The dry air kept the chicken coop fresh and the hard floor didn't bother him overmuch, but the new, strident voices did. His peace was shattered. Conversation hummed on the night air, poisoning the desert wind and reminding him of the blinding moment when God had plucked him off the telephone wires. He fell asleep weeping.

*   *   *

"Someone has really kept this place lovely," exclaimed Violetta, looking at the polished floor, the brightly-patterned curtains, the freshly dusted fetishes hanging from the ceiling. A black cat rubbed against her legs.

"I wonder where he is," said Tom. Cezare had placed

kerosene lamps around the room and the golden light made everything look especially nice.

Phaedra and Jeronimo carried in bowls of chili, rice and string beans. The dining room was extremely crowded, even with Bogomil eating outside as he preferred, but no one objected except Mr. Yee. They were all so used to his caustic remarks that he faded into the background like a distant wood chipper.

"I found someone to build us a proper cookhouse with an oven," said Cezare, tearing off part of a crusty loaf of bread he had bought in town. "I was amazed at how many crafts people live here—carpenters, bakers, weavers, tailors, glass makers. It's like going back in time."

"Can any of them string electric lines?" said Cubby.

"I don't know," said Cezare.

"One step at a time," said Tom, hoping to avoid Cubby's gentle but persistent nagging. Tom tossed a chunk of beef to the cat prowling beneath his chair.

"How many of those are there?" Frietchie asked. "They keep moving."

"Uncle Shumba said there were between five and nine at any one time. Occasionally kittens are born and adults disappear."

"They get eaten by the goddamn coyotes," said Mr. Yee. "You can bet I'm never sleeping outside. I'm not turning myself into puppy chow."

"You don't have to sleep outside," Tom said wearily. Mr. Yee's bed, a large ornate construction once owned by a Chinese emperor, almost filled one of the bedrooms in the main house. Mr. Yee was too old to stay in one of the cabins. He needed help getting in and out of bed, and he demanded special treatment at all times. Thaís had been drafted to help him, but when she returned to the city Tom didn't know what they would do.

Other worries descended on him as he mechanically shoveled chili into his mouth. Cubby wasn't going to give up on the electric lines, and Tom knew that the town's power station wasn't big enough to supply the ranch. He hadn't thought it important at first—after all, the goal was to escape the Youth Patrol—but Cubby really wanted his computer. He said it would help him take over the government.

My God, Frietchie was batting her eyelashes at

Jeronimo! Tom realized it was her automatic reaction to any presentable male, but it was completely inappropriate. She was old enough to be his grandmother. Tom hoped Jeronimo hadn't picked up on the signals.

And how were they going to keep Bogomil occupied? The *Mhondoro* had said that the task was for the elders to solve, but Bogomil's muscle power had been too tempting to pass up. Now Tom realized that he'd made a mistake. What could you do with someone who went in for recreational bullying?

The only bright spot was Violetta. She was blissfully happy. The more crowded the house was the better she liked it.

In spite of his concerns, Tom slept extremely well that night and so did everyone else. Before retiring, Frietchie took a nude swim in the hot tub. She toyed with the idea of luring Jeronimo out, but rejected the plan. The poor darling had only been married a few months and she hated to spoil a fresh marriage.

The moon rose very late, casting a pale radiance over the ground. In the city a half-moon would hardly have been noticeable, but here in the desert it was like a beacon. It was enough to galvanize the coyotes. They complained to one another about the invasion of their territory. There were more humans than they had ever seen before and they didn't like it.

They circled the cabins and the main house. They tried and failed to get into the vegetable garden. They sniffed at the shed with the hens. Nothing pleased them and so they gave themselves up to outraged howls until the big daddy of all howls rose up and made them bristle with terror.

Bogomil had awakened. He remembered the wolves that had prowled outside his hovel as a child and how his great-grandmother had told him that wolf-blood ran in their family. That was why he need never fear these hunters of the night. Atavistic pleasure bloomed in Bogomil's mind and he left his bed, a heap of blankets near the back door, to snuff the air and let the vapor rising from a nearby hot spring fan over his hide. He gave tongue to a cry that had not been heard in the valley since the Dire Wolf went extinct millennia ago. But the coyotes recognized it. They fled to the safety of the Farther Hills.

The valley seemed asleep, but it was in fact extremely busy. Most of the activity was in Nigh where myriads of insects were enjoying the warm night. Midges, mosquitoes, crickets and katydids emerged. A great horned owl floated over the fields, watching for the bow-wave of mice in the grass. A cloud of moths surrounding a light exploded as they were dive-bombed by a bat. A dog barked half-heartedly at the half moon.

The plain of Far was quieter, but not deserted. Pygmy rabbits came out of their burrows to forage on sagebrush. They were soft little bundles of gray fur, nearly extinct in most of America, but abundant in Far. Many rare things had found the place to their liking. Pallid bats crept out of rocky crevices where they had spent the day. Unlike most of their kind, they didn't like hunting in the air. They preferred to scuttle along the ground after anemic-looking cockroaches and spiders.

A flock of ghost moths slowly rose and fell over a moon-bleached oval of earth. It was a gathering of males, known as a *lek*, engaging in a competitive mating display, much as teenage boys display for girls outside a high school. The moths flew in formation, seductively and hypnotically, watching for the females who were hiding in nearby sagebrush.

The moon inclined to the west and disappeared behind the Mirage Mountains. The eastern sky changed from starry blackness to deep blue. The creatures of the night returned to their burrows. Bogomil slunk back to bed exhausted, but happier than he'd been in years.

At dawn a weird sound broke out over Far. A mob of sage grouse males strutted in a salt pan, *lekking* their little hearts out. They fanned their tail feathers, swished their wings and swelled their chests to reveal air sacs disturbingly shaped like human female breasts. By inflating and deflating these interesting structures, they produced a call—*coo-oopoink!*—that made the hens nearby tremble with desire.

Thirty-One: *THE GOD BUNKER*

FRIETCHIE WOKE UP abruptly. What in hell was making that awful racket? *Coo-oopoink! Coo-oopoink!* It sounded like something being sick out in the desert. Frietchie got up but she couldn't see anything from the window except sagebrush.

After she showered and dressed, she went to the house to find Thaís slumped despondently in a chair. "Mr. Yee kept me up all night," the girl lamented. "Up and down, up and down. First he wanted hot chocolate and swore at me when I couldn't figure out how to light the stove. Then he wanted me to find his wallet so he could make sure none of the money was stolen. God, I can't wait to get back to the city!"

"I'll take care of him now," Frietchie said kindly. "You go and sleep."

"Watch his hands," said Thaís. "He says he's practicing an old Chinese therapy. Don't believe him."

Frietchie went into the kitchen and lit the stove. She soon had a pot of coffee going and the aroma drifted through the house, arousing sleepy murmurs here and there. By now the sun had broken over the Farther Hills and flooded the plain. It was such a bright, hopeful light that Frietchie felt happy in spite of leaving the salon she had worked on so hard.

Cubby wandered in, drawn by the odor of coffee. "I can't find the White Mountain," he said, breathing deeply at the steaming cup Frietchie handed him. "I put up the telescope, but there's nothing out there."

"There's probably too much mist, dearest. Drink your

coffee."

"It's the desert and there isn't any mist," said Cubby, ever logical.

He helped Frietchie put out bowls of cereal and glasses of orange juice. They would have to restock frequently, she realized, because there was no way to refrigerate anything. And the stove was too small to easily feed eleven people. Frietchie thought regretfully of her well-ordered kitchen in the city.

"Thaís! Thaís!" came a querulous voice from Mr. Yee's bedroom.

"On my way," called Frietchie. She found him lying down with his arms raised, like a spoiled infant waiting to be cared for. She was almost certain he could do better than that, but he *was* ninety.

"You aren't Thaís," Mr. Yee said accusingly.

"She needed a break." Frietchie got him to his feet and steered him toward the bathroom.

"From what?" Mr. Yee demanded. "She was asleep every time I called her. Ning and Fan used to take turns staying awake."

"I'll bet that was fun," Frietchie said. "Do you want them to come here?"

"They're taking care of my business, probably letting it go to hell, the lazy parasites."

Frietchie doubted it very much. All the Yee children seemed extremely industrious. They had been hired by the Willows Trust with a clear schedule as to salary increases. That had been her idea and she'd neglected to tell Mr. Yee about it.

She closed the bathroom door and waited. Some of Mr. Yee's slowness was due to age, but a lot of it was spite. What *were* they going to do with him when Thaís went home? Frietchie could hear Mr. Yee's stealthy movements. He was doing *tai chi* exercises in there, the bastard, just to make her wait.

No one was in a mood to hurry over breakfast. It was pleasant merely to sit around and savor the fresh air and good company. Phaedra had one of her migraines, but she had rallied enough to eat. "I think I saw the monk," Cezare commented. "He was letting chickens out of a shed. He ran when he saw me."

"He must be starving," Violetta said, concerned. "I wonder why he's so frightened."

"We could send Bogomil after him," said Atalanta. "Then he'd know what real fear looks like."

"Shame on you," Violetta reproved.

A chorus of mournful honks overhead told everyone that the Canada geese had returned. A few of them landed in the yard. They flapped their wings and hissed, and a second later one of the black cats streaked through a window with its ears flat against its head.

"That poor monk will starve if we don't do something," said Violetta. "By the way, where is Bogomil?"

"Asleep," Atalanta said. "He looked like he'd had a rough night. My inclination is to let sleeping Bogomils lie." Everyone agreed.

*   *   *

The Lineman *was* hungry, crouching in the shadow of a distant shed where water pipes were stored. He wasn't actually a monk, but a postulant since it wasn't clear that he understood the theology necessary to take the final step. And he didn't understand it. He merely appreciated the orderly lives the monks led. He didn't know what they kept trying to tell him and his eyes blurred when they handed him books. But he was good at copying what the others did.

Water was a much more pressing concern to him now. He'd managed to drink from the chicken's supply until that huge black man had yelled at him. Now they knew he was here, whoever *they* were. They'd drag him into the house and assault him the way the monks had after he'd torn up the monastery.

The monks hadn't understood. It wasn't a thunderstorm looming over the monastery. It was God. Once upon a time God had plucked the Lineman off the telephone wires for listening to whoopee talk and now all he could hear was *buzz buzz buzz*. God had scared him spitless, so naturally he went a little wild when the lightning started forking down.

There had been thunderstorms at the ranch, too, but the Lineman had constructed an underground room to escape them. He called it the God Bunker. He wanted to hide in it now, but unfortunately the entrance was too close to the house. It was next to the hot tub where that woman had been skinny dipping last night. The Lineman had watched her, entranced, until he thought about where God might strike him next.

He had returned to the chicken house just before that new creature turned up. The Lineman was used to coyotes. Their voices were perfectly clear to him, as were the high-pitched chirps of bats. In fact, all the insects and animals talked to the Lineman, telling him their hopes and fears. It was only humans he couldn't understand. But the new animal! The hair prickled on the Lineman's arms when he thought about it. Some large, new predator had made its way into the valley and the coyotes were utterly spooked.

The Lineman was very, very thirsty. He could drink from one of the ponds, but they were full of goose shit and would make him sick. As things stood, he would die of thirst anyway after a few days. He would dry up and the wind would blow his bones across the plain like all those other dry bones next to the Farther Hills.

Thirty-Two: *MANTIS MIND*

AFTER BREAKFAST Frietchie, Tom and Mr. Yee decided to go to town for supplies. Frietchie wanted to leave Mr. Yee behind, but the old man wanted to get out of the house. He was bored, he said. He knew life was going to be pissy at the ranch, but not *this* goddamn pissy.

"Drive slow," ordered Mr. Yee. "I want to see more than a fucking blur." And so Tom had slowed down to a crawl and Frietchie bit her lip in frustration.

The lake was beautiful, however, in slow motion. It was dotted with waterfowl and delicately rippled like a sheet of silk. It was also pleasant to watch the emerald fields of Nigh slowly approach. There were many orchards there: peaches, plums, apples and cherries. The soil was fertile and lavishly watered by streams that poured out of the Mirage Mountains. To the south (Frietchie hadn't noticed it the day before) a huge water wheel turned above the monastery.

"What's that for?" she wondered.

"Believe it or not that's where the town gets electricity," replied Tom. "They have hydroelectric power."

"Wow! Any chance we could get it at the ranch?"

"There's only enough for Nigh," said Tom. "Funny, I never thought of electricity having limits before. In the city you just plugged something in. Here you have to measure power like water. Each house gets so much and when it's gone, it's gone."

The town was just as pretty close up as it had been in the distance. There was a grocery store, an old-fashioned gas station and garage, a hardware store and many, many small work-shops. As Cezare had noticed, there was an astonishing number of crafts people—saddle makers, metal smiths, cobblers. Everywhere they looked there were more surprising little enterprises that had disappeared in the outside world. All the shops were surrounded by trees and grass.

A few townspeople waved at them as they drove to the grocery. "It's so friendly," said Frietchie. "I forgot how nice things used to be."

"Don't be deceived," said Mr. Yee. "I've seen movies about small towns like this. They all belong to a cult."

"You know, you're one of the reasons city life is so grim," said Frietchie and was rewarded with Mr. Yee's rat-chewing laugh.

They bought bags of fruit, fresh milk, bread and Mirage wine. The girl at the checkout stand smiled at them. Then, because the day was still young, they drove around the back streets. They found a library, a clinic and a school surrounded by a small park. Children were playing hide-and-seek among the trees.

"I haven't seen kids do that for years," Frietchie said. "In the city, schools have abolished recess altogether. Kids are force-fed information all day long and the instant they get home they're plugged into electronic equipment. Maybe that's why they turn out vicious."

"You can't let children run around in the city," Tom said. "There's too many molesters and drug dealers. If I idled my motor outside a schoolyard there, the cops would swarm all over me."

"*I* ran around like that," Frietchie remembered. "I had a lovely childhood."

"Why are there so few of the brats?" commented Mr. Yee.

He was right. Frietchie didn't know the population of the valley, but twenty children between the ages of five and ten were far too few. A bell rang and the children flocked back to their classrooms, laughing and chattering. The bright sound disappeared like a rain shower pattering across a lake.

Somewhat subdued, Tom, Frietchie and Mr. Yee drove north along the country lane, and soon they saw little shrines that could have come from Japan, carvings that might have been Chinese and rainbow flags that were definitely from San Francisco. Most of the land was taken up by agriculture, but a few small factories were clustered around a large building with rammed-earth walls and ornately carved wooden doors. In front was a garden with fanciful walkways, a pond and a curved bridge.

"Stop! Stop!" cried Mr. Yee. Tom pulled over and Mr. Yee slowly climbed out of the van. He walked to a bench facing the pond and sat down. Frietchie and Tom looked at each other. They were startled by the gentle expression on the old man's face.

"This is a moon-viewing garden," he said in a faraway voice. "My mother took me to a such a place when I was a boy. You see that curved bridge? Together with its reflection, it makes a moon shape. But at night it's even better. The fireflies come out. And when the moon rises, it is reflected on the water, surrounded by stars like heavenly fireflies."

"Why, Mr. Yee, you old softie," said Frietchie. She had never seen him look so vulnerable before.

"My mother used to recite poetry. She was quite well educated, but made a bad marriage. My father threw her out because she nagged him. This is the poem she told me in the moon-viewing garden:

> *Holding a jug of wine among the flowers,*
> *Drinking alone, not a soul keeping me company,*
> *I raise my cup and invite the moon to drink with me.*
> *Together, with my shadow, we make three.*"

Mr. Yee's face was wet with tears. "I left her in China. She died. I did not raise a gravestone for her or honor her memory."

"I'm sure she forgives you. Mothers do," said Tom softly.

A tall, thin, white man wearing a brown robe was coming toward them on one of the walkways. "Welcome, honored elder," he said, bowing to Mr. Yee. "I see you are enjoying our moon-viewing garden."

"Who are you?" Mr. Yee said suspiciously.

"I'm the abbot of the Buddhist monastery."

"Oh, goody. Monks."

"We aren't all monks," the man said, not taking offense. "We're a community of like-minded people who have found our way to this refuge. We come from all branches of Buddhism. You may have noticed our pottery factory and dairy. We live organically, walking carefully upon mother Earth. Would any of you like to visit our community center? I can offer you tea."

"Yeah, sure. Why not?" said Mr. Yee.

Frietchie saw to her delight that the community center was furnished with a restaurant, an old-fashioned soda shop and a central meeting hall with comfortable chairs. There were so many potted trees, it was as though a small forest had moved indoors, and birds flew in and out of open windows, unafraid of the people. In side rooms Frietchie could see monks praying, women sewing, and a play pen with two toddlers. Altogether, it was an attractive place.

The abbot, who was called Ginsberg Roshi, served them cups of tea that smelled like musty second-hand books. Frietchie and Tom bravely choked it down, but Mr. Yee spat it out. "What's in this stuff? Dead lamas?" he demanded. "Haven't you got anything better?"

"We grow our own traditional tea," the Roshi said.

"Take my advice and spray for stink bugs."

"Mr. Yee . . . " began Frietchie. How was she ever going to shut him up? The old man had a gift for picking fights.

But Tom took over then, describing how he'd inherited the Seaworthy ranch and asking genial questions about the Buddhist community. "We produce most of what we need right here," said the Roshi. "For other things, we trade dairy products and handcrafts with people in the valley."

"Don't you use money?" said Mr. Yee in a scandalized tone.

"As little as possible. Money can't buy happiness."

"Since when?"

The Roshi smiled gently. "A man dying of thirst cannot be satisfied with a mouthful of gold."

"Yeah, right. Quality of life is worth more than money, blah, blah, blah. A lot of things are worth more than money," said Mr. Yee.

"Not, apparently, to you."

"Yes, to me. I like poetry and looking at snow-covered mountains and drinking under a full moon. I like friends. These things can't be bought, except for some of the friends. But even more than that, although I hate to admit it, is the pleasure to be found in children." By the pained expression that flashed across the Roshi's face, Mr. Yee knew he'd struck pay dirt. "You two take a hike," he ordered Tom and Frietchie. "Go spin a prayer wheel or something. The abbot and I want to have a private conversation."

Tom, after an initial surge of anger, pulled Frietchie to her feet and stalked outside. "The Roshi must think Mr. Yee is some kind of Chinese sage," he fumed. "Did you see how he bowed to him? And ignored us?"

"He can look pretty spiritual," said Frietchie.

"Until he opens his mouth," said Tom.

Tom and Frietchie walked through a garden at the back of the community center. Tom maintained a stony silence and Frietchie watched him with concern. The Roshi *had* ignored them, and Tom was sensitive to slights. "I don't think the Roshi meant any insult," she said carefully. "My second husband became a Buddhist monk after I left him. He meditated in a cave for three years and could barely string two words together when he came out. But he was a much nicer person."

"I don't really worry about insults," Tom admitted. "After all, I had enough of them at Burton, Barton, Gerbill and Slithe. But it seems I have too much on my plate. I feel responsible for making everyone happy and I have something I don't know how to do." Tom fell silent. He'd been about to tell Frietchie about the old gods of Africa and stopped just in time. It wasn't that she wouldn't have understood. It was the feeling that the knowledge was secret, and might be harmed if pulled out into the light of day.

"If you need help on anything, I'm sure the rest of us can pitch in. You're not alone," Frietchie said warmly. Tom took her hand and they continued walking.

The paths were laid out like a maze, with trees alternately hiding and revealing views. It was cleverly done to make a small landscape look like an endless vista. Prayer wheels turned in the branches like so many well-oiled weather vanes. "How did Mr. Yee know about those?" said Tom at last, looking at the devices.

"Cubby says Mr. Yee knows everything about religion and poetry," said Frietchie. "What do you think he's up to in there? I hope he isn't making more enemies." They continued following the path, unknowingly treading the Tibetan letters of a prayer worked out in stone, while above and all around the wheels turned restlessly.

Back in the community center, the Roshi leaned toward Mr. Yee and spoke in a confidential tone. "There used to be several hundred of us, but our numbers have dwindled."

"Because you can't have kids," Mr. Yee said.

"Not many," the Roshi admitted. "I would welcome the advice of your advanced years." The sound of women in the sewing room murmured in the background. The laughter of the two toddlers echoed like birdsong.

"A family without offspring is like a dry tree waiting to blow over in a storm," said Mr. Yee.

"I know, and yet the highest path for mankind is to free oneself from the wheel of existence," argued the Roshi.

"That's okay for monks. They've already checked out of the hotel so to speak, but what about ordinary people? They *like* being on the wheel. They don't want to give up the pleasure of hearing the first cry of a baby boy, or even a girl."

Mr. Yee had the man now. He knew it. He'd been observing carefully in the town and along the road. There were adults in the shops and fields, there were adults everywhere, but almost no children. For some reason the numb nuts in this valley couldn't get it up.

Somewhere in the building, Mr. Yee heard the bumblebee drone of Tibetan lamas saying prayers and the clink of glasses in the restaurant. The juxtaposition of piety with commerce wasn't as jarring to him as it would be to Tom and Frietchie. It was Life with all its discordant features mixed up together.

"Have you ever heard of Ten Thousand Happiness Elixir?" said Mr. Yee, assuming a benevolent expression. "I invented it."

A profound silence fell. The Roshi was transfixed. Mr. Yee waited. He had perfected, early in his career, Mantis Mind Awareness. It was that quality of attention that looks like sleep but is in fact the zenith of predatory intent. The mantis does not pursue. It does not show impatience. It hovers at the still center of the turning universe. And eventually the business contract, property deal or woman comes within reach.

"*You* invented Ten Thousand Happiness Elixir?" said the Roshi. "I've been trying to order it from Luga Chuga—not for me, of course, but for the wider community. Unfortunately, we Buddhists don't have the required money."

"No problem," said Mr. Yee. "I can get as much as I like."

"I heard it was a secret Tantric recipe that allows a man to satisfy a hundred women."

Which could be true, Mr. Yee thought, over the average life span. There was no mention on the label of how *long* it would take for you to round up a hundred women.

"And that it contains a potent ginseng that only grows in a remote Tibetan valley. Does it really work?"

"Work? It puts the ram back in Rameses," Mr. Yee said. "Listen, I can get the stuff here within a week if we can work out a deal."

"What do you want?" said the Roshi.

Mr. Yee told him.

By the time Tom and Frietchie returned, Mr. Yee had attracted a crowd of young men and women. A full-scale party was going on, with chip dip and snacks from the restaurant. "Here's the second part of my plan," announced Mr. Yee, slapping Frietchie on the rump. She turned on him and pulled her punch at the last minute. He *was* ninety years old. "Men are only part of the problem," Mr. Yee told his audience. "They need objects worthy of their interest.

"Hear! Hear!" bellowed one of the men.

"Fortunately, Frietchie is the world expert on Tantric temptation."

Everyone cheered.

"What in hell are you up to?" Frietchie hissed into Mr. Yee's ear.

"I'm setting you up in the beauty business. Don't tell me you're going to be happy sitting in a rocking chair for the next twenty years. You're like me. You need a challenge. You're going to open up a salon in the middle of town and give beauty treatments to love-starved Buddhists and farm girls. I'll explain later."

It was impossible to hold a conversation over the din and so Tom and Frietchie gave in and joined the festivities. It was late afternoon before they managed to extract Mr. Yee—and then only for one night—for the old man had weaseled his way into the Buddhists' hearts. He was moving into their community. He would be a mentor (Frietchie snorted) and would be waited on hand and foot as befitted an honored elder.

The geese were already taking off for the fields of Nigh when they drove across the causeway. The lake was turning pink, and in the distance the White Mountain shone above the haze.

Frietchie had got over her initial anger at Mr. Yee. The longer she thought about it, the more sense his scheme made. The old man needed a lot of care and he wouldn't get it once Thaís went home. As for herself, she couldn't spend the rest of her life soaking in a hot tub. The local girls *did* need her, the poor ragamuffins. Mr. Yee with his usual astuteness had discovered a flaw in the Valley of Nigh and Far.

It was a dreamy place, a haven for contemplation. But it wasn't up to much in the sex department. Men lost themselves in gazing at the purple distances of Far. Even in the midst of daily chores—prying a stone out of a horse's hoof or baling alfalfa—they would stop and look toward the White Mountain on the edge of forever.

For it is a little-known fact that men do not really like excitement. Most of them want a tranquil existence with no surprises. Men, let's face it, want to drift along in happy amnesia without all the ferment women bring into their lives. And the women, if neglected long enough, let themselves slide into a bovine indifference.

Once there had been a theater and a dance hall. Once there had been a beauty salon. No more. The Buddhists had been full of vigor when they crossed the mountains, but the will to enter the dangerous arena of sex had faded. As it had throughout the whole valley. Only the sage grouse *lekking* in the salt pans and the ghost moths rising and falling in formation, kept the flame burning brightly.

This was about to change.

Tom, Mr. Yee and Frietchie were filled with a comfortable tiredness and a sense that the day had been well-spent. They looked forward to a peaceful evening. They didn't know what mayhem had broken out at the ranch during their absence.

Thirty-Three: *BOGOMIL SLIPS HIS LEASH*

VIOLETTA STARTED IT. She was worried about the monk. At first she hoped he'd gone back to the monastery. It was a fifteen mile walk, but perfectly doable, and so she sent Atalanta to check. No, the monk had not returned, said the Dominican abbot. And he wasn't a monk, only a postulant. And he wasn't a good postulant either. He had a tendency to slam his fist into a wall when the others talked—not that they talked much, but now and then even a monk needs to communicate.

And he had a thing about wires. He curled up in a ball when someone plugged in a lamp. During the thunderstorm, the abbot said, he hurled beds around like ping-pong balls and smashed dishes. Everyone called him the Wichita Lineman.

"The Wichita Lineman," murmured Violetta, her eyes wide. "Poor man, he doesn't even have a proper name."

"Mom, he trashed the monastery," said Atalanta. "He's dangerous and he's probably insane."

"He can't be all bad," her mother said. "Look how nice he kept this house—and the hot tub! He built that on his own initiative."

"I don't think monks are supposed to have hot tubs."

"He's not a monk yet, dear. He's a postulant. Anyhow, I don't see why monks can't have hot tubs. Frietchie says they're very good for your health."

Atalanta gave up the argument. Her mother saw good in everyone and she was completely unsuspicious. Frietchie's idea of things that were good for you would have uncurled Violetta's hair if she'd understood them. At that moment Bogomil staggered in, rumpled and filthy.

"*You* certainly had a restless night," Violetta said kindly. "I'm sure you'll feel much better with oatmeal inside you." She went off to the kitchen and Bogomil slumped over a chair. He stared at Atalanta with red-rimmed eyes.

Sweet Jesus, how are we ever going to leave Mom and Dad alone out here? thought Atalanta. *I wish Frietchie hadn't gone into town. She seems to be the only one who can order this monster around.* She heard Cezare and Jeronimo calling her and reluctantly left.

Cezare and Jeronimo were next to the hot tub, staring down into a hole. It had been covered with a door cleverly disguised with sagebrush, and Jeronimo had only found it when he tripped over the edge. "Is that a mine shaft?" enquired Cezare.

Jeronimo shone a flashlight into a large room at the bottom of a ladder. Light reflected off bottles and cans. A bed was jammed against a wall. "Looks like a hidey hole. Who'd need a thing like that out here?"

"The monk?" said Cezare.

"I can see water bottles, beef jerky and cans of stew"

Atalanta arrived and said she was worried about Bogomil.

"I don't think he's that dangerous," said Cezare. "Bogomil is like a pit bull. You feed him Spam, keep him chained up and throw him an occasional burglar. Besides, Frietchie warned him not to hurt anyone in the house."

"That doesn't exactly put my mind at rest," said Atalanta.

Meanwhile, Violetta had brought out a bowl of oatmeal with raisins and brown sugar for Bogomil. She gave him a spoon, but he ignored it and buried his face in the bowl, slurping for all he was worth. In two seconds he had licked it clean. In his dim mind (it was still prowling the plain by moonlight) Bogomil registered that the food wasn't quite satisfactory. It needed something more. Something wet. *Blood.*

"Would you like seconds?" Violetta inquired.

Rrrroooooooo, said Bogomil, scratching an ear with a long, dirty fingernail.

"I'll take that for a yes. A big fellow like you probably needs an omelet. Just you wait and I'll rustle one up." Violetta padded back to the kitchen.

Bogomil snuffed the air. Like his long-ago ancestor, the Dire Wolf, he had a supernatural sense of smell. He could smell lightning a hundred miles away. He could detect the progress of a herd of mastodons across a steppe. But most of all he could sense fear, and fear was pouring off something nearby—not Violetta, fortunately. She was humming contentedly to herself over the propane stove.

She brought out the omelet, flavored with bacon, and was gratified to see Bogomil polish it off with the same alacrity as he had the oatmeal. And then she remembered the Lineman. Poor man, he must be starving! Violetta caught her breath. Perhaps he was too weak to move!! Perhaps he was dying right now! "Bogomil, I need your help," she said, putting her hand on his shoulder.

He almost snapped at her, but deeply buried in his mind was the memory of Frietchie. She no longer appeared human to him, but took on the hulking persona of the ancestral female of his species, the Dire Bitch. The Dire Bitch snarled, displaying an impressive set of canines, and drove him from his intended prey. Bogomil fled whimpering down the long dark valleys of time.

"I'll find the Lineman and you can carry him to the house," Violetta said. She led Bogomil outside. The fear-smell leapt at him. The source was cowering behind a shed, its scent forming an outline that gave tongue to a thousand ancestral memories. Yes! This prey was Outside! It was permitted! The Dire Bitch would not punish him if he ate it!

Rrrroooooooo, howled Bogomil, lunging from beneath Violetta's hand.

Earlier that morning the Lineman had watched the van with Tom, Mr. Yee and Frietchie disappear in the direction of town. Then he saw Atalanta leave and return. By now the sun was high and his throat ached with thirst. He felt chills and when he moved lights flashed in front of his eyes. *Keawww*, said one of the hens, pecking near him. *Are you ill?* she asked.

I'm thirsty, answered the Lineman, figuring that the chicken couldn't help. But the hen trotted off to a garden hose and began dipping and warbling the way such creatures do when they've discovered a tasty insect. The Lineman understood and thanked her with his mind. *Buck-buck-buck*, she replied, acknowledging his gratitude. He looked around cautiously. Everyone was either in the house or working out of sight. He could hear a cluster of voices near the God Bunker.

He crept forward, grabbed the muddy nozzle of the hose and emptied its contents into his mouth.

Ahh! Relief! But only temporarily. The trickle of water only intensified his longing and so he followed the hose to the tap. In a trice he had it off and the tap open. He threw himself on the ground, letting the water gush over his face. It soaked his robe, but he didn't care. He was in a delirium of joy, drinking until he heard a noise over the cascading water.

Rrrroooooooo!

It was that new animal and it was coming for him! The Lineman leapt to his feet, but he was weighted down by his soggy robe and before he could escape the animal had him. They fought one another desperately, slipping and sliding in the mud. The Lineman tried to jab his fingers into the Beast's eyes. The Beast opened its jaws—

When Atalanta and the others heard Violetta scream, they ran to the back yard. Thaís and Phaedra came out of the house. They saw Violetta wielding a rake, trying to separate Bogomil and a strange man. "Mom!" screamed Atalanta. Her brothers pounced on the struggling men.

"Bad Bogomil!" yelled Cezare. "No eat! Frietchie angry." For it was clear to him that the ex-prison guard had slipped the fragile leash that had connected him to humanity.

The only word that penetrated Bogomil's skull was *Frietchie*, but it was enough. He dropped his quarry and fled. Heat waves blurred his shape as he pounded across the desert, and soon no one could tell which was sagebrush and which was man.

The Lineman slumped to the ground. Cezare and Jeronimo dragged him to his feet. He tried to flee, but they were too strong. *Please,* he begged them with his eyes. *Let me go to the God Bunker. I won't bother you.* But they couldn't understand him.

"Mom, are you all right?" cried Atalanta. Phaedra and Thaís hugged Violetta.

"I'm fine. Goodness, don't make a fuss over me. It's Bogomil and the Lineman we should worry about."

"They're both crazy," said Atalanta.

"Now dear," said her mother. "We mustn't judge anyone until we've walked a mile in his moccasins."

The sisters exchanged glances over their mother's head. There was no arguing with Violetta once she'd decided to take someone under her wing. "At least we got rid of one of them," muttered Phaedra, shading her eyes at the heat haze where Bogomil had disappeared.

"We haven't 'got rid' of anyone," her mother said reprovingly. "I'm sure Bogomil will come back when he's feeling better. Now what do we do about you?" She turned her big, welcoming smile on the Lineman, but to him it looked like a snarl.

"I say we take him back to the monastery," said Cezare.

"They don't want him," Atalanta said.

Violetta frowned. "That doesn't mean *we* have to throw him out. We certainly owe the poor soul something for looking after this place."

"Mom, he's got a bunker in the front yard. For all I know, it's full of grenades."

"Then we'll simply have to throw those nasty old grenades away," Violetta declared.

The Lineman stopped struggling and went limp. Going limp had made the monks stop beating him after he trashed the monastery, and it had worked on the cops in Luga Chuga. There were other cops in other places that were hazy in his mind, but all of them had stopped beating him when he went limp. They were working for God, of course, but fortunately they weren't as smart as God was. As soon as their guard was down he could make a run for it.

The black men dragged him to the front of the house, never loosening their grip, and one of the women went down into the God Bunker. The Lineman remembered a story he'd heard as a child, about a wily rabbit and a briar patch. *Oh, no no no. Don't throw me into that briar patch*, he said with his eyes. He must have communicated something because when the woman came out again, he was lowered into the God Bunker where he wanted to be.

Except that the ladder was removed and the hatch was left open. The Lineman didn't like that one bit (*oh, no no no*). If a storm blew up he'd be a sitting duck. Even now God's blue eye shone into the opening, never blinking, never sleeping. The Lineman retreated to his bed and pulled the covers over his head.

"I didn't find any grenades," said Atalanta, dusting off her hands, "but I did see some disgusting pictures."

"We can't keep him down there forever," Cezare said.

"We'll ask Dad about it when he gets home," his sister said.

Thirty-Four: *CUBBY MAKES A FRIEND*

AFTER BREAKFAST, Cubby had gone for a walk across the plain. He was puzzled by the absence of the White Mountain and thought he might be able to detect it better close up. The plain was much larger than he thought, however. He wasn't used to such open spaces and traveled a long way before he realized that the Farther Hills weren't getting much closer. He had gone quite a distance because when he looked back the ranch had shrunk considerably. The lake was a ribbon of blue against the misty green of Nigh, and the Mirage Mountains, cloaked in cedars, formed a barrier against the western sky.

Cubby wasn't worried. He knew it would be impossible to get lost with such easy landmarks. He noticed a line of ants carrying eggs. They were moving their nest, for whatever reason ants did such things—overcrowding, invasion, the craving for a more upscale neighborhood. They detoured around an alkaline pond steaming gently in the clear morning light. The plain was dotted with such ponds, some cool and amenable to fish, and some, like this one, fed by the runoff from a hot spring.

A band of brine flies pullulated at the edge and flew up at Cubby's approach. It was wonderful, he thought, how life flourished no matter how grim the setting. This water, for example, was close to 110 degrees. (One of Cubby's many skills was to gauge temperature accurately by sticking a finger into whatever it was.) Dark green bacteria formed a mat on the surface while at the bottom of the pond, where the temperature was hotter, red and orange microbes flourished.

The flies fed on the surface mat. They in turn were devoured by spiders that ran over the steaming mat to catch them. As long as the spiders kept moving they were safe from the heat, much as people who walk over hot coals are fine as long as they don't slow down.

"This reminds me of our trip to Mono Lake," said Gerbill, settling companionably on the ground beside Cubby.

"You're back," Cubby said, delighted.

"I intended to come earlier but Sybille vanted to explore the monastery. It is a splendid place, this valley. I feel quite young." And indeed Gerbill looked somewhere between the ages when he'd known Sybille and when he'd known Cubby.

"Do you remember the *cuchabee* patties we made for the lab?" Cubby asked.

"That vas even less popular than the spider soup."

The two scientists had spent a happy fortnight harvesting fly pupae. Tons of brine fly larvae and pupae grow on the shores of Mono Lake every year, and storm waves sometimes pile them up in heaps on the beaches. Long ago they had provided a rich food source for the Kuzadika Indians.

The Kuzadikas were also known as the *Monos*, or fly eaters, a label that didn't upset them because everyone liked eating flies. The pupae were gathered in nets and rubbed to remove the exoskeletons. The resulting morsels looked like grains of yellow rice.

Modern Americans don't understand how much work is involved in getting the food necessary to survive. The organization required to assemble a 2,000 calorie megaburger at a favorite fast-food restaurant is hazy in their minds. Not only is a half pound of hamburger with two slices of cheese covered with mayonnaise between sesame buns required, but also the farms necessary to grow cattle, to plant wheat, and to raise chickens for the eggs in the mayonnaise. You need refrigerators and ovens to store and process the ingredients. You need lettuce flown from Arizona and tomatoes from Mexico. You need airplanes fueled by oil pumped from surly Middle Eastern kingdoms. All these must be coordinated to satisfy the munchies in under ten minutes.

The Kuzadika Indians knew exactly where their food came from: Never-ending toil. There were no fat Kuzadikas.

How could you gain weight when you spent half your time chasing jackrabbits? Thus, the massive appearance of fly larvae, each one containing 12.4 lip-smacking calories of fat, was cause for wild celebration. The Indians mixed them with acorns, berries and grass seeds, and made *cuchabee* patties. Fried in fly fat, *cuchabee* patties are said to resemble pork rinds.

Cubby and Gerbill had made such a dish for the laboratory. By then all the scientists were wary of any snack the pair brought in, but there was always a new exchange student or secretary. Even they wouldn't have thrown up if Cubby had kept the list of ingredients to himself.

"Is that Bogomil?" said Cubby, squinting to make out the dark shape approaching them.

Gerbill, being dead, could detect the soul inside. "It is und it isn't," he said carefully. The ex-prison guard loped by with a gait suitable for long distance traveling. His tongue lolled and his eyes were fixed steadfastly on the Farther Hills. "I vould not try to stop him," the older man advised. "He is going where he belongs und good riddance."

Cubby was puzzled, but he was used to accepting Gerbill's opinions. "I should probably go back," he said.

"Race you," teased Gerbill and Cubby smiled. When they were both alive there was no question about who would win a race. The dead, however, are swifter than eagles. No one can outpace them, or should try.

Cubby walked back through the salt pans and sagebrush. By now the sun was high and he regretted not bringing a hat. The ranch slowly drew nearer. He saw the Seaworthy children washing vans in the back yard. Violetta was feeding a flock of chickens.

He made his way to the cabin and ran his fingers across the dust on the lab bench. Everything was covered with it. Cubby's computers and television were stored in plastic bags to protect them, their homeless little plugs trailing outside.

I've got to have electricity, he thought. The memory of the Alzheimer's patients nagged at him like a bad tooth. Also, there were the Senior Laws to get rid of and the government to overthrow. So many chores, so little time. He went outside again.

Strange. There was a hole in the ground next to the hot tub. Cubby could see a room below, with orderly shelves and a bed. Curious, he levered a ladder he found into the opening. It was wobbly, but far easier to navigate than the fire escape he had used in the city.

The dwelling—for it was clearly meant for occupation—had the closed, secret feel of an old house where generations of mice have made their home. Unlike the ranch above it was devoid of ghosts. In the main house Cubby always had the feeling that something was going on just around the corner. He knew what it was, of course—Tom's ancestors. They didn't show themselves openly to Cubby because their business wasn't with him. Gerbill had the same delicacy about appearing before strangers.

Cubby was extremely sensitive to atmosphere, an ability honed by decades of communing with insects. He could tell the mood of a beehive by listening to its hum. A chirping sound, for example, meant the bees were starving. A thin, high-pitched drone meant the queen was dead. Cubby could detect the nose-prickling smell of ant-fear and the acrid stench of lacewing rage. He understood the meditative mood of a grasshopper turned sideways to a rising sun. He knew now that the emotion permeating this underground room was despair.

Bogomil, by comparison, was only able to detect fear. Like the Dire Wolf, he reacted to signals that were of importance to him. His interior life was made up of simple building blocks: *Fear = prey.* And: *Things that are bigger than me = no prey.* Despair was too complex an emotion for his mind.

This complexity is what Cubby sensed at the bottom of the ladder. He saw a table and chair, an iron bedstead draped by an army surplus blanket—which was moving. It rose and fell as something beneath it breathed. *Keeawww?* said a hen, looking down into the opening. Cubby knew that she was concerned, too. Her head darted this way and that as she tried to make out the objects in the gloom. "Don't worry," Cubby told her. "I'm not going to hurt anything."

A corner of the blanket lifted and a pair of eyes in a bloodless face peered out. The Wichita Lineman and Cubby regarded each other with astonishment, but it was Cubby who recovered first. "I'm sorry. I should have knocked," he apologized.

*　　*　　*

When the Lineman heard the ladder being put down, he scrunched himself up as small as possible. If only he'd thought to hide under the bed or had made a tunnel, like the one he'd used to escape from the asylum. Now they were going to kill him. In the asylum they'd killed him again and again with electricity, not realizing that God had been there before them. Once you've been zapped by God nothing else makes an impression.

After the Lineman died he came back to life and for a short period he understood human voices again. "Who's the President of the United States?" they kept asking him. "Who's the President of the United States?" Why were they bothering him with such stupid questions? Couldn't they look it up? Their voices quickly faded into a monotonous hum.

Now the Lineman heard someone come down the ladder and pause, no doubt deciding how to attack him. *Keeawww?* said a hen from up above. *What are you up to?*

But then—miracle of miracles—someone answered: "Don't worry. I'm not going to hurt anything." It was a real voice, not the buzz of human conversation. It had a bell-like clarity that made the Lineman shiver all the way down to his toes. He peeked out and saw a thin, elderly man with the sweetest expression he'd ever seen. "I'm sorry," said the elderly man. "I should have knocked."

The Lineman came all the way out of his covers. *No kill*, he pleaded.

"I wouldn't hurt a flea," replied Cubby. "Especially a flea. It's a very interesting animal. Did you know it can leap thirty-five times its height?"

No, I did not know that, said the Lineman, charmed.

"I imagine you're the monk everyone's been talking about. Violetta's been worried about you—well, we all have. My name's Cubby, by the way. Would you like me to get you something from the kitchen?"

Yes, please, the Lineman said.

Cubby climbed the ladder and ambled to the kitchen. It didn't surprise him that someone would choose to live in a dark, underground hole. Tarantulas did it all the time, except in the fall when the males roamed in search of mates. Those intrepid romantics could travel for miles, occasionally winding up as eight-legged decorations on the freeways.

Cubby made grilled cheese sandwiches and collected bottles of orange juice. "Having a picnic?" called Phaedra from an easy chair in the living room. The fine weather was making her feel ill.

"Something like that," said Cubby.

"You'd better wear a hat. It's really hot out there."

But in fact the God Bunker was delightfully cool. The Lineman devoured his cheese sandwiches gratefully. Cubby ate more slowly and carefully. He saved the bread crusts. "For the hens," he explained.

They'll like that, said the Lineman, putting aside one of his own.

Cubby inspected the pictures on the walls. They were mostly underwear ads, spotted and mildewed where ground water had seeped in. "Do you like underwear?" he enquired.

The Lineman was deeply ashamed until he realized there was no censure in Cubby's voice. *Yes*, he replied. *The pictures make me feel as though I have visitors.*

"I used to live alone," Cubby said sympathetically. "The only visitors I had were cockroaches and dead people until I met Frietchie. She's in town now, but I'll introduce you when she gets back."

Is she the one who was in the hot tub last night? said the Lineman with a glimmer of interest.

Cubby nodded. "She really likes hot tubs. We all want to thank you for the way you've kept things up. Tom had us convinced the ranch was a mess, but you've turned it into a resort."

The Lineman basked in the praise.

"Well, I should get back to the house. Violetta wants me to check for weevils in the pantry."

After Cubby left, the Lineman went back to bed, but his mind was no longer in turmoil. With the ladder in place he could put the top down if a storm blew up. He mused happily on projects he'd planned around the ranch—a greenhouse for winter crops, a larger water tank, a perimeter fence. He would sleep in the bunker and leave the rest of the property to the new tenants. One of the hens came to the opening to ask whether he was all right, and the Lineman brought her down for a feast of bread crumbs.

Thirty-Five: *THE VALLEY OF DRY BONES*

VIOLETTA HAD SPRAYED the curtains with water to cool the desert air. It was too hot to work outside, and everyone had congregated in the living room to wait out the heat. The fetishes swayed gently from the ceiling and the cats lay panting on the floor, their bellies turned up to catch an errant breeze.

"Poor darling," Violetta said sympathetically to Phaedra, who had a wet cloth on her head. "Is it really bad?"

"Yes, Mom. It's really bad. If only it would rain!"

"I don't think it rains much here," said Violetta, looking out at the shimmering desert.

When the shadows lengthened and the geese began to depart, they heard Tom's van in the distance. "I hope he brought ice," said Atalanta.

"Where would we keep it?" said Cezare. They forced themselves to rise and that was when Atalanta noticed the ladder sticking out of the God Bunker.

"Damn! He's escaped!" She saw the Lineman in the distance herding hens toward a shed. He waved at her. Uncertainly, she waved back. "Shouldn't we try to catch him?"

"It's too hot," said Cezare. By now Tom's van was rolling to a stop in the front yard.

Frietchie hopped out. "You'll never guess what happened," she exulted. "Mr. Yee's moving in with the Buddhists and I'm opening a beauty salon. God, I'm exhausted! All I want is to curl up with a good author—oh, and we've brought Tsingtao. I think it's still cold."

"Hey! Come and get me out of the van," complained Mr. Yee. "I'm the one who made everything happen." Cezare lifted him down. "Where's Thaís? I want a bath."

"They're going to love you in the Buddhist community," said Frietchie.

Jeronimo and the others unloaded supplies, including a stack of pizzas picked up just before leaving town. "Who's that by the shed?" said Tom.

"Oh, Dad, you have no idea what's been going on," Atalanta began. "Bogomil went crazy and tried to kill the monk, only he isn't really a monk. He's a postulant. Everyone calls him the Wichita Lineman. Mom tried to get between them with a rake and Bogomil took off. Then the Lineman acted weird so we put him into a cellar, but somehow he got out—"

"Whoa! One thing at a time," said Tom, holding up his hand. "You say Letta tried to get between them with a rake?"

"I'm fine," said Violetta. "It's Bogomil we have to worry about."

"Where did he go? When?" said Tom, trying to sort things out.

Atalanta pointed toward the White Mountain. "He left about eight hours ago."

"Jesus Christ! It's a desert out there. Didn't anyone go looking for him?"

"Dad, he went postal," said Atalanta. "He was *growling* and he tried to bite out the Lineman's throat. I'm glad he's gone. I hope the coyotes eat him."

"He's a human being," said Tom. "You can't leave him out there to die."

"The jury's out on whether he's human," Atalanta said sullenly.

By now Cubby had wandered into the front yard, slightly bleary from an afternoon nap. He saw Jeronimo unloading crates of beer and Phaedra carrying a stack of pizza boxes to a table. The odor of sausage and hot cheese drifted out.

"I saw Bogomil this morning," he remarked, causing Tom and the others to turn around. "I think he was going to the Farther Hills. Gerbill told me to leave him alone."

"*Gerbill* told you that," emphasized Tom. By now he

was used to Cubby giving bulletins from dead people.

"He said Bogomil was going where he belonged and good riddance." Cubby yawned. "That pizza smells really good. Can I share some of it with my new friend?"

"What new friend?" Tom said warily.

"The monk," said Cubby.

"So you're the one who let him out," Atalanta accused.

"I didn't know he was supposed to be in. Anyhow, he likes living underground. He'll go back when he's finished herding the chickens." Cubby helped himself to food.

"We should drink the beer while it's still cool," said Frietchie. "I've known Bogomil a long time and if anyone knows how to survive in the wild it's him."

"It's just not right," Tom said, looking unhappily at the White Mountain. Shadows had crept across the plain and only a slim band of brightness lay between them and the Farther Hills. "I won't be able to settle unless I look for him. I'll open a can of Spam and see if I can lure him into the van."

*   *   *

What in hell am I getting into? thought Tom a few minutes later, driving along the road to the east. A plume of dust rose behind him, dark against the sunset, and before him the way was a pale ribbon scarcely distinguishable from the surrounding desert. It deteriorated as he went on. Dry washes appeared suddenly and more than once he had to detour through sage brush. The Farther Hills faded to purple, but the White Mountain still shone like a beacon against the evening sky.

Tom fished a slice of pizza from the box on the seat next to him. The Spam, as yet unopened, sat on the floor along with a bottle of vodka—although judging by Bogomil's behavior that morning, he might have graduated to bigger game. For the first time Tom felt a twinge of uneasiness. Just how was he going to cope with Bogomil Rex if the Spam ran out before they got back to the ranch?

I should have brought Frietchie, he thought, but she'd been so tired. Dealing with Mr. Yee all day would take the starch out of anyone. The old tyrant had ordered his special chair, the one with carved dragons, to be dragged into the yard. From there he had messily devoured pizza, stripping off the top and throwing aside the bread portion.

What was that? Something darted in front of the van and Tom swerved into deep sand. The wheels spun uselessly as he tried to reverse.

Great.

He would have to find branches for traction. Except that branches seemed to be scarce in this part of the desert. Scrubby sagebrush made hardly any difference to the tires and Tom, sighing, got out a machete and a heavy-duty flashlight. The sky was brighter in the Farther Hills than he expected. Even so, he turned on the van's emergency beacon, to be sure of finding his way back.

Tom thought he saw junipers in a fold of rock ahead. The terrain was made of friable granite filled with many unexpected holes and he nearly fell more than once. When he finally reached the trees, they were too tough to cut, and he heard something slither through the gravel. He shone his light around. Nothing. But beyond the grove was a trail going up to a crag that still caught the sunset light.

What makes a trail in such a deserted spot?

At the top, temptingly, were pieces of wood that looked exactly right to place under the back wheels of the van. Tom looked around to check the position of the beacon. It was farther away than he thought, a dot of security in an otherwise gray (and turning grayer) wasteland. He continued on. The trail was clear enough, although covered with scree, but on one side was a rock wall and on the other a sheer cliff. *I should go back*, thought Tom. The odd thing was that having embarked on this course he felt impelled to go on. It was as though he were being drawn toward some conclusion.

Just before the top his feet slid out from under him. The machete went flying and the flashlight fell, but he managed, by slamming himself onto the ground, to grab it before it rolled over the side.

Great.

Tom lay on the scree, trying to stave off panic. What would have happened if he'd fallen off the cliff? How long would it have taken for anyone to find him? Blood dripped from his forehead and onto the dirt. *Head wounds always bleed a lot*, he told himself. *It's no biggie.*

A coyote barked somewhere in the juniper grove. It was answered by another. How big were coyote packs, or did they run in packs? Did it matter? If they found a food source wouldn't they all pile in together like buzzards over a dead cow?

Tom carefully got to his hands and knees. He was light-headed and didn't trust himself to stand, and now he saw that the dry wood he'd glimpsed at the top of the crag was in fact bones. Big ones. He crept forward, fascinated and alarmed at the same time. The flashlight beam bobbed ahead of him. Night was finally settling in and the twilight seeped away into the western sky.

They were the leg bones of some large beast that had struggled to this spot, trying to escape a predator Tom could only guess at. With them was the scattered rubble of a life, bits of fur, shreds of flesh, a horn. But most of it was bones. Tom connected them.

The leg bone connected to the knee bone, the knee bone connected to the thigh bone. Tom shone his flashlight into the gorge and saw that it was full of skeletons, thousands of them flowing up the valley, going all the way up to the White Mountain. It had to be a hallucination. His head was throbbing and his eyes went in and out of focus.

The bones were of all sizes and shapes, and among them bobbed (but of course they weren't really bobbing, that was a hallucination) skulls. Most of these were the elongated heads of wild sheep, but some were rounded and intelligent-looking.

Rrrroooooo! said a voice far off in the night. Excited yips rose all around as the animals acknowledged the *Übercoyote* that had entered their realm.

Tom slid down the slope with the leg bones and flashlight clutched to his chest. He crashed through the junipers and ran, tripping and cursing over the ragged granite. He jammed the bones under the back wheels of the van and—after a heart-stopping second when he heard the bones crack—jolted the van out of the sand pit and back onto the road.

He stopped briefly, panting. Sweat, or perhaps blood, dripped down his face and his heart thudded. There was one last task to perform before he could return with a clear conscience.

He got out and opened the can of Spam. He perched it on a rock as an offering, with the bottle of vodka by its side.

When Tom returned to the ranch he found everyone waiting anxiously, and Violetta responded with heart-warming alarm to the wounds on his face. "I think Cubby's right," she said as she dabbed his forehead with disinfectant and kisses. "Bogomil is where he belongs."

"It was actually Gerbill's opinion," said Cubby, a stickler for accuracy.

Thirty-Six: *DEAR AVATAR*

MR. YEE LOOKED around with pleasure at his new dwelling in the Buddhist community. It had ample space for his possessions and, most importantly, it had electricity. He was also supplied with a Jacuzzi, a radio (the valley did not get TV) and a pair of satisfyingly meek servants. Okay, they were supposed to be volunteers, but in Mr. Yee's mind anyone he could dominate was a servant. Not like that lizard-tongued Thaís who refused to give him back rubs in the middle of the night. These young women were totally respectful.

"Make me tea," he told them. "Not that shit that tastes like Chairman Mao's sneakers. I want vintage *pu erh*. You'll find the canister in the kitchen. Heat the pot first."

The two scurried off. Mr. Yee stretched comfortably in his cushioned chair. He contemplated his favorite pictures on the wall—a sage meditating among misty mountains, Li Po raising a wine cup to the moon, Miss Shanghai in a bikini. All his favorite things were here and the Ten Thousand Happiness Elixir was stored in a safe, to be doled out as Mr. Yee saw fit. Life was good.

And yet he missed the ranch. He missed the lively conversation and Frietchie's stimulating presence. *Ai-ya!* You didn't need Ten Thousand Happiness Elixir with her around. Most of all, he missed Cubby. How that man could cut through to the things that really mattered! His words appeared simple but, as Lao Tzu said so long ago: *The sayings of the great sages are ordinary.*

Once, when Mr. Yee was trying to explain how the government should be run, Cubby interrupted him with, "Did you know that a cockroach can only run a short distance without over-heating? It doesn't matter how motivated the insect is, it begins staggering and follows an erratic path."

Some people might have thought that Cubby had been wool-gathering, but Mr. Yee knew better. The man was actually saying, *It is through not meddling that the empire is won.* In other words, if you tried to control the government by force, you became over-heated like the cockroach and followed an erratic path.

Cubby constantly brought Mr. Yee up short with jewels of wisdom. It was his idea to construct a shrine to Mr. Yee's mother, and the old man felt happy every time he visited it. He burned incense and paper representations of all the things his mother needed in the spirit world—houses, clothes, money. For the first time in many years he felt a lessening of the sorrow he experienced whenever he thought of her.

The tea was acceptable and Mr. Yee did not spit it out. "One of you fire up the laptop," he commanded the women. He adjusted his glasses and read the latest letter from the Buddhist flock.

Mr. Yee was not only the supplier (or *pusher,* as Frietchie referred to it) of Ten Thousand Happiness, he provided counsel in a newsletter distributed to the Buddhist community of the United States. His words were taken by road to Luga Chuga on the weekly runs to pick up elixir. His column was titled *Dear Avatar* and offered advice to the elderly.

For there was no point imparting wisdom to the young, whose brains were like kitty litter and incapable of absorbing any-thing but shit. What young people needed was a swift kick up the backside. Then maybe they'd catch on that one day they, too, would be old and the Senior Laws would apply to them.

Mr. Yee took a deep breath to clear his mind, and began reading:

> *Dear Avatar,*
>
> *My daughter Melissa is the single mom of three chil-dren. She is unemployed and for the past five years has lived with my husband and me. Our house is very small, but we love her and our grandchildren. The problem is that she brings strange men home every night. When that happens she insists that we go to bed straight*

away. It doesn't matter whether we've had dinner or not. The minute she arrives we have to disappear. Also, I'm afraid Melissa's friends aren't as honest as they should be. The last one stole my husband's Purple Heart medal and we later saw it for sale on the internet. Sadly, Melissa's attitude has communicated to her children. They call us ca-ca head and poo-poo face if we don't obey them. It has made us feel quite depressed.

Should we move into an old folks home?
Mama Bear in Minneapolis

Yee took a swig of tea and proceeded to answer the letter.

Dear Mama Bear,

You don't seem to know much about the habits of bears. After two years they kick their offspring out of the den. Not only that, Papa Bear eats the cubs if he runs into them. My advice is to call the vice squad and tell them Melissa is running a brothel. This serves two purposes: Not only will she end up in the slammer, but the welfare department will take those ca-ca faced brats away. Old people deserve a nice, quiet retirement without parasites sucking the life out of them.

Yours in Buddha,
The Avatar

Mr. Yee smiled. When you had the genius touch, you had it. He could still shed a little sunlight into people's lives. He told the women that he wished to do *tai chi* in the garden and they respectfully cleared a path for him. Soon he was moving harmoniously under the shade of a wisteria vine, the prayer wheels whirling vigorously in the branches around him.

*   *   *

Violetta helped Frietchie set up her new salon. Frietchie had offered to do another make-over for her, but Violetta had refused. She said it made her nervous having every stray tomcat follow her down the street when the only person she was interested in was her own dear Tom. And so Frietchie had limited herself to exchanging Violetta's sneakers for sandals and her muumuu for a flowing caftan.

In fact, the new social life Violetta was experiencing gave more of a glow to her skin than any beauty treatment. Now she contentedly swept, dusted and arranged the furnishings of the new salon. She would not work there permanently—a pair of photogenic young men had been hired for that.

"Care for a movie tonight?" enquired Frietchie.

"A movie?" cried Violetta, who'd been confined to TV for years.

"Mr. Yee says we need a place for young couples to meet. He discovered where the old theater was and the Buddhists have been cleaning it up. Tonight is just a trial run to see if the popcorn machine works."

"Popcorn," murmured Violetta, remembering the exquisite pleasure of digging her fingers into its hot, buttery depths. The memory of a neon-lit palace wafted into her mind. It had been a summer night and the sky had been full of stars. You could still see stars in the city then

"Violetta?" said Frietchie.

"Oh! I'm sorry. I'd love to go. The kids are busy packing and I'd only get in the way."

"You'll miss them, won't you."

"They have their own families, except Phaedra. She's staying, although I'm worried about her migraines. We've offered to help out at the town school. I'm teaching gardening. It's so inspiring to watch kids dig vegetable beds and get their hands muddy."

Frietchie shuddered, thinking of grubby fingerprints all over her new salon furniture.

That evening, as the sun slid behind the Mirage Mountains and the fields turned a deeper green, the two women strolled to the new movie theater. The Buddhists had painted the front in Dayglo colors and the marquee was outlined in Christmas tree lights.

Only a few people were there on its inaugural night—those who had worked on it and a few shy couples from the farms. The interior still smelled of paint and only half the seats were repaired, but Frietchie could see how beautiful it would be when finished. Violetta got herself a huge bucket of popcorn and at the last minute Mr. Yee was carried in by his caretakers. They brought his special chair and he insisted on being in the center of the theater where he would block the view of several seats behind him.

"I'm sick of listening to hillbilly music," he grumbled to Frietchie and Violetta. "That's all I can get on my goddamned radio."

"Poor you," Frietchie said. "At least you can plug it in."

The lights flickered. The red velvet curtains drew back, releasing a fume of dust, and the movie started. The Roshi had found a trove of old films and the evening began with Roadrunner cartoons. Wile E. Coyote, strapped onto Acme jet-powered roller skates, sailed off into the Grand Canyon. This was followed by an old newsreel from the 1950s. It showed a group of children hiding under their desks during an atom bomb drill. *Always wear dark glasses when looking at atom bombs,* the teacher warned them.

"Isn't it strange that we don't get news here?" Frietchie remarked while the main feature was being loaded. "This town is in a time warp."

"That's why it's so nice," said Violetta. "Cubby says that civilizations decline because people keep tinkering with perfection. Maybe the citizens of Nigh and Far knew when to stop."

"Are they citizens of anything?" Frietchie wondered. "They never talk about the outside world. I never hear about elections or the Senior Laws—"

"Thank God for that!"

"I know I shouldn't complain, but sometimes I feel like one of Cubby's ghosts."

"The Mirage Mountains block TV signals," Mr. Yee told them. "You could get TV with a satellite dish, but no one here is interested enough to put one up."

The movie started while Mr. Yee was speaking and several people tried to shush him. "What? I can't have a conversation with my friends?" he said loudly. "Who made you president of the United States?"

The main feature was in French with subtitles. There was a groan of disappointment in the theater, to which Mr. Yee retorted, "I guess you bozos don't know how to read." But in fact, the plot was so simple no one needed a translation. It was a movie from World War II called *La Cigale*, or *The Cicada*.

"Good thing Cubby isn't here," whispered Frietchie. "He'd give us a lecture on bugs."

"Oh!" said Violetta, squeezing Frietchie's arm. "I know that actress!"

Frietchie was amazed to see Josephine Baker dancing across the screen, wearing nothing more than a few palm fronds. Josephine Baker was Frietchie's role model. She enjoyed every little drop of honey that life dripped onto her willing tongue and was an inspiration to all free-spirited ladies. Frietchie had watched every one of her movies. This one, however, was new.

It started, as all Baker movies did, with the actress cavorting through an African landscape. Her vitality leapt out at you from the screen. You knew that someone like her could never die and that she had simply danced beyond the blue horizon where her nakedness would never suffer another goose bump.

"Just listen to her voice," murmured Violetta.

Frietchie had forgotten how beautiful the actress's voice was. Generally, what you noticed was the gratuitous nudity, but when Baker sang there was so much feeling in it that you got a knot in your throat. *La Cigale* was about a child of nature who was whisked out of her idyllic African setting and plunked down in a depressing Parisian slum.

Baker made her living washing sheets in an underground laundry, while her brutal husband drank away everything she earned. She no longer sang or danced. She was exiled from sunlight as surely as her namesake, the cicada, was exiled to a twilight lasting seventeen years.

But then the Nazis invaded France. After they shot Baker's husband (cheers from the audience) Josephine suddenly came to life. She whisked up all the local children and led them to freedom through the French countryside. (She entertained them at night by singing and dancing because you simply can't have a Josephine Baker movie without singing and dancing). There, a sea captain took them back to Africa. The last scene was of Baker in her old village, surrounded by a mob of rainbow-hued children.

People drifted out of the theater in ones and twos. Mr. Yee made his slow way to the front while his caretakers dutifully carried the chair behind. "Tell Cubby to visit me," he called to Frietchie and Violetta.

The women waited outside for Cezare to pick them up. Violetta still felt spangled with happiness. Frietchie was uncharacteristically silent.

"I wonder if I'll ever see Africa," Violetta said, putting on a sweater. Several weeks had passed since they had arrived in the valley, and the nights were growing cooler. "Tom used to talk about it, but we never went."

"What did you think of the movie?" Frietchie asked.

"I loved it! Oh, I know it was a silly plot, but it made me happy."

"Josephine Baker didn't make it," said Frietchie.

"Of course she did. That was her on the screen."

"I've seen everything she was in and read all her biographies," said Frietchie. "This was the film she wanted to make and never did."

Violetta drew the sweater tighter against the evening chill.

"I don't know what's going on," said Frietchie slowly, "but something about this valley isn't quite real. Look how neatly everyone has settled into a role, like we're characters in a movie *we* always wanted to make. Tom has the ranch. You'll soon be surrounded by children at the school. I'm uplifting the manhood of the valley one makeover at a time. Mr. Yee is writing those spiteful *Dear Avatar* columns. Probably even Bogomil is happy devouring antelopes."

"Cubby isn't happy," Violetta said.

Frietchie paused, thinking. "You're right. He can't find anyone to bring electricity to the ranch. And he says he needs the internet and TV as well, to accomplish his mission."

Violetta laughed softly. "You don't really think he can overthrow the government?" Cezare had stopped across the street and the two women walked toward him.

"If it was anyone else, I'd say no. But with Cubby you never know," said Frietchie, opening the door for her friend. "He's awfully persistent."

Thirty-Seven: *THE THUNDERSTORM*

M R. YEE WAS touchingly grateful for Cubby's visit and immediately ordered the women to make tea. "I have a new kind, harvested only last week," he said. "*Ta ma de*! You brewed it too long!" he bellowed, spitting out the liquid a woman had brought to him. "Try again! I said thirty seconds and I mean it." She fled to the kitchen.

"You shouldn't yell at people," Cubby said mildly.

"You're right. It's bad for my blood pressure. What do you think of my new computer?" Mr. Yee proudly displayed the state-of-the-art equipment he'd ordered to write his column. *Dear Avatar* was becoming a nation-wide hit. It gave Mr. Yee bragging rights with all his relatives and business rivals.

"I hope it works better than mine," Cubby said. "I tried accessing the internet from town and failed."

Mr. Yee looked uneasy. "Yeah, I noticed that. There's no internet here. I have to send everything out by car." The tea reappeared from the kitchen and this time the old man passed a cup on to Cubby. "Taste that. Smooth as a virgin's thigh. You pick newly opened buds at sunrise and they have to be used within two weeks."

Cubby sipped appreciatively. There were many secrets science hadn't explained, many of them based on the delicate interplay of organic molecules. The aging of wine, for example, or of cheese. It wasn't just a matter of sloshing chemicals together and getting instant results. (Although the flavor of Yee's tea *did* depend on instant results. It was a matter of catching youth on the wing.) For most things patience was required. Time worked its slow magic on people, too. The older they got, the more satisfying they were.

Up to a point.

As happened a dozen times a day Cubby remembered the Alzheimer's patients. If only he could explain to them why they were afraid, that what was happening was a gradual lightening of accumulated baggage. In the end they would be as clear as water. They would be ready to step over the blue horizon.

"I can't get my work done," Cubby said, as though Mr. Yee knew what had been passing through his mind. But Mr. Yee did understand. It was the one topic to which Cubby returned again and again.

"The Roshi says that our isolation protects us," the old man explained. "This valley is a sanctuary for a way of life that has vanished from the rest of the country. It's a place for people who don't fit in. *Are you too tall, too short, too gloomy, too happy. We have pills to make you like everyone else. Are you too old? Do we have a hospice for you!* So far the fucking do-gooders have stayed on their side of the mountain. They haven't tried to haul us off to their gulags, where they can pump us full of drugs and blast our frontal lobes with electricity."

"Shock therapy," said Cubby. "Do you suppose that the Wichita Lineman—?"

"I'm sure of it," said Mr. Yee. "He's a certified gulag graduate. Once, maybe, he was merely eccentric, the square peg that didn't fit. He has his collection of underwear ads, remember."

"The Lineman says they make him feel like he has visitors."

"Yeah, right. The kind that charge by the hour. He might really have been a lineman because he has one hell of a burn scar. But when the do-gooders got him to the gulag they gave him worse scars, the kind you can't see because they're inside. Now he's really a dingbat. Not dangerous, though. Not like Bogomil."

"Bogomil got a bighorn sheep the other night," Cubby remarked. "Tom found the carcass."

"I hope he gets a cow and the farmers shoot him. Would you like to hear my latest *Dear Avatar*?" said Mr. Yee.

"Yes, please," said Cubby.

Mr. Yee pulled out yesterday's column.

Dear Avatar,

For years we nurtured our children's self-esteem and did everything we could to empower them. We negotiated bedtimes and household chores (although I must admit they never did any). We lived to make them happy. Unfortunately, they turned into nasty, lazy, insulting, little brutes that made every second of our lives miserable. When we complained to the school psychiatrist, she said we were being too judgmental and prescribed tranquillizers.

Now our children are grown and have kids of their own. They say we messed up their lives and that they are too emotionally damaged to take on the task of parenting. Therefore, we must make amends by taking over the responsibility. They dumped all five grandkids on our doorstep. Dear Avatar, the oldest is only six! We can't face another fifteen years of tranquillizers.

Pooped Out in Palo Alto

"You'll like my answer," said Yee. "I mention bugs in it."

Dear Pooped,

Asking a child's opinion about anything is like asking Hitler if he wants another slice of Poland. Children are ravening beasts. They aren't even human until they reach the age of forty. Here are the Avatar's suggestions for dealing with them:

First of all, teach them fear. At a very early age instill a sense that all hell will break loose if you are disturbed in any way. Smash the less expensive toys as a demonstration. Remind the little snots that the boogeyman works for you, and that only you can get him out from under the bed. You may compliment them for subservient behavior, but don't make a habit of it.

Remember that your word is law. Bedtime is when you say it is. Chores are a natural duty, in repayment for the gift of life. Insure that they understand that this debt can never be fully repaid. There's no such thing as being too judgmental.

Once the little ones' spirits are broken, you,

as king and queen bee of the family hive, can sit back and enjoy a tranquil old age. P.S. If you can't face parenthood a second time you can always dump the brats anonymously on someone else's doorstep.
 Yours in Buddha,
 The Avatar

"Strictly speaking, there are no king bees," said Cubby. "Drones exist solely for procreation and are thrown out of the hive in winter."

"Sounds like the average marriage to me. Anyhow, the central message is good," said Mr. Yee.

"No it isn't. It's wrong to frighten children." Cubby had fond memories of his own childhood when all his relatives had devoted their lives to making *him* happy. "Dumping kids on doorsteps . . . that's going too far."

"Do you really think so?" said Mr. Yee, worried. Of all the people in the world, only Cubby's opinion mattered to him. "What would you do with five brats?"

"Love them, I guess."

Mr. Yee smiled tenderly. That Cubby! What would he do with five kids? He didn't know the first thing about child-rearing, but the Immortal's heart was in the right place. "I'll update my answer in the next column," Mr. Yee promised. "I'll put in something about love."

That would be nice," said Cubby.

*   *   *

Phaedra was thirty, unmarried, and between jobs, and so there was no compelling reason for her to return with the others. Violetta was pleased of course, and took her along on visits to the grade school, but Phaedra wasn't particularly fond of small children. She had a make-over at Frietchie's salon and reacted in much the same way as Violetta had to the overwhelming male attention.

She was waiting—what *was* she waiting for? She didn't know, but something made her hesitate every time she tried to go back to the city.

Phaedra took a pan of brownies out of the new wood-fired oven and put it on a picnic table to cool. Everyone was in town, except for Cubby, who was in his cabin, and the Lineman, who was taking the chickens for a walk. Her head ached as it always did these days. She needed the rainy climate of the coast where storms blew in regularly to give her relief. If only there was electricity, she thought. It would make it so much easier to leave Mom and Dad alone. The giant waterwheel next to the Dominican monastery churned out power for the farms and businesses of Nigh, but not a glimmer of it reached Far.

She went indoors. One of the cats twined around Phaedra's legs. The animals didn't mew like normal felines, they hissed. It was like having snakes in the house and they made her uneasy, as though they were trading evil secrets.

Unseen by her, Balthazar, Melchior and Caspar were playing poker at the dining room table, while Shumba smoked *ganja* in an easy chair. The Mhondoro lay on the sofa with the rest of the cats on top of him. The cats absolutely adored the Mhondoro. They were purring in unison like little race car engines.

Phaedra might not be able to see the spirits, but she was not without influence in their world. Her one experience with the Rain Queens had opened her up to new abilities. She could tell when negative ions were building up in the atmosphere. She could sense a humidity gradient as well as Cubby. And when the great packets of air moved like ocean liners overhead, she knew when they would collide and bring forth rain. The problem was, it rarely happened here.

Oh crap, she thought as her vision began to ripple. It was a migraine aura. For at least an hour her sight would be full of twinkling lights and she would be incapable of walking. Then the headache would begin. Phaedra felt her way to the sofa. "Move, you damn pussies," she muttered, swiping at them. They fled, hissing. The Mhondoro good naturedly removed himself to the ceiling.

She feels that the land needs rain, he said approvingly to the poker players.

Yebo, Sekuru, replied Balthazar. *You said it, Big Daddy.*

Soon she will understand what she must do, Melchior said, displaying a full house and raking in the chips. Phaedra distantly registered the sound and thought it was a hallucination.

You can do it, Baby Girl, said Shumba, taking an extra-big hit on his spirit bong.

The water supply in Far had dropped steadily during the long hot summer. The holding tanks, both the Lineman's original and the larger one he had constructed recently, were nearly empty. The garden was suffering and the distress calls of two hundred pea, bean, tomato, squash and pumpkin plants vibrated in the ether. Phaedra picked them up subliminally and they made her head feel like it was about to explode.

And then she heard a whispery voice: *You can do it, Baby Girl. You can pull the clouds out of the sea.*

She lay on the sofa with a wet towel over her face. She cried for relief and the sky responded. A breeze flowed over the Mirage Mountains, laden with life-giving moisture. Clouds began to build. Thunder rumbled in the distance.

Cubby was studying a manual on how to generate electricity using geothermal energy. He sat in his comfortable easy chair in front of his grandfather's roll-top desk. Frietchie had hung new curtains, remodeled the kitchen and covered the floor with expensive Turkish rugs, but Cubby had resisted her attempts to replace the old, saggy bed.

It was still the domain of the Willows ancestors. They didn't approve of Frietchie poking around with a carpet sweeper and gave her an allergy attack she wouldn't soon forget. They liked the Turkish carpets the way they were, for these had a sad aura of vanished sunsets and hushed voices.

The wind rattled a Venetian blind and Cubby noticed the dampness in the air for the first time. He looked outside to check on the welfare of his telescope. The wind gusted again, prickling his nose with the sharp odor of wet dust.

Cubby spent much time studying astronomy now. It seemed wasteful to ignore the magnificent star-strewn nights. He made careful photographs of galaxies and plotted the progress of asteroids through the crystalline desert sky. During the day he looked for the White Mountain. It eluded him in the morning, but by late afternoon it had appeared, hovering beyond the violet shadows of the Farther Hills. A white river appeared to wind through the hills until it flowed up the White Mountain to form a standing wave against the eastern sky.

Cubby quickly hauled his telescope and other equipment out of the dust swirling before the approaching storm. On the last trip he gathered up a tray of brownies cooling on a picnic table.

Thunder rolled closer and closer. The sky turned the color of slate and as Cubby was positioning a camera in a window to take a picture, a blinding flash followed by a ground-shuddering thunderclap, almost knocked him off his feet. And then he heard a scream.

Thirty-Eight: *FORGIVENESS*

MOST MORNINGS the Lineman took the hens for a stroll. It was a welcome break for them from the shed. Both he and they liked to wander far out into the sagebrush wilderness where the hens could feast on caterpillars and grasshoppers.

Now, out in the bushes, he lay on his back with God's blue eye looking down. He felt perfectly comfortable. He was no higher than a hen and God, who loved chickens, would see his humility and not smite him.

Skrrrrk, said a hen, craning her neck at the sky.

Is something wrong? enquired the Lineman.

Skrrrk keaww, she replied. *The air is changing.*

He sat up and felt a cool breeze. Monster clouds were piling up over the Mirage Mountains. They made his heart bounce in his chest and the scar burn along his back. A thunderstorm was coming!

The Lineman's first impulse was to flee, but he couldn't abandon the hens. *Come quickly*, he called. *Danger.* The hens responded instantly. They clustered around him, flapping and clucking loudly. He herded them toward the ranch, constantly checking the sky and flinching every time he saw lightning. Unfortunately, the birds had trouble focusing. There were only two settings in their brains—hysteria and amnesia. They kept stopping to peck and wander off into the bushes.

Meanwhile, the clouds were coming on faster than the Lineman believed possible. This was no normal storm. God was truly and thoroughly pissed. The Lineman tried to remember what sins he'd committed recently. There was the night he spied on Frietchie, and yesterday the new underwear ads from Macy's had arrived. They covered his walls now—slips, panties, bras and thongs. Christ! The thongs! No wonder God was pissed!

I'll take them down. I won't look at them again, he promised, urging the hens to hurry. God grumbled in the clouds. He wasn't buying it. He'd been lied to before.

Don't stop, the Lineman begged a wayward hen. *Danger! Hawks!* The word *hawk* communicated and the hen bolted from the bushes, keening with fear. Lightning struck somewhere in town. The Lineman broke into a run, checked himself and came back for the hens. *Faster! Faster!* he implored.

At last he got them into the chicken shed and slammed the door. Then he sprinted for the God Bunker, praying and making promises as he went. The first drops of rain splashed down. He skidded around the house and bolted through the fanciful Moorish gateway Frietchie had designed for the courtyard. He rounded the hot tub. Home stretch now. He dove for the God Bunker—

A van was parked on the closed hatch. Tom had warned everyone about driving over it, but someone had forgotten. It was a miracle the vehicle hadn't fallen through.

The Lineman, sobbing, tried to move it. He got behind and pushed, but he might as well have been an ant trying to shift a boulder. He stepped away and at that instant the thunderbolt Cubby had heard struck. It went down the side of the hot tub, snaked along the ground and disappeared into the God Bunker under the Lineman's feet.

The Lineman screamed.

Phaedra heard it in the house. She ran to the back door and saw that the courtyard was almost invisible in the downpour. "Hello?" she called. "Anyone there?" Two shapes moved away in the distance. *Oh crap*, she remembered. *I left the brownies out in the rain.*

Cubby had gone in search of whoever had screamed. He knew the cry had come from the courtyard because he was extremely good at zeroing in on sounds. He could locate a single cricket in an alfalfa field at midnight. Nor did he notice obstacles when he was homing in on a target, a habit that had ruined more than one set of clothes. Now Cubby sloshed through the teeming storm, completely unaware that he was getting soaked, until he saw the Lineman standing by the hot tub.

Rain lashed the Lineman's body and blew into his open mouth. For a second Cubby thought he'd been struck by lightning, but then he saw the van blocking the God Bunker. Cubby understood that his friend was distraught because he couldn't reach his nest under the ground, much as a honeybee can despair if it is barred from its hive. Cubby took the Lineman's hand and led him away.

"You sit there and I'll make coffee," he said, settling the Lineman into a chair in the cabin. Water dripped ruinously onto Frietchie's antique Turkish carpets. Lightning flared outside and thunder rolled around the horizon. Cubby lit a small propane stove. "This rain is going to fill the water tanks right up," he said cheerfully. "I imagine the springs will start running again, too."

The Lineman stared. His mind was frozen in that instant when God had sent His wrath into the bunker. It didn't matter that the ads were hidden in darkness with a van guarding the door. God saw everything. He'd peeled the ads right off the wall and if the Lineman had been any closer, he'd be a heap of ashes right now.

"Put your hands around the cup," Cubby instructed. "That rainwater was chilly."

The Lineman felt the warmth and his mind cleared slightly. Why was this strange elderly person concerned about him? Cubby's face reminded him of something, a pamphlet he'd seen in Sunday School long ago. The Lineman had memorized a verse for the teacher and been rewarded with a cookie. He struggled to remember. First you saw through a glass darkly and then —mumble, mumble. Oh, yes. And then you saw face to face. *What* did you see face to face?

"I hope the chickens are all right," Cubby said, sipping his coffee.

The Lineman's mind cleared a little more. It was all so simple, himself and the hens. It was like Sunday School before the bad things happened. If he had a cookie now, he'd share it with them. *I put the hens into the shed*, he said.

"That's good. They can drown in a storm like this."

I love chickens, the Lineman said.

"And they love you. Not only that, they respect you. I

can tell by the way they follow you around."

A light shone on the Lineman then, not like the horrible destroying bolt that had plucked him off the wires and sent him from asylum to asylum. This was a pure radiance that poured from God's heavenly throne. It was a ray of forgiveness that washed away the murky sins of the past.

The Lineman understood at last. The chickens had interceded for him. They had gone before God, clucking and *keeawing* in their good-hearted way, and God had listened to them. He had sent this elderly messenger to draw him from the pit of despair just as surely as the prophet Jeremiah had been drawn from the pit of wicked king Zedekiah.

Now he remembered the picture on that pamphlet from Sunday School. It was a painting of an angel, a thin, fragile being who radiated goodness, and who reached out to the child who had held that pamphlet. Beneath were the verses the Lineman was supposed to memorize that Sunday: *Once I was a child and thought as a child. I saw through a glass darkly, but now—*

"Brownie?" Cubby said, brightly, passing him the tray.

The Lineman ate, filled with joy and a desire to reciprocate such divine grace. *Is there anything you'd like?* he said shyly. *Anything at all?*

"I wouldn't say no to an electric line and internet connection," Cubby said.

*   *   *

Streams burst out of the Mirage Mountains and filled the reservoirs and cisterns of Nigh. Phaedra, sensing that the mission she'd been waiting for was done, took tearful leave of Violetta and promised to return as often as possible. The long lake rose, nudging the boundaries of fields and driving water birds out until they invaded Tom's ranch. They settled all over the tile roofs. They clambered hungrily over the chicken wire protecting the garden. A few hardy ducks swam in the hot tub until Frietchie chased them out.

On the whole, they weren't unwelcome. Tom enjoyed watching the amazing influx of mallards, teals, loons, pelicans, herons, and the Canada geese that strutted around importantly. It was a temporary situation. As soon as the cold weather set in, the birds would go elsewhere.

Most interesting was their reaction to Cubby. As soon as he emerged from his cottage, the birds flocked to observe what he was doing. As far as Tom could see they never got fed, but they showed an endless fascination with the man. Even when he was reading, the ducks crowded around and nibbled at his pant legs. They just seemed to like him.

Cubby spent much time at a table outdoors, drawing up plans and communing with the Wichita Lineman. Although how much communing you could do with that loony was anyone's guess. Tom had seen the specifications of a waterwheel. It was covered with notations like *powered by the grace of God* and *insert smite-proof wiring here.* The Dominican abbot, who would be directing the project, said most of the plan made less sense than an astrologer's chart, but that the Lineman understood electricity.

The Lineman was also going to put a satellite dish at the top of Jedediah Bidwell Pass and run a cable line from Luga Chuga. Tom smiled lazily and sipped a cup of tea. He didn't miss TV or the internet, but anything that kept Cubby happy had his vote.

Speaking of votes, wasn't there an election coming up? It was hard to keep track in the Nigh and Far Valley. Anyhow, Tom figured his ballot didn't count for much. The last time he'd used it a power fluctuation had erased all the returns for Northern California.

Who would have thought things would turn out this well? Tom thought, gazing out over the sagebrush sea. Not long ago he'd been just another senior waiting to be shuffled off the old coil. Now he was master and commander of all he could see, even with his glasses on.

The ranch was no longer the rural slum Uncle Shumba had maintained. With the help of artisans from town, everything had been repaired. Five new cottages were scattered around the grounds, one of which had been turned into a library. His kids and grandkids could visit whenever they liked. Best of all, Violetta was happy. The ancestors had done well by them.

But of course, there was more to it than that. Tom couldn't congratulate himself that the task they had given him had been accomplished. The spirits only appeared to Seaworthys to alter the course of history and last time Tom looked, history was just the same. The ancestors were waiting for something more to happen.

Tom hadn't seen them since he left the city, but he knew they were around. Too many beers went missing and too many things went bump in the night. The cats piled up in a heap on the sofa, purring loudly for someone only they could see.

He looked idly at the date on the wristwatch Violetta had given him for his birthday. September 21. Son of a bitch. The equinox, when day and night were perfectly balanced. Astronomical events like that had always interested Tom. The equinoxes were big *juju* back in Stonehenge, when everyone painted himself with *woad* and danced naked under the stars. *Wonder what Uncle Shumba used to do*, Tom thought, sipping his tea.

Uncle Shumba used to play his drums and throw a party. He saw no reason to give up the practice just because he was dead. After September 21 darkness grew and prolonged the visiting hours of spooks, haunts, shades, *loas* and other folk. It was a fine opportunity to invite guests to Far.

Mhoro, Sekuru, Shumba said to the Mhondoro sitting on the living room sofa. Big Daddy was surrounded by purring cats.

Mhoro, young one, the Mhondoro replied. *Have you eaten well?*

I have done so if you have done so, Shumba said politely, after the manner of his ancestors. *Violetta made barbequed ribs.*

I saw them. Big Daddy smacked spectral lips.

Shumba waited until everyone had gone to bed before playing the drums. Spirit drums don't sound like living ones. They cause a vibration in the blood and a ripple along the nerves, and they spread like dark sunlight through the astral world. Tom, Violetta and Frietchie tossed in their beds, not knowing why they were so disturbed. The hens huddled together with visions of hawks circling in their heads. The Wichita Lineman twitched as he slept in the God Bunker. A thousand telephone calls murmured in his dreams.

The *loas* arrived at the fashionable hour of midnight. They were naturalized Americans, having come over on the first slave vessels to land in Haiti. Damballah the Great Serpent, Erzulie the Love Goddess, and Baron Samedi, Lord of the

Graveyard, had changed their African aspects, being influenced by new landscapes and conditions, but beneath their American exteriors lurked the shadows of an ancient world.

Damballah slithered around Tom and Violetta's bed, inspiring troubled moans. Erzulie stroked Frietchie's face and aroused a complicated dream involving husbands #2 through #6. Baron Samedi blew stale breath into Tom's nostrils and sent him fleeing through a valley of dry bones. Eventually the *loas* left their entertainment and joined the other dancers in the courtyard, twisting and jittering around the hot tub.

In Central Africa lives a parasite known as the Loa Loa Worm. It spends much of its fifteen-year lifespan under a victim's skin, traveling continuously through a person's connective tissue. The host experiences a strange sensation that he is not alone, that something else resides within his body. Hence, the name, *loa*, or *spirit*. Occasionally, the adult worm—two and a half inches long—ripples across an eye ball, causing panic. But the worm is soon on its way, wriggling up a tear duct to new adventures.

One of the most interesting habits of these creatures, and there may be many living in one host, occurs on chilly nights. When the host tries to warm himself at a fire, the worms migrate as a group to the front, giving new meaning to the phrase *feeling one's skin crawl*.

All night the *loas*, spooks, haunts and shades celebrated. They finished off the rest of Violetta's barbequed ribs and made a start on the ham she intended for the next day. The fetishes came down from the ceiling and the cats chased them around. But when the first hint of dawn touched the sky, the party was over. The drums fell silent. A cool wind blew out of the east. The fetishes returned to their posts, where they froze into menacing postures. The visitors thanked Shumba for his hospitality and withdrew before the brightening day.

Don't be a stranger, called the Mhondoro after their departing shadows.

The living woke up with low fevers—all except for Cubby, that is. He had slept like a baby, immune to the nightmares that had plagued the others. He had no fear of dead people and dreamed of mayflies dancing over a sunlit pond.

Thirty-Nine: *THE BIG WHEEL AND THE LITTLE WHEEL*

THERE WERE FEW mayflies at the foot of the Mirage Mountains, but enough mosquitoes to start a blood bank, Tom thought morosely. Clouds of insects rose every time a bush was disturbed and descended in starving mats on the work crew. Cubby said the mosquitoes were breeding in puddles left by the rain. "The water in a single hollow log can produce hundreds," he informed the workers. "There must be thousands of hollow logs lying around, which means—"

"Please skip the math," said Tom. He had been lured out to see Cubby's progress and now regretted it.

They were following a path up the mountain. On one side the huge waterwheel that provided electricity to Nigh creaked and wobbled dangerously as flood water spilled over it. It had been built long ago. From the mismatched slabs of wood and rusty infrastructure, Tom thought it must run by faith alone. Someday the whole structure would come tumbling down.

Or not, depending on how strong the Dominican faith was. Ever since the valley of dry bones, Tom had been undergoing a kind of spiritual rebirth. Sometimes he caught himself watching the sun shine through a drop of dew or a fly rub its paws back and forth. The wonder of these things held him spellbound. How perfectly the sun fit into the dewdrop! How human were the actions of the fly! He knew there was a deep meaning here, but he couldn't say what it was. *Maybe I'm just turning into another Lineman*, he thought, smacking a fly attempting to dig its proboscis into his arm.

"*Chrysops discalis*, the common deer fly," said Cubby. "Sometimes it carries tularemia."

"Tularemia?" Tom said, realizing his mistake even as he made it. Cubby never missed a chance to impart data.

"Also known as rabbit fever. One of the most infectious diseases in existence. Mortality is about 7% for untreated cases, due to multiple organ system failure—"

"Why doesn't anything bite you?" interrupted Tom. Of all the people on this fool's errand, only Cubby seemed immune to the cloud of bloodthirsty insects.

"Gerbill says it's because I've been *used up*," Cubby explained. "I was bitten thousands of times as a young man. Insects inject a fragment of themselves every time they feed, and after a while—this is Gerbill's theory—an entomologist's blood becomes half insect DNA. I no longer smell like food."

"In other words, you're half mosquito. Remind me not to get too close to you," Tom said.

Cubby smiled delightedly, the kind of expression you might see on a happy baby, and Tom was ashamed of trying to bait him. It was impossible to stay annoyed at the man. He might talk to ghosts and to the Lineman, who talked to *chickens*, for Christ's sake, but—

There was that smile. You couldn't fight against it. The smile was strong enough to make Genghis Khan fold up his tents and go back to Mongolia.

"*Culex pipiens* and *Aedes hexodontus*." Cubby correctly identified the mosquitoes now settling on Tom's arms. "They'll disappear when the weather gets colder."

"That's good, isn't it?"

"To be replaced by *Culiseta inornata*, a much larger and more aggressive species."

The Lineman indicated, with much arm waving, the stream they would be using for the small waterwheel's power. The work crew, the same individuals who had repaired the theater, gathered around to discuss strategy. Tom studied the new stream that had burst out of the mountain after the last storm. The Dominican abbot said it had never appeared before. It was beautifully strong and showed every indication of being permanent. A miracle, in fact.

Tom didn't believe in miracles and yet, in the fresh, invigorating air of the valley, reality itself seemed poised on a knife edge. Tip slightly to one side and something magical might happen. The spray of the new waterfall dampened Cubby's gray hair. "You mustn't catch cold," Tom said, pulling him away. For the first time he noticed how much the entomologist had aged since arriving in Nigh and Far. He didn't look sick exactly, but he was certainly thinner. More transparent.

At any rate Cubby's part in the construction was over. Younger men would assemble the waterwheel and install the turbines that would bring electricity to the ranch. The cables were the Lineman's responsibility, and if he got the job done without getting everyone fried, Tom would definitely start believing in miracles.

*   *   *

Tom drove Cubby to Jedediah Bidwell Pass and waited in the van while the Lineman showed Cubby where he'd placed the satellite dish. Tom guessed that the man had pirated cable feeds from Luga Chuga, but he didn't much care. He wasn't interested in the TV reception, and that was strange considering how much he'd watched in the city.

The valley had that effect on you. Football, soap operas, news—it was all remote now. Were grown men still competing to see how hard you could hit a ball with a stick? How could something like that matter when you saw your parents beckoning to you from beyond the blue horizon? Tom could see the White Mountain now as he gazed out the front window of the van. It was more distinct these days, perhaps because the autumn air was clearer.

Cubby had to sit down to rest several times on the way. The Lineman was so eager to show him the dish that he bounced up and down like a puppy when they stopped. *You'll get everything you want, even the whoopee channel*, he boasted.

"Whoopee channel?" said Cubby.

The Lineman was immediately contrite. Angels didn't watch those things. *You'll get the election news*, he amended.

"I wonder who's running?" Cubby remembered President Mogador, whose face had shifted eerily as he (or she) spoke. President. That word had meant so much when Cubby was a boy. Now a computer-generated face smiled benignly at its audience, bleating the words *No Senior left behind. We're there. We care. We're the Empowerment Party.*

Or Fairness Party or Diversity Party. It hardly mattered. Frietchie and the others made the mistake of thinking Cubby didn't register half of what he was told, but they were wrong. He had an incredible ability to hold onto things that mattered. For forty years the number of dots on a wasp's abdomen or the natural enemies of aphids had been important. Now he had put away childish things. His focused mind did not forget a single item relating to his mission.

"Have you ever voted in an election?" Cubby asked the Lineman. "No, of course you haven't. They probably asked you who's president of the United States like they did me, to assess my sanity. And you said you didn't know."

The Lineman nodded.

"The joke is, they don't know either. Even if they allowed you to vote, your ballot could disappear in a power overload."

The Lineman smiled. He understood overloads.

"The government is ruled by hungry ghosts," Cubby said, "not real ghosts who remember the earth and are still involved with it. Not them." He pointed at Jedediah Bidwell and the Modoc warriors, who were sniffing around the new satellite dish, as suspicious as a troop of coyotes. One of the warriors pissed on the dish. "The kind of entities that drag old people off to Alzheimer's hospitals, the kind that sent lightning through your brain, have never been alive. They don't understand life, and that's why they've filled the world with bad replicas of it."

The Lineman didn't understand what Cubby was talking about and he couldn't see the spirits, but he responded to the kindness in the man's voice. He wanted to contribute something to the conversation. *I wouldn't cast a ballot unless they gave the vote to chickens,* he offered.

Cubby's delighted whoop of laughter sent a pair of scrub jays flying from the blackberry bush where they'd been feeding. Tom heard it in the van and felt happy. "I wouldn't vote either, unless they enfranchised chickens," Cubby declared, patting the Lineman on the back. "And cockroaches, too."

Forty: *MR. YEE MAKES A MISTAKE*

A FTER MONTHS WITHOUT electricity, Tom was almost sorry to see the lights go on. He'd got used to the yellow flame of kerosene lamps. His daily rhythm had adjusted to waking a half-hour before sunrise and going to bed not long after sunset.

When Tom woke in the night—and like most elderly people, his sleep was broken—he went outside to watch a plume of steam rising from a nearby hot spring. It was forever changing, sometimes a faint breath over the sagebrush and sometimes a white fountain reaching for the stars. Cubby said it had to do with magma moving within the earth, but Tom thought of it as a living presence. It woke and slept as he did.

Tom liked listening to the night noises. They were so much more soothing than the gunshots and sirens of the city. Occasionally a loon lifted its ghostly lament from the lake. A mouse squeaked as it encountered a pallid bat hunting on the ground. (To be honest, Tom was capable of uttering a squeak himself when he came across one of those weird creatures scuttling along.) When he tired of solitude, Tom would knock on Cubby's door.

Cubby slept very little and was always willing to talk, although his discourse often rambled into odd corners. Tom learned much about the habits of katydids and silverfish. He'd been charmed by the female burying beetle (*Necrophorus vaspillo*) feeding her larvae in a nest of carrion. And who couldn't love the weaver ants (*Oecophilla longinoda*) who wove tree leaves together by moving their silk-producing larvae back and forth like animated shuttles?

Since the arrival of electricity, though, Cubby had only talked about current events. Tom sighed. What good were current events in the lonely, loon-haunted reaches of Far? Even Nigh had turned its back on the outside world. The Dominicans might sell Mirage Wine and import the few items local people couldn't make, but beyond that, they had no interest in what happened elsewhere. Only Cubby sat up night after night, watching television and surfing the internet.

He'd been hunched in front of the computer so long it was beginning to tell on his health. He'd aged visibly and had the beginning of a stoop. He forgot to eat. Violetta placed meals on the keyboard and stood over him while he chewed mechanically, staring at the monitor.

"If you don't start taking breaks, I'm going to drop that computer into a hot spring," Tom said one night.

Cubby blinked at him. "I'd only get another one," he said logically.

"Then I'll destroy that one, too. Shit, Cubby, you can't live like this. You're acting like a goddamn robot." Tom yanked the surge protector out of the wall and threw it out the door. "Get up," he said gruffly, lifting Cubby to his feet. He walked him outside where a star-strewn sky shone bright enough to cast a faint shadow.

"It's nighttime," said Cubby, wondering.

"Christ, you don't even know when it gets dark. Look at that sky, man! Biggest free show in the universe. Cast of thousands. And smell that air."

"It's cold," said Cubby.

"Damn straight. Summer's gone and we're most of the way through Fall. Want me to get you a coat?" Tom didn't wait for an answer. He returned to Cubby's cabin and fetched the army surplus coat the entomologist had worn for forty years.

"It *is* nice out here," Cubby conceded. "You can see the Orion Nebula. Did you know that when the stars in Orion's Belt set, they mark the exact compass position of west?"

"No, I did not know that," said Tom, placing the coat around the man's shoulders.

"Gerbill taught me how to navigate by the stars. He learned it in the Hitler Youth."

"Amazing where you can pick up things. How is old Gerbill these days?" Tom said.

"I haven't seen him," Cubby said, concerned. "I hope nothing's happened to him."

What could possibly happen to dead people, thought Tom. "Maybe he got reincarnated."

"He would have said good-bye first," Cubby said.

And he would have, too, Tom thought. Gerbill was a stickler for manners.

"Anyhow, I'm glad you came by because I've discovered something so disturbing I don't know what to do about it," Cubby continued. "I was looking around a Belarus website, the same group who gave me the Golden Aphid Award, and discovered that they were experimenting with antihistamines. They've diversified since the fall of Communism. They make contraceptives and foot spray, as well as—"

Cubby warbled on with his usual enthusiasm for arcane topics and Tom zoned out. It was enough to hear the vitality in the entomologist's voice. Tom should have thought of distracting him earlier, because it was easy to fall into a trance in Far. Tom did it himself sometimes.

The ranch was entirely too quiet these days. Friends from town visited, but Tom could see them glancing at the road as though calculating how soon they could decently leave. It wasn't him, it was the emptiness of Far that unsettled them. Nigh was where things happened. It was a bustling place now, with parties on the weekends. The population was recovering, to go by the number of pregnancies. Everyone had things to do, places to go, people to see.

When Tom first arrived he couldn't understand why folks didn't have picnics in Far. It was such a beautiful place. There were birds to watch and pools to swim in (and pools that would scald the hide off you if you weren't careful). The view went on forever. Then Tom noticed the strange enervation that crept over him when he crossed the causeway. The green smell of fields fell behind, to be replaced with mineral dust. The sky was taller, emptier, deeper, until nightfall came when it was almost too full of stars.

Far was where you turned away from the fleeting,

trivial, utterly desirable affairs of the world. It wasn't a place for picnics.

"—they have a cure for Alzheimer's and our government won't let them use it," said Cubby.

"What?" said Tom, jolted awake.

"The Belarusans have an antihistamine that staves off the onset of Alzheimer's. Our government has threatened them with *regime change* if they dare to export it." Cubby was more animated than Tom had ever seen him. His voice trembled with emotion. "Those poor people in the hospital should never have gone there. Not only that, Alzheimer's is on the increase. The medicine the government hands out is contaminated with chemicals that trigger the symptoms."

Tom's mind raced over the medications he'd consumed. "Are you telling me we're all doomed? You? Violetta? Frietchie?"

"There's a genetic component," said Cubby. "You have to have a hereditary predisposition."

"But . . . but . . . why would they do such a terrible thing?"

"The social security system is broken," Cubby said simply. "Every year more seniors enter the system and fewer children are born. Once there were nine working adults to support one person over sixty-five, then four, then two. No politicians wanted to deal with the problem. It was the political third rail, and so they pretended it wasn't there until half of everyone's salary went to care for old people."

"I never thought about it," admitted Tom. He wanted badly to lose himself in the peacefulness of Far, to turn *his* back on the problem. But that wasn't how he was raised. Seaworthys didn't walk away from righteous causes.

"I never thought about it either," Cubby said. "The population imbalance has changed the government of this country. That's why laws are made by opinion polls—no one person can be held responsible. Our senators, representatives and president are icons who change shape hourly. I'm not even sure if there are any real people left in Washington. One thing is certain: The Senior Laws were enacted to fix the social security problem by removing the imbalance. By removing us."

"Son of a bitch," murmured Tom. A cold wind started

up from the east. A single coyote howled in the Farther Hills. "That explains the Diminished Culpability Act. That's why it's okay to murder old folks."

"Or declare them insane or give them poisoned medicine. There's more."

"I know I'm not going to like this," said Tom.

"We're days away from an election," Cubby said. His gentle voice was blown away by the wind and so Tom steered him back to the cabin, privately blessing the Lineman for the electric current that fueled the new space heaters. "All three parties are running on the platform that seniors need protection from violence," said Cubby.

"That's good, isn't it?"

"The most popular solution is to resettle people over sixty-five in "protected villages", where their every need will be catered to. *All* seniors. No exceptions. The villages are being constructed now, as though the outcome of the election was a given. Which of course it is. You can imagine the level of care we'll receive."

Tom was so shocked he couldn't speak. *Surely we're safe here*, he thought. *No one bothers with what lies beyond the Mirage Mountains. But what if the government found out about us?*

Cubby and Tom sat in front of the TV, which was more-or-less constantly tuned to the Homeland Channel. Right now it was showing a group of seniors getting out of a bus. The camera panned over a housing estate, complete with miniature golf course, spa and enrichment center. The seniors all looked deliriously happy or perhaps they were drugged. They were aided by attendants in perky uniforms. Joy Meadows all over again.

Security! There can never be enough of it, the voice from the screen proclaimed. *You can find it in this gated, fully guarded community.* The camera zeroed in on a state-of-the-art fence with an electric wire humming around the top. *Give your seniors the gift of safety. Vote for the Empowerment Party. We're here! We care!*

"If you'd like to watch sports, I can get anything," offered Cubby.

"No, thanks," said Tom. "I don't think I'll ever watch another football game."

*   *   *

In the morning Mr. Yee and the Roshi arrived. Violetta was serving breakfast and immediately fetched two more plates. But Mr. Yee was in no mood for breakfast. "God-rotting, putrid duck egg fucking government!" he shouted.

"Whoa! What's the matter?" cried Tom. Frietchie and Cubby looked up.

"They're here!"

"Who's here?" said Tom.

"Please sit down, Mr. Yee," implored the Roshi. "I'm sorry. He's been beside himself since he found out."

"Do you know my column *Dear Avatar?*" Mr. Yee could hardly get the words out, he was so enraged. Violetta slid a plate of biscuits and gravy in front of him. In her opinion, biscuits and gravy could fix anything.

"I've seen it," Tom said noncommittally. Privately, he was disgusted by the advice the old man handed out.

"*Dear Avatar* has been so popular that Mr. Yee collected the letters into a book and published it," said the Roshi

"Did he make much?"

"I'll say!" said the Roshi. "He has funded all sorts of projects in our community, including an old Lamas' home." The Roshi gratefully accepted a plate of biscuits and gravy. "We brought several of them into the valley because they were in danger of being sent to an asylum. They might look like they're mumbling prayers, but frankly they're just mumbling."

"They're like living prayer wheels," said Tom.

"That's exactly what Mr. Yee thinks," agreed the Roshi. "He believes such venerables must be conversing with the next world."

"Plus we can collect their social security income," said Mr. Yee.

"Oh, no, you didn't!" cried Frietchie.

"Why not? They're better off here and we can use the cash."

"You left a money trail," said Frietchie. "My God! We go to all the trouble to escape and you've given us away."

"I didn't think it all the way through," admitted Mr. Yee, somewhat shamefaced.

Cubby laid down the scalpel with which he'd been dissecting his sunny-side-up egg. He was proud of his ability to remove the white from a yolk so runny the slightest touch would rupture it. He also dissected fat strips from meat in bacon and crust from toast. This was a skill perfected by years of performing autopsies on insects. The few times Gerbill had lured Cubby to a restaurant, other diners had removed themselves to more distant locations.

"I noticed an influx of money into the Willows Trust," said Cubby. "There was more than half a million dollars."

"That's amazing," marveled Violetta.

"Mr. Yee is a first class money-seeking missile," the Roshi said admiringly. "But that's the problem. No one in the Nigh and Far Valley has ever had a reportable income. We barter and money has almost never changed hands. Therefore we have never paid taxes."

"Uh oh," said Tom.

"The IRS noticed a stream of profits flowing into a blank spot on the map and decided to investigate. They followed a pirate cable feed from Luga Chuga and discovered the Nigh and Far Valley spread out before them. Homeland Security visited me last night," said the Roshi. "They know there's an unregulated colony of seniors here. Furthermore, they claim that Mr. Yee is inciting terrorism."

"You've been a busy boy, Mr. Yee," said Tom.

"Yeah, yeah. It's not my fault. A group of retired terrorists read my book and decided to take to the streets. It's their problem."

"It's our problem now," said Frietchie, cradling her head with her arms.

Forty-One: *TRUST IN CHICKENS*

C UBBY FIRED UP the computer when he reached his cabin and continued his relentless tracking of the coming election. He knew that they were all in extreme danger. The government had discovered the valley and when the election was over it would send the Youth Patrol to round them up. Once subtracted from view, the memory of their existence would fade.

Governments can suffer from Alzheimer's, too.

In less than a week, the electorate would vote on an avalanche of initiatives known as the Omega Laws, to distinguish them from the earlier Senior Laws. Proposition $\Omega 11$: All people over sixty-five should be disenfranchised. Proposition $\Omega 12$: All people over sixty-five should be removed to protected villages and their assets seized. Proposition $\Omega 13$: All people over sixty-five should no longer be entitled to medical care.

Every day there were more. It would take a voter hours to read the ballot, but that wouldn't be a problem because at the bottom was a single box: *All of the Above.* No one had thought it necessary to add another box: *None of the Above.*

Cubby's heart beat slowly and painfully as he looked at the evidence. The aim was to make the country *altenrein*—a variation of the old Nazi word *judenrein*, or Jew-free. Once the old had been disposed of, the young could empty out their parents' and grandparents' bank accounts. They could do anything they wanted because for them, consequences did not exist. They believed that bank accounts were refilled automatically. They had never known anything else. The government could always print more money.

Altenrein: Free of old people, with overtones of cleanliness as though age itself was dirty.

"I'll shiver their timbers," Cubby whispered, but for once the old pirate persona failed to encourage him. Even Captain Tarantula was appalled by the tidal wave looming over his ship. The electoral system was no longer based on the needs and desires of the people who had created it. It was ruled by opinion polls taken over the internet and dispersed over the internet. The Empowerment, Fairness, and Diversity Parties had all been corrupted. Cubby didn't know who was staging these polls and where were they coming from.

The election was less than one week away.

Cubby slumped over the keyboard. His eyes ached from hours of work and his hands had gone arthritic. He was just one man and he couldn't defeat a whole government.

The door opened and the Lineman tip-toed in, careful not to disturb his hero in the middle of work. One of the hens followed him and settled on the carpet. Frietchie had screamed herself hoarse when she discovered chickens on her Turkish rugs, but it hadn't done any good. Cubby didn't have the heart to ban them. They couldn't help not being housebroken.

Keeaww, said this one, cocking her head. *You look depressed.*

"I am depressed," admitted Cubby, rousing himself from the keyboard.

Buk-buk keeaww. I always eat a grasshopper and take a dust bath when I'm feeling down, she offered.

Humans don't do things like that, said the Lineman.

"I do," said Cubby, who had eaten toasted grasshoppers and experimented with dust baths as a way to combat fleas.

There, you see? cawed the hen triumphantly.

"But I don't think grasshoppers are going to cheer me up now." Cubby leaned back in his chair and saw spots before his eyes.

You could ask God for help. You're on good terms with Him. The Lineman hadn't worked up the courage to approach God himself, although he'd filled in the God Bunker as a gesture of good will. He'd thrown out the Macy's underwear ads, too, but who knew how long God could harbor a grudge? The Lineman preferred to trust in chickens and so far he had not been proven wrong.

"I'm simply worn out," said Cubby. "I keep watching the election escalate and the candidates shift and I don't understand what's happening. Yesterday all three icons were women. Today they're men. The number of Omega Laws keeps rising. There's over a hundred now and by election time there might be a thousand."

The Lineman watched, concerned, as Cubby groped his way to the easy chair and clicked on the TV. His hero didn't look well today, not at all. It was that computer nonsense and that nasty Homeland channel. The Lineman couldn't see the channel because they had burned out the back of his eyes in the asylum. He couldn't see anything that wasn't alive and the Homeland channel had been reduced to zigzag patterns.

This didn't bother him because most things on TV were alive (such as mountains) and some things were twice as alive (such as chickens) and therefore twice as visible. But election news only produced jagged lines.

After the doctors had blasted the Lineman's brain, they had hounded him with the question: *Who's the President of the United States? Who's the President of the United States? Who's the President of the United States?* Answering it correctly would have qualified him to cross over the great gulf that separated him from the saved. But try as he would, the Lineman never got it right. *Is it Mickey Mouse?* he cried. *Is it Gorbachev? Is it the Dalai Lama?*

Now Cubby was asking the same thing as he stared at the jittery screen, "Who's the President of the United States? Who's running this mess?"

The Lineman knew the jagged lines were trying to kill his friend and that it was up to him to outwit them. *Let me change the picture,* he suggested.

"I have to keep working," murmured Cubby, but he didn't resist when the Lineman slid the remote out of his hand and began to flip through the channels. Half of them were zigzags because election news was everywhere: Zigzag, car ads, zigzag, zigzag, western, soap opera, zigzag, underwear ads (*move,*

move, move moaned the Lineman, punching the remote) zigzag, televangelist, zigzag, insects—

That one! cried the hen. She loved insects.

It was a nature program about the pine processionary caterpillar, or *Thaumetopoea pityocampa*. This creature, explained the invisible narrator, was in the habit of traveling over the ground from one tasty tree to the next. It formed long head-to-tail processions that sometimes contained 300 individuals. The film showed them plodding along, each head pressed firmly against the welcoming ass in front.

For such delicate animals their mandibles were remarkably strong, as indeed they had to be to munch up pine needles. Even more interesting were the times they chose to feed. Most caterpillars flourish in summer because, like all cold-blooded creatures, they need external heat to be active.

But the pine processionary caterpillar preferred winter and darkness. When the chill nights fell they departed from their silken nests and traveled to feeding sites, and when dawn approached they returned. Even at sub-zero temperatures they crept over the frosty ground like a trickle of cold molasses.

The Lineman noted that Cubby was watching the screen intently and smiled to himself. There was nothing like bugs to bring the roses back into the entomologist's cheeks. Bugs aplenty frolicked in the sagebrush, he thought, and after the show the Lineman would suggest that they take the chickens for a walk.

As the caterpillars moved they laid down a trail of silk and pheromones. Pheromones are the language of the insect world. Different odors form the alphabet of this speech, and combinations form the words. This ability is most highly developed in the social insects, the ants and bees, but caterpillars are not entirely illiterate. The odor trail of the pine processionary caterpillar was redolent of fellowship. It was irresistible.

But occasionally mistakes happened. The line of caterpillars, so like a length of twine, could curve back on itself. The lead insect could encounter the tail end and begin to follow it, closing the loop. Round and round they would go, believing they were approaching the promised pine tree. But they were only going in circles.

The screen showed the unlucky insects following one

another around a parking lot. Days came and went. They did not stop. They could not stop. The trail grew ever stronger, marking all else as wilderness. Slowly they began to starve and eventually the caterpillars lay down for the last time. The wind blew their desiccated bodies across the tarmac.

Following orders blindly isn't good even in the insect world.

"That's it!" shouted Cubby.

Skeeaw! shrieked the hen, jumping straight into the air. The Lineman caught her and held her tightly to keep her from fluttering around the room.

"I'm sorry," apologized Cubby. "It's just that I finally understood what's happening with the election polls. Oh dear, she's been indiscreet on the carpet. Frietchie will be upset."

I'll clean it up, said the Lineman, grabbing a dish towel and smearing the spot with one hand as he cradled the bird in his other arm. *There, there. He didn't mean it*, he told the hen.

I thought hawks were after me, she said resentfully, but she quickly forgave Cubby. Hens don't hold grudges even when they can remember them.

"I've been working on this problem for weeks," said Cubby. "Every poll has been worse—first, five percent were in favor of the Omega Laws, then ten percent. Now it's unanimous, and yet I couldn't understand the mechanism. Who was posing the questions? Who was answering them? "

Cubby's eyes glittered with a feverishness that the Lineman didn't like. It was like a fire burning at the heart of a tree when the leaves still appeared green. *We should go for a walk*, he said.

The entomologist laughed wildly. "Oh, no! I can't postpone this. Don't you see? The original poll influenced the outcome of the next poll. The next poll influenced the poll after that, and so on. *The hip bone connected to the thigh bone, the thigh bone connected to the knee bone, la la*—that's how it worked. Then the bones got up and walked around. The poll results, one after the other, fed into party headquarters and changed the agenda. The icons shifted to accommodate new data. Only, it wasn't data. It was a computer-generated feedback loop!"

The Lineman understood none of this, but he knew Cubby was spiraling out of control. *Please stop. Please take a rest*, he begged.

"I can't rest! This is what I was born for. This is what I've been waiting for."

The Lineman considered fetching Violetta to help him get Cubby outside.

"I'm not crazy," said Cubby, suddenly coming out of his mania. "Try to understand. The government is about to invade this valley. They're going to drag the old people away. They'll get Tom and Violetta. They'll take them to an asylum and smite them with lightning."

Now he had the Lineman's attention. Now the man understood the danger they were in. Even the hen looked up, bemused, at the sudden tension in the Lineman's arms.

"All decisions are being made by machines—*mad machines*," explained Cubby. "It's as though they decided people weren't reliable enough to govern themselves, and so they removed people from the equation. *Machines* are asking and answering the questions, except that they've trapped themselves into a loop like the caterpillars. They're going round and round, getting less coherent and more lethal."

Are we doomed? said the Lineman, seeing the caterpillars being blown away like dry leaves.

"No," said Cubby, laughing again. "We've waked up just in time. Captain Tarantula is on the deck, matey, and he's got his spy glass trained on the enemy. We're going to shiver their timbers. We're going to open up that loop and feed it through the Nigh and Far Valley."

Forty-Two: *ELECTION NIGHT*

CUBBY HAD BOUGHT another TV for the main house and everyone was sitting around it with cups of mulled cider—everyone, that is, except Cubby and the Lineman. Cubby had been working feverishly for days, eating little and sleeping erratically. Frietchie managed to get a few meals into him, but for the rest she had to depend on the Lineman.

Winter had at last come to the Nigh and Far Valley. It didn't arrive with tree-lashing winds, as it did on the other side of the Mirage Mountains. Rather, it settled quietly on field and desert in a sparkling layer of frost. The long lake had turned into a shield of ice. The sky emptied itself of birds as they fled south, and the myriad creatures that could not so escape burrowed into the earth.

A great stillness had descended over the valley, so that when a coyote howled in the Farther Hills it was shocking to the watchers in front of the TV. It was answered by another coyote, and another until a much deeper howl shuddered on the keen air and silenced them all. "Dear God, Bogomil's still alive," murmured Frietchie, retreating more deeply into her down comforter. "How can he survive the cold?"

"The farmers baited a trap for him," said Mr. Yee. "He tore it apart and stole the bait. I told them you can't kill a demon with traps. You need Unending Wall Total Misery Demon Repellent, which I sell. But they wouldn't listen."

Frietchie shivered.

Mr. Yee was seated in his favorite chair, with Ginzberg Roshi and the Dominican Abbot on the sofa beside him. Tom and Violetta completed the circle.

None of them had any hope. They had discussed many escape plans and found all of them impossible. In the first place, where could they go? By tomorrow nowhere would be safe for them. By tomorrow Proposition $\Omega57$ would require all old people to be micro-chipped. Their every movement would be tracked and scanners were already in place in Luga Chuga. The only path left was to the east, to the Farther Hills. No one knew what lay there.

At any rate they were too old. Their feet would stumble on the rocks. The frost would slow their already sluggish blood and darkness would confuse their dimming eyes.

"To think it would end like this," said Frietchie. "I have enjoyed life so much."

"We're not licked yet," said Tom, holding Violetta's hand. "We can always join the Gray Ghosts." On the screen retired terrorists, white-haired men and women, were shown setting fire to a playground.

"Now that's just wrong," Violetta said. "I wouldn't burn a child's playground for anything."

"Why give them toys in the first place?" argued Mr. Yee. "Big waste of money. The only entertainment a kid needs is a job."

Tom went to the kitchen to fetch more cider. He looked out the back window to Cubby's cabin. The lights were on and maybe Cubby and the Lineman were watching the election results there. Or maybe not. It was hard to tell with those two. The Lineman was a complete loony and Cubby was getting stranger as time went on. Once Tom saw him in a lawn chair, reading aloud to ducks. The ducks crowded around him as though they were hanging onto every word.

"Oh! The election results are coming in," cried Frietchie as Tom returned with a pitcher of cider.

They all bent forward to watch the news anchor—a computer simulation, of course. Simulations were cheaper than actresses and more reliable. No drug scandals or crotch shots to worry about. This one had a perky smile and tossed her hair coquettishly as she parroted the news. Only a few polling stations had closed, she said, but they already had the exit polls. The probability was (she half-closed her eyes and made love to the camera), all reliable trends indicated (she thrust her bosom at the screen), that the Omega Laws would pass with a resounding landslide. "Won't that be wonderful for all you guys and gals who took the trouble to vote?"

"You know who that reminds me of?" said Violetta. "Princess Diana before she got her heart trashed."

"The voice is Marilyn Monroe's," said Frietchie.

"Numbers don't mean squat," growled Tom. *Probability? Reliable trends?* The election was decided before the first vote was cast!" Nevertheless, they watched the screen with increasing depression as poll after poll came in. But after a while, something strange began to happen. The perky smile wavered and the image blurred.

"Must be a thunderstorm in the Midwest," remarked Violetta. All at once—*poof!*—the news anchor vanished and in her place was an old man with white hair. He was dressed in a shabby brown suit and had a lapel pin with the double G logo of the Gray Ghosts, the retired terrorists' organization.

"Guess what," said the old man. "All those projected trends were so much ca-ca. The actual results from the east coast show a landslide defeat for the Omega Laws. A new day is dawning, kiddies. That fat allowance in your back pocket is going to be put on a diet. It's Time for a Time out!" This was the motto of the Gray Ghosts.

The camera panned around the anchor room. It was no longer a glittering stage set with klieg lights and sexy reporters. It was a dingy shed festooned with wires. A spotlight shone on a table where the white-haired man and two elderly women sat. Behind them, fading into the shadows, was an immense crowd of seniors.

Mr. Yee burst out laughing.

"That can't be real," cried Tom.

Frietchie clicked the remote, but on channel after channel the chirpy anchorettes had disappeared, to be replaced by grimly amused Gray Ghosts. Each station was different, another indication that these weren't computer-generated. In many places hastily painted banners proclaimed *It's Time for a Time Out.*

Most of the newscasters were amateurs. Their voices had that reedy quality common to old age. Their clothes were frumpy. They sometimes forgot to look at the camera, but they were unmistakably real and they were all seniors.

Tom, Violetta and the others stared spellbound as election results poured in. Hours passed. No one moved. No one got up to replace the cider. It was too enthralling, even though by midnight it was clear what the results would be.

They weren't the only ones who were delighted. The back of the room thronged with dead people. "Seaworthys always come through for you," said the Mhondoro, raising a bottle of Eight Ball Stout from the top of a bookcase.

"*Yebo, Sekuru,*" chorused Balthazar, Caspar and Melchior scattered among the fetishes. Shumba floated in midair with his spirit drum, his crazy smile almost splitting his face in half.

Mr. Yee's mother was filled with pride. *Ai-ya*! By himself her son had roused the elders to do battle. He had outdone all her sisters' sons, who'd had their mouths filled with gold at birth and been given one thousand yuan notes to wipe their worthless bottoms. Her prestige had risen enormously in the spirit world and she wasn't going to let anyone forget it.

Other shades jostled for position· Jedediah Bidwell and the Modocs, Mr. Strickland and Miss Feeny, Bogomil's great-grandmother, who preferred a warm room to coyotes, and even, right at the back because he liked being alone, Eric Hoffer.

Gerbill, loyally, had chosen to watch the election results with Cubby. All the spirits were pleased as punch with the way things were turning out and there would be a fiesta in the halls of the dead later.

The Omega Laws had been swept away. A new law gave the new president and his cabinet sweeping powers to restore order and right wrongs. After four years there would be another election with real paper ballots and real people.

*   *   *

Traditionally, doctors ask a question of patients they wish to test for Alzheimer's: *Who's the president of the United States?* If they'd asked it several hours before, every single person in the country would have flunked. Now the correct answer appeared on Tom's screen: *The new president of the United States is Dr. Wolfgang Willows.*

Time for a Time out.

*   *   *

Cubby lay glassy-eyed on the bed with Gerbill sitting at the old roll-top desk nearby. The Lineman had left an hour before. He was curled up in the chicken house under a heap of hens.

"That vas truly outstanding," exclaimed Gerbill for the fifth or sixth time. "The election vas a computer program und you rewrote it! If I could have destroyed Hitler that way—but I was only a boy when he came to power. I vas seven years old."

"My father gave me a dog when I was seven," Cubby murmured. "She was called Jingle Bell because it was Christmas." He was so tired he thought he could never move again. But at the same time a pleasant dreaminess softened the light in the room. The air trembled like a veil and beyond it he saw a group of elderly men and women around a piano, listening to a woman sing.

"Cubby!" shrieked Frietchie, bursting into the cabin. A blast of cold air followed her and the veil wavered and dissolved. "Cubby! What have you done?"

He blinked at her, trying to remember who she was.

"Oh dear God, look at you," she raged. "When was the last time you ate? You're wasting away! I told that Lineman to feed you—"

"Frietchie," said Cubby, finally putting a name to this attractive person. "Oh, good. I wanted you to meet Gerbill." But when Cubby looked, his friend had already gone.

"I can't see anyone," Frietchie said, half-way between tears and hysteria. "Oh, God, how did you do it? The Omega Laws have been defeated and a new government created out of thin air—"

"Strictly speaking, air isn't thin," said Cubby, musing, "at least this close to sea level. You could make the argument if we were standing on Mount Everest."

"I'm going to scream if you go off on one of your tangents. How in hell did you take over the government?"

By now Tom and the others had arrived, with Mr. Yee moving slowly to the most comfortable chair. The rest gathered around the bed, gazing down at the new President of the United States.

"It wasn't really a government," Cubby explained. "It was a feedback loop that started when opinion polls began to influence each other. You see, the pine processionary caterpillar—" He went on to describe the behavior of this curious insect. Most of the time, when Cubby got onto his favorite topic of bugs, people's eyes glazed over. No one dreamed of wool-gathering now. This was the President of the United States with an army, navy and air force at his disposal.

They all felt a little shell-shocked. None of them had paid attention to how the country was run, except to agree that it was run badly. They had no idea how this unworldly being had got his hands on the reins of power or what he intended to do with them.

"So I broke open the feedback loop and fed it through my computer," Cubby said. "After that it was easy to construct a new political party, draft a platform and rewrite the ballot. Oh, and I deleted the votes of everyone under sixty-five. That was Gerbill's idea and I must say it worked very well."

"You—deleted—votes?" said Tom, horrified.

"Big deal. Don't think it hasn't been done before," jeered Mr. Yee.

Cubby closed his eyes briefly and Frietchie immediately bent over him. "You absolutely have to rest, dearest. I don't know how you're going to run a government in the state you're in." She smoothed his gray hair and kissed him gently on the forehead.

"I'm not going to," he said, smiling faintly. "You are. My cabinet." He was clearly fading and unable to stay awake much longer. "What do I know? I've been studying insects for forty years, but all the talent we need is here in the Nigh and Far Valley. Who knows more about organization than the Abbot and the Roshi? Who understands women's issues better than Frietchie? Violetta is our expert on human relations. Mr. Yee is our financial genius. But most of all we need you, Tom. You've often said that mainte-nance is the mark of a high civilization. What America needs now is a Secretary of Maintenance. And now . . . please excuse me." Cubby closed his eyes for the last time. Frietchie anxiously checked his pulse, but he was only sleeping.

The members of the new government looked at each other, stunned. One by one they departed to confer in the main ranch house. Only Frietchie stayed to sleep on Cubby's sofa. "The first thing I'm going to do as a member of the cabinet," she said, savagely pulling a blanket over herself, "is take these Turkish carpets to the cleaners. Goddamn that Lineman and his chickens."

Forty-Three: *THE TIME OUT*

U NLIKE PREVIOUS governments, there was no time lag before the new rulers were installed. President Mogador and the Senators and Representatives simply vanished, after the manner of deleted computer programs. They had been, after all, only icons.

The new cabinet immediately repealed the Senior Laws and disbanded the Youth Patrol. The Gray Ghosts were enlisted to disarm the Youth Patrol, and if their methods were messy, they were at least thorough.

Tom worried about a breakdown of law and order, but surprisingly, the transition was fairly easy. For one thing, young people had almost no idea how to organize themselves and more than half of them were functionally illiterate. Nor were they capable of rebellion. Years of idleness had sapped their will.

The infrastructure of police, fire fighters and military held up during The Time Out, as Cubby's years of presidency were called. Libraries, schools, shopping centers, bus systems and hospitals still existed, if in shrunken and distorted forms. They could be rehabilitated. Underneath them lay the strong bones of American culture.

For advice, Tom turned frequently to the writings of Eric Hoffer. "So long as a country has courage and a passion for excellence, it can face the future confidently, no matter how fearsome its difficulties," wrote the great man. One of the great strengths of America had been its attitude to work. It was this respect for labor that set it apart from the febrile aristocracies of earlier times.

People needed to live meaningful lives and they could not do that by merely sitting around. They needed jobs. And the most meaningful jobs, accessible to everyone no matter what his or her ability was, were those that required one to learn a skill. "Since man has no inborn skills," said Hoffer, "the survival of the species has depended on the ability to acquire and perfect them. Hence the mastery of skills is a uniquely human activity and yields deep satisfaction."

It was here that Hoffer advocated combing the world for little-known or half-forgotten crafts in order to revive them. He would have children of five—for who is more eager to try new things than a young child?—apprenticed to these masters. "It is most fitting that in an automated world," he wrote, "the human hand, a most unique organ, should come back into its own and again perform wonders."

Tom was reminded of that long-ago day when he'd shared fettuccini with Eric Hoffer. He looked at his hands again and thought *yes, they are wonderful.*

The elderly, who had retreated to hidden valleys like the Wollemi pines, ventured forth. The hands that had built the machines in Cubby's old factory found that their skill and knowledge had not deserted them. They knew how to make manifest the workings of the human mind. It was for them to liberate the young from sloth and show them the beauty of a well-made bridge or a wheat field or a house.

Cubby maintained that civilizations decayed because people keep tinkering with perfection. They didn't realize that there was a point at which change only made things worse. Therefore, the corridors and conduits were allowed to fall into ruin and country roads came back into existence. Silence was allowed to be reborn. Cell phones were banished.

Of course there were disagreements. There always are during such momentous eras, but the important thing was to make a beginning.

Cubby interfered very little, trusting in the good sense of his cabinet and the myriads of helpers they enlisted to run the country. He did issue a presidential order about the National Insect. There were many heated arguments over the importance of honey bees, monarch butterflies and ladybugs. But in the end Cubby prevailed and the new National Insect for the United States became the cockroach. The Mexican embassy complained, stating that *La Cucaracha* was practically their national anthem.

"Cry babies," scoffed Mr. Yee. "They had their chance. You're either a winner or a loser in this world."

The only other major change Cubby made—and he did this immediately—was to make anti-Alzheimer's drugs available and free to whoever needed them. For the rest, he left the reins of government in more capable hands. He had accomplished his goal. Like the cicada that spends years sheltering in darkness, he had emerged for one brief season to sing. Now that season was over.

Next page: The President of the United States reading to ducks.

Forty-Four: *EASTER MORNING*

SPRING CAME SUDDENLY to the valley. In other places the departure of winter was marked by a gradual uncurling of leaves, a new bird's nest or a single iris displaying its gaudy purple in the shade of a laurel. But not here. One day the fields of Nigh were powdered with frost and the next they were splashed with green. A haze of bees searched out alfalfa blooms and squirrels chased one another madly around tree trunks.

In Far the air heated up equally fast. Tom was wearing a short-sleeved cotton shirt today and he already found it too warm. "I wish we could parcel up this weather and dole it out during winter," he grumbled to Violetta over the breakfast table.

"You'd find it boring," she said, cutting herself another slice of the Lineman's excellent bread.

The Lineman had been hoarding eggs from his beloved hens for the past week and now he was dyeing them for the Easter party. Red, green, yellow, purple or just plain white. Nothing could compare with an ordinary chicken's egg for sheer beauty in his opinion.

Overnight, the sky had filled with birds winging their way back to the Long Lake. Canada geese uttered cries at dawn and dusk. Swallows swirled around the eaves of Tom's cabins, now occupied by his visiting children and grandchildren. The United States government was taking a Time Out to celebrate an old-fashioned Easter.

First they went to church and a score of Seaworthy grand-children overwhelmed the pancake breakfast. Violetta had donated honey from the Lineman's hives and so the children were forgiven. Afterwards, she left them behind to enjoy pony rides and greased pig events, so she could immerse herself in cooking. She had very little time for this, what with visiting schools and nurseries around the country. She relished the opportunity.

By afternoon Violetta, the Lineman, Frietchie, Ezekiel and Lourenço had filled the house with delicious smells, and Bulbul had unloaded several crates of Mirage wine from the monastery. Then Mr. Yee appeared with a pair of Buddhist acolytes carrying crates of Tsingtao. "You know what's happened?" said Mr. Yee, accepting a bottle an acolyte had respectfully opened. "My son wants to move into my house in the Buddhist community."

"You mean Lucky?" said Frietchie, wiping her hands on a towel.

"Yeah, yeah. That's the one, unless the paternity tests lied." Mr. Yee gave his rat-chewing laugh.

"So what's the matter?"

"He's sixty-five, damn it! He's a senior. Imagine how old that makes me feel."

"Maybe you can change the locks," Frietchie suggested.

"Aw, I don't really want to discourage him," said Mr. Yee with uncharacteristic charity. "He's my son. Besides, his third wife dumped him and took the kids."

Frietchie went to the window and looked across the lawn the Lineman had claimed from the desert with great effort. Cubby was sitting in a chair with a magazine in his lap. All around him ducks craned their necks and watched him lovingly. "I wish he wouldn't sit in the sun," she murmured. "He'll get heat stroke."

"He says it keeps his blood warm," said Violetta, shading her eyes. "Poor man, his heart is failing. He won't go to the hospital. He says it's his time and he won't interfere."

"He's reading to ducks," Mr. Yee said. "Do you realize that's the President of the United States and he's reading to *ducks*?"

"It does no one harm," Frietchie said softly.

*　　*　　*

The sun poured all around him and yet Cubby still felt cold. He had to remind himself to breathe, too, a problem he was having more and more frequently these days. It was strange, forgetting a habit he'd had since—well, since forever.

He looked beyond the ducks and saw Gerbill approaching him from the plain of Far. The air dimpled with heat and the old German's feet seemed to hover over the ground. But then he was dead, Cubby reminded himself. Dead people's feet tended to do that.

"Vat a wonderful day!" said Gerbill, floating over the lawn.

"I haven't seen you for a while. Have you been touring Austria?" Cubby enquired.

"A bit of this und that. Sybille, you know. She loves the spring. I left her on a hillside in Switzerland."

"I hope she doesn't mind being left behind," said Cubby.

"Not at all. This is a special day. Come, they're waiting for you."

"They?" said Cubby, feeling a pain in his chest, but in the next instant it was gone and he realized that he, too, was floating over the lawn.

"You see? That's better. You are going to love my surprise."

They walked away and Cubby felt himself more invigorated than he'd been for ages. It was a beautiful day and the birds wheeled through the sky, singing for all they were worth. Ahead of them, a veil of rain trembled in the air, but when Cubby stepped through it he didn't get wet at all. It smelled wonderful, like all the spring times of his life.

"You're going to make a lot of people happy," said Gerbill.

Cubby looked ahead and saw a neat, white house. The door opened and his grandmother came out. "Oh! Oh! Look who's here," she cried. More of his relatives came onto the porch, delightedly waving and laughing. "You bad boy," his grandmother said with mock severity. "Look what you did to that nice tablecloth I made you." She held it out, all brown and moldy from the bucket where Cubby had left it.

"I'm sorry—" he began.

"Oh, hen feathers! It doesn't matter. I've made you a new one." And she handed him a spotless white tablecloth covered with the fine embroidery that was her pride and joy. "Come in! Everyone's expecting you."

Cubby looked back and saw Gerbill retreating into the distance. "Wait!" he called. "Aren't you coming with me?"

"Later," the voice floated back to him. "Ve have lots of time. This is their occasion."

Cubby was ferried into the parlor by his joyful relatives, and just as he stepped inside he was mobbed by an ecstatic dog. "Jingle Bell!" he cried. So all dogs *did* go to Heaven, he thought, and all cockroaches, too, by the look of it. He saw one slyly waving its feelers at him from a dark corner.

"Well done, Cubby," said his father, looking exactly as he had on that night when they'd watched a meteor shower in the back yard. "We always expected you to win the Nobel Prize, but being President of the United States is even better." Cubby flushed with pleasure as his father tousled his hair.

He could see his grandmother's dining room through a farther door and a grand meal set out on her willowware dishes. But here in the parlor his great-uncle was playing at the old piano that never was quite tuned and that had strings missing on a couple of the high notes. A woman was singing.

It was his mother, but heavens! How young she was! Cubby looked down and saw that he was young, too, perhaps ten years old. He looked back through the open front door. Beyond a rain curtain an old man appeared to be dozing in a chair. A magazine had dropped from his hand and a mob of excited ducks milled around. Cubby liked the man—he had always liked old people—and he also liked the ducks.

The colors in that other world were muted, like an old photograph left out in the sun, while on this side the hues were saturated with light. Fields of living green were crossed by clouds as fleecy as those in a child's picture book. The sky beyond was so blue that Cubby's eyes blurred with tears.

But then the piano played again and he turned away. He forgot about the photograph. He lay down on the old Navajo rug with his head on his hands and listened to his mother's sweet, young voice.

CUBBY AND JINGLE BELL

ABOUT THE AUTHOR

Nancy Farmer grew up in a hotel in Yuma on the Arizona-Mexico border. After dark, she explored rooftops in the center of town and discovered an opening into the local cinema, where she could watch free movies. During the day she explored the old state prison and the banks of the Colorado River. She attended Reed College in Portland, Oregon. Instead of taking a regular job, she joined the Peace Corps and was sent to India (1963-1965). When she returned, she moved into a commune in Berkeley and sold newspapers on the street.

Her first trip to Africa ended in disaster. She and a friend tried to hitchhike on a yacht, but the ship they'd selected was actually being stolen by the captain. It was boarded by the Coast Guard just outside the Golden Gate Bridge. Nancy got a job in the Entomology department at UC Berkeley. After a few years, she decided to explore Africa legally, with a real ticket. She spent more than a year on Lake Cabora Bassa in Mozambique, monitoring water weeds. Next she was hired to help control tsetse fly in the dense bush on the banks of the Zambezi in Zimbabwe.

Nancy was introduced to her soon-to-be husband by his soon-to-be ex-girlfriend. He proposed a week later. Harold and Nancy now live in the Chiricahua Mountains of Arizona on a major drug route for the Sinaloa Cartel. They have a son, Daniel, who is in the U.S. navy.

Nancy's honors include the National Book Award for *The House of the Scorpion* and Newbery Honors for *The Ear, the Eye and The Arm, A Girl Named Disaster* and *The House of the Scorpion*. She is the author of nine novels, three picture books and a number of short stories. Her books have been translated into twenty-six languages.

Made in the USA
Middletown, DE
10 August 2019